PRAISE FOR THE NOVELS
OF KATE HEWITT

"Pulled me in and never let me go. . . . Hewitt writes about the complex emotions of family relationships with sensitivity and realism."

—Marie Bostwick, *New York Times* bestselling author of *The Second Sister*

"A moving look at what family can look like and how much it can mean."　　　—Wendy Wax, *USA Today* bestselling author of *Sunshine Beach*

"A lushly imagined, deeply moving story . . . stunning . . . the perfect book to lose yourself in!"

—Sarah Morgan, *USA Today* bestselling author of *First Time in Forever*

"As deeply satisfying as a fragrant kitchen, a warm cup of tea, and a heart-to-heart chat in the midst of a Cumbrian downpour."

—Emilie Richards, *USA Today* bestselling author of *The Color of Light*

"Completely and totally charming. . . . I read this book straight through, in pajamas, eating brownies, on a rainy day in Oregon. I don't think I left my couch. That's how much I loved it."

—Cathy Lamb, author of *My Very Best Friend*

ALSO BY KATE HEWITT

Rainy Day Sisters

Now and Then *Friends*

A HARTLEY-BY-THE-SEA NOVEL

KATE HEWITT

NAL NEW AMERICAN LIBRARY

NEW AMERICAN LIBRARY
Published by New American Library,
an imprint of Penguin Random House LLC
375 Hudson Street, New York, New York 10014

This book is an original publication of New American Library.

First Printing, July 2016

Copyright © Kate Hewitt Limited, 2016
Readers guide copyright © Penguin Random House, 2016
Excerpt from *Rainy Day Sisters* copyright © Kate Hewitt Limited, 2015
Penguin Random House supports copyright. Copyright fuels creativity, encourages diverse voices, promotes free speech, and creates a vibrant culture. Thank you for buying an authorized edition of this book and for complying with copyright laws by not reproducing, scanning, or distributing any part of it in any form without permission. You are supporting writers and allowing Penguin Random House to continue to publish books for every reader.

New American Library and the New American Library colophon are registered trademarks of Penguin Random House LLC.

For more information about Penguin Random House, visit penguin.com.

LIBRARY OF CONGRESS CATALOGING-IN-PUBLICATION DATA:

Names: Hewitt, Kate, author.
Title: Now and then friends/Kate Hewitt.
Description: New York City: New American Library, [2016] | Series: A
Hartley-by-the-sea novel; 2
Identifiers: LCCN 2015041938 (print) | LCCN 2015045293 (ebook) | ISBN
9780451475596 (softcover) | ISBN 9780698195349 (ebook)
Subjects: LCSH: Female friendship—Fiction. | Domestic fiction. | BISAC:
FICTION/Contemporary Women. | FICTION/Romance/Contemporary. |
FICTION/Family Life.
Classification: LCC PS3619.W368 N69 2016 (print) | LCC PS3619.W368 (ebook) |
DDC 813/.6—dc23
LC record available at http://lccn.loc.gov/2015041938

Printed in the United States of America
10 9 8 7 6 5 4 3 2 1

Penguin
Random
House

To my parents, George and Margot Berry,
for showing both faith and fortitude in the midst of difficult circumstances,
and giving me a wonderful model of marriage. With much love, Katie

Now and Then
Friends

1

~

Rachel

"MY CORNS ARE BOTHERING me terribly today."

"Are they?" Rachel Campbell managed to combine a bright smile with a look of sympathy for ninety-three-year-old Iris Fairley. "Cup of tea, then?" she suggested, and maneuvered around the tiny kitchen with its cracked linoleum tile to fill the brass kettle Iris's father had bought in a Turkish bazaar before the First World War. She had no intention of examining Iris's corns, which was undoubtedly what the elderly lady wanted her to do.

"Biscuit?" Iris suggested hopefully, and Rachel reached for the packet of custard creams she'd brought.

"Can't have a cuppa without a biscuit."

"You shouldn't have sugar. You *know* that, Iris," Edith, her twin sister, called from the sitting room.

Rachel winked and slipped Iris a custard cream. She'd been cleaning house for the Fairley twins for eight years, and she'd long ago learned that tea and biscuits were just as important as, if not more than, wiping counters or mopping floors. The twins didn't get out much, and they loved a bit of a chat over a cuppa, especially Edith. Iris just liked the biscuits.

Rachel glanced out the window at the pale blue sky, fleecy clouds scudding across it. Muddy pasture stretched out to the sea, winking

1

gray-blue in the distance. Although it was late March, it still felt wintry in this cold corner of Cumbria, and there had been frost on the tiny patch of grass outside Rachel's house that morning.

The kettle began to whistle shrilly, and Rachel whisked it off the ancient cooker as Edith stumped into the kitchen.

"Have you had a biscuit?" she asked Iris accusingly, and Rachel busied herself making the tea.

"I haven't," Iris said, and Edith pointed a finger at her face.

"You have *crumbs* on your chin."

"Oh, give way now, Edith," Rachel said cheerfully as Iris brushed at her chin. "A biscuit or two won't hurt anybody." She slid Iris another one with a small smile. "Anyway, they're low calorie. I bought them specially." Rachel slid the opened packet back into the cupboard before Edith could get too close a look at it. "Now, let's all have a cup of tea before I get on with the hoovering." Low calorie or not, Rachel figured at ninety-three you were entitled to a few cookies.

Two hours later she let herself out of the tiny terraced cottage at the top of the village and breathed in the chilly, damp air. The blue sky of a few hours ago had predictably given way to gray, with dark clouds hovering low over the horizon. Rachel turned up the collar of her coat and checked her phone: nothing from Meghan about their mother and nothing from her little sister, Lily, who had headed off to sixth-form college after Rachel had gone on her first cleaning job of the day. No messages was a good thing; her sisters only called her in a crisis. And they'd had more than their share of crises over the years.

She climbed into her car and headed down through Hartley-by-the-Sea, past the primary school, the post office, and the pub, to where the steep, narrow street opened onto a muddy sheep pasture, the square church tower visible in the distance. She'd lived in Hartley-by-the-Sea her whole life, save two precious, fleeting weeks in Durham, and its cozy charm charmed and depressed her in turns.

Rachel turned down the beach road and up the steep lane that led to Four Gables, her next cleaning job. The house would thankfully be empty, as the Wests lived in London for most of the year, and Rachel was looking forward to a few hours of peace and quiet. The Fairley twins were lovely, but they could be hard work.

She unlocked the door, breathing in the slightly stale scent of lavender potpourri and lemon furniture polish. The kitchen was as pristine as ever, untouched from week to week, and so Rachel decided to do the bathrooms. The house had five.

She'd just opened the door to the first en suite bathroom when she stopped, nonplussed. There was a wet towel on the floor.

After a few surprised seconds she took in the other details of the room: the condensation on the mirror, the streaks of water on the glassed-in shower, the warm humidity of the air. Someone had just taken a shower.

Rachel put down her mop and pail filled with cleaning supplies, the back of her neck prickling with alarm. There had been no car in the driveway, and she knew the Wests were in London; they always let her know in advance when they were coming back, as Marie West tended to be very particular about the cleanliness of her house.

Their son, Andrew, was doing something related to engineering in America; their daughter, Claire, was partying her way through Portugal.

So who had just taken what must have been a very long hot shower?

"Hi, Rachel."

Rachel spun around, stiffening at the sight of Claire West coming around the corner of the bedroom. Her hair was wrapped in one towel, her body in another.

"Claire!" Rachel's voice sounded loud, even jolly, and it made her inwardly cringe. "The prodigal daughter returns." Claire flinched a little, and Rachel quickly clarified. "I thought you were in Portugal. It's been what . . . four, five years?"

"I'm not sure when I was last here," Claire answered, a note of uncertainty entering her voice. Rachel remembered that hesitant lilt and then the shy smile from primary school and how it had made her seven-year-old self want to protect Claire West. "It's been a while," Claire said, and there was the smile.

Rachel nodded, trying to remember the last time she'd seen Claire. From a distance, maybe, six years ago when her parents had thrown her a party for graduating from university, complete with a live band and a fountain spurting Bollinger. Rachel had helped out with the catering, serving champagne and canapés and shooting glances at Claire, who had, as usual, been surrounded by admirers.

But when had Rachel last actually *talked* to Claire? She'd have to go back decades, maybe even to those days in primary school, when they'd been best friends standing shoulder to shoulder—or rather, shoulder to waist since Rachel had always been about a foot taller than Claire— against the bullies of Year Two.

Rob Telford, who now ran the Hangman's Noose in the village, had once pushed Claire in the school yard and Rachel had given him a bloody nose in retaliation. She'd been called into the office of the head teacher, who had telephoned her mother, who had clipped her on the ear, but she hadn't cared about the consequences because she'd protected Claire.

It had been a long, long time since she'd stood up for Claire West.

"So how are you?" she asked, trying to pitch her tone somewhere between friendly and polite. "Back from Portugal?" Obviously.

"Yeah . . . for a few months." Claire tugged the towel a little higher up on her body.

"Well . . . great." Rachel nodded several times as she put her hands on her hips and then dropped them; suddenly her body had become awkward, as if she had too many limbs. "Huh. Wow." The last she'd heard, Claire had been engaged to some hotshot property developer, someone with a double-barreled name and a father who was a baronet. Claire's mother—after telling Rachel to clean the bathrooms "just a touch more thoroughly"—had regaled her with the endless wedding plans for her only daughter. An afternoon reception at the fancy hotel overlooking Derwentwater. An evening ball at another hotel in Windermere. And then a whole raft of events down in London.

"Have you come back to plan the wedding?" Rachel asked.

"Um, no." Claire's smile slipped. "The engagement's off, unfortunately."

"Oh." Rachel squashed the inevitable schadenfreude she felt at knowing that at least one thing had not gone well for Claire. "I'm sorry."

"Yeah, me too."

Claire shifted where she stood, dripping water onto the carpet Rachel would have to vacuum later. "Sorry," Rachel said. "I'll get out of your way."

"No, don't bother," Claire said quickly. "You're obviously busy. I'll just . . ." She gestured to the bedroom, one of the house's four guest rooms, although perhaps this one had been Claire's as a child. Rachel didn't know; she'd never been invited to Claire's house when they were friends. She was the riffraff whose father was sometimes on the dole and whose mother cleaned houses. Definitely not good enough to be Marie West's only daughter's friend, even though they'd been inseparable during school for four years.

"It's fine," she said, and scooping up her mop and pail, she moved past Claire. "I'll do one of the other bathrooms," she called over her shoulder. "Just let me know when you're done."

She opened the door to another of the en suites, flicking on the switch before she sat down hard on the toilet seat. Distantly she could hear Claire moving around, turning on taps.

Claire. Claire West. For a second Rachel pictured Claire as she'd been the first time she'd seen her. They'd both been six years old, starting Year Two, taking off their coats in the crowded cloakroom at school. Claire had shrunk back from the noisy press of children and parents, and Rachel had seen from the corner of her eye how shiny her black patent Mary Janes were, her coat a kind no self-respecting six-year-old would wear, made of red wool with black epaulets and a Peter Pan collar. She wore a matching tam o'shanter, red with a black silk bobble on top, and she'd looked like an overdressed extra from a Shirley Temple film. Rachel had seen how the other girls in their sparkly jean jackets and puffy pink parkas had kept shooting her incredulous, disparaging looks. Her dark, silky hair had been neatly braided into two plaits, with shiny red ribbons tied into big bows on the ends. One of the boys had leaned forward and yanked one of those ribbons, and Claire had jerked back as if she'd been slapped.

Rachel had stepped forward, elbowing the boy—had it been Rob Telford or Oliver Bradley?—out of the way, and then she'd turned to Claire and asked if she needed help with her buttons. Claire had nodded wordlessly, and Rachel had stooped to undo each button of her coat while Claire had remained still and accepting, her gaze averted. Then Rachel had said, kindly, "Maybe you shouldn't wear that coat tomorrow."

Claire had blinked at her, surprised, and then she'd given her a shy smile of gratitude and whispered, "I think you're right."

From that day on they'd stayed together. Claire had clung to Rachel, and Rachel had anchored her to her side. It had been wonderful to have someone you could count on, a forever partner in PE, someone who would always save you a seat at lunch. And more than that, someone who listened.

Claire had always been good at listening. At recess they'd often run off to a rhododendron bush on the side of the school yard. They'd wriggle underneath its tangled branches and sit there on their knees, mindless of the dirt or mud. Under that bush Rachel had admitted how she wished her father had a proper job, and Claire had whispered how she wished her mother wouldn't worry so much. Rachel had secretly wished she'd had a mother who worried; her mother was too busy cleaning houses and keeping them afloat financially to worry whether Rachel was having a good day at school.

For four and a half years they'd wriggled under the rhododendron, sat together during lunch, and said goodbye at the bottom of the school lane because Rachel had known, without Claire ever having to say anything, that she would never be invited up to Four Gables to play. She'd told herself she didn't mind, and she hadn't, until their friendship had come to an abrupt halt in Year Six, when they were eleven years old.

When Rachel looked back, it felt as if one day she had been linking arms with Claire as they'd walked into school from the playground; the next Claire had been surrounded by the in girls, who had formed a protective circle around her Rachel had been too proud to attempt to breach. But maybe it hadn't been that quick. Memories had a way of blurring together, especially then. So much had been going wrong.

Rachel hadn't talked to Claire since; in all those intervening years they hadn't exchanged more than a few stilted words, a frozen smile, a nod in the street. Sometimes not even that.

Rachel let out a breath and rose from the toilet seat. This bathroom didn't need cleaning, but she spritzed it all the same. Marie West was the kind of woman who sniffed a room upon entering it to make sure it smelled like lemon polish. Once, when Rachel had been talking to her about her work schedule, Marie had slowly run her finger along the top of a very tall curio cabinet. When it had come away covered with a thin film of dust, she'd given Rachel a silent, pointed look.

"Rachel?" Claire's voice floated down the hallway. "I'm done in here, if you . . ."

Rachel stuffed her supplies back in her pail and came out into the hallway. Claire stood by the doorway to her bedroom, dressed in jeans and a fleece, her damp hair tucked behind her ears. Even in such standard-issue clothes Claire looked expensive and put together. The jeans were skinny designer ones; the fleece, with its chunky buttons and signature stripe, was from one of the pricey mountain-gear shops in Keswick or Windermere. Still, with her feet bare and her hair damp, Claire looked much as she had back in school, fragile and uncertain, and Rachel felt a tug of protectiveness that she resolutely ignored.

"Great, thanks." Rachel slipped past Claire into the bedroom and scooped up the wet towels Claire had left in a sodden pile on the floor. She tried not to do it as pointedly as Marie West had with her dust-grimed finger, but Claire muttered an apology, so maybe she had.

She was starting to feel a tingling sense of annoyance, like a toothache she just couldn't keep from probing with her tongue, as other memories came back in lightning-streak flashes. Claire at sixteen, walking down the high street of Whitehaven on a Saturday night with a gaggle of private-school girls in tight skirts and tottering heels. Rachel had been standing outside the fish-and-chips shop, waiting for her father to finish his evening shift. She'd folded her arms and stared straight ahead as the girls had bent their heads close together and giggled behind their hands. Claire's vacant gaze had skimmed right over Rachel. She hadn't been ignoring her; she simply hadn't registered her at all. Rachel hadn't known which was worse.

Claire at nineteen, coming back from university at Christmas. They'd both attended the Christmas Eve carol service at church, Claire seated near the front with her parents and brother, Andrew, Rachel in back with Mum, who had needed a walker to get her through the door but had insisted on going, wheezing all the way, and left halfway through to have a smoke. Her father had been gone for three months by then, three bitter months when every day had been nothing but something to struggle through. Three months of seeing the life she'd hoped to have, a place at university, *dreams*, trickle away to nothing.

Sitting in the back of the church, Rachel had watched as Claire had taken off her cashmere coat, flicked her long glossy hair over her shoulders, and whispered something to her brother. Rachel had suppressed a pang of envy so fierce and terrible it had felt like an ulcer eating away her insides. Her envy didn't arise from Claire's *things*; it had never been about material possessions. So Claire was rich. Lots of people were. No, it had been about the *freedom*. The ease with which Claire sat there smiling and didn't seem to have a single worry in the world. The family that surrounded her, protective, loving, *there*. Claire didn't know how lucky she was.

From what Rachel had seen now, she didn't think Claire had changed. But why was she back in Hartley-by-the-Sea, and for a couple of *months*?

"I'll just take these downstairs," she murmured to Claire, nodding towards the towels, and after an awkward pause Claire stepped out of the way.

Rachel was switching on the washing machine when she realized Claire had followed her down to the utility room off the kitchen. She'd put her hands in the back pockets of her jeans and rocked back and forth on her heels. "So, Rachel." She cleared her throat. "How are you?"

"Fine, thanks." Rachel needlessly rearranged a few of the bottles and rags in her bucket of cleaning supplies, her head bent so her hair fell in front of her face and hid her expression, which she knew she couldn't trust at that moment. "Never better."

"How's your mum?" Claire asked, and Rachel stiffened. Claire had never talked about her mother; they'd stopped being friends right before Janice Campbell had had her accident.

"Fine. I mean, the same." When Rachel was eleven, Janice Campbell had fallen down the stairs of one of the houses she'd been cleaning and broken her back. She'd been virtually bedridden since.

"And . . . your sister?" Claire asked hesitantly, and Rachel knew she was feeling her way through the dark, trying to be polite.

"Sisters," she corrected. "They're both fine. Thank you for asking." She forced a bright smile. "How are you? Broken engagement aside, I mean."

Claire let out a soft, hesitant laugh. "Truthfully? I don't know."

It didn't really surprise Rachel that Claire didn't know how she was feeling; she'd always been like that, waffling over everything, even whom she was friends with. And now Rachel no longer cared.

"Well, then." She hoisted her mop and pail. "I'd better get back upstairs."

"Right." Claire moved out of the way again, and Rachel brushed past her before heading upstairs. She cleaned the bathroom Claire had used, spritzing the mirrors and sink, opening the window to let out the steam, half listening to Claire move around downstairs.

When she was finished, she came back down and found Claire in the center of the sitting room, standing there as if she were lost in her own house.

"So I'll be back next week," Rachel announced, "unless you'd like me to come sooner than that? Since you're staying? Normally I just do a quick tidy because there's no one here." She didn't relish the thought of cleaning up after Claire, but she could use the money. She could always use the money.

"Oh, once a week is fine. I'm not . . . I mean . . ." She shrugged, and Rachel remembered how Claire hadn't always finished her sentences.

"Okay, then. See you next week."

Rachel loaded her cleaning supplies into the back of the hatchback she used to get to her various jobs; CAMPBELL CLEANERS was painted on the side, along with her mobile phone number. Her sister Meghan had protested the advertisement, since the car was the only one they had, but Rachel had ignored her.

"When you're making as much money as I am," she'd stated, "then you can buy your own car, or at least contribute more to the family finances."

Meghan had rolled her eyes, caught as ever between laughing it off and being annoyed. Lily had looked guilty, and her mother had pretended not to hear the whole exchange.

Now Rachel slid into the driver's seat of her car and headed down the steep, winding lane from the Wests' house to the beach road. The wind had started up again, blowing off the sea, and the clumps of daffodils that lined the road huddled against its onslaught. She had ten minutes to get to her cleaning job for the Browns, a busy family with two working parents and three school-age children, and then she'd drop the ironing she'd done for Juliet Bagshaw at Tarn House Bed-and-Breakfast before heading back home to see to dinner, tidy up, and make sure Lily, who was only two months away from doing her A levels, put in at least three hours of study. She was predicted for three As, maybe even an A star in biology, and if she got the marks, she would be going to the University of Durham in the autumn. Rachel was determined to see that happen.

Three hours later Rachel pulled up to the terraced house on the upper end of Hartley-by-the-Sea's high street that had been her home since she was a baby. The gutters were crooked, the paint on the front door was peeling, and the once-white net curtains framing the front window were the color of weak tea. Her house was definitely not an advertisement for her cleaning services, but then, she didn't have time to clean her own house. Rachel hauled her cleaning supplies from the back of the car and headed inside.

The first thing she heard was three-year-old Nathan's shrieking. She walked into the kitchen, tossing the mop and pail into a corner, and glanced at her sister Meghan. Nathan was clinging to Meghan's legs while she sat at the table, flicking through a magazine. Rachel glanced at the lurid titles on the cover: *My Child's Past Lives* and *My Fur Stole's Haunted by the Fox!*

She rolled her eyes. "Seriously, Meghan?"

Her sister looked up from the magazine. "What?"

"You're reading rubbish while Nathan is screaming his head off." At that moment Nathan chose to go silent, staring at Rachel with wide eyes.

"He's been screaming all day. He's getting teeth."

"He's three. He has all his teeth."

"His molars or something. Trust me, I know." She dropped her magazine onto the table and leaned forward. "Nath, open your mouth."

Solemnly Nathan opened his mouth wide, and Meghan peered inside. "See? Molars," she said triumphantly, picking up her magazine once more, and Rachel spared a sympathetic glance for her nephew's reddened, swollen gums before she shrugged off her coat.

"He should have some Calpol." She fished in the cupboard for a bottle of children's medicine, the lid sticky with residue, and handed it and a spoon to Meghan, who took it with a sigh, dropping her magazine on the table.

Rachel turned to Lily, who was standing in front of the stove, her red hair, the same color as Rachel's, caught in a messy knot as she hummed tunelessly and stirred the sauce.

"Lily, you should be studying."

"I did some homework at school—," Lily began.

"That's great, but you could get a little more in—"

"Oh, give it a rest, Rach," Meghan cut in. "You're always on her case."

Rachel stiffened. "I don't mean to nag, but this is a very important year—"

"And so was last year, and the year before that. Lily's fine."

"Of course you would say that," Rachel answered with a sigh. Meghan had left school at sixteen with only a handful of barely passing marks. "Seriously, Lily," she said, and she gently elbowed her sister out of the way. "Let me do this. You can get a half hour of revision in before tea."

Lily hesitated. "I don't actually have that much to do. . . ."

"Lily, your exams begin in—" Rachel glanced at the calendar above the sink. "Seven weeks. You need to keep at it. You know that. It's hard, I know, but it's so worthwhile."

"She can have a twenty-minute break, can't she?" Meghan interjected, and tossed the *Fate & Fortune* magazine to Lily. "Here you go."

"Meghan—"

"There's biology in it," Meghan answered, wide-eyed. "Animals and stuff."

"The fox haunting someone's fur stole?" Rachel said, rolling her eyes, but Lily had already hurried upstairs, the magazine clutched to her chest. Rachel turned back to the spaghetti Bolognese that was bubbling away on the stove, two tins of chopped tomatoes and half a kilo of beef mince mushed together, the beef only half cooked. Sighing, she reached for the oregano.

"So what's got you in such a crap mood?" Meghan asked. Nathan had scrambled onto her lap and was now sucking his thumb, the other hand wrapped around a tendril of Meghan's hair, which he tugged rhythmically.

"Who says I'm in a crap mood?"

"I do, but now that I think about it, it's no more crap than usual. You just usually hide it better."

"I'm fine. And you should watch your language," Rachel said with a meaningful nod towards Nathan.

"Oh, Nath knows what 'crap' means," Meghan answered, and ruffled her son's hair. "So? What's bothering you?"

"You mean, besides coming home to the house an utter tip and dinner not made even though it's gone half six?" Rachel answered, keeping her tone flippant. She and Meghan always bickered, but they tried not to draw blood.

"Is that really that unusual?" Meghan countered. "Anyway, the house isn't that much of a tip. I actually hoovered, you know."

"Mummy spilled her crisps," Nathan volunteered, and she tapped his nose.

"That was meant to be our little secret, Nath."

"So, what have you been doing today, Meghan?" Rachel asked conversationally. "Besides eating crisps and watching rubbish telly?"

"*Real Housewives of Cheshire* is *not* rubbish."

Rachel shook her head, too tired to press her sister. As usual, she couldn't tell if Meghan was being thoughtless or just taking the mick. Her sister walked a fine line between the two. "How's Mum been getting on today?"

"Brilliantly. She loves *Real Housewives of Cheshire*."

"Well, that's a relief." Rachel prodded the sauce without enthusiasm. "But she's been all right?"

"As all right as she ever is."

Rachel nodded, her mind already elsewhere. From upstairs she could hear Lily moving around, and then the tinny sound of techno music. Her sister was definitely not studying.

"Did you know Claire West is back in the village?" she asked abruptly.

"Claire West?" Meghan wrinkled her nose, uninterested. "Wasn't she in Spain or something?"

"Portugal. The Algarve."

"Some people have all the luck," Meghan answered with a shrug. "What's she doing back here?"

"Her engagement's off, apparently."

"You saw her?"

"I clean the Wests' house every other Wednesday."

"Right." Meghan yawned. "I so do not feel like working tonight," she said, stretching, and Nathan nearly fell off her lap. Rachel managed to keep herself from saying her sister never felt like working; she only did three nights a week at the Hangman's Noose. "I'd better get on, then." She stood up, settling Nathan onto her hip. "Time for the tub, Nath. Aunt Rachel won't want to bathe you. She's too grumpy."

"I'll read you a story after tea tonight," Rachel promised Nathan, who smiled hopefully in response. Meghan headed upstairs with Nathan, and Rachel listened, wincing, as the taps went on and the pipes screeched. She imagined the headline on the cover of *Fate & Fortune: Help, There's a Banshee in My Water Pipes!*

She turned the sauce on to simmer and went into the sitting room; it was as much of a mess as the kitchen, with half-drunk cups of tea making damp rings on the coffee table, along with a towering Play-Doh creation of Nathan's and two Lottery scratch cards, a vice of her mother's that Meghan happily enabled even though Rachel had forbidden it. They couldn't afford to play the Lottery, and it was a waste of money. She'd tried to explain the ridiculous odds of winning to Meghan, and her sister had rolled her eyes.

"You don't get it, do you, Rachel?" she'd said, to which Rachel had replied tartly, "I was just about to say the same to you."

Now, as she collected the mugs and worthless cards, Rachel wondered what Claire West was doing up at Four Gables. She pictured her in that endless gourmet kitchen with its Sub-Zero fridge and pristine Aga, cooking an elegant meal for one. If Claire was staying for months, she must have left her job in Portugal showing rich retirees newly built villas in the Algarve. What would she do in poky Hartley-by-the-Sea? Rachel was surprised she'd come here at all, instead of going to London to stay with her parents.

Not that she cared what Claire did, or why. Rachel straightened, gazing around the little sitting room with its saggy sofa and warped coffee table, bits of hardened Play-Doh littering the carpet, despite Meghan's hoovering. Upstairs Lily's music blared with a relentless, pulsing beat, and from the dining room—turned-bedroom she heard the squeak of bedsprings as her mother shifted her weight. No, she had far too many people in her life to manage to waste a single brain cell wondering or worrying about Claire West.

2

Claire

CLAIRE LISTENED TO THE door click shut behind Rachel, leaving the house empty and silent. She stood for a moment in the center of the sitting room, the cream carpet stretching out in every direction in a pristine sea, the still air smelling faintly of lemon polish and lavender potpourri. Home, even if it didn't feel like it.

After a moment she went to one of the huge overstuffed sofas and sat down gingerly, because even though her mother was three hundred miles away in London, Claire could imagine her hovering, clucking her tongue and plumping the pillows.

She tucked her legs up and wrapped her arms around them, resting her chin on top. Her mother would screech in alarm to see her bare feet on the silk sofa cushions, and sitting like this felt like a tiny but important act of defiance.

She savored the silence for a few minutes, because after four weeks at Lansdowne Hills, where the noise had been soft but persistent, the company constant, she was glad of a little solitary time. No one chirpily telling her it was time for the discussion group or counseling session or a massage. No supposedly soothing sound of water trickling over rocks playing incessantly in the background. Lansdowne Hills had been elegant and expensive, but it had still been a prison.

Now that she'd escaped, she wasn't entirely sure what to do with herself. She had no intention of going back to Portugal; Hugh hadn't called her in the four weeks she'd been at Lansdowne Hills, and she didn't particularly want him to call her now, although she supposed she'd have to have a conversation with him at some point. They were, technically at least, still engaged. The ostentatious diamond Hugh had bought her was in her toiletry bag; she'd taken it off on the plane from Portugal, after Hugh had staged his intervention.

Grimacing, Claire rose from the sofa and paced the elegant confines of the sitting room. She wasn't sure why she'd come back to Cumbria; she didn't have too many happy memories of living here. Home had been miserable and school had been a blur. Her parents had moved to London five years ago, and Claire hadn't been back to Hartley-by-the-Sea since.

But when it had been a choice between Hartley-by-the-Sea or living with her parents in London . . .

Cumbria won, hands down.

And yet she'd been in Hartley-by-the-Sea for only two hours and she was already starting to feel restless and uncertain. What on earth was she going to do here, or anywhere? She had no job, no fiancé, no future. She had no plans whatsoever, and she didn't know how to go about making them.

The phone rang, breaking the stillness, and Claire didn't move. She listened to the answering machine pick up; she could hear her mother's recorded message, the tone nasal and sharp, although Claire couldn't make out the words. Then a second's silence followed by the long *beep* of someone having hung up.

Then the phone rang again.

It had to be either her parents or her brother, and none of them was likely to give up calling. With a sigh Claire rose from the sofa and went to answer it.

"Hello?"

"Claire?"

"Hi, Andrew." Claire leaned against the kitchen wall and closed her eyes. She was glad it was her brother rather than her parents, although he could be almost as bossy.

"You got there all right," he said unnecessarily.

"Yes."

A little sigh of disappointment, the sound track to her family life. "Mum wanted you in London, Claire."

"I know." Her parents had insisted she come to stay with them after she'd been released from the clinic; in an extraordinary and unprecedented act of rebellion, Claire had turned away the limo they'd arranged to collect her and had taken the train up to Cumbria instead. She'd felt like a twenty-eight-year-old runaway, watching the placid coastline stream by as the train clattered towards Hartley-by-the-Sea. She'd turned off her phone and enjoyed the fact that no one actually knew where she was.

"They're worried about you," Andrew said. "We all are."

"I know. But I can't stand Mum hovering over me, Andrew. I just can't."

"She means well—"

"I *know*." As the high-achieving older brother, Andrew had never been subjected to the relentless concern that Marie West lavished on her only daughter. He had no idea what it felt like to be under the microscope of a mother's love and yet always feel so disappointing to her, so feeble. "I'm fine here," Claire said.

"You shouldn't be alone."

She stiffened, because she knew what he meant. He was afraid, as her parents were, that left alone she'd *regress*. She'd fall off the wagon she'd been flung onto four weeks ago, when Hugh had phoned her parents and insisted she had a *problem*. Rehab had been the obvious answer, and blinking and bewildered, Claire had followed their wishes, because when had she ever done anything else?

But after four weeks of bucolic prison in Hampshire, she was done with being a dormouse. She wasn't sure how to change, or even if she could, but she wanted to. Coming to Cumbria had been the first step.

"I'm fine, Andrew," she began, only to have him cut her off, his voice taking on the schoolteacherish tone she knew well.

"Look, Claire. I know Mum can be a bit much sometimes. But at this vulnerable time, you really shouldn't be by yourself—"

"I want to be by myself," Claire interjected. "Trust me, Andrew. I'm not going to go raiding Dad's liquor cabinet. He's locked it, anyway, to keep the staff from having a nip." As a joke it fell abominably flat, and it made Claire think of Rachel.

For a second she pictured Rachel as she'd been in primary school, six inches taller than the tallest boy, with her flaming hair and freckles and reckless, brassy confidence. Why Rachel had chosen to take Claire, an overdressed shadow, as her best friend, Claire had no idea. But she'd been grateful. She'd been overwhelmingly grateful.

"I'm going to call you every day," Andrew said, and Claire made a murmuring noise of agreement. "And I want you to answer your phone. Your mobile's turned off, you know."

"I'm aware." With a sigh of resignation she slid her phone out of the deep pocket of her fleece and powered it up.

"What are you going to do up there, Claire?" Andrew asked. "Hartley-by-the-Sea is . . ."

"Home."

"It hasn't been home for years. And it's in the middle of nowhere."

"The edge of nowhere, maybe," Claire answered. "Considering it's on the sea."

"You know what I mean."

"Yes, I do, but I told you already I don't want to go to London, and I don't have anywhere else to go."

"You could come here, to Minneapolis—"

"No, thanks." Andrew worked as a civil engineer, traveling around the world, building bridges and canals and dams, living in corporate flats and eating takeaway. Claire had no intention of being on the periphery of his transient life.

"But what are you going to *do*, Claire?"

"Maybe I'll get a job," Claire answered before she'd really thought such a possibility through. Hartley-by-the-Sea didn't have many jobs, and she was qualified for basically nothing. A third in art history, a couple of positions where she'd been meant to look decorative and not much else. But it would be nice to feel useful. Productive.

"A job? Doing what? Checkout at Tesco?"

"Why not?" Claire returned. "It's a decent job."

"You're better than that."

"You sound like a snob."

"Fine," Andrew conceded. "But I'm ringing tomorrow."

"Fine."

"And turn your mobile on, for goodness' sake."

"I already did," Claire told him, and hung up. She had five voice mails from her mother. Resolutely, she deleted them all. She didn't need to hear Marie West's histrionics about how she should have come to London, and she couldn't face an actual conversation with her mother yet. Hugh, unsurprisingly, hadn't called. Claire wondered if he ever would.

She gazed around the huge kitchen and wondered when any of her family had last been there. She opened the fridge, and the gleaming, empty expanse seemed to mock her.

She needed food, and since she didn't have a car, she'd have to get it at the poky village shop.

At least it would get her out of the house and the silent accusation every spotless carpet and plumped-up pillow was making.

She went upstairs for her socks and shoes and then grabbed her coat and keys before heading out into a brisk March day. After three years in Portugal, she'd forgotten how chilly Cumbria was. Her parents' house was at the end of a long private drive at the top of the

village, with a view of the winding high street and its cluster of terraced houses, the beach a wide expanse of smooth beige sand in the
distance, the sea glinting on the horizon, gray-blue and ruffled with
white. If she turned she could see the sloping fields, dotted with sheep,
that led to the dark, jagged gray-green humps of the distant fells.

It was a stunning sight in every direction, and for a few moments
Claire simply stood there, taking it all in. She'd never looked back on
her years in Hartley-by-the-Sea with anything close to affection, but
in that moment she was glad to be there. She was grateful to be free.

She started walking down the lane that led to the beach road, the
wind buffeting her hard as soon as she stepped out into the open
street. A few sheep glanced up balefully as she passed, the ewes' stom-
achs swollen with the lambs that would come in April.

No one was about, and for that Claire was glad. She didn't think she
could handle any more awkward reunions; seeing Rachel Campbell had
been hard enough. Had she been imagining that slight note of hostility
from Rachel? After she'd been away for so many years, it felt a little
surprising, but then she and Rachel hadn't been friends for a long time.

The beach road joined up with the high street at the train station; a
woman wearing a waterproof parka and Wellingtons despite the sunshine was walking a small dog. She gave her a smile, and Claire smiled
back, glad it was a stranger. How many people were still living in
Hartley-by-the-Sea that she'd know, or who would remember her? A
few acquaintances from primary school at most, probably. The realization was a relief.

She turned right up the high street, digging her hands deep into
her pockets and lowering her head against the wind. She'd forgotten
how relentless the wind in Hartley-by-the-Sea was. When she'd walked
to school as a little girl, she'd felt as if it had been pushing her forward,
like a strong hand at her back. She'd needed the push; she'd often
dreaded school, the teachers whose questions she never managed to
hear and the children who thought she was ridiculous. Rachel had

been the only one who had had time for her, at least until Year Six. But collecting a gaggle of gossipy girls as pseudo-friends hadn't been nearly as fun as it had first appeared.

Claire slowed as she came to the little stucco-fronted post office shop with its windows full of advertisements and dusty tinned goods. She glanced at the notices taped to the inside: cleaning services, a lost cat, help wanted.

She thought of Andrew's remark about Tesco and wondered what he would think if she told him she was working at the village shop. Not that she wanted to work right in the middle of the village. She craved a bit of anonymity, and standing behind the till, ringing up her neighbors' newspapers and milk, surely wasn't the way to get it.

And yet, a job. One small way to sort her life.

She opened the door and stepped inside, blinking for a few seconds to get used to the gloom of the little room. The shop looked like it hadn't changed much in the five or more years since she'd last been in it: a few shelves with basic food items, a tiny refrigerated section, a rack of sweets, another of magazines. There was a post office counter tucked away in the back and a counter of old, scarred wood with an ancient-looking cash register at the front.

And behind the cash register scowling at her was a giant of a man with tattoos down both folded forearms.

"Hi," Claire ventured hesitantly, and the man's black eyebrows snapped together.

"Are you coming in, then?" he asked, and Claire realized she hadn't closed the door behind her. She did so now, a sudden gust of wind causing it to slam with enough force to rattle the glass. She winced, and then braced herself to turn around and face the man.

His scowl had deepened, his arms still ominously folded, biceps bulging. With a quick, apologetic smile, Claire started to wander the shop's three aisles, conscious the whole time of the man's hostility. It emanated from him like a bad smell or a malevolent force. No wonder he needed staff. He probably couldn't keep anyone working for him for more than two minutes.

She stared blindly at a tin of baked beans in tomato sauce and then grabbed it as well as a loaf of white bread. Beans on toast she could manage, and at this point she wanted to get out of the shop as quickly as possible. First Rachel, now this guy. No one, it seemed, was happy for her to be back in Hartley-by-the-Sea, which wasn't too surprising, considering she wasn't sure if she was.

Claire took the beans and bread to the counter and waited while the man rang them up silently.

"Three pounds and fifty-four pence," he told her, and his voice was exactly what Claire would have expected. Gruff, gravelly, and without a shred of warmth. She fumbled in the pockets of her coat for the money, hating that her fingers actually trembled. She was such a *mouse*. But she'd been one for a long time.

"There you are." She laid the coins on the counter and then gathered her items, clutching them to her chest as she blurted, "Are you . . . ? Are you still looking for help?"

The man gave her a flat stare. "Maybe."

Not the most encouraging of responses, but since she'd drummed up the courage—or the foolishness—to ask about the job, she thought she might as well continue. "It's just I'm looking for work."

"Haven't seen you here before."

"I've been away. In Portugal. But I'm back now, for . . . for a while."

"And how long is a while?"

"I'm . . . I'm not sure."

"I'm looking for someone who can commit," he stated, and handed her a penny in change.

"I see." Claire took the penny, nearly dropping the beans in the process, and then turned to leave.

She was so busy trying to manage her purchases and closing the door without it slamming again that she nearly collided with a woman coming into the shop.

"Oh, my fault, my fault," the woman exclaimed, and caught the tin of beans that was slipping out of Claire's grasp.

"Sorry," Claire said, and looked up to see the woman—about her age, with frizzing, sandy hair and an open, friendly expression—scrutinizing her.

"I don't think I know you."

"I'm Claire. Claire West. I've just . . . moved back into the village."

"That explains it, then. I've been living here since August, more or less. Lucy Bagshaw." She stuck out a hand, and Claire attempted to shake it, transferring the tin of beans to her other hand.

"Nice to meet you."

"Moved back, you said? You lived here before?"

"I grew up here." Now that she'd said more than a few words, Lucy's American accent was recognizable. "You obviously didn't," Claire ventured, and Lucy grinned.

"Nope, although I actually am British, if you can believe it. I know I don't sound it. I moved here from Boston. I live down at Tarn House, the bed-and-breakfast? With my sister, Juliet."

"Right." Claire hadn't heard of either.

"Well, I'm sure we'll run into each other again. I work at the primary school, teaching art. It's only part-time, but it's a start."

"Right," Claire said again.

Lucy gave a goodbye sort of nod and started to move past Claire before turning around suddenly. "You ought to come out with us some evening," she said. "We go to the pub quiz on a Thursday evening. Have you ever been? Of course, you probably know loads of people, but if you don't . . ."

"I don't really know anyone anymore," Claire admitted, and Lucy touched her arm, a spontaneous, friendly gesture that made Claire feel oddly moved.

"Then come out with us. We're down one anyway, because Juliet's going somewhere with Peter. He's taking her out to a fancy restaurant somewhere in Keswick. Do you know Peter Lanford? Sheep farmer?" Claire shook her head. "Anyway, the quiz is tomorrow night, seven thirty at the Hangman's Noose. You will come?"

"I . . ." Claire shrugged, overwhelmed by the exuberant force of Lucy Bagshaw's personality. "Sure. Thanks for the invite."

"Good. That's settled, then." Lucy headed into the shop, and Claire watched her go, bemused and yet grateful for the American's overwhelming friendliness. God knew she could use a friend.

3

Rachel

THE PUB QUIZ WAS the highlight of Rachel's week. For an hour she escaped the stifling confines of her house, dressed up, drank wine, and got to feel smart. Four ways to win.

She hummed under her breath as she put on mascara and wondered if her new magenta sweater was too clingy. There was trying and then there was trying too hard. She definitely didn't want to be in the latter camp, but she liked looking nice, and Rob Telford had been giving her the eye the other week, if she wasn't mistaken.

She hadn't dated much in the last ten years—a few fumbled attempts hardly counted—and she wasn't sure she wanted to date Rob Telford. But she wouldn't mind flirting a little tonight. She could use the distraction. She'd been in a bad mood since yesterday, when Claire West had waltzed back into Hartley-by-the-Sea.

Although, actually, Claire wasn't the waltzing type. Mincing, perhaps. Or maybe tiptoeing. But the fact remained she was here, and it made a lot of old, hard memories resurface. Memories that didn't directly have to do with Claire, but hurt all the same. The loneliness and isolation and pure desperation of the years after her mother's accident. The struggle to hold on to her dreams, and then watching them all scatter.

But she wasn't going to think about any of that tonight. She was going to flirt and drink wine and maybe even win the pub quiz for once.

"What are you smiling about?"

Rachel met Meghan's speculative gaze in the mirror. "Nothing."

"You seem in a good mood," Meghan remarked, and came to sit down on the edge of Rachel's bed, bouncing lightly on the mattress. "And you're wearing a tight sweater that shows off your boobs. Who's that for?"

Rachel pressed her lips together and concentrated on her mascara. "I like to look nice," she said. "And I'm in a good mood because I'm going out for a change."

"For a change? You go out every Thursday."

"Can we not do this, Meghan?"

"Do what?"

Rachel slipped the mascara wand back into the tube with more force than needed and was rewarded with a smear of black across her fingers. "This. This bickering. I'm not in the mood."

"You call this bickering? Clearly you don't remember our childhood."

"Actually, I do. I remember you being monumentally lazy, eating crisps and watching telly while I did all the bloody work. Oh, wait. Nothing's changed."

Her sister simply raised her eyebrows and gave her a gratingly familiar catlike smile. "Ouch. That's harsh, even for you."

"Sorry," Rachel muttered. "I'm just . . . tense."

"Why?"

Rachel knew she couldn't tell Meghan about Claire. She couldn't even articulate it to herself, and in any case, she and Meghan never talked about that time. They'd both drawn a line across it, kept their heads down and soldiered on. "Where's Nathan?" she asked as she grabbed a tissue and scrubbed at her fingers.

"I put him to bed early. He was tired from playgroup."

Meghan and Nathan shared the biggest bedroom in their three-bedroom terraced house. Lily had had the little box room, but a year ago Rachel had taken it and given Lily the other double, so she had room for a desk. Now Rachel squeezed past Meghan and reached for her coat. With her bed and bureau crammed in the six-by-six space, there was barely room to breathe. There certainly wasn't room for both her and Meghan to be in there comfortably. Sharing the same house was bad enough.

"I need to go," she said pointedly. "I don't want to be late."

"Have fun," Meghan trilled.

"Make sure Lily does her homework."

"You doubt me?"

"Don't forget to check on Mum, either." When it came to Meghan, Rachel couldn't help but give instructions. She'd been bossing her sister around since she was twelve and Meghan was eight, when she'd stepped up and taken over from their mother, while Meghan had come home late from school and hidden in her room and their father had done his best to find work.

"I *will*, Rachel," Meghan answered, and for once she actually sounded impatient rather than breezy.

Rachel hesitated, caught between wanting to escape and needing to stay, to make sure everything was under control. Finally she relented. "Okay, then," she said. "Thanks."

She was at the front door when she heard her mother call from her bedroom.

"Rachel? Love?"

Slowly Rachel turned around and cracked open the door to the dining room; her father had turned it into a bedroom for her mother more than ten years ago, when stairs had become too difficult for her to manage on a regular basis.

"Hey, Mum." Rachel stood in the doorway, trying not to breathe in the stale smell of sickness and cigarette smoke that permeated the air. Her mother had refused to quit her pack-a-day habit despite the doctor's repeated urgings. She claimed it was one of the few comforts left her, which Rachel could reluctantly understand.

Now Janice Campbell sat propped up in bed, a couple of pillows behind her back, her face puffy from prescription pills and gray with pain. "Sweetheart," she said, and sank back into the pillows with a wheezy sigh.

They stared at each other for a moment, both of them helpless in their silence, because what was there to say? Janice never left the house. Rachel didn't do anything but work. They'd never had much in common to begin with; Rachel had been a determined Daddy's girl ever since she was small, wearing dungarees and a flat cap, avidly watching her dad work a lathe.

Joss Campbell had been a carpenter by trade, although he'd never been employed regularly. He'd supplemented his income with stints on the dole and shifts at various restaurants and shops. When he'd been younger he'd wanted to study architecture, but he'd told Rachel university hadn't been for the likes of him. He'd promised it would be for her. Too bad he'd reneged on that one, along with a dozen others. Like in sickness and in health.

To make up for the silence now, Rachel busied herself as she always did. She plumped her mother's pillows and then poured her a glass of water from the pitcher on the table, which Janice probably wouldn't drink. She rearranged the bottles of prescription painkillers her mother had been on for fifteen years and aligned the box of tissues so the bottles and box made a right angle. Finally, having run out of ways to look and feel useful, she stepped back.

"You're going out?" Janice asked, wheezing, and Rachel nodded.

"It's Thursday. Pub quiz."

"Right." Rachel shifted where she stood and then glanced down at her top; maybe it really was too clingy. "You look nice, love."

"Thanks, Mum."

Her mother gave a grimace that Rachel suspected was meant to be a playful smile. "You wearing that for someone special?"

"No. I just wanted to look nice." Rachel pulled at her sweater and then took a step towards the door. "Sorry. I should go. I don't want to be late."

"Of course, love. You have a good time. I know how hard you work." Janice plucked at the bedcover with plump fingers. "Everything's all right, isn't it, Rach?" she asked.

Rachel tensed, one hand on the doorknob. "Why wouldn't it be?"

"It's only that you've seemed a bit distracted these last few days."

"Distracted? Not really." She managed a smile. "Not more than usual."

"Okay, then." Janice smiled, and suppressing the uncomfortable pang of guilt she always felt at leaving her mother stranded in her bed, Rachel left the room.

Outside the sun was just starting to set, and Rachel could feel a gathering chill in the air. She dug her hands into the pockets of her coat and hurried down the street towards the Hangman's Noose.

As soon as she entered the pub, the warmth and noise fell over her like a comforting blanket. She smiled and nodded to several people already clustered around the small tables and shouldered her way to the long bar of scarred oak, propping her elbows on its surface as she gazed up at Rob Telford.

He was pulling pints with practiced ease, and his gaze flicked to Rachel's sweater for a millisecond before returning to her face. "What can I get you, Rach?"

"Don't you know my order yet?" Rachel answered with a flirty smile, and she saw surprise flicker in his eyes. She didn't usually flirt with Rob, or with anyone, and her question had probably come out a bit aggressively. She was definitely out of practice with this kind of thing. Then Rob gave a slow smile in response. Maybe she could do this, after all. Rob wasn't a bad-looking bloke, with dark hair and a slightly gap-toothed smile. He'd been a tearaway in school, but he'd settled down since taking over the pub.

"Lucy's already ordered your table a bottle of red," he said as he pushed two foaming pints of ale across the bar to a stony-faced sheep farmer in a flat cap and mud-splattered dungarees. "You're late."

"Not that late." Rachel glanced towards the table in the corner that had always belonged to her team. She, Juliet and Lucy Bagshaw, and Abby Rhodes from the beach café had been coming every Thursday for the quiz for nearly six months now. They hadn't won yet, but they'd come close. And more importantly, they'd all had a laugh.

She could see Lucy's cloud of frizzy hair above the crowds, and as she caught sight of Rachel, Lucy waved enthusiastically, gesturing to the bottle of wine already on the table.

"Looks like you've got an extra at your table tonight," Rob remarked.

"An extra?"

He nodded towards the table in the corner. "Lucy's one for picking up strays, isn't she? Although that was your brief, back in school."

Rachel stiffened. "What on earth are you talking about?"

Rob pulled another pint. "Claire West," he said, and feeling as if she'd swallowed a stone, Rachel turned back to look at the table in the corner and saw what she'd missed before: Claire West seated next to Lucy.

4

Claire

THIS HAD BEEN A mistake. Claire realized that as soon as she stepped into the pub and the noise of the place hit her like a smack in the face. She nearly stumbled right back out the door, because she'd never been good with crowds. When Hugh had taken her to parties, she'd spent the whole time either in the ladies' or craning her head forward, attempting to catch what everyone was saying, trying to keep up, or at least appear as if she were.

Before she could move, Lucy was calling to her from across the entire pub. "Claire! Claire, over here."

The crowd of people blurred before her into one unfriendly mass; she saw a few farmers hunched over their pints, looking resolutely uninterested, a couple of women dolled up and avidly curious. She lifted her chin and started to move through the crowds.

"You came." Lucy looked delighted, which seemed a bit weird. Claire barely knew this woman, and she hadn't done much to recommend herself to Lucy Bagshaw, except for not dropping a tin of beans on her foot.

"I came," she agreed inanely, and sat down on the stool next to Lucy's. Lucy was still scanning the pub, so Claire introduced herself to the other woman at the table.

"Abby Rhodes." The woman, small with long, dark hair, eyed her in a knowing way that made Claire tense. She didn't recognize the name, but . . . "We were in school at the same time," Abby explained. Her voice was soft, and Claire had to lean forward to listen. "I was in Year Two to your Year Six." She offered a teasing smile. "You were one of the in girls."

The in girls. Claire shook her head as if to deny it, although she knew she couldn't. She had been one of those popular girls, even though it had felt like a bewildering joke at the time, something she neither understood nor trusted.

"Well," she said, because she had nothing else to say, but Abby seemed to want a response.

Lucy sat down with a sigh of satisfaction and started pouring them all glasses of wine. "I hope red's all right," she said to Claire. "It's what we usually get, but if you want something else——"

"Actually," Claire said, "I'll just have some sparkling water."

Lucy stopped in midpour, and then she said quickly, "Of course, sorry. I should have asked first."

"No, no, it's fine. I'll just go up to the bar and order." Claire rose awkwardly from the little table, while Lucy attempted to pour the wine from her glass into Abby's. Murmuring an apology, Claire made her way to the bar.

What on earth had possessed her to agree to come to the pub, of all places? Her parents would be appalled. Andrew would pontificate how she shouldn't put herself in the way of temptation. All because she'd gotten drunk rather publicly and embarrassingly and Hugh had decided she had a *problem.*

Maybe she did. Maybe she had a lot of problems.

She came up to the bar, only to stifle a groan as she realized she was standing next to Rachel Campbell.

Rachel was ignoring her and chatting with the man behind the bar, who looked vaguely familiar. Someone else who recognized her, for he smiled as he turned to her and said, "Hello, Claire. What can I do for you?"

"A glass of sparkling water, please."

The man smiled slowly as he reached for the bottle. "You don't remember me, do you?"

Claire forced an apologetic smile. "Sorry, no."

"Why should she?" Rachel said. "Although you did make her life a misery."

"Ah, come now, Rach. That's a bit harsh." Rachel shrugged, and Claire looked at them both blankly, trying to remember whatever it was they were referring to.

"I might have pulled your plaits a time or two," the man said to her as he handed her a glass of water. "But it was nowt more than what any seven-year-old boy would do. And you paid me back by ignoring me completely in Year Six."

Claire could feel her smile turning strained. "I suppose we're even, then," she said, and he stuck out his hand for her to shake.

"Rob Telford, since you obviously don't remember. That stings a little, by the way. I thought I'd made quite an impression." He winked at her, and Claire managed to smile back.

"I'm afraid primary school is a bit of a blur to me," she said. "It was so long ago." And she'd been so unhappy for most of it.

"That it was," Rachel agreed, and straightened, giving Claire a direct look for the first time. "We ought to sit down. The quiz will be starting in a minute. You are joining our team, aren't you?"

Rachel was on Lucy's team? Claire tried for another smile. "Brilliant." She reached for her purse. "How much do I owe you?" she asked Rob.

"On the house, Claire," he said. "Welcome back to Hartley-by-the-Sea."

She smiled her uncertain thanks and followed Rachel back to their table, wishing with every step that she was back at Four Gables, safe and alone. Navigating all these old, half-forgotten relationships was way too fraught.

"Oh, good, you two have met," Lucy said as Claire and Rachel sat down at the table. Rachel reached for the wine.

"Actually, Claire and I go way back," she said as she poured herself a full glass. "To primary school. But apparently it's a blur to Claire." Rachel spoke lightly, smiling, but Claire still felt rebuked.

"Oh, it's a blur to me too," Lucy said. "Thankfully."

"Does anyone have a good time in primary school?" Abby asked. "I was terrified of my Year Two teacher, Miss Marsden. Did you have her, Claire? Rachel?"

"No. She was after our time," Rachel answered. "Mrs. Lennox was our Year Two teacher."

Mrs. Lennox. Claire had a sudden memory of a tall woman with a bosom like the prow of a battleship and a thunderous voice to match. "I was terrified of Mrs. Lennox," she told Abby. "She was always so impatient."

"Yes, she was, although to be fair, you were a bit slow." Rachel still spoke lightly, smiling even. "Do you remember? I used to help you unbutton your coat."

It was the first time Rachel had made a reference to their childhood friendship, and it made Claire feel an uncomfortable welter of guilt and sorrow. "I remember," she said, and Lucy began to hand out the pencils and slips of paper.

She was hopeless at the quiz. Claire had known she would be. She had absolutely no head for trivia, and she'd been fairly useless at school. Maybe it had been starting late, or having trouble hearing the teachers, or the simple fact that she wasn't a brain box like her brother.

Lucy tried to involve her in the first few questions, but after Claire had apologetically shaken her head several times, having no clue as to any of the answers, she gave up. Claire sat back and sipped her water, wondering when she would be able to call it a night without offending anyone.

Rachel already seemed offended. Actually, Rachel had seemed irritated by her presence from the moment she'd seen her coming out of the bathroom yesterday. Claire glanced sideways at her; Rachel was hunched over her piece of paper, scribbling. She obviously knew the answers to the quiz, but then, she'd always been clever.

Rob Telford, who was directing the quiz, asked another question. "What countries border Spain?"

"France, of course," Rachel said quickly.

"Any others?"

"Portugal," Claire blurted, pleased she actually knew something. "Portugal borders Spain to the west."

"Of course." Rachel wrote it down. "Claire used to live in Portugal," she told the others, and Lucy and Abby swiveled to face her with expressions of polite interest.

"That must have been brilliant," Lucy said. "Far better weather than here."

"It was hot," Claire answered, and wondered if she was the only one who thought she sounded so inane.

Rob Telford called for a five-minute break, and it seemed like a good time to make her departure. "Look, I'm really sorry," she said. "But I'm still tired from . . . everything, and I ought to get to bed."

Rachel pushed back from the table, tilting her head up to gaze at Claire. "Busy day tomorrow?"

"Are you working locally?" Lucy asked.

"No, no . . . just . . ." What was she doing tomorrow? Wandering around the house or the village, trying to fill up all her empty hours. "Actually, I'm looking for a job," Claire said. "So if you know of anything going . . ."

"The real estate market isn't too big here," Rachel said. "Not like in Portugal."

"It doesn't have to be real estate. I'd do just about anything, actually."

"Dan Trenton at the post office needs an assistant," Lucy suggested, and Claire couldn't keep herself from grimacing.

"I've already tried the post office," she said. "Dan Trenton wasn't too impressed with me, I'm afraid."

"Oh, Dan's a big softy really," Lucy said, and Rachel snorted. "You should try again. He could use a little company in the shop."

"You seem to know everyone, for only having been here six months," Claire said.

"That's Lucy for you," Abby chimed in. "She's the friendliest person I know."

Lucy blushed and smiled and Rachel rose from the table. "Right, more wine," she announced. "While there's time." She gave Claire a goodbye type of smile, and Claire murmured something about how nice it was to see her again. Even though it wasn't.

She watched Rachel head over to the bar and wondered just what it was about her that bothered Rachel so much. They'd been friends once, even if they'd stopped in Year Six. There had never been a falling-out, no big argument or tears or tantrums. Just a casual, gradual drifting away, but Claire supposed that was natural. They'd been very different, and they'd been heading to different secondary schools. Still, it made her sad, both then and now.

"Rachel can be a bit prickly," Lucy said. "She's got a lot on."

Claire turned back to Lucy. "Has she?"

"With her mother bedridden and her younger sisters . . . Rachel manages everyone, and she works like a devil." Lucy glanced at Rachel thoughtfully; she was leaning against the bar, chatting with Rob with a look of almost fervent determination on her face. "She wasn't on top form tonight, though."

"I think that was because of me." Lucy and Abby turned to stare at her in surprise, and Claire explained, "We were friends in primary school, a long time ago. But I think I annoy her now."

"No," Lucy protested, but she sounded unconvinced.

"Thanks for inviting me," Claire said, and made her way through the tables to the door. As she was reaching for the handle, she glanced back at Rachel and felt a jolt of uneasy surprise to see Rachel gazing back at her. She started to smile, but Rachel simply moved her gaze on, as if she hadn't seen her at all.

Early the next morning she woke to the phone ringing shrilly, clicking over to voice mail, and then ringing ahead. With a groan Claire reached for the receiver by her bed and managed a groggy hello.

"Claire." Her mother's voice was breathy, melodramatic, and made her wince. "Do you *know* how many times I've called you?"

"Five?" Claire answered. Five voice mails on her mobile that she'd deleted.

"Do you realize how *worried* we've been about you?" Marie demanded. "We were expecting you *here*. We sent a *car*." Her mother always spoke in accusing italics.

Claire rolled over onto her back and stared at the ceiling. Sunlight filtered through the curtains, and in the distance she could hear the train coming into the village, clattering across the tracks.

"I'm sorry, Mum," she said, "but I didn't want to come to London. I needed a little space."

"Dr. Bryson said you shouldn't be alone."

"For heaven's sake, I'm not suicidal."

"Claire." As usual whenever Claire dared to raise her voice, her mother sounded shocked and so very disappointed. "We're *concerned*. We want to *help* you."

"I know. I appreciate that." She took a deep, even breath. "I'm sorry."

"Daddy's sending a car to get you," Marie informed her briskly. "And this time you'll get in it, Claire, and come back to where you belong. Where we can keep an eye on you."

"Mum, I'm twenty-eight, not eight," Claire said. She could feel a lump forming in her throat, her default response to her mother's commands. "I don't need looking after."

"You're in a vulnerable state. The doctors at the clinic insisted you should be with people—"

"There are people here," Claire interjected. "Last night I went to a pub quiz—"

A second of shocked silence followed. "You were at the *pub?*"

"I had water. Seriously, Mum, I am not about to fall off the wagon." She almost added that she didn't think she actually *had* a drinking problem, but she kept herself from it. Her mother would just start pontificating about denial. And maybe she did have a problem. She'd gotten drunk. Roaring drunk, according to Hugh, and Claire supposed she had to believe him since she didn't remember much of the party. She might have started singing at some point. And dancing. Completely and utterly unlike quiet, malleable Claire, which had no doubt appalled and humiliated Hugh.

"The car should be there by noon," Marie said. "You can be in London by dinnertime."

For a second Claire pictured it: the sleek black sedan pulling up the lane, the driver holding the door open, all obsequious charm. She'd slide inside and doze her way down to London, arrive at her parents' flat in South Kensington, sleep in the second guest room; the first they kept for more important guests. And then what? Slot into some kind of life her parents had arranged? A job at an art gallery or museum, something barely paid but seemingly prestigious. She'd meet up with the group of catty acquaintances she'd called friends, daughters and nieces and grandchildren of her mother's socialite cronies. And endure and endure and endure.

"I don't want to be in London by dinnertime," she said quietly. Just this much defiance took more strength than she feared she had. "Please, Mum, just let me be, for a little while at least. You can call me every day. You can send someone over to check on me. Just . . . let me be." Her voice ended on something close to a whimper, making her cringe.

Marie was silent for a long moment. "I am not happy with this, Claire," she said sternly, and then let out a long, weary sigh. "Fine, since you are being so *difficult*. But if at any moment I feel like things aren't going well, I'm sending someone to get you. Is that clear?"

"Very."

"I'll call you tonight," Marie promised, and Claire murmured her thanks and goodbye before hanging up and rolling over onto her side, a pillow clutched to her stomach.

So this was freedom. She didn't know why she'd been so determined to stay here. It wasn't as if Hartley-by-the-Sea had anything to offer her. It was better than being micromanaged in London by her mother, but only just. She couldn't stand the thought of staying in the house all day, wandering through its elegant, empty rooms, feeling anchorless and adrift.

But she didn't need to stay inside, hiding. It was a beautiful, if chilly, day, and it had been years since she'd been down to the beach. Claire showered and dressed and then headed outside, the brisk wind making her eyes water as she started down the lane towards the main road and then turned right towards the beach.

Sheep pasture bordered the road on both sides, the tufty grass touched with frost. Puffy white clouds studded a fragile blue sky, and by the time she'd reached the promenade, her eyes were streaming from the wind.

The tide was in, so Claire stood on the concrete promenade and watched the white-tipped waves crash against the railings before turning towards the shabby little beach café up on the promontory. She'd hardly ever been inside; her parents had preferred to go farther afield, to the more fashionable towns of Cockermouth or Keswick, for refreshment.

There weren't many people in the café; Claire saw a couple of elderly ladies chatting as they dipped their shortbread biscuits into cups of milky tea. A little boy was playing in a corner that had been set up as a play area, with a blanket and some books and toys.

A dark-haired woman emerged from the kitchen and Claire realized it was Abby, whom she'd met at the pub quiz last night.

"Hello," Abby exclaimed. "Fancy seeing you here."

"I didn't know you worked here." Claire came towards the till and perused the plastic-covered menu self-consciously.

"My grandmother owns the place," Abby explained, "but she's been unwell. Noah and I are living with her until she gets back on her feet."

"Noah . . . ?"

Abby nodded towards the little boy playing in the corner. "My son," she said, a slight note of proud challenge entering her voice.

"Of course." Claire smiled at the boy, who, at the mention of his name, had looked up from his toys. "Well," she said, only half joking, "you don't have a job going, do you?"

Abby made a face. "Sorry. I wish I did. I wish I had enough business to warrant the help."

"It was worth a shot," Claire said. "How about an egg-and-bacon sandwich and a cup of tea instead?"

"That I can do," Abby said, and rang up the order. Claire paid and then wandered to a table by the window, where she could watch the sea surge and swell. She propped her chin on her hands and wondered where else she could look for a job, and then she wondered if she really *wanted* a job.

Did she want to stay in Hartley-by-the-Sea? Maybe only by default, because she had nowhere else to go. But to get a job, actually settle down here, if only for a while?

She turned the thought over in her mind, trying to imagine it. Working here, making friends here, building a life. Something she'd never actually done before, not really.

She'd spent four years in Portugal, but it hadn't felt like a life or a home. She'd had a job that had felt like being a show pony, a glamorous, soulless executive flat, and a fiancé who had sometimes felt like a stranger. A charming, handsome stranger but someone she didn't really know or miss.

The thought brought a sense of shame, that she'd come so close to tying her life to a man she didn't actually care about. But then she didn't know if Hugh had even cared about her. She'd never really understood why he'd wanted to marry her, except that she looked good on his arm and always did what he said. Not exactly the stuff of romantic dreams.

He hadn't called her once since she'd left Portugal a month ago, hadn't sent so much as a text. It was as if he'd disappeared from her life, and the worst thing was she didn't feel hurt or even disappointed. She only felt relief.

"Here you go." Abby put down her sandwich, along with a little tin pot of tea and a jug of milk.

"Thanks."

She stood there while Claire poured the tea and milk, starting to feel self-conscious under the women's scrutiny.

"I think you should try the post office shop again," Abby said. "I know Dan Trenton can be a bit unfriendly, but honestly, he's like that with everyone."

"Is he?" Claire took a sip of tea. "I don't actually have any experience working in that kind of environment."

"You don't need much. Just ringing up the till, stocking shelves, I imagine." Abby hesitated. "What did you do out in Portugal, then?"

"I worked in real estate." It sounded far more important than it had been. "Really, I just showed retirees a new estate of villas my fiancé was developing. It didn't involve much more than walking around an empty house, opening doors and talking about the stunning ocean views and dual-aspect kitchen." She grimaced at the memory, and Abby cocked her head.

"Didn't like it much, did you?"

"Not really."

"What happened to the fiancé?" Abby asked. "If you don't mind me asking?"

"We broke up." Claire felt her face heat. "Actually, he dumped me. I think."

"You think?"

"Well." Claire grimaced. "We left it a bit . . . undecided. I was coming to England, and we haven't spoken in a month. So."

"You don't seem too disappointed."

She let out a laugh, surprised at Abby's bluntness. "No, I'm not. And yet I stayed with him for nearly four years. I'm not sure what that says about me."

"Maybe that you're very patient?" Abby suggested with a smile. "Enjoy your sandwich." She turned away to tend to a pair of hikers who had come into the café, stomping mud from their caked boots and brandishing elaborate-looking walking sticks. Claire stared out at the sea.

Perhaps she would try Dan Trenton again. Why not? She'd made two sort-of friends since she'd come back to Hartley-by-the-Sea, and as she sipped her tea she could almost imagine what it would feel like to live here. To have a life. To be free and independent and happy.

Three things she'd never really felt before, but maybe, just maybe, she could feel them—be them—here.

5

Rachel

RACHEL GAZED IN WEARY dismay at the en suite bathroom she was cleaning. Four wet towels in a sodden heap on the floor; coarse, dark hair filling up the drains of both the shower and the sink; and as for the toilet . . .

"Oy, Juliet," she called. "Who did you have staying here? A pair of gorillas?"

"Some hikers who are in uni," Juliet called back up. "They weren't the tidiest blokes."

"You should have charged extra," Rachel answered as she started spritzing the shower stall. "*I* should charge extra."

"Shall I put the kettle on?"

"You'd better, and make it a double."

Twenty minutes later Rachel came downstairs to the kitchen of Tarn House, with its cheerful green Aga and the view of the sheep pasture leading to the dark green fells in the distance. Juliet Bagshaw stood at the sink, rinsing out a teapot, as Rachel bundled the wet towels into the washer.

"You survived," she said, humor glinting in her gray eyes, and Rachel grimaced.

"Only just. The toilet almost defeated me."

Juliet held up a hand. "I really don't want to know."

"I'm sure you don't." The kettle started whistling, and Juliet whisked it off the Aga's hot plate while Rachel made herself comfortable at the kitchen table. Juliet was always good for a cup of tea and a chat.

"So," Juliet said as she poured water into the teapot, "what's going on with you?"

"What do you mean?"

"Lucy said you weren't yourself at the pub quiz last week."

"Wasn't myself?" Rachel tried to joke. "Who was I, then?"

"'Not on top form' were her actual words."

"I single-handedly answered seventeen of the twenty questions. I'd say that was top form, or close to it."

Juliet turned around, planting her hands on her hips as she gave Rachel a stern look. "Rachel. Quit it. You know what I mean."

"Who says I do?" Rachel challenged grumpily. Six months ago Juliet had minded her own business well enough; it was only since her half sister, Lucy, had come to stay, and she'd begun dating Peter Lanford, that she'd started *emoting*. Right now Rachel didn't like it.

"Seriously," Juliet said as she poured the tea into mugs and brought them to the table. She pushed the milk jug towards Rachel. "Is something going on?"

"Nothing more than usual. Lily doesn't want to study and Meghan is being a lazy pain in the backside. But what else is new?" Rachel poured milk into her tea and stirred it vigorously.

"And what about this Claire West, then?"

"Oh, for heaven's sake. What about her?" Juliet raised her eyebrows, an eloquent response, and Rachel blew out a breath. "All right, fine. Maybe I was a bit snippy with Claire at the pub quiz, but only because she's so bloody useless." Juliet sipped her tea, waiting for more, and annoyed now, Rachel gave it to her. "Look, I know Lucy's taken Claire under her wing because Lucy's like that. She's always looking to fix people. But that doesn't mean I have to."

"Of course you don't," Juliet answered mildly. "How do you even know Claire?"

"Didn't Lucy tell you that? We went to primary school together." Juliet cocked her head, waiting, and Rachel groaned.

"Oh, honestly, Juliet. We used to be friends, all right? Best friends, way back when."

"And what happened?" Juliet sounded uncharacteristically gentle rather than her usual acerbic self. Letting both Lucy and Peter into her life had softened Juliet, so now Rachel felt like the one with brittle edges, the hard angles.

"We stopped being friends," she answered. "As you do."

"Do you?"

"Come on, Juliet. Are you still friends with your bestie from Year Two?"

"I didn't have a *bestie*," Juliet said with a grimace.

"Your BFF, then."

"Oh, please."

Rachel grinned, but Juliet kept giving her a knowing, beady look, and with a sigh she continued. "We just . . . grew apart. I guess." Or rather, Claire grew apart from her. Quite abruptly. At least it had felt abrupt, but maybe it hadn't been. Maybe it had been more of a drifting as the reality of secondary school approached, and Claire had naturally gravitated towards the girls who would be going to Wyndham. Rachel had a distinct memory of coming into the school yard and seeing Claire surrounded. She'd stopped short, and Claire had looked away. Even now, nearly twenty years later, that memory made her chest hurt. "It was a long time ago," she said to Juliet.

"But she still gets under your skin."

"Maybe a bit . . ." Rachel stared down at the milky depths of her tea, embarrassed by the admission. What had happened between her and Claire was ancient history, virtually irrelevant. What grown woman was still bothered by a breakup with a childhood friend? Before last week she hadn't spoken to Claire West since they'd both been in school pinafores. She'd hardly spared her a thought in the last ten years. So why all the angst and anger now? It didn't make sense.

"She really gets to you," Juliet observed.

"No." The denial was both instinctive and necessary. "She doesn't. Honestly. We were best friends, I know, but I'm not so pathetic that it matters or hurts me now. It's just . . ." Rachel hesitated. She didn't talk about her childhood very much. She never mentioned her father, or the way he'd left without a hug, a note, or even a backwards glance. In the ten years since his abrupt departure, all of the Campbell women had preferred to pretend he'd never existed. "That time in my life was hard," she finally told Juliet, each word drawn from her with reluctance. "My mum broke her back right as I was leaving Year Six and Lily was only tiny and my dad was out of work. It was *hard*. Anyway," she said, her tone turning deliberately dismissive, "I think seeing Claire again after all this time brought it back. So it's not her. It's just . . . that time of life."

Which sounded plausible, although Juliet didn't look as if she was buying it. And the truth was, it *was* about Claire, at least in part. Claire with her perfect hair and teeth and clothes and family; Claire with parents who'd bought her a car and a flat in London and who were *there*. Who took care of her. Who made her life easy.

But that was a dangerous way to start thinking. "Anyway," Rachel said, injecting a cheerfully brisk note of moving-on-now into her voice, "what's up with you? How are things with Peter?"

Just the mention of Peter Lanford's name caused Juliet's cheeks to turn pink and her eyes to brighten. Rachel suppressed a laugh. Before Peter, Juliet had never been so obvious. So *happy*. It was cute, if a little saccharine.

"They're fine," she said. "Just fine."

"That's all you're going to tell me?"

"What do you want, *details?*"

"Well, yes, actually. A few, at least. Come on, Juliet. For ten years you've lived in this village and barely said boo to anyone."

"That's not fair—"

"All right," Rachel conceded, "you've growled boo to a few people. You haven't been the friendliest—"

"I tried," Juliet protested. "I'm still trying. No one changes overnight, you know. And if you think I'm going to just go ahead and spill all the details of my love life—"

"Ooh," Rachel couldn't resist teasing. *"Love life."*

Color deepened in Juliet's cheeks as she rose from the table. "Right, then. This conversation is officially over."

"Are you and Peter serious?" Rachel pressed. "I mean, it has been six months, and neither of you is getting any younger—"

"Thanks very much for reminding me."

"Are you thinking marriage yet?" Rachel asked, grinning. "The whole nappies-and-bottle routine? You know . . ." She propped her elbows on the table, leaning forward as she made her eyes go wide. *"Babies."*

Juliet gave a shudder. *"Don't* mention babies."

"You don't long for the pitter-patter of little feet?"

Juliet stared out the window at the muddy pasture, her gaze turning distant. "It's not that. But it's . . . complicated. I'm not sure babies are in the cards for me. I've got limited fertility as it is."

"Oh, I didn't know that," Rachel said, dropping the joking tone. "I'm sorry."

"It's fine, honestly." Juliet cleared their mugs and dumped them in the sink. Rachel saw something brittle in the way she moved, and she wished she hadn't pressed quite so much. Clearly Juliet had sorrows in her life she hadn't shared with Rachel, which was hardly unexpected. The woman had been a completely closed book until six months ago.

"What about you?" Juliet asked. "I hear you were getting rather cozy with Rob Telford at the pub quiz."

"What!" Rachel sat up straight. "Lucy again, I suppose?"

"No, not Lucy." Juliet's mouth curved in a small smile. "Kate Barton, from Hillside Farm. I buy eggs off her."

Rachel let out a groan. "She was in the year above me at school. Is *nothing* private in this place?"

"You've lived in this village all your life and you're only realizing that now?"

"No," Rachel conceded with sigh. "Just having a moan about it."

"Kate said you were wearing a sexy top and leaning over the bar while you talked to Rob."

Rachel could tell her friend was enjoying this. "And that constitutes flirting, I suppose."

"Not just flirting. Kate's mother is wondering when you're getting married."

"Juliet."

"You know how things are in Hartley-by-the-Sea," Juliet answered, unrepentant. "Really, you ought to be surprised there isn't a notice in the parish magazine, grateful that the church hasn't been booked. Yet."

"Thank heavens for small mercies."

"Exactly."

"I'm not really interested in Rob Telford," Rachel said as she traced a pattern in the weathered wood of the kitchen table with one finger. "I just wanted a distraction."

"Poor Rob, then."

"I'm not all that sure Rob Telford is interested in me. Anyway, I don't have time to date."

"What about the whole nappies-and-bottles routine for you?" Juliet challenged. "You're getting close to thirty, after all."

"I'm twenty-eight," Rachel answered indignantly. "In any case, I've already done the nappies and bottles with my sister Lily, and I still help out with Nathan."

"They say it's different when it's your own."

"I don't think it is." Rachel rose from the table. "I should go. The Harts are expecting me at three."

"Are they the new family that's moved up to the top of the village?"

"They have toddler twins. Which makes me all the more certain about not having kids of my own." Rachel had meant it to come out flippantly, but she had a feeling she sounded bitter. And she wasn't bitter. Not about Lily, anyway. She'd never regret taking care of Lily, or having Nathan in her life.

"Rachel." The compassion in Juliet's voice had her tensing by the door, her back to Juliet. "Look, I understand about someone blowing into your life unexpectedly and stirring up all sorts of memories," Juliet said. "Trust me on that."

"I know," Rachel said, although she didn't really. She knew Lucy and Juliet had had issues, that until Lucy had come to live with Juliet, their relationship as half sisters had been nonexistent and then fraught, but not any of the details. In any case, it was strong now, and Lucy and Juliet had each found happiness with a bloke to boot. Juliet might have once understood how Rachel was feeling, but she was in a different, better place now.

"When Lucy first knocked on my door," Juliet persisted, as stubborn as ever, "I wanted to slam it in her face. Even though I was the one who invited her."

"But you didn't," Rachel said. "And it's all good now."

"That doesn't mean it wasn't hard."

Slowly she turned around. "What are you trying to tell me, Juliet? To give Claire a chance? We aren't *sisters*. We were friends about twenty years ago, when we were children. We've both moved on. And like I told you, my . . . issues have nothing to do with Claire."

Juliet regarded her evenly, her gray eyes seeming far too shrewd. "As you like," she said, and whistled for her dogs, two greyhounds who came scurrying towards her, to come with her outside.

It was obvious that Juliet didn't believe her, and unfortunately Rachel didn't believe herself either. She drove up the high street to the top of the village and parked in the drive of the Harts' neat new build, two stories of smart red brick with a slate roof and a fenced-in garden of runty trees and anemic-looking shrubbery.

Rachel collected her pail of supplies from the back of the car and headed towards the house, knocking once and calling hello before she stepped inside.

The smell hit her first: a full nappy pail that clearly hadn't been emptied all day. Then the noise: nearly two-year-old twins who sounded like they were in a screaming contest.

"Sorry," Emily Hart called as she came from the kitchen. She had a smear of jam on one cheek and a stain on the front of her jumper, which looked alarmingly like sick. "The twins are teething and they've just been horrid all day. If I could, I'd post them back to wherever they came from."

"If you could do that, the Royal Mail would go on strike," Rachel answered. "Imagine all the kiddies people would be trying to cram into the postbox." She put her pail by the stairs and headed into the kitchen, the granite surfaces covered in the maternal detritus of half-empty sippy cups and biscuit crumbs. Rachel felt something squish under her foot and retrieved a graying half-eaten banana from the floor. "Cup of tea?" she called over her shoulder, and Emily slumped against the doorway.

"Yes, please. You're a saint, Rachel."

"Saint of the tea bags." She took the kettle, a modern triangular thing of gleaming chrome, and filled it at the sink. From the sitting room she could hear the toe-tapping theme song of *Fireman Sam*.

"They seem quiet now," she remarked to Emily as she opened the cupboard and took out two mugs. Emily was, like the Fairley sisters, one of her clients who needed a bit of looking after; Rachel spent at least twenty minutes of her three hours at the Harts' house chatting with Emily or making tea. More than once she'd changed Riley's or Rogan's nappy; Emily had looked so pathetically grateful that Rachel hadn't been able to keep from offering. Between the twins and Nathan at home, she'd changed a lot of nappies for someone who didn't have kids and professed not to want them.

"I put on the telly," Emily confessed in a whisper, as if the parenting police were going to jump out of a cupboard and arrest her for giving a two-year-old too much screen time. "Just for half an hour," she added, a pleading note entering her voice. "I don't do it all that often, honestly."

The kettle began to whistle, and Rachel lifted it off the gleaming black hob. "Plug them into the matrix all day long as far as I'm concerned," she said. "They won't be watching *Fireman Sam* when they're sixteen, I promise you."

Emily gave a small smile. "No, but you know what they say about too much telly. It suppresses their creative development, leads to childhood obesity. . . ."

"And gives a mother a much-needed break. Trust me, the way Riley and Rogan career about this place, you don't need to worry about obesity. I burn calories just watching them." She poured the water into the mugs and dunked the tea bags a couple of times before she flicked them into the sink with a spoon. It would be her job to clean up the mess later.

Sitting at the table, cradling a mug of tea, Emily Hart started to look and no doubt feel human again. "You're lucky you don't have any kids," she said as she took a sip of tea.

Rachel sat down across from her. "Having a kid sister is almost the same. I practically raised Lily."

Emily eyed her curiously, and Rachel wondered what had made her say that. She didn't normally confide in her clients, or in anyone. First Juliet, now Emily. Seeing Claire West had shaken her up way too much, made her *say* things.

"How come you raised her?" Emily asked. "What about your parents?"

"My mum broke her back when I was eleven, just after Lily was born. She's pretty much been an invalid since then."

"Oh, I'm so sorry. . . ."

This was why she didn't share details with anyone. Pity was awful; it felt like a kind of well-meaning violence. "Thanks, but it's fine now. We're all fine. Lily is eighteen and about to do her A levels. She's going to Durham University next year." If she got three As, which she would.

Rachel would make sure of it. And an A star in biology, because her sister really was that clever.

"Still, it must have been difficult," Emily ventured, and Rachel rose from the table.

"For a little while, yes, of course. But it was a long time ago. Now, clearly the kitchen needs sorting," she continued as she poured the rest of her tea out in the sink. "And the bathrooms, I'm sure. Anything else at the top of the list?"

Emily cringed guiltily. "The nappy pail . . ."

"First thing," Rachel agreed. "And maybe I'll open a few windows while I'm at it."

Three hours later she'd left the Harts' house with Riley and Rogan chucking wooden trains around the newly cleaned kitchen and Emily defrosting a pack of chicken breasts for dinner. It had all been oddly domestic and cozy as Rachel had buttoned up her coat and stuffed her supplies back into her pail. Maybe it made a difference that the kitchen was three times the size of her own, with granite counters and top-of-the-line appliances.

For a second she imagined living in this kind of house, pottering around this kind of kitchen. The kids she could take or leave, but the privacy, the space, the freedom . . .

Those were attractive.

Grimacing, Rachel headed towards her car. The fragile blue sky of that morning had darkened to pewter, and rain was spitting down like an insult. She threw her stuff in the back of the car before getting in and sitting there a moment, her hands on the steering wheel.

"Right," she said aloud. "Get over it, Rachel. Move on, for heaven's sake."

She had to, because Claire was here to stay, at least for a little while, and tomorrow she was cleaning her house.

6

Claire

IT TOOK CLAIRE FOUR days of moping around the house, venturing into Whitehaven by train for supplies, and randomly surfing the Internet for job opportunities before she worked up the courage to try the village shop again on Tuesday morning.

She wasn't sure she wanted to deal with Dan Trenton on a daily basis, but since she didn't have a car and train times were irregular, a job in the village really was ideal.

And if she got a job, even one stocking shelves at the post office shop, she'd have something to show her parents and brother, something to prove that she was actually making a life for herself here.

Even if it didn't feel that way. She hadn't seen Lucy or Abby or really anyone since her walk to the beach; the weather had been horrendous, at least compared to Portugal. Gusty wind and spitting rain, although that morning the sky had been blue. For about fifteen minutes. She'd forgotten how absolutely awful the weather could be here, although there was something strangely cozy about it too. Sitting snugly inside with a cup of tea while the heavens opened did make one feel safe.

Now Claire stood in front of the village shop and checked that the help-wanted sign was still in the window. Of course it was. Who really wanted this job?

Rain blew into her face, and she wiped her cheeks of moisture before stiffening her spine along with her resolve and heading inside.

No one was by the till, and the shop had an empty feel to it. Claire stood there for a moment, her gaze wandering around the shelves of dusty packets and tins, before she decided to go around to the back, where the post office was.

Dan Trenton was just coming from behind the post office counter with its wall of Plexiglas, and he was moving at a clip that nearly had Claire smacking into his concrete wall of a chest.

She took a hasty step backwards and Dan grabbed her by the arm. "Whoa." He righted her even though she hadn't actually been losing her balance and then released her with a scowl. "You again."

"Yes, me again. I wanted to ask about the job. Again."

Dan moved past her to the till and then turned, his arms folded. Claire glanced at one of the tattoos: the name "Daphne" with an intricate design of vines and flowers around it.

"I thought you weren't sure how long you were staying."

"At least six months," Claire said firmly. "Probably longer." She was lying, because she had no idea how long she'd end up being here. But she wanted this job. The more Dan resisted, the more determined she felt to get it, to actually achieve something on her own merit.

"Do you have retail experience?"

"I worked in real estate for the last four years, showing villas to prospective buyers. That's kind of like retail."

His lip actually curled. "You don't need to showcase a tin of beans. I'm talking about handling money. Working a cash register. Basic stuff."

"Well, then, no. But I could learn. I'm a quick learner." Dan looked unconvinced and no wonder. She was a decidedly slow learner. "I could really use a job," she added, hating that she'd resorted to begging, and so quickly. Dan Trenton did not seem like the kind of man who would be moved by pity. "And I'll work hard. Promise." Still nothing. "It's not like you've a queue of people lining up to interview," she finally burst out.

"I'm choosy."

"Clearly."

She held his gaze even though it was hard, and her breath too because this was incredibly nerve-racking. Then he gave one short, terse nod.

"Fine. You can work on probation for a fortnight, four days a week, at minimum wage. Monday, Wednesday, Thursday, Friday do you?"

"Yes—"

"You can start tomorrow?"

"Yes, definitely."

"Eight o'clock sharp."

"Okay. Thank you. You won't regret it."

Dan Trenton didn't answer.

She headed back up to Four Gables without seeing anyone. The misting rain had upgraded to a downpour and the wind was starting to gust, which meant the handful of commuters trickling from the train station was walking with their shoulders hunched and heads down. One man was uselessly holding a soaked newspaper over his head, the thin paper coming apart in his hands, and a woman had made the mistake of opening her umbrella, which immediately blew inside out, revealing its bent spines.

Claire tried to give her a smile of sympathy, but the woman wasn't looking. No one was in this weather, and so she hurried down the street towards the beach road and then up to her house.

She had a job. After wrestling with the latch in the wind, Claire closed the front door of Four Gables behind her and leaned against it. She actually had a *job*. The first job she'd gotten all by herself. She knew her parents would scoff at her working in a shop; so would Andrew, for that matter. They were all ruthless academics, but working in a shop was more her speed, surly Dan Trenton aside.

"Claire?"

Andrew came around the corner from the kitchen, and Claire gaped, feeling as if she'd conjured him from her mind. "Andrew . . . what are you doing here?"

"How about 'welcome home'?" he responded wryly, and Claire moved forward to hug him. Awkwardly, because her family didn't really do hugs.

"Sorry. Welcome home. But I didn't know you were coming. Last time we talked you were in Minneapolis."

"That job finished." Andrew's arms had closed around her for one brief, tight hug before he stepped back. Claire hadn't actually seen her brother in more than two years; with her in Portugal and Andrew in America, their holiday times hadn't crossed. Or maybe they just hadn't wanted to come home for a West Family Christmas, with all the awful, excessive trimmings.

"You didn't say anything . . ." Claire began.

"Actually, I texted you. Do you ever check your phone?"

"Oh. No, not really." She moved past him into the kitchen, and Andrew followed.

"Why not?"

"Because there's no one I want to talk to on it."

"Ouch."

"Sorry," she said as she turned around and leaned against the kitchen counter. "I didn't think you'd call. You usually don't."

She hadn't meant it as an accusation, but Andrew must have taken it as one because he answered, "I know I should be in better touch."

"I didn't mean it like that. But why are you here, Andrew? It's not like you to come back to Cumbria. You were rubbishing Hartley-by-the-Sea to me a few days ago." She gazed at him, trying to see something in his expression, but as ever, Andrew was blank-faced, unsmiling, his dark hair a little damp from the rain.

"I have a couple days before my next project, which happens to be near Manchester," he said. "So I decided to come back for a bit."

"How long?"

"Four days."

She nodded, taking a deep breath before voicing her fear. "Are you checking up on me?"

"Would that be such a bad thing?"

"I'm not a baby."

"I didn't say you were."

Claire expelled a frustrated breath. This was how conversations with Andrew always went. He won everything, even Monopoly. "I don't need anyone being worried about me."

"Sorry, but that's not your choice."

"I'm fine—"

"Really, Claire?" The words were a challenge, but his voice was gentle.

Claire's strength to stand up to her brother evaporated. "I wish you hadn't come," she mumbled.

"Do you want me to leave?"

She didn't know if the question was genuine—when did Andrew ever do what she wanted?—but she pretended it was. "No, not now that you're here." She realized she meant it, stupidly perhaps. Four Gables was huge, but it was going to feel very small with Andrew watching her all the time, measuring how much vodka and whiskey was in their dad's dusty bottles, thinking she was on the brink of toppling into alcoholism. She hadn't even been tempted to have a drink in the four weeks of rehab. She'd barely drunk anything during university; hard liquor had made her sick. But Andrew wasn't going to listen to her feeble protests. No one was.

"You don't sound convinced," he remarked, and she sighed.

"I'm not. But like I said, you're here." Her earlier euphoria about landing a job had started to trickle away. It was such a small, silly thing. "What are you doing in Manchester, anyway?"

"Working on some repairs to the Ridgegate Reservoir near Macclesfield."

"Right." Which made putting bread on shelves for a wage definitely feel a bit *less than*.

"Claire . . ." Andrew's voice was uncharacteristically hesitant. "Look, I know you've been through a difficult time. . . ."

Claire winced at the prospect of some emotive spiel from her brother. Or worse, yet another warning about how she shouldn't be alone. "Look, I need to shower and change," she said. "I'm soaked just from walking here from the post office. I forgot how wet and windy Cumbria is."

"You didn't get water in your ear?"

For a second she was propelled back to school days, when Andrew had been charged with Making Sure Claire Didn't Do Something Stupid.

"No, but in any case, a few drops of water won't actually—"

"Remember, the doctor said you could go completely deaf if you got water in your bad ear."

As if she'd ever forget. "I'm going to shower," Claire said, and left the kitchen without waiting for a response.

Upstairs she turned on the shower full blast and reached for the earplugs she'd been required to wear since she was four. It didn't usually bother her; it was just her thing. Claire's thing, to be deaf in one ear, missing its middle bones, having had countless surgeries and procedures over the years. No one in her family ever talked about it and hardly anyone knew. Hugh hadn't even known. As for being deaf in one ear, Claire had long ago learned to listen carefully and pretend she'd heard something when she hadn't. Usually it worked.

She showered and changed into yoga pants and a hoodie, gazing out at the shrubs and flower beds below. The hedges were clipped to military precision and the flower beds looked ruthlessly weeded. Absently Claire wondered how much her parents spent on gardening, and why, when they came to Hartley-by-the-Sea for a couple of weekends a year. Maybe.

The answer, of course, was obvious. Appearances.

"Claire?" Andrew knocked on the door but didn't open it. "Fancy a takeaway?"

"From where? You're not in Manchester, you know."

"There's a chippy in Egremont, if I remember correctly. Or an Indian place in Whitehaven. How about a curry?"

For the first time since her brother had arrived Claire felt genuinely glad he was there. Sharing a takeaway sounded so cozy, so *normal*. And she could use someone to talk to, even stodgy Andrew. "Okay," she said. "Let's have a curry."

An hour later—takeaway in Cumbria was not, by any means, fast food—they were sitting at the kitchen table with Andrew dividing the basmati rice into precise halves.

Claire glanced at the fine china and crystal glasses Andrew had put out as she tore off a strip of naan bread. "Pretty fancy for a takeaway."

"It's always worth doing something properly."

"Of course." Andrew was definitely their mother's son.

"I can't remember the last time we were here together," Claire remarked. Andrew sat back in his chair, reflecting.

"Your graduation from uni maybe?" He glanced around the kitchen with its top-end appliances. "It hasn't felt like home for a while."

"I know. It's strange to me, in a way, that it ever was home. I thought Mum and Dad would sell it."

Andrew's mouth twisted wryly. "I think they like having a second home in the Lake District, even if we're two hours away from the tony part."

"Maybe. Funny, though, that they never really got involved here."

"I don't know." Andrew ladled some chicken korma onto both of their plates. "Dad was busy in Leeds, and Mum was busy with you."

Claire grimaced. "Yes, I know." She'd been her mother's full-time job. "So, were you sad to leave Minneapolis?" she asked as they both started eating.

"Not particularly. Were you sad to leave Portugal?"

"Not particularly." They smiled at each other, strangely conspiratorial, and then being Andrew, he got serious again.

"Have you heard from Hugh?"

"Nope." Claire swallowed a piece of chicken that seemed poised to stick in her throat. "I think I've been officially dumped."

"Mum seemed to think the two of you might get back together."

Claire grimaced. "Of course Mum thinks that. She loved Hugh. Probably still loves him." Hugh ticked all of her mother's boxes: wealthy, intelligent, good-looking, successful, charming. Shallow and with a hidden cruel streak too, although those qualities might not have bothered her mother, if she'd ever noticed them.

"And presumably, you loved Hugh," Andrew remarked.

"Of course I did." The answer came automatically. How could she say otherwise, when she'd agreed to marry him? "But things went sour. Obviously."

"Maybe he was just looking out for you, Claire. He had to have been worried. We all were. . . ."

"Maybe," she allowed, and then wondered why she'd said that. She didn't actually believe Hugh had been looking out for her. He'd been embarrassed by her, humiliated, and suggesting her parents send her to rehab had been her punishment. Claire had suspected that from the beginning, and four weeks in unnecessary rehab had crystallized the notion. He'd stood aside while her parents had made the arrangements; when he'd mailed her things to Lansdowne Hills, he hadn't even included a note.

"Maybe you should reach out to him," Andrew suggested. His voice was kind, which only made Claire angry. "Perhaps he'd like to hear from you."

"I don't think so."

"You were engaged for a year. It stands to reckon—"

"Please drop it, Andrew," Claire cut him off with uncharacteristic sharpness. "It's not going to happen." If she called Hugh, she'd probably end up apologizing. He would give a long-suffering sigh and then what? Take her back, on certain conditions? Or tell her it really was over? Either way, it was a conversation Claire didn't want to have.

Andrew didn't answer, just picked at his chicken, and the ensuing silence was stiff with the kind of disapproval Claire hated.

"Actually, I'm not hungry," she said, and taking her plate to the sink first, she walked out of the kitchen.

Upstairs she had to fight the urge to go downstairs and say sorry. She paced her bedroom for a few minutes before she turned and went back down.

Andrew was still sitting at the table, finishing his dinner, looking completely unruffled, and for some reason that annoyed her.

Here she was, practically panting in agitation, and her brother was calmly cutting his naan bread into squares.

"I'm sorry."

He glanced at her, clearly surprised by her blurted apology. "It's obviously a sore point. I shouldn't have mentioned it."

And that, apparently, was that. Claire stood there for a moment, uncertain as ever, because in her life that was never that. But then she didn't usually apologize to Andrew. It was to her mother, her father, Hugh. And they all accepted it with long-suffering sighs, as their due.

"I think I'll go to bed."

"Okay."

"I have to get up kind of early. I start work in the morning."

"So you did get a job?"

"I'm working at the village shop."

Andrew made a little grimace, and Claire grimaced right back at him. "I'm never going to be a civil engineer, Andrew."

"I wouldn't want you to be one. But that doesn't mean you have to work in a shop."

"Maybe I'll like it."

"You're intelligent, Claire—"

"And intelligent people can't work in shops?" She shook her head, holding up a hand to forestall Andrew's reply. "Never mind. I really should go to bed." And in any case, she didn't believe what he'd said. He thought she had to be intelligent because everyone else in her family was. Between her parents and her brother they had a whole wall of framed advanced degrees in her father's study: Four MAs, two PhDs, one MD. And meanwhile Claire had barely scraped through uni.

Claire headed upstairs, shivering slightly as the wind rattled the windowpanes and rain sleeted against the glass. The house still felt big and empty, but a little less so with Andrew downstairs. She was still glad he'd arrived, and yet as she climbed into bed, Claire wondered when he was going to leave.

She lay in the dark for a long time, listening to the rain and the wind and then the creak of stairs and the click of a door as Andrew went to his bedroom down the hall. She finally fell asleep, only to awake with a start, her heart pounding as she glanced at the clock and saw it was already ten past eight in the morning.

7

Rachel

FOUR GABLES *LOOKED* EMPTY as Rachel drove up on Wednesday. She hoped it was empty, because it would be easier for both women if her former friend made herself scarce while she cleaned. Rachel definitely didn't relish another run-in with Claire, just-showered or otherwise, and she could certainly live without Claire skulking around, caught, as she often seemed to be, between apology and arrogance while she hoovered and dusted.

Rachel tried the handle of the front door, relieved when it was locked because that meant Claire probably was out, and then she sucked in a surprised breath when the lock was turned from the inside and the door swung open to reveal not Claire, but her older brother, Andrew.

Rachel had never liked Andrew all that much. He'd been four years above them in school, always looking a bit bored and indifferent, a little smug.

She'd seen him occasionally over the years, from a distance, but seeing him now, like this, standing in a doorway, brought her back to the moment when she'd been twelve, two months after she and Claire had stopped being friends. She'd rung the doorbell, teary and snot-nosed, only to have Andrew coolly inform her that Claire was busy with her birthday party, the party Rachel hadn't even known about. Then he had, without a qualm, shut the door in her face.

Old memories. Kid stuff. Rachel shouldered her mop and gave him a quick smile. "Hello, Andrew. I didn't know you were back."

Cue the blank, bored look. "I'm sorry. You are . . . ?" He sounded just like his mother, with that slight, telling sniff of disdain.

"Rachel Campbell. I clean the house." She raised her eyebrows, willing him to move aside, but he simply stood there. "This mop is heavy, you know," she said, and Andrew finally moved. Then he followed her into the kitchen and watched as she started to unpack her cleaning supplies.

"How long have you been cleaning the house?"

"About five years. I do a quick whiz round once a week but if you're staying along with Claire, I can do more."

"No. I'm sure whatever you're doing will be fine. I'm leaving in a few days."

"Right." She started spritzing cleaning spray over the vast black granite island, and still Andrew just stood there, watching. Rachel kept an alert, cheerful expression on her face with effort. She felt as if she were performing a role, the chirpy housekeeper on some BBC drama. Next she'd be calling him "love" and boiling him a cup of tea. But, no, Andrew West was no Emily Hart or Iris Fairley.

"Sorry," he said after a moment. "It's just you look familiar."

"I grew up here, went to school a few years below you," Rachel answered as she started wiping down the island. "Same year as Claire."

"Oh, right. I must have seen you around, then."

"Must have."

He stood there for a few more minutes while Rachel went about her business, head down, spraying and swiping. Finally he left.

She let out a breath, glad to relinquish the role she'd been playing— and for whose benefit? Andrew West's? Annoyed, Rachel spritzed the sink and swiped it with vigor. Maybe she should stop coming to Four Gables until the West children were no longer in residence. She could do without the stress they caused her, bringing back memories she'd far rather leave buried deep in her subconscious.

Except those memories were already starting to slither out.

She stopped wiping, her elbows propped on the sink, her gaze on the rain-soaked garden outside even as she remembered another scene entirely. A chilly April evening, a month after her mother's accident, her father walking out. Rachel had watched him go down the high street to the pub. It had only been half five, and Lily, not even a year old, had needed feeding and bathing. Her mother's sheets had to be changed. And Meghan had been hiding upstairs.

Rachel had done it all, and then, when her father had come in at eight, reeking of beer and knowing full well that the hard work had already been done, he'd given Rachel a shamefaced smile and slouched upstairs.

Rachel had stood by the door for a long moment, consumed by a rage that she, at not quite twelve, didn't fully understand. All she'd known was that she'd been doing her father's job, and it wasn't fair.

She'd slunk out of the house and run up to Claire's. She'd never been there before, but she'd known where it was. Everyone in the village did. If you stood on the high street and tilted your head back, you could see it perched on the hill above the beach, a Victorian monstrosity that had looked to Rachel, with its gables and turrets, like some kind of over-grown gargoyle.

She'd knocked on the door, her heart beating hard, her nose running from the cold, and tears already starting in her eyes. All she'd wanted was to talk to Claire, to talk to someone who, even if she didn't understand, might at least listen. Out of desperation she'd put her pride aside; then Andrew had opened the door, told her about the party, and then promptly shut it in her face.

It shouldn't matter now, but it still hurt, especially when she considered that not much had changed in the sixteen years since then. The only thing that was different was her dad wasn't at the pub; he was gone for good. And instead of standing on the stoop, she was cleaning the Wests' house.

"You were friends with Claire, weren't you?"

She turned around; Andrew had come back into the kitchen, hands stuffed in the pockets of his jeans as he rocked back and forth on his bare feet.

"A long time ago," she answered. "Back in primary." A shrug to show she barely remembered. Then she turned her back on him and got out the Hoover.

"How come you didn't keep in touch?"

"How do you know we didn't?" Rachel challenged as she unwound the endless cord. "Anyway, do you keep in touch with your primary school friends?"

"So you didn't," Andrew stated, and Rachel gritted her teeth. Andrew West could be even more aggravating than his sister.

"No, we didn't."

"Why not?"

"You didn't answer my question."

"About my primary school friends? No, I haven't kept in touch with any of them. I left this village when I was eighteen and I didn't come back very much." A shrug to dismiss the village and all of its residents as unimportant, or at least it felt that way to Rachel. "But you haven't left."

"Obviously."

"So?"

"Claire was the one who left," Rachel responded. "Anyway, we stopped being friends long before that. She went to Wyndham, same as you did, if I'm remembering correctly?" The elite private school in Keswick that sent a blue-and-gold bus to the village to pick up its exalted pupils. Wyndham kids stuck to themselves and always had; the kids who went to Cumberland always seemed a bit raggedy and rough in comparison.

"Right. Of course." Andrew didn't move, and Rachel decided to ignore him. She plugged in the Hoover and started vacuuming the hessian carpet under the breakfast table.

He waited there until she'd finished and turned the machine off before he spoke again. "I'm only asking because I think Claire could use a friend right now."

"Oh, could she?" Andrew raised his eyebrows and she turned away, lugging the Hoover across to the hall. "Sorry, but I'm here to clean, and since I get paid by the hour, it's in your family's best interest to let me do my job."

After a second's pause where he seemed as if he were debating whether to say something, Andrew stepped aside. "I'll let you get on with it, then," he murmured as she passed.

Rachel spent the next two hours cleaning at hyper speed, working up a sweat and trying to suppress the stupid guilt she felt at the way she'd smacked Andrew down. It should have felt good to wipe that supercilious look off his face. As if she were going to become pals with Claire again.

When she had needed a friend, where had Claire been for her?

Of course, they'd only been eleven at the time. She wasn't really going to hold a childhood grudge, was she? That would be pathetic.

Looking around at the Wests' huge house, with a whole parade of photos of Claire through the years marching up the wall along the stairs, Rachel decided that yes, maybe she was going to.

She was just leaving when Andrew appeared again in the hallway. He must have been listening, waiting for her to start packing up.

"I'm sorry if my suggestion was offensive."

"I'm not offended." She was tired and grimy and her self-righteous anger had disappeared sometime between cleaning the toilets and stripping the beds. "I'm sure Claire could use a friend. She told me the last time I was here that she'd broken up with her fiancé, so yes, I get that she's having a tough time. But so am I, as it happens, and I'm afraid I don't have it in me to look out for her. Not again."

Then, realizing she'd probably said too much, Rachel grabbed her mop and pail of supplies and left. She was just throwing them into the back when her phone buzzed with an incoming call. With a queasy feeling she saw it was from Cumberland Academy, Lily's school.

"Hello?"

"Mrs. Campbell?"

"Yes?" Rachel had long ago stopped correcting the parade of teachers who assumed she was Lily's mother. It was easier all around if she simply pretended she was.

"I'm ringing about Lily's parent-teacher conference yesterday—"

"What?" Rachel slammed the lid of the boot and hurried around to the driver's side and slid in, out of the rain. "I didn't realize she had a conference last night."

"Lily didn't tell you?"

"She must have done." Rachel closed her eyes and leaned her head against the back of the seat. "I must have forgotten. I'm sorry." Why hadn't she written it on the calendar? She couldn't remember Lily telling her about it, but then she often felt as if she were doing four things at once, and none of them well. Lily might have told her and she hadn't registered it.

Sighing, she turned on the car and put the heat on high. "Could I make it up? Sometime this week, perhaps?"

"I'm free tomorrow afternoon, if you'd like to come in."

She cleaned two holiday cottages tomorrow afternoon, but she could do it in half the time if she hustled. "Of course."

"I'll see you at four."

"Thank you, Miss—" Too late Rachel realized she didn't actually know the woman's name.

"Taylor," the woman said, and Rachel heard a note of reproof in the woman's voice. What kind of mother didn't know the name of her daughter's teacher? Except Rachel wasn't Lily's mother. "I'm Lily's biology teacher. The other teachers might want to see you, too, if you want to make the arrangements."

When the call ended, Rachel sat there for a moment, the phone cradled in her hand, exhaustion crashing over her. She saw a movement in the front window of the Wests' house, and the pale sliver of a face between curtains before it moved away. Andrew, no doubt, wondering what she was doing, sitting in his driveway. She reversed out of the Wests' sweeping drive and headed down the beach road.

Four hours later Rachel pulled up outside her house, reversing into a parking space that gave her two inches on either end and hitting her neighbor's bumper in the process. With a groan she got out to assess the damage and saw that it was a tiny scratch that could be buffed out with a rag and some polish, but Edgar Lacey would read her the riot act about it anyway. He was incredibly precious about his old banger, polishing it to a tired shine every Saturday morning while wearing nothing more than a vest and gym shorts. Not a sight Rachel liked to look at while eating her Shreddies.

She decided to tackle him later and headed inside to the chaos that was the Campbell home. The noise hit her first: Nathan screaming at the top of his lungs, Lily's pulsing techno music, and her mother calling for something, a chaotic orchestra of her family life whose tune she usually didn't mind. Today she found it nearly unbearable.

Rachel dumped her stuff in the cupboard under the stairs and headed first for her mother, poking her head around the doorway.

"Mum?"

"Sorry, love," Janice wheezed. She was lying flat on her back as she did whenever the pain was really bad, her face pale and gray. "It's just I've run out of pills and my back is aching something fierce."

"You shouldn't have run out," Rachel said with a frown. She retrieved the brown plastic bottle from the bedside table and squinted to read the instructions. "Meghan had this filled only last week, and they're meant to last a month."

Her mother smiled in apology. "Poor Meghan spilled some in the toilet of all things, when she went to get me a glass of water. She forgot she had the open bottle in her hand."

Which sounded a lot like Meghan. Rachel put the bottle back on the table. "I'll phone the chemist's emergency number." Which would cost money they couldn't afford, as well as a drive into Whitehaven. "Can you manage with ibuprofen till then?"

Her mother winced but then lifted her chin in what looked like a pantomime of bravado. "I suppose I'll have to, won't I?"

"Yes, I'm afraid you will." Her voice came out sharper than she had meant for it to. She was starting to feel savage; everything today seemed to be crowding her in, reminding her of how small and suffocating her life was and always would be.

She fetched a bottle of ibuprofen and poured her mother a glass of water. Janice Campbell heaved herself up against the pillows.

"Sorry, love."

"It's not your fault." Bloody Meghan. With an impatient breath, Rachel helped her mother to rest against the pillows and then handed her two tablets.

"Better make it three."

Wordlessly Rachel shook out a third and handed it over. After her mother had swallowed the pills, she headed upstairs to where Lily's music and Nathan's wailing were competing in both volume and aggravation. Rachel decided to tackle Meghan first.

"Meghan, why didn't you deal with the prescription before I came home?"

"Say again?" Meghan glanced up from the mirror propped on top of her dresser, a lipstick in one hand. Nathan was wrapped around her legs, his head peeking out between her knees. At Rachel's entrance, he'd stopped crying, at least for a second.

"Ray-Ray!"

"Hey, Nath." She patted his head before turning back to Meghan.

"Mum's prescriptions. She said you dropped half the pills down the toilet this morning. But you had all day to deal with it, and you didn't."

Meghan stared at her for a moment, nonplussed, and then turned back to gaze at her reflection. "Oh. Yeah." Slowly she leaned forward and outlined her lips in carmine red.

"*Meghan.* Seriously? That's all you're going to say?"

Meghan shrugged, her eyes still on her reflection. "What would you like me to say?"

"Oh, I don't know. Sorry, maybe?"

"Okay. Sorry." She smacked her lips together, unrepentant.

"Why didn't you phone the prescription in, or text me? I could have picked it up on the way home." Meghan didn't answer, and for the first time since she'd come into the room, Rachel registered her sister's outfit: tight miniskirt, clingy top, and way too much makeup. "You're not working at the pub tonight, are you?"

"Nope."

"Then why . . . ?" Nathan started crying again, a halfhearted attempt that told Rachel he was either exhausted or knew it wouldn't get him anywhere. Probably both.

"I'm going out." Meghan nudged Nathan with her foot. "Oy. A little quieter."

"Going out? And I'm babysitting Nathan, I suppose?"

Meghan flicked her gaze from her reflection to Rachel. "I'll put Nathan to sleep first, if you can't be arsed."

"He's your son," Rachel snapped, then took a deep breath. This wasn't Nathan's fault. "Sorry."

"You should be."

Meghan hauled Nathan up onto her hip, and he hooked one hand around the neckline of her top so Rachel could see the strap of a cherry red bra underneath. It looked new.

"Are you going out on a *date?*"

"Maybe."

Meghan had always been tight-lipped about her love life. No one even knew who Nathan's father was, only that he wasn't in the picture and never had been. One day she'd announced she was pregnant, she was keeping the baby, and no one was to question or even discuss it. Rachel had been overwhelmed at the thought of coping with a newborn along with their mother and Lily, but she could hardly demand Meghan not have the baby. And she loved Nathan, even if she felt as if her maternal affection had been spent on Lily.

Since Nathan's birth Meghan had gone out on the occasional Saturday night with some girlfriends, but never on a Wednesday and never looking like . . . that. "You're not dressed like a maybe," Rachel said, and Meghan smiled smugly.

"Just because you haven't been able to get it on with Rob Telford doesn't mean I can't try."

"You're going on a date with *Rob Telford*?"

"No, but then neither are you."

Rachel shook her head, exasperated. "So who, then?"

"Never you mind. Come on, Nath." Meghan yanked a pair of Thomas the Tank Engine pajamas from the top drawer of the bureau she shared with her son. "Time to get ready for bed."

"I haven't even started tea yet——"

"Nathan and I had toasties down at the beach café."

"In this weather?" It was still raining outside, the drops hitting the windows like bullets.

Meghan shrugged. "It gave us something to do, and Nathan likes to play with Noah." She picked Nathan up and plopped him on the bed, stripping the clothes from his toddler-belly body with practiced speed.

"If you need something to do, how about cleaning the house? Or making tea? Or getting Mum's prescription refilled?"

For a second Meghan's eyes flashed with ire. "I took care of my own tea, and you'll find the sitting room is actually decent."

"And Mum's prescription——"

"I forgot. I'm sorry, okay?" Her voice rose, and alarmed, Nathan let out an experimental cry they both ignored. Meghan took a deep breath and flipped her hair over her shoulders. "Look, I told you I'll put Nathan to bed before I go out. What's the big deal?"

The big deal was Rachel wanted to go out. She wanted to escape the confines of her life for an evening, flirt with Rob Telford or anyone, *forget* for a few minutes. She stared at Meghan for a few seconds and then sighed. "There's no big deal. Come on, Nathan." She scooped the little boy up into her arms. "How about we do some coloring?"

"He could use some Calpol before bed," Meghan said as she grabbed her jacket, a red scrap of cotton that looked as skimpy as her top. "He's still teething."

"I believe you," Rachel said, and started for the hallway.

"Rachel?" Meghan called, and for once her voice sounded uncertain. "Thank you."

"You're welcome." Rachel set Nathan up with a coloring book and crayons while she tidied the kitchen; the sitting room might have been decent, but the kitchen was not. Then she put some sausages in the oven for dinner and went back upstairs to confront Lily. Meghan had already left, banging the front door behind her.

"Lily?" Rachel poked her head into her sister's bedroom. Lily was lying on her stomach on her bed, music blaring, a sketch pad in front of her.

She looked up warily. "Yeah?"

Rachel leaned against the doorframe, trying to summon the energy for what had the potential to be another difficult conversation. "Hey, your parent-teacher conference was yesterday. Why didn't you remind me?"

Guilt flashed across her sister's face. "You seemed tired."

"I still wanted to go," Rachel said. She studied Lily's face; her sister looked as if she was hiding something. Rachel recognized the downcast gaze, the bit lip, from when Lily had been small. But this wasn't a case of sneaking a sweet. "Did you tell me about the conference in the first place?" she asked carefully.

"No," Lily said after a second's pause. "I didn't want to."

"Lily." Rachel tried to keep the hurt from her voice. "Why not?"

"Because I knew what the teachers were going to say. You didn't need to hear it."

"Maybe I should be the one to make that decision. And I am going to hear it, because your biology teacher called me this afternoon. I want to be involved, Lily."

Lily's face took on a closed, pinched look. "What did she say?"

"Just that I missed the conference. I'm seeing her tomorrow afternoon. And I'll see the others too, if you give me their details." Besides biology, Lily took further maths and business studies. She'd dropped Design and Technology after she'd completed her AS level.

Wordlessly, Lily wrote some names down on her sketch pad, tore off the strip of paper, and handed it to Rachel. "Their e-mail addresses are on the school Web site."

"Thank you," Rachel said, wishing this wasn't such a battle. Didn't Lily realize how lucky she was? How much opportunity she had? She knew Lily wouldn't appreciate her reminders, and so she said nothing.

The smell of burning sausages brought her back downstairs. She had just taken them out of the oven—blackened on one side, raw on the other—when the front doorbell rang.

With a groan Rachel dumped the tray of sausages onto the stove top and went to the door.

Her mouth opened in shock and no words came out when she saw Andrew West standing there, his expression as serious as ever.

"Hello, Rachel," he said. "Can we talk?"

8

Claire

AFTER THROWING ON HER clothes and grabbing a banana, Claire bolted out of the house and sprinted down the lane towards the village shop. She was going to be at least twenty minutes late for her first day of work. She'd probably be fired.

She weaved between the trickle of late commuters heading for the station and squeezed past a farmer coming out of the shop with a loaf of bread under one arm and then stood in front of the till, panting, disheveled, and twenty-five minutes late.

"Sorry."

Dan Trenton didn't even look up from the till. "You're late."

"I know. I overslept. I didn't hear the alarm." She'd slept on her good ear, which she hardly ever did, but the persistent pattering of the rain last night had bothered her, and if she slept that way, she couldn't hear anything, including the alarm. Somehow she didn't think Dan was interested in her excuses. "I'm really sorry. It will never happen again."

Finally he closed the drawer of the cash register and looked up, his expression as unwelcoming as ever. "You can start on the newspapers."

"The newspapers?"

He nodded towards the empty rack to the right of the counter. Several stacks of freshly printed and delivered newspapers were pushed up against the wall, each one bound with plastic cord. "They need to go on the shelves. The *Telegraph* at the top, the *Times* underneath, then the *Guardian* and the local papers at the bottom. Think you can manage that?"

"*Telegraph, Times, Guardian,* local. Yes. Right."

Dan handed her a pair of scissors. "To cut the cords," he explained when she looked at him blankly.

"Okay. Thanks." He'd turned away even though no one had entered the shop, and so Claire went to work.

It wasn't particularly interesting work to cut the cords binding the stacks and then slide the newspapers onto the shelves. She glanced at some of the headlines on the national papers; they were the usual dreck about the royal family, an MP who was accused of corruption, troubles with a large bank.

She glanced back at Dan, who was ringing up a loaf of bread and a tin of cat food for a middle-aged woman Claire vaguely recognized. When the woman had gone, she decided to try a little light conversation.

"Do you carry any tabloids?"

"No."

"They must sell pretty well, though."

"So does porn, and I don't sell that either."

Startled, Claire tried for light. "A man of morals, then."

"Principles, maybe." Finally he glanced over at her. "When you're finished there, you can unload the milk."

Claire glanced around the little shop; the refrigerated section that usually held milk, butter, and a few pots of yogurt was nearly empty. "Where's the milk?"

"It hasn't arrived yet."

A jogger decked out in a lot of bright spandex came in for a bottle of Vitaminwater and Claire got back to stacking.

By the time she'd finished, she felt tired and dirty, and it was only a little after nine o'clock in the morning. Still, she'd accomplished something, and that felt good. While she'd been working, the milkman had arrived, wearing the Cumbrian farmer's uniform of flat cap, wool jacket, plus fours, and mud-splattered Wellington boots. He unloaded the milk from a huge plastic crate, chatted with Dan in a nearly incomprehensible accent, and then disappeared.

With the newspapers finished, she started on the milk, developing a rhythm of lifting, swinging, and putting down. She'd finished about half the crate when Dan's voice, sharp with irritation, stopped her cold.

"What the bloody hell do you think you're doing?"

Claire's mouth dried and her mind spun. She *hated* confrontation. And Dan Trenton was looking extremely confrontational, with his massive hands planted on his hips, biceps bulging, and his face contorted into the darkest scowl Claire had yet to see him make.

"Stacking the milk?"

"You've smeared the newspaper ink all over the bottles," Dan exclaimed. "Don't you even look at what you're doing?"

Claire blinked, and then saw the black ink smeared across the glass of the pint bottles. She looked down at her hands and realized they were covered in ink smudges from the freshly printed newspapers. "Sorry," she said. "I didn't realize . . ."

"Obviously."

She could feel heat surging into her face. "I'll wipe it off—"

"Go wash your hands," Dan ordered. "There's a sink in the back." He pointed towards a door in the back of the shop, by the post office counter.

Feeling like a scolded schoolgirl, Claire went. The door opened onto a narrow passage that led to the area behind the post office on one side and on the other to what she realized must be Dan's living quarters.

She was just stepping through to the kitchen when she heard Dan call, "Mind the dog."

"Dog . . . ?" She looked around nervously; she really wasn't a dog person, and Dan Trenton didn't seem like the type to have one of those cute little keep-in-your-handbag ones.

"She doesn't bite," Dan called, which wasn't all that reassuring. "Just don't pet her."

Claire stepped cautiously into the kitchen, but she didn't see any dog. She breathed a sigh of relief and then glanced around, taking in the tiny room with its ancient appliances and big stone farmhouse sink, a window overlooking a small courtyard of cracked concrete. The kitchen was tidy to the point of barrenness, the only sign that anyone actually lived here a single bowl and spoon drying in the dish drainer.

Claire washed her hands at the sink, her gaze moving around the room. She was curious, wanting to pry a little into Dan's life, but there was nothing to see. As she dried her hands on the tea towel hanging on the railing of the small cooker, she saw a flight of steep, narrow stairs leading to the second floor. She couldn't see what was at the top, and she wondered if the rest of Dan Trenton's little house was as clean and empty as his kitchen.

Deciding she'd spent enough time speculating, she turned to go back into the shop, and that was when she saw the dog cowering under the table.

"Oh . . ." She felt a surprising dart of sympathy for the animal. It was trembling with what could only be terror. "Hey," she said softly to the dog, and it cringed back. It was white with brown and black patches and looked like some kind of springer. Maybe. She'd never been good at identifying breeds.

She heeded Dan's warning about not petting it and hurried back into the shop. An elderly woman was standing by the newspapers, squinting at the cover of the *Telegraph*.

"Can I help you?" Claire asked, and the woman's head jerked up.

"I can pick out my own paper, thank you," she snapped, and tucking the paper under her arm, she reached for a pint of milk.

Dan must have polished the bottles, for there were no traces of smeared ink to be seen on the glass. Claire stood there uncertainly while the woman took her purchases to the counter.

"That will be two pounds twenty," Dan said. He wasn't friendly to anyone, it seemed, except maybe the milkman.

The woman retrieved a little coin purse of faded embroidered silk. "I knew your mother," she said as she counted out several twenty-pence coins. "We were both in the embroidery club."

It wasn't until the woman had pushed the coins across to Dan that Claire realized she'd been speaking to her.

"Oh, did you? I didn't know Mum embroidered."

"Every Tuesday for ten years," the woman said as she collected her paper and milk. "Until she moved down to London." She glanced at Claire, her eyes small and shrewd in her wrinkled face. "You can tell her Eleanor Carwell says hello."

"Yes, of course I will, Mrs. Carwell," Claire answered.

"It's 'Miss,'" she said, and left the shop.

Claire sagged a little. She'd been at this job for less than two hours and already she wanted to go home. She didn't think she could stand Dan Trenton's unfriendliness along with a potential parade of villagers who knew her or her family, not to mention the fact that she'd done a rubbish job at the most basic thing Dan had asked of her.

Resolutely she turned to him. She wasn't going to give up now. "Thank you for wiping off the milk bottles. I would have done it, though." Dan grunted in reply. "What should I do now?" Claire asked.

For a second she thought she saw something flicker on his face, some semipositive emotion, but it was gone so quickly she couldn't be sure. "You can check the expiration dates on all the tins," Dan said, and pointed to a shelf of baked beans, tomato soup, and other basic items. "Throw out anything that's expired." He reached under the counter and produced a cardboard box. "Think you can manage that?"

"Yes," Claire answered a bit sharply. She could only take so much sarcasm. "I know I am new to this, but I'm not an idiot." Dan didn't reply.

"I didn't know you had a dog," she remarked as she started searching for the expiration dates stamped on a variety of unappealing-looking tins.

"Why would you?"

"I don't know. He never comes into the shop?"

"She, and no. That wouldn't be hygienic."

Claire pictured the dog cringing under the table. "But she must get lonely."

"I take care of her fine. I walk her at lunchtime and at the end of the day."

"I . . . I didn't mean . . ." Claire began, and Dan sighed.

"I know you didn't," he said, and turned away.

A few hours into her first day and Claire ached with exhaustion, not just from bending and straightening from hours of stacking or checking and then chucking tins, but from sharing the same small space with a man who radiated tension. Dan Trenton seemed like the most unlikely person to run a cozy little shop. He should be smiling and chatty and leaning over the counter as he talked to people. Instead he simmered with latent anger, seeming almost to resent anyone who dared come through the doors. She wondered what had possessed him to take this job, but she didn't have the courage to ask.

She'd certainly seen enough tinned goods to last a lifetime. "Tinned golden syrup pudding?" she asked as she chucked a tin into the nearly full box at her feet. "It expired three months ago. Does anyone buy this stuff?"

"I stock a full range of tinned items," Dan answered. He was feeding scratch cards into the Lottery ticket dispenser.

"I know, but if no one buys it, surely you shouldn't stock it?" Claire returned. "Tinned deviled eggs . . . How do they even *do* that? And does anyone eat Spam anymore?"

"I do," Dan said, and she didn't think he was joking.

"What about getting in some different things?" she suggested. "Something people actually want to eat?"

"Like caviar or black truffles?" Dan filled in. "You might be used to such luxury items, but most people in Hartley-by-the-Sea are a little more plebeian."

She turned around, pressing her hands to the pulsing ache in the small of her back. "You think I eat truffles and caviar?"

"You know what I mean. You're wealthy."

"My parents are wealthy," she corrected. "I'm not really." Although her parents had always subsidized her lifestyle, so she couldn't quibble too much. "I certainly don't eat caviar. Anyway," she said, trying for brightness, "here I am working in a shop."

"Your choice."

"I know." She gazed at him for a moment, wondering if he had a particular problem with her or just with everyone. "Sorry I said anything about the tins," she said at last. "Clearly you're not looking for suggestions."

Dan didn't answer.

At noon he gave her a half-hour break for lunch. She bought a meat-and-potato pie from the warming oven that was propped on one end of the counter. The pies, she'd already learned, were delivered by a local baker at eleven.

She'd eaten the pie standing outside, under the awning, because the rain had still been sleeting down, and watched a few people hurry down the pavement, heads ducked low as if somehow that helped in avoiding the rain. The pie was mushy and tasteless, but at least it was hot, and the street seemed to be washed in gray, a muted landscape of somewhat dingy-looking terraced houses under a heavy, dark sky. She'd grown up here, walked down this street a thousand times during her five years at the primary school, but it felt unfamiliar to her now. The years at uni, and then in London and Portugal, had separated her from the life she'd once had in Hartley-by-the-Sea. She felt as if she were looking through the wrong end of a kaleidoscope when she recalled her years here.

And yet, for a second, she could picture herself, as if watching an old film, walking up the street in her pinafore and plaits. She could see Rachel at the top by the school lane, waiting for her. They always went in together, linking arms. That sense of solidarity had been so welcome, so needed. Claire didn't think she'd experienced it since.

And yet she'd been the one to turn away from Rachel, even if Rachel had let her. Sighing, she chucked the empty foil container into the bin and went back into the shop. Ancient history. Half-forgotten memories. She doubted she and Rachel could be friends again now.

At three fifteen the shop, which had been empty for the last hour, filled with children from the primary school, all of them squealing and squabbling over the rack of sweets. Dan had asked her to make sure none of the children pocketed a sweet, which had seemed cynical to Claire until she'd seen just that. She'd tapped the boy tentatively on the shoulder, and he'd scowled at her before shoving it back on the rack, making Claire feel both vindicated and a little guilty, as if she'd been the one to do something wrong.

The children lined up at the till, snapping gum and grabbing cans of soda from the refrigerated section, while Claire stayed out of the way. She never did well in crowds; the background noise made it nearly impossible for her to hear anything. A crowd of children seemed even more intimidating than one of adults; children could be so blunt, so cuttingly direct. They hadn't yet learned to have a filter.

"Oy. *Oy.*" Too late she realized Dan was shouting at her.

"Oh, sorry! Yes?"

He called something to her, but she couldn't make it out over the chattering children, and so she shook her head helplessly. Scowling, Dan stalked across the shop to the rear storeroom, where he hauled out an enormous box of Haribo sweet ten-pence bags. "I'm not paying you to stand about," he grumbled as he headed back to the till, and Claire mumbled another apology.

Finally the children trickled out, and at Dan's instruction Claire started restocking the much-depleted sweet rack. Then at quarter to four Lucy Bagshaw breezed in, giving Dan a cheery hello, to which he actually cracked a smile. Claire was counting the minutes until she could go home.

"Claire!" Lucy's voice rang out cheerfully. "So Dan took you on, after all. I knew he would." She threw a playful look at Dan, who did not acknowledge it.

Claire could only wonder at Lucy's indefatigable cheer. Did not even Dan Trenton's surly stare put a dent in her mood?

Lucy grabbed the local paper and slapped it on the counter before turning to look at Claire. "Pub quiz tomorrow night?"

"Oh, um. Didn't your fourth person come back? Juliet . . . ?" She plucked the name out of her memory and Lucy's smile faltered only slightly.

"Well, ye-es, but Juliet could make up another table with Peter and some others." She nibbled her lip in frowning thought, and Claire took the obvious opening.

"No, no, it's fine. I'm not much of a pub quiz person, actually. Neither pub nor quiz, and as for both together . . ." She let out an uncertain laugh. Had she even made a joke?

"Well, if you're sure," Lucy said, and Claire thought she sounded a little relieved.

"Honestly, I'm fine. After today I think I'll just go home and have a long soak in a huge bubble bath." Which sounded heavenly.

"When do you end your shift?"

"At four. I think." Claire glanced at Dan for confirmation and he gave a terse nod. "And back tomorrow at eight?" she added, making it a question. Although why she wanted to come back, Claire didn't even know. Another eight hours of stacking tins and smearing ink, all with Dan Trenton silently glowering at her.

"Don't be late this time," Dan said.

"Why don't you stop by Tarn House for a cup of tea when you're finished here?" Lucy suggested. "It's the white house with the black door, down at the end of the street, near the station. But you must know it."

She let out a laugh. "I keep forgetting you're from here. You're far less of an offcomer than I am."

Offcomer. Claire had always hated that word, how unfriendly it sounded. "Actually," she said, "I'm not sure I am. But yes, okay. Thanks for the offer. I'd love a cup of tea."

Which wasn't strictly true. She'd love to go home and run a bath and stay in it for hours, hiding from the world. But it was hard, if not completely impossible, to say no to Lucy Bagshaw.

"Great!" Lucy gave a smile and nod of satisfaction, as if she'd managed everything just as she'd intended. "I'll see you in a bit, then." She took her paper and fluttered her fingers at Dan. "Bye, Dan."

"Bye," Dan answered, and put her change in the till.

"So you're friendly with at least one person in this village," Claire said before she could think better of it. Eight hours of surly silence had taken its toll.

Dan gave her his usual stare. "That's about right."

"Are you from here?" Claire asked. "Or are you an offcomer like Lucy?"

"Offcomer," Dan answered, and Claire couldn't say she was surprised.

9

Rachel

RACHEL STARED AT ANDREW West standing on her doorstep and said the first thing that came into her head. "Oh no. Not you."

"May I come in?"

She really, really did not want Andrew West in her house. Not with the burned sausages on the stove top and Lily's music blasting and her mother groaning faintly from the downstairs bedroom. Plus she was pretty sure Meghan's underthings, including several lacy thongs, were draped over the radiator in the sitting room to dry.

"Okay," Rachel said after a moment, without any grace. She stepped aside so he could enter.

Andrew ducked his head to avoid the low stone lintel and then stood in the tiny hallway, cluttered with shoes and discarded hats and scarves and a whole lot of LEGOs.

Rachel picked up a woolly beanie that always seemed to be lying on the floor even though no one ever wore it and hung it on one of the coat hooks. "Come into the kitchen," she said. "I'm just burning our tea."

Andrew followed her into the kitchen, which was little bigger than the hall, his quiet gaze taking in everything Rachel never wanted someone like him to see. The peeling linoleum, the ancient cooker and wheezing fridge, the dripping tap and the burned sausages, their greasy smell hanging in the air and clinging to her skin.

Nathan looked up from his coloring book, his expression turning alert at the sight of a stranger.

"Hello," Andrew said to Nathan, and then he shoved his hands in the pockets of his parka, clearly ill at ease, which gave Rachel a twist of savage amusement. Let him be a little uncomfortable in her domain. Let him see how close and constricting her life was. Fine. It would be worse for him than for her. Maybe.

"I'm not sure why you're here." She banged a pot on the stove and reached for a bag of peas from the freezer. Unfortunately she hadn't realized it was open and as she jerked it out of the freezer, peas sprayed across the kitchen floor like tiny green bullets.

"Oops, Ray-Ray," Nathan said, looking pleased by the mess.

Rachel sighed and pushed the peas into a pile with her foot. "Never mind, Nathan. I'll clean them up later."

"I wanted to talk to you about Claire," Andrew said. "But if you're busy . . ."

Rachel arched an eyebrow. "Oh, you think I'm busy?" she said as she poured the rest of the peas into the pan. "Why on earth would you think that?"

Andrew neither apologized nor rose to the bait. "I can come back later."

"I'd rather you didn't."

Nathan's face crumpled a bit. Clearly he was sensing the hostility. Rachel took a deep breath, forcing herself to stay calm. She didn't want Nathan dissolving into tears, and frankly, she shouldn't care what Andrew West thought of anything. Being so openly aggressive showed him she did.

"Sorry. I'm not actually trying to be rude. But is it important? Because I have a lot going on at the moment. As I told you before."

"Actually, it is," Andrew said. "I wouldn't have come here otherwise. I can tell you have a lot going on, Rachel."

The quietly spoken words deflated her a bit. "Right, then." No doubt he wanted to tell the details of Claire's sob story. And a tiny, mean little part of her wanted to hear them. "We can talk, but not here." She was fighting the urge to push Andrew out of her house before he saw any more of her sad little life. She'd thought she could take it, but now she didn't think she could. "Let me sort things here and then we can talk outside, okay?"

"It's bucketing down at the moment," Andrew pointed out. "How about I buy you a drink at the pub?"

Which would be the closest thing she'd had to a date in more than five years. "Not the pub," Rachel said. She couldn't bear everyone's speculative gazes when she came into the Hangman's Noose with Andrew, the good-natured but uncomfortably pointed ribbing she'd get. "Let's go somewhere else."

"Raymond's?" he suggested, which was the classy bistro that had opened in the old train station a handful of years ago. Rachel had never been inside.

"Can you go there just for a drink?"

Andrew gave her a look of polite disbelief. "Of course you can."

And of course he would know these things. "Fine," she said. "Just give me a minute."

She ran upstairs and begged Lily to put Nathan to bed, and then checked on her mother, who had thankfully fallen into a doze.

"Damn, the prescription," she said aloud, and Andrew, who was waiting in the hall, answered politely, "Can I help?"

"No. I just . . ." She fished her mobile out of her bag and scrolled through her contacts for the number of the out-of-hours pharmacy. "We'd better make this quick," she told him. "I have to drive into White-haven to pick up my mother's prescription."

"Why don't I drive you? We can just as easily have a drink in White-haven as in Hartley-by-the-Sea. Raymond's is overrated, anyway."

"Oh, is it?" Her mouth twitched in a sardonic smile. "All right, then. Let's go into Whitehaven."

She grabbed her jacket, and they walked in silence to his car, parked down the street by the post office shop. Andrew nodded towards the shuttered windows. "Claire took a job there. Today was her first day."

"She said she was looking for a job," Rachel answered as Andrew pressed a button on his key ring to unlock a navy blue Lexus. "Glad she found one."

"Yes, although I don't know how long she'll last. She came home today absolutely knackered. Stacking newspapers isn't really her thing."

"Is it anyone's?" Rachel countered. "Most people have a job to make money."

"Personal fulfillment is important too."

"Must be nice for some," Rachel answered, and then, annoyed she'd reverted to being snippy again, she turned her face towards the window.

"Yes," Andrew agreed after a moment. He'd started the car and pulled away from the curb, driving up the steep hill that led to the A-road. "Not everyone can afford to work in a job they enjoy, I do realize."

"Well-done." The words slipped out before she could suppress them.

Andrew didn't respond for a moment. "You really have a chip on your shoulder, don't you?" he finally remarked mildly.

Rachel turned to face him. "A *chip* on my shoulder?"

"About money. Or privilege. Whatever." He shrugged, the movement so dismissive Rachel wanted to slap him.

"Yes, I suppose I do have a chip on my shoulder," she said, her voice rising. "A bloody great Grand Canyon. But it's easy for you, isn't it?"

"Maybe from where you're standing," Andrew answered. "Yes. I can see that things aren't easy for you. Like you said, you have a lot going on."

Rachel didn't answer. She'd wanted him to stay smug and condescending, because then she could feel justified in being angry. Instead she felt petty and mean.

"Do you enjoy your job?" Andrew asked. "Housecleaning?"

With effort she kept herself from a snippy retort. "I enjoy some things. Providing for my family—"

"The money aside, though," Andrew interjected. "Do you enjoy the work?"

"Cleaning toilets and scrubbing floors? No, can't say I do." Rachel paused, thinking of Iris Fairley's conspiratorial grin when she'd slipped her a custard cream. "I like the people," she admitted. "Helping them, and I don't mean just by cleaning their houses."

"How, then?"

She shrugged. "I give people the odd cup of tea, a chance to talk to someone. It's like free therapy for some, I suppose."

Andrew was silent, and too late Rachel realized where he'd so neatly led her—right to helping Claire.

"Where exactly are we going?" she asked before he made the obvious suggestion.

"How about the Harborside?"

It was a swanky bar on the harbor that was another place Rachel had never been to. "Sure," she said with a shrug. "Sounds good."

They didn't speak for the rest of the three-mile drive into Whitehaven. Andrew parked the car in the lot by the harbor, and as Rachel stepped out into the damp evening—the rain had stopped, at least—she felt a sudden pinprick of excitement at the prospect of going to a nice place with a fairly attractive man. Even if it was Andrew West.

She glanced at him, his navy blue parka zipped up although she could see the collar of a dark green fleece underneath. He wore dark chinos, ridiculously pressed, and hiking boots. The outdoor version of preppy.

But no matter what his clothes, it was turning into a nice evening, the clouds scudding across a deep violet sky and moonlight glimmering on the placid sea. Rachel stood for a moment, breathing in the fresh, still-damp air, enjoying the simple fact that she wasn't in her kitchen cutting sausages into Nathan-sized bites.

"Shall we?" Andrew asked, and with his hand on the small of her back, he guided her towards the bar's entrance.

It was a classy place, a far cry from the crowded pubs on King Street, which stank of old beer and sweat with the TV blaring football at all hours of the day, farmers and shift workers lined up at the counter, heads hung low over their second or third pints.

The Harborside had big velvet armchairs and sofas and low tables of dark, polished wood. The only sound was the murmuring of voices and the occasional clink of crystal, with a background of soft piano music.

"I didn't know places like this existed in Whitehaven," Rachel quipped, and then wished she hadn't. She'd sounded a little too awed.

"It's nice enough," Andrew agreed as he shrugged out of his parka. Rachel took off her coat and, unable to hang it on the back of her armchair, she stuffed it underneath.

"What can I get you?"

"A glass of red, please." She watched as Andrew headed for the bar, utterly at ease while she was sitting on the edge of her enormous chair, her hands folded primly in her lap. She wanted to enjoy this, even if she was with Andrew West, but she felt too tightly wired. Then she remembered she still needed to call in the prescription, and so she did that while Andrew got their drinks, slipping her phone into her bag as he brought back a fishbowl-sized glass of wine for her and a half-pint of lager for himself. No self-respecting male acquaintance of Rachel's would ever order half a pint, yet Andrew hardly seemed like the type of bloke to go in for a drinking contest.

"Cheers," she said, and took a sip of the wine, which was velvety smooth and tasted better than any bottle of plonk she'd ever picked up at Tesco.

Andrew sipped his own lager before setting it on the table between them. "I'm sorry for bringing you out here like this. I know you're busy."

"It's not every day I get to drink wine in a classy bar," Rachel answered. Two sips of wine and she was already starting to feel mellow, but maybe it was the atmosphere. She leaned her head back against the velvet armchair and glanced at Andrew; he was staring at his hands, frowning in thought.

"What do you do, exactly?" she asked. She didn't want to talk about Claire just yet.

"I'm a civil engineer."

"Impressive. You go to uni for that?" Of course he had, but she wanted to hear it anyway.

"Yes."

"Where?"

"Cambridge." He looked slightly discomfited, and Rachel smiled.

"I think I've heard of it."

He smiled back, self-consciously, but at least he'd recognized she was joking. She almost wanted to tell him that she'd had a scholarship place at Durham, that she'd gone there for all of two weeks. Thankfully she resisted that temptation.

"And an MA too, I suppose?"

He nodded. "Also at Cambridge."

"PhD?"

"Same."

Seven or eight years of advanced education, then. She refused to give in to the petty impulse to feel jealous. "So why are you back in Hartley-by-the-Sea?"

"I have a couple days before my next project starts, down near Manchester. And I wanted to see Claire."

They were already back to Claire. So much for chitchat. "So why are you so worried about her?" Rachel asked.

Andrew didn't answer for a moment. "As you know, she's been

through a difficult time," he said finally. "But there's more to it than just her breaking up with her fiancé. I'm not even sure they are broken up, permanently, but . . ." He sighed. "Claire should tell you herself what's going on—"

"Claire and I really don't have that kind of relationship," Rachel cut him off. "We were friends when we were children. Before last week I hadn't seen her since her graduation party, and then only because I helped with the catering."

Andrew looked up from his study of his drink. "Even so. I don't see any other friends queuing up, do you?"

"Claire had plenty of friends in primary." Rachel spoke matter-of-factly. "She was the most popular girl in Year Six, and as far as I could tell, she kept that status at Wyndham."

"I don't know if any of those girls were actually real friends."

And I was. She'd been a good friend to Claire West until she'd been unceremoniously dumped. Rachel sighed. "So what do you want me to do, exactly?"

"Just keep an eye on her. It would be better for her not to be alone right now."

As if Rachel needed one more person in her life to watch over. "I'm happy to check up on her when I come to clean," she said, although happy was stretching it. "But other than that . . ."

"Couldn't you drop in every day or two?" Andrew asked. "I know you're busy—"

"You keep saying that, but I'm starting to think you don't mean it."

"Sorry." He gave her a rueful smile as he raked a hand through his hair, and Rachel's stomach did a surprising little flip. When he dropped the whole pompous thing, Andrew West was actually good-looking, in an uptight, nerdy sort of way. Although there was nothing nerdy about his wavy dark hair or deep blue eyes, or even the broad shoulders she could detect under the fleece. No, unfortunately it was just his personality.

"Does Claire think she needs checking up on?" Rachel asked.

"She's . . . resistant."

"And she's also an adult. So maybe I should let her make her own decisions."

"Claire's never been good at making her own decisions."

Which was a horribly patronizing thing to say, and yet Rachel could see the truth in it. When they were little Claire had always let Rachel make her decisions. At school Rachel had even carried Claire's lunch tray and picked out which meal she'd eat. But she'd liked taking care of Claire. And Claire had been so grateful, smiling up at her, relief evident in her face whenever Rachel stepped in and took over.

"Claire is never going to learn to make her own decisions if everyone keeps insisting on making them for her," Rachel said. "She's twenty-eight years old. Maybe it's time for her to grow up."

"I take your point," Andrew answered, "but now's not the time for that particular life lesson."

What was it about Claire that made everyone want to look out for her? Was it her sense of fragility, or did simply being chronically helpless make proactive people step in and take control? Rachel couldn't say, even for herself. What she did know was that she didn't want to help Claire now nearly as much as she had when they were seven.

"I'm not sure there's ever a good time for that life lesson," Rachel said as she downed the last of her wine. "I had to learn it when I was twelve."

Andrew frowned. "What happened when you were twelve?"

"My mother broke her back." Rachel wished she hadn't mentioned anything; she couldn't stand pity, especially from someone who could spare it so easily. "Everyone's life sucks sometimes, you know."

"Yet you seem to think only yours does." Andrew spoke mildly, but Rachel recoiled all the same. Heat rushed into her face, and she put her wineglass on the table with a decidedly loud *thunk*.

"I think I'll get that prescription now." She reached under the chair for her coat and yanked it on. Andrew watched her, unperturbed.

"I've upset you."

"Well-done, Sherlock." Rachel stood up, hugging herself, all the things she'd liked about this place now jarring, irritating her. This was not her life.

Andrew put his half-pint of lager, barely drunk, on the table. "Where do you need to pick up the prescription?"

"Lowther Street. There's a late-night pharmacy."

"All right." He left a pound on the table and then walked out of the bar, holding the door open for her first. Rachel went through, averting her head. She felt stiff and jerky, and while she knew her hurt was obvious, she couldn't make herself relax. It was an overemotional reaction, considering she barely knew Andrew West and he barely knew her. But in that case, how dared he make such an assumption about her?

"You know," she said as they walked towards the car, "you don't know anything about my life."

"I'd say I know a little at this point," Andrew answered. "But essentially you're right."

"So you really have no right to make a judgment like that," she continued, keeping her voice even.

Andrew opened her door, ever the gentleman. And didn't agree with her.

"Do you?" Rachel pressed as he got in the driver's side.

"Perhaps not. I was simply responding to what I've experienced of you so far."

"You're very blunt, you know."

His mouth twitched in a tiny wry smile. "I have been told that before."

They didn't speak as he drove through the empty streets of Whitehaven and parked in front of the pharmacy on Lowther Street, its plate window fogged with rain, halogen lights glowing inside.

"I'll be right back," Rachel said, and slipped out of the car. It took only a few minutes to get her mother's prescription, a four-week supply of OxyContin that cost nearly two hundred pounds. And half of that had gone down the toilet, thanks to Meghan. Rachel handed her debit card over with a grimace, breathing a tiny sigh of relief when the amount went through.

Back in Andrew's car she clutched the bag to her while he pulled out onto the empty street. Neither of them spoke on the way back to Hartley-by-the-Sea.

"So you'll check on Claire?" he asked when he'd parked in front of her house. Rachel didn't know whether to laugh or groan.

"I'll try," she said on a sigh.

He paused and then said carefully, "If you'd prefer to think of this as part of your housekeeping . . . I could pay you the hourly rate."

Rachel stared at him for a moment, offended by the suggestion even though practically it made sense. She would be going out of her way, spending time she didn't have running around after Claire. And she could certainly use the money. "That's not necessary," she managed, and got out of the car.

Inside, the house still smelled of burned sausages and Rachel could hear Nathan's pitiful sobs from upstairs. He sounded utterly exhausted.

"Finally." Lily appeared at the top of the stairs, looking harassed. "Nathan has been crying for hours."

"Did you give him Calpol?"

"No. You didn't tell me—"

"Sorry," Rachel said wearily. "I'll go to him. Can you give Mum her prescription?" She nodded towards the white bag she'd left on the hall table, and Lily gave a little grimace.

Lily didn't spend much time with their mother. Since Janice had injured her back when Lily was only a newborn, they'd never had a lot of time together, and they hadn't really bonded. Rachel and Meghan handled their mother's care, wanting to shield Lily from it, and now Lily was eighteen and usually avoided her mother as much as she could.

"Okay," she said reluctantly, and went downstairs. Rachel kicked off her shoes and headed into Meghan's bedroom. Nathan was kneeling on the bed, tears running down his snot-smeared face.

"Hey there, Nath," Rachel said softly. She put her hands on his thin shoulders and pulled him to her; he came with a loud sniff, tucking his head into her shoulder. "How about some yummy medicine?"

He nodded against her chest, hiccupping, and she eased away and went to retrieve the bottle of bubble-gum-pink Calpol from the bathroom as well as a sticky spoon, which looked like it hadn't been washed between doses.

She gave him two spoonfuls and then tucked him into the double bed he shared with Meghan.

"Ray-Ray stay?" he asked hopefully, and with a sigh she stretched out next to him.

"Okay, Nath."

Nathan snuggled into her again, smearing snot across her sweater, and Rachel put her arm around him, resting her chin on the top of his head. He smelled like baby shampoo and Calpol with a hint of sausage. She kissed his head and closed her eyes and tried to ignore the tug of longing for something in her life to be different.

10

Claire

ON THURSDAY CLAIRE SET her alarm and slept on her bad ear so she would hear it. She felt cautiously optimistic as she dressed, buoyed by the cup of tea she'd had with Lucy and Juliet Bagshaw yesterday afternoon.

There had been something so pleasant and welcoming about their kitchen, with its green Aga and a jar of early daffodils on the windowsill and the B&B guests going in and out. Lucy's good humor was, as ever, infectious, although her half sister, Juliet, had taken a bit more getting used to. Her smile reminded Claire of a crack in a plate, and she'd given her several speculative looks that had left Claire squirming. But she'd been friendly enough in the end, and Lucy's warmth certainly made up for any lack on her half sister's part.

Sitting with them, listening to their good-natured bickering, Claire had felt a part of things. At least, she'd felt as if she could be a part of things, eventually. Maybe.

Buoyant, Claire made it to the village shop by ten minutes to eight, and this time she stepped inside with a cheery smile for the man at the counter.

"Morning, boss."

"Just call me Dan."

"Okay. Dan." Claire glanced around, but the newspapers and milk hadn't arrived yet. "What would you like me to . . . ?"

"I thought I'd teach you how to operate the till. That'll be most helpful, when I need to be at the post office counter."

"Okay." She eyed the cash register, telling herself it couldn't be that difficult. It was nothing but an oversized calculator.

"You need to come around this side," Dan said.

"Oh. Right." Claire moved around the counter with its racks of sweets and crisps to the small space behind it. There was barely room for both her and Dan, especially considering how huge he was. Claire didn't even come up to his shoulder.

"So it's a basic machine," he said. "You check the price sticker. You input it into the machine." He pointed to the number buttons. "Then you hit the tab and the drawer opens. Take the money, make the change, close the drawer, and give the receipt. Simple." He eyed her expectantly, and after a second Claire recited, "Money, change, drawer, receipt. I think I've got it."

Dan didn't look convinced. Standing this close to him made him seem even more intimidating. He had a tattoo on the inside of his forearm that said "sapper" in curly script, surrounded by clouds of fire. Claire realized she was staring at it, and she moved her gaze up to Dan's face. This close to him she could see that his eyes were brown with flecks of gold. From a distance, narrowed in his usual glare, they'd just looked dark.

"Why don't we practice?" he said, and moved past her to the front of the shop, his large body brushing against her as he did so. He smelled of soap.

"Okay." She stood in front of the cash register as if it were an undetonated bomb. She could do this. She really could. She tucked her hair behind her ears and wished her heart hadn't started pounding. All she was doing was operating a till, for heaven's sake. It didn't have to be hard.

Dan plunked a bar of chocolate onto the counter. "Ring that up, then."

"Right." Gingerly Claire picked up the bar of Bournville. "Okay.

Eighty-nine pence. Got it." Her voice sounded squeaky. She stabbed the eight and nine buttons on the till, and Dan made an impatient harrumphing sound.

"You just charged me eighty-nine pounds for a bar of chocolate. You need to put a zero and decimal point first. Everything is rung up in pounds."

"You didn't tell me that," Claire protested.

"I thought it was obvious."

"Well, it wasn't." She bit her lip and searched the keypad of the register. "Is there a delete button?"

"Oh, for . . ." Dan muttered under his breath, and then moved around to join her behind the counter. He pushed the "clear" button and then rang the order up himself. The drawer opened with a jolly-sounding *brrrng* that was at odds with the tension emanating from the man operating the register.

"Sorry," Claire said, and he shoved the drawer closed and ripped off the receipt before flinging it into the bin.

"Don't be so sorry all the time. I'm the one who hired you."

"Yes, but you probably thought I wasn't quite as useless as I am."

"Actually, I did. Why don't we try again?"

This time Claire managed to ring up the bar of chocolate without any problem, and the sound of the drawer opening made her nearly weak-kneed with relief.

The newspapers and milk had arrived while they'd both been behind the counter, and after tossing the second receipt in the bin, Dan handed her the bar of Bournville. "Keep it," he said tersely, and then headed for the post office counter. "You can stack the papers until someone comes in. Don't attempt to do cigarettes or Lottery cards, though, all right? Those are handled differently."

"Okay," Claire said, and watched while he opened up the post office, wondering if this meant she was actually in charge.

The first person to come into the shop was Eleanor Carwell, dressed in the same twinset and tweed skirt she'd worn yesterday, looking just as sniffily imperious. She collected her milk and *Telegraph* and placed them both on the counter, clearing her throat unnecessarily as Claire hurried over.

"Behind the till now, are you?"

"Yes, just started." Claire smiled brightly before picking up the paper and scanning it for the price. Considering she'd been staring at the newspapers for the last half hour, she should know where it was, but in her nervousness the lines of print blurred before her.

"It's a pound forty, dear," Eleanor said tartly.

"Right." She looked up. "Seems expensive for a daily newspaper."

"I quite agree. Perhaps your employer would care to lower the price?"

"Oh, well . . . It's a national thing, isn't it?" Claire rang up the newspaper with a tiny sigh of relief and then glanced at the pint bottle of milk. There was no price sticker on it.

"Eighty pence," Eleanor said with a slightly martyred air. "Do you not know the price of anything?"

"Not yet. I've just started. That's two pounds twenty, please."

Eleanor took out her change purse and counted out eleven twenty-pence pieces before sliding them across the counter. "Have you spoken to your mother about me?" she asked.

"Oh. No, I'm sorry. I haven't spoken to my mother for a few days." Although she'd seen that her mother had left two more voice mails, she hadn't listened to them yet. Dealing with Marie West took a level of fortitude Claire never seemed able to work up to.

"Well, I hope you improve in time," Eleanor said with a nod towards the cash register, her tone implying she very much doubted it, and Claire sagged against the counter as she left the shop in a cloud of stale Yardley's lavender water.

The rest of the day passed in silence until lunchtime, when Dan dismissed her for half an hour. "What about your lunch?" Claire asked. "Don't you want a break?"

"I can't have you in the shop alone," he answered. "Not until you've learned a bit more, anyway."

It wasn't raining for once, so Claire walked down to the beach café. It took longer than she'd expected, so by the time she stepped into the muggy warmth of the café, she realized she had only five minutes to eat if she wanted to make it back on time.

"Claire!" Abby greeted her from behind the counter. "Lucy told me you got the job at the post office shop."

"Word travels fast here, doesn't it?"

"You should know that by now," Abby answered with a smile. "What can I get for you?"

"I only have about five minutes," Claire said, a note of apology in her voice. "I didn't realize how long it would take me to get down here. Do you have anything ready-made?"

"Only the kids' picnic baskets," Abby said, and pointed to a row of luridly colored cardboard boxes that held, according to the sign above them, a sandwich, a juice box, a packet of raisins, and a biscuit.

"That's fine. I'll take one of those," Claire said, and after paying and thanking Abby, she walked back outside, feeling more than a little ridiculous holding the little box with a picture of Buzz Lightyear on it. She found a park bench overlooking the sea and ate the jam sandwich, tilting her face up to the sun. She'd forgotten how beautiful it could be here when the sun actually came out. She'd hardly ever come down to the beach when she was younger; her parents had never been walkers, and when she was a teenager she'd always gone with the Wyndham girls into Whitehaven, to pursue the more alluring pleasures of the town's dodgy nightclubs. She would have preferred to go to the beach, but she'd never gone against the crowd.

It annoyed her now, how little backbone she'd had. How little she still had, if she was honest with herself. She'd done everything everyone had asked of her, even gone into a clinic to dry out when she was pretty sure she didn't actually have a drinking problem. The trouble was, after so many years of obeying other people while you doubted yourself, Claire wasn't sure she knew how to be different. She definitely didn't think she had the strength.

But coming back to Cumbria had been a strong decision, even if it looked from the outside like merely running home. She just hoped she could keep at it. She knew the pressure from her parents would only get worse. Her mother was too used to managing her to stop now, and Claire was used to being managed. Not having someone arranging her movements, telling her what to do and even what to think, felt like dangling in midair, feet kicking uselessly.

It was only as she took these first few tentative steps that she realized there might actually be a foundation beneath her feet, even if she didn't know how strong or safe it was.

With a start Claire realized she'd spent ten minutes staring into space, half a jam sandwich dangling from her fingertips. She stuffed the bright box with its kiddie contents into the bin and hurried up the beach road, back to the shop.

She was late. Of course. Dan glowered at her but didn't say anything, and then pointed to the till. "You can manage that while I do the post office. There's usually a rush after lunch."

There hadn't been yesterday, but obediently Claire went behind the till. She rang up four purchases in three hours, when Dan took over the mad rush of pupils from the primary. This time she managed to tap a bit more firmly on the shoulder of a boisterous-looking lad who had been trying to put a cherry bootlace in the pocket of his trousers, and he grinned sheepishly before putting it back. Progress.

Lucy came in just as she had before, after the children had left, as cheery as ever.

"Oh, Claire, I'm glad I caught you. Rachel's backed out of the pub quiz tonight, and so we're desperate for a fourth. You wouldn't mind coming, would you?"

"Oh . . . no, I suppose not." Actually, she would mind. She couldn't think of anything worse than facing the loud scrum of the pub on quiz night, as well as twenty questions she knew she wouldn't be able to answer. "Why did Rachel back out?"

"She's not feeling well. Which means she must *really* not be feeling well, because Rachel never misses a quiz. But you'll come?"

"Well, I . . ." Dread seeped into Claire's stomach. Abby and Lucy and even Juliet were friendly, but the whole experience was an endurance test. The crowds, the noise, the feeling of ignorance and then the awkwardness at only drinking water while everyone was swilling wine. Although, actually, she'd like a glass of wine. "I suppose . . ."

"Great—"

"Can't you tell she doesn't want to go?"

Both Lucy and Claire turned in astonishment to see Dan leaning over the counter, scowling as usual, although this time it was at Lucy. "Stop pestering her. She said no yesterday and she's trying to say it today."

"Oh." Lucy's face crumpled a bit, and Claire felt a rush of sympathy.

"No, I don't mind . . ." she began, unconvincingly.

"Oh, I didn't realize," Lucy said. "I'm sorry." She turned to Claire with an uncertain smile. "I do rush on sometimes, I know, and I'm not always clued in to what's really going on . . . but if you don't want to go, you mustn't. I mean, we can always find a fourth. I just thought . . . "

Claire was torn between appeasing a disappointed Lucy and taking the exit Dan had so surprisingly provided. In the end she chose to escape. "I'm sorry. I'm just not a party kind of person. But maybe something else, some other time, would be . . ." She trailed off, and Lucy nodded.

"Yes, of course. Sure. Brilliant." She slapped a coin on the counter, waved at them both, and then hurried out of the shop.

Claire turned slowly to Dan. "Thank you," she said. "I think?"

He arched an eyebrow, unsmiling. "What's to think?"

"You might have just lost me my one friend in this village."

"Lucy? That won't put her off. But you should stick up for yourself. Learn to say no."

"I know I should," Claire said quietly. "But thank you for saying it for me."

"Don't expect me to again," Dan said, and walked back towards the kitchen, no doubt to walk his dog. Claire watched him go, wondering if he did have a soft side like Lucy had said, or if he'd simply got tired of her waffling. Probably just tired.

I I

Rachel

THE DAY HAD NOT started well. The night hadn't been that great, either. Rachel had fallen asleep with Nathan drooling on her shoulder and occasionally flinging his arm across her face until Meghan had crept in around four o'clock in the morning, smelling of beer and cigarettes and giggling tipsily.

"Oh, I'll just sleep in your bed," she'd whispered before Rachel, blinking blearily, had fully woken up.

"No . . ." she began, but Meghan was already creeping out of the room. Rachel sank back onto the bed and spent the next three hours being alternately kicked in the face and the kidneys until Nathan woke up at six thirty and demanded his Weetabix.

The morning was beautiful, with the birds twittering in the two runty trees in the back wedge of garden, the golden light filtering through their barely unfurled leaves. Rachel stood at the sink and tried to enjoy the moment, but Nathan was banging his spoon on the table, and she realized the grass hadn't been mowed in forever.

She poured milk into her coffee and then into Nathan's cereal as he looked up balefully.

"Mummy gives me sugar too, on top."

Rachel dumped a spoonful of sugar over his Weetabix without a word. She sat at the kitchen table and sipped her coffee, trying not to feel irritated that she'd spent the night in bed with a toddler *and* she had to work all day. Meanwhile Meghan had wasted a hundred pounds' worth of prescription pills and partied all night. And would no doubt be unrepentant about both when she finally stumbled downstairs that morning.

Rachel finished her coffee as Nathan turned his Weetabix into a brown, sugary mush without eating much of it. She'd never been a morning person, and usually slept in as late as she could, only to rush around grabbing coffee and banging dishes while Lily, Nathan, and Meghan tiptoed around her. She would actually enjoy this moment's fragile peace, if she weren't so tired.

Reluctantly she thought of last night's drink with Andrew, his nasty assessment of her. *You seem to think only yours does.* It had been a bloody rude thing for him to say. He didn't know anything about her life; he didn't know how hard it was.

And yet she *had* been rude to Andrew, and even to Claire, since she'd clapped eyes on the pair of them. Seeing them again had made her take a hard look at her life and realize just about none of it was going to change. Would she be cleaning houses and taking care of her mother when she was fifty? Probably. It could be worse, she knew. If she hadn't had that brief taste of freedom and opportunity at Durham, she'd be fine with the way things had turned out. It was just she knew how different they could have been.

"Hey, you're not usually up this early," Lily said as she came into the kitchen, knotting the belt of the ratty *Doctor Who* dressing gown that Meghan had given her for Christmas last year. Rachel hadn't even realized Lily liked *Doctor Who*; she'd felt a jolt of surprised uncertainty when she'd seen how pleased Lily had been with it.

"There's the culprit," Rachel answered, and pointed a finger at Nathan as she gave him a reassuring grin. He grinned back and then shoveled a spoonful of mushy Weetabix into his mouth.

"Where's Meghan?"

"Sleeping off last night."

"Ah." Lily switched the kettle on and retrieved her favorite mug, a chipped bowl-sized pottery one, from the cupboard. Rachel watched her, noting how she'd dyed the tips of her hair fuchsia, and she had three piercings in one ear. When had she done those things? Why hadn't Rachel noticed? Lily certainly hadn't consulted her, and with an unpleasant jolt Rachel realized how little Lily consulted her about anything these days.

When Lily had been a baby, Rachel had done nearly everything for her. Changed her, bathed her, fed her, tickled her tummy. Her father had looked after her while Rachel had been at school, and when he'd had work, she'd gone to the nursery in Egremont. But whenever Rachel had been home, Lily had been hers. At first she'd liked having her own baby doll to play with. It had felt like a game, and there was nothing quite like the feeling of chubby baby arms wrapped around your neck, a sweet, plump cheek pressed to yours. But then her mother had fallen and her father had had to take any job he could, and suddenly taking care of Lily had stopped being such a game.

But she hadn't minded. She'd never minded sacrificing her social life so she could be there for Lily. She'd seen all her milestones: first steps, first word, first lost tooth. She'd been the one to put the pound under her pillow; she'd bought her Christmas and birthday presents and helped her write invitations in her painstaking best joined-up script for the party she'd had when she was ten. She'd baked the birthday cake, and greeted the children at the door. She'd done everything a mother would.

But sometime in the last few years she'd stopped being so involved in Lily's life. When Rachel had come back from Durham, after Dad had left, she and Meghan had made a deal. Meghan would quit school that summer, after Year Ten, and get a nighttime job so she could look after Mum and Lily during the day. Rachel would restart Mum's house-cleaning business. Even though she'd been working ten-hour days,

Rachel had made time back then for Lily. She'd gone to her parent-teacher conferences and cricket matches, and she'd kept her weekends clear.

So when had it all changed? Perhaps when Lily had become a teenager and had naturally become more secretive, more hidden. Perhaps it had happened gradually, and Rachel had been too busy and tired to notice. Yet in that moment, in the dawn light of an April morning, Rachel realized she really didn't know her sister at all.

Lily had her own life now, her own friends, whose names Rachel didn't even know: a couple of pimply boys with hair that always got in their eyes, chunky glasses, and ironic T-shirts. The arty, geeky crowd, and Rachel couldn't tell one of them from another.

"So," she said, her voice a little too loud and bright as Lily dunked her tea bag a couple of times. "I'm meeting your biology teacher this afternoon. I e-mailed your other teachers, but they haven't gotten back to me."

Lily shrugged and tossed the soggy tea bag into the bin. "They're busy, I suppose."

"You're doing well in all your subjects, though," Rachel said. The trial exams in January had given Lily predictions of two As and an A star in biology. She had a conditional offer from Durham for biology as long as she got the grades, and three other backups if she didn't. "I don't think she'll have anything important to say," Rachel continued. "But it's good to check in."

Lily shrugged, her thin shoulders hunching under the pilled fleece of her dressing gown. Rachel stared at her, wishing Lily would say something. Wishing she knew what to say to her. When had this tense silence started? Maybe last year, when Rachel had insisted Lily drop Design and Technology. Lily had wanted to drop one of her other subjects, but no serious university was interested in what was generally considered a soft option.

"You can go almost anywhere you want," Rachel had said. "Why hamper yourself with a subject good universities don't take seriously?"

"Maybe they should take it seriously," Lily had said, and Rachel had shrugged her words aside. The fact was, they didn't.

Last autumn she'd taken Lily on a tour of universities, including Durham. It had felt amazing and yet agonizing to stroll down those narrow, cobbled streets, walk across the footbridge that spanned the River Wear to the student union. Her two weeks at Durham had been the best of her life, but she didn't talk about them to anyone, and certainly not to Lily. Rachel didn't think Lily even remembered that she'd gone there.

Lily had been quiet during that trip, although she'd seemed to enjoy the meals out, and she'd liked the student union with its walls full of students' artwork, all self-consciously stark lines and messy blobs of paint. But at the end of the trip Lily had told Rachel she wasn't sure university was for her, and Rachel had replied that it most certainly was. Lily hadn't answered, and in the six months since, she'd worked hard and filled out her university application online, smiled when she'd gotten her offers. Rachel had assumed all the uncertainty and teenage angst was behind her.

Now, as Lily picked at her black nail varnish and sipped her tea, Rachel wondered if it wasn't.

"What have you got on this weekend?" she asked.

"Revision, I know," Lily answered with a sigh.

"I'm trying not to nag, you know," Rachel answered lightly. "It's only that it's so important, Lily——"

"I know it is."

She couldn't keep herself from giving Lily these pep talks. "You'll thank me one day," she said, and Lily rolled her eyes. Rachel couldn't blame her. She sounded as sanctimonious as Andrew West. "Maybe we could do something this weekend. Go to the cinema."

"There's only rubbish on."

"I don't mind rubbish." She couldn't remember the last time she'd gone to the cinema, or done anything fun with Lily. "Do you want to check the times?"

"I'm going out on Saturday night," Lily said. A few flakes of black nail varnish drifted to the floor. "With some friends from school."

"Oh?" Rachel tried to pitch her voice light and interested. "Where to?"

"Just Will's house." Lily shrugged, and Rachel decided not to press. She didn't know who Will was, but Lily went out a lot of weekends, usually to someone's house to hang out or watch a DVD. Rachel didn't keep tabs on her social life; during the weekend she was usually too busy catching up on errands and bills, before the week and all of its demands and pressures rolled around again. It hadn't bothered her before, but now she felt the loss.

"Well," she said. "Maybe next weekend." Lily didn't answer.

It was after seven and Meghan still wasn't up. Nathan had finished his cereal, and so Rachel dumped his dishes in the sink and wiped him down with a wet cloth. "I think you got more on you than in you," she remarked. "Better go wake up Mummy, Nath. Ray-Ray has to work."

Lily had disappeared upstairs, no doubt to grab the shower first, and Rachel took Nathan by the hand and led him to her bedroom, where Meghan was stretched out on her bed, drooling onto her pillow.

"Wake up, Snow White," she said, trying to keep her voice light. "Your prince is here." She deposited a wriggling Nathan onto Meghan's stomach, and her sister groaned. Nathan squealed.

"You have no heart."

"I let you sleep in my bed. I think a thank-you is in order."

Meghan let out an enormous yawn and then reached up to snuggle Nathan, who wrapped his arms around her neck. "I'm completely shattered."

"Where were you last night?"

"Out."

"Obviously, but where—"

"Ask me no questions, I'll tell you no lies." Meghan rolled over onto her side, bringing Nathan with her as she tickled his tummy. "Thanks for giving him breakfast. I assume that's what you did, since there's Weetabix all down his front?"

And now in her bed. "I need to get ready for work," Rachel said. "Could you please move?"

Half an hour later she was heading out to clean Henry Price's two-up-two-down terraced house at the top of the village. A single man in his forties, he had her clean only once a fortnight, and Rachel didn't think he so much as rinsed a dish in the interval. She wiped two weeks' worth of shaving bristle from the sink in the bathroom and stripped sheets that felt grimy and smelled stale.

After Henry's place she had two holiday cottages and then her meeting with Lily's teacher. A knot of tension had taken up residence in Rachel's stomach, although she couldn't precisely identify its source. Maybe it was everything: her mother's lost pills, Meghan's insouciance about being away most of the night, Lily's unnerving silences. Andrew West asking her to watch over Claire and telling her she had a bloody chip on her shoulder. He had no idea.

By the time she arrived at Lily's school, having cleaned three houses in a handful of hours, Rachel was tired and sweaty and felt nearly as grimy as Henry Price's sheets. She took a moment in the car to brush her hair, apply some lip gloss and deodorant, and then change her work T-shirt for a button-down blouse she hardly ever wore. Too late she noticed the three boys sneaking a smoke behind the rubbish bins at the back of the school. They'd goggled at her speedy striptease, and now one leered as she left the car.

"Shut it," she barked, and headed inside the school.

Miss Taylor's classroom was quiet and empty of students, and for a second Rachel stood in the doorway, relishing a moment of relative peace. Then the woman looked up from her marking, and Rachel stepped forward.

"Hi, I'm Rachel Campbell, Lily's . . ."

"Mother, yes——"

"Actually, I'm her sister." Rachel put her bag on the floor and sat in the chair the teacher had already pulled up to her desk. "Our mother is bedridden, so I get to do the honors."

"Right, of course." Miss Taylor rifled through some papers before drawing out Lily's exercise book.

"Lily does excellent work, as you know," she said, and Rachel nodded, her hands knotted in her lap. "She is a very intelligent young woman, very capable. I rang you yesterday because, unfortunately, she hasn't handed in her last three assignments."

"Lily hasn't?" Rachel clarified stupidly. As if the teacher would be talking about some other kid.

"No, Lily hasn't. And she's offered no reason when I've asked her for them."

"But . . ." Rachel shook her head slowly. Lily had been a straight-A student since reception, had received ten A stars on her GCSEs, had never missed or forgotten anything. All right, maybe she'd been a little quiet lately, a little morose even, but forgetting assignments in Upper Sixth, when you'd been accepted to Durham University? "I don't understand."

Miss Taylor folded her hands on top of her desk and gave Rachel a look that felt too compassionate. "The truth is, Miss . . ."

"Rachel."

"Rachel, I don't think Lily actually likes biology."

"But she's so good at it." The protest came instinctively. "And she's never *said* she doesn't like it."

"I think the missing assignments might speak for themselves."

"Maybe she just forgot."

"She didn't say she forgot," the teacher said gently. "And she didn't take up my offer to hand them in late. She just said sorry and pushed past me."

"That doesn't sound like Lily."

"I know."

Rachel shook her head again, flummoxed. Lily was ruining her chances by doing this. Sabotaging them, and for what? "I'll talk to her. I'll see what's going on. Are the assignments important? Will they affect her grades?"

"They don't count towards her final mark, but it's important I see that she understands the concepts. Her final lab work for her fifth paper is next week. That's important."

"Right." Rachel knew Lily was doing her final research paper on soil content and the effect of sand dune erosion on its properties. Or something like that. She'd taken a bunch of samples near the beach and brought them in to school to analyze. Rachel had talked to her about it a little bit, had tried to reclaim some of the scientific knowledge from the crowded fog of her mind. She'd even felt a tiny spark of intellectual curiosity; it had almost felt painful, when she considered how much she'd once known, how interested in everything she'd once been.

Maybe that had been why she hadn't asked Lily more about her research project, been more involved. Because it had hurt. "I'll talk to her about it," she said, and then realizing she was already five minutes late for her next client, she said a hasty goodbye and hurried out of the school.

Back in the car she saw a text from Lucy confirming the pub quiz for that night, and impatiently Rachel texted back, canceling. As much as she loved her one evening out, she knew she wasn't up for it then. Not when everything in her life felt poised to explode.

When Rachel arrived back home a little after six, Meghan was asleep on the sofa while Nathan sat on the floor, picking his nose and watching *Teletubbies*. Lily was nowhere in sight.

Rachel popped her head around the doorway to check on her mother; she was sitting propped up in bed, looking a bit more cheerful, although her breathing was labored.

"You all right, Mum?"

"Good day today," Janice half panted. "A little short of breath, but I got up and watched telly in the living room. Even went out in the garden to sit in the sun for a bit. The tulips are coming out."

"Are they?" Rachel smiled distractedly as she checked the bottle of OxyContin she'd bought last night. "You've had your pills today?"

"All two of them." Janice smiled up at her and reached out to put one hand over Rachel's. "Don't worry about me, love," she said, and took the bottle from her.

"I'm not worried," Rachel lied. "Just checking, that's all." The truth was, ten years of bed rest hadn't done Janice Campbell any favors. She'd never been a thin woman, and now she was verging on morbidly obese. Her shortness of breath came no doubt from being overweight as well as from thirty years of smoking. "Can I get you anything?"

Janice shook her head. "I'm fine, love, fine."

Rachel was coming out of her mother's bedroom when the front door opened and Lily slipped inside, clearly trying not to be noticed. She gave Rachel a quick, guilty smile and then hurried up the stairs before Rachel could say a word.

"Lily . . ." she called, and hurried after her. The bedroom door was already closed, music pounding. Rachel stood there for a moment, trying to summon the energy to have a confrontation with Lily. But maybe it wouldn't be an argument; maybe there was a reason why Lily hadn't done her course work. "Lily," she called again, and opened the door.

Lily was just taking off her school blouse and she let out a yelp as Rachel came in. "Can't you *knock*?"

"Sorry," Rachel said even though she was pretty sure Lily had heard her call. "Can we talk?"

"Fine." Lily yanked her blouse closed, glaring, and Rachel folded her arms. So this was going to be a confrontation.

"Miss Taylor told me you haven't handed in some of your course work." She waited, but Lily didn't say anything. "*Lily*. Is this true?"

"I doubt Miss Taylor would lie about it."

Rachel forced herself to ignore her sister's snarky tone. "But why haven't you handed them in? You know how important it is—"

"I know. I *know*." Lily let out a huffy sigh. "You tell me often enough. I was busy, okay? It won't happen again."

"Busy?" Rachel stared at her sister, at her fringe falling into her face, her eyes wide and dark with too much black eyeliner, her shoulders almost as bony as they'd been when she'd been little, in her too-big secondhand uniform, her little hand in Rachel's as they'd walked up the school lane. "How can you be too busy to do course work?" Rachel asked, striving to keep her voice level. "All you have to do is study. That's *it*. And you can't hand in your course work?"

"I know, Rachel. You're a saint," Lily said, her voice tired now. "I'm sorry I'm not up there with the angels with you."

"I don't mean it like that. But what have you been doing with your time, if not studying?" Lily shrugged. "Lily, come on. Tell me what is going on, please." Still nothing. *"Lily."*

Rachel looked around the bedroom for clues, but all she saw was the typical detritus of an eighteen-year-old girl's room: laddered tights kicked onto the floor, half a dozen pairs of shoes in an untidy jumble, makeup spilled across the desk meant for her books, sheets of paper flung all over the floor. Then she noticed that the papers had intricate drawings all over them. "What is this?" Rachel muttered, and picked up a sheet that was lying on the desk, covering Lily's dusty biology textbook.

"Don't . . ." Lily began, but she sounded halfhearted.

Rachel stared down at the drawing in confusion. It was a cartoon done in black ink, of a girl with crazy hair and big glasses, wearing a lab coat. Rachel saw the title in Harry Potter–like script at the top: *Adventures of the Mad Scientist Girl.* "Did you do this?" she asked.

"Yes," Lily answered, and Rachel didn't miss the note of shy pride in her voice. It made her angrier.

"So let me see if I have this right. Instead of actually *doing* your biology course work, you're drawing doodles about it instead?"

Her sister didn't say anything, just folded her arms and hunched her shoulders. Rachel wasn't an idiot; she understood this was important to Lily, that her sister had wanted her to be impressed and admiring of her creativity. But a *cartoon*. And assignments left incomplete. "Lily, look." She took a deep breath, forcing the fury down. "I get that you like this stuff. It's fun, and you can do it, but not at the expense of your schoolwork." She tried to keep her voice reasonable, but she could tell the damage had already been done. "You can't make a career out of this," she said, waving the paper. "It won't get you into university. You can't *live* off it—"

"Maybe I could," Lily said in a low voice. "If you'd let me."

"I'm trying to give you the best chance in life—"

"Maybe I should decide what the best chance *is*."

"What are you saying?" Rachel demanded. "That you don't want to go to university? You want to live at home and draw cartoons for the rest of your life, maybe take a few shifts at the pub, like Meghan?"

Lily's face crumpled, and with a rush of remorse Rachel realized what a child she still was. Children had dreams, and she didn't want to crush Lily's, but it killed her that her sister could have so much if she just tried for it. She could have everything Rachel had wanted but been denied. Lily might not think she wanted it now, but in a couple of years, when all that was on offer was lousy shift work? Rachel knew better than Lily. It was only that Lily didn't realize it.

"It doesn't have to be like that," Lily muttered.

"You're right. It doesn't. You can do your work, go to a fantastic university, get a degree and a job, and *then* you can do your damned doodles." She thrust the paper back at Lily, who clutched it to her chest. Rachel felt as if she'd hit her. She was being mean, and to *Lily*, whom she'd cuddled and burped and treated like her own daughter.

Which was why she was so angry now.

"I'm going to make tea," she said, and went downstairs. Meghan was just waking up on the sofa, and her mother had started calling for something again, her voice a faint, pathetic entreaty.

Gritting her teeth, Rachel grabbed a pan and thwacked it on the stove as hard as she could. The loud clatter was a satisfying sound, but it didn't actually make her feel any better.

"So what's your problem?" Meghan asked as she strolled, yawning, into the kitchen. She still had the traces of last night's makeup on her face, and her hair was flattened on one side and sticking up on the other. "Hmm?" she asked, and stretched. "Bad day, or are you just in your usual pissy mood?"

Rachel took a deep breath and didn't answer.

12

Claire

CLAIRE HAD BEEN WORKING at the village shop for a week—four days a week, anyway—and she was starting to feel as if she'd gotten the hang of it. She could manage the till, and Dan had even taught her the trick about Lottery cards and cigarettes and how to add the tax. She'd survived the rush of schoolchildren every afternoon, and Eleanor Carwell's beady precision every morning. She didn't particularly enjoy stacking newspapers or milk, but after a while she could appreciate the steady rhythm, and at the end of the week, when Dan paid her, she felt satisfied if surprised at the small amount.

"I did tell you it was minimum wage," he said, and Claire realized she must have looked disappointed.

"Yes, of course you did." She tucked the check into her bag. "Thank you."

"That will buy a pair of shoes, I suppose?" Dan said without looking at her. Claire couldn't tell if he was being serious or not.

"Maybe one shoe," she answered flippantly as she went back to dusting the tins on the shelves. In London and Portugal she'd spent hundreds of pounds on a single pair of shoes at a time. Her parents had been giving her a clothing allowance since she was thirteen. It hadn't stopped when she'd graduated from university or gotten a job; she hadn't thought about it either way. She had just expected the money to be there, and it had been. The realization made her feel uncomfortably guilty now. Maybe she really was the spoiled princess Dan and Rachel and who knew who else seemed to think she was.

"So one shoe," Dan answered. "Maybe you can buy the other one next week."

So maybe he could joke, after all. Claire took a deep breath. "You really do have me pegged as some spoiled rich girl, don't you?"

"Can you deny it?"

"No, I don't suppose I can. No one can help what they were. But I'm trying to be independent now. To change." She'd been dusting the tins, taking her time with each one. "Do you know this tin of lamb stew with minty peas has been here since I started?"

"You mean one week?"

"How long have you been running this shop?"

"Three years."

"And in all that time," Claire asked, hefting the tin aloft, "has anyone bought a tin of lamb stew with minty peas?"

Dan stared at her, his arms folded. "How am I supposed to remember something like that?"

"I'd remember." Claire put the tin back on the shelf. "I can't imagine wanting to eat an entire meal that comes out of a single tin."

"It's convenient."

Appalled realization rushed through her. "*Oh.* Is that what you . . . ?"

"I can cook," Dan answered shortly. "But don't judge it. A lot of the old folks find these tins helpful. They can't manage to cook for themselves anymore."

"Oh." She stared at him in surprise. He'd almost sounded sensitive. "Right. I suppose I didn't think of that." But since she'd started in the shop, no one had bought any of it. Not the lamb stew or treacle pudding or the Fray Bentos "Boozy" steak-and-ale pie, which came in a pie-shaped tin with a lid you peeled back. She decided not to point that out to Dan.

She'd been in a surprisingly good mood these last few days, almost buoyant. Andrew had left for Manchester several days ago, and it wasn't until his Lexus had disappeared down the lane that she'd realized how oppressive she'd found his well-meant concern.

Her mother had called only once yesterday, and Claire had actually listened to the voice mail. She hadn't flinched when she'd heard her mother's needling tone, demanding she ring her back, saying that Andrew had told her she'd found "a little job." Maybe she'd actually phone her mother back today. She almost felt strong enough.

Yesterday Lucy had come by and invited her into Whitehaven to go shopping over the weekend for craft supplies for the art stall at the Easter Fair.

"Easter Fair?"

"Yes, it's next week. The school puts on an Easter Fair every year, with stalls and games and all sorts. Best Decorated Egg, a fancy hat competition, you know."

"Right." A vague memory had surfaced in her mind like a soap bubble: decorating a hat with Rachel, both of them giggling as they tied a pink ribbon Claire had brought from home around its straw brim.

So much of her school years had been a miserable blur as she'd been caught between her mother's concern and disappointment, in and out of hospitals with procedures for her ear or illnesses as a result of it.

"Everyone says the Easter Fair is good fun," Lucy had told her. "Although I've never actually been. I only moved here in August. But Alex said that some of the local businesses and charities come and set up stalls," Lucy had added. "The Hangman's Noose puts on some food, a bookshop in Whitehaven brings some kiddie books to sell, and the Lifeboat Institute does their thing about water safety. They give away key rings and fridge magnets, that sort of stuff."

Now, as Claire dusted a row of tins of hot dogs in brine—yuck—an idea came to her. "Why don't you do a stall at the Easter Fair?" she asked Dan.

"The what?" It was the end of the day, and Dan was balancing the cash register, an intricate procedure of matching receipts to cash amounts, which Claire had not yet been invited to learn.

"The Easter Fair, up at the primary school. Lucy said a bunch of local businesses set up stalls. Why don't you?"

He didn't even look up from the receipts. "Who would run the shop while I was up at the school?"

"I could."

Dan gave her a quick, quelling glance. "I don't think so."

"Don't you think it's important to have a presence in the village?" Claire pressed.

"I do have a presence. My shop is on the high street."

"But a community presence. The shop is almost like a church or a community center, a place where people meet. . . ."

Dan stared at her disbelievingly. "It's a place to buy things."

"You could sell sweets and crisps and fizzy drinks up at the school," Claire suggested. "The kids would love it."

"I'm sure the head teacher will thank me for that. They've banned fizzy drinks from the school."

"All right, no fizzy drinks, then. But sweets or biscuits or even fruit, for goodness' sake—"

"No." Dan's voice was flat and final, even for him.

Claire took a deep breath. "Why not?"

"Because I don't want to."

"You don't want to get to know people?"

"No."

She fell silent, because there wasn't much she could say to that. And really, why should she argue for him to have a stall at the fair? She didn't want to get to know people, either. At least, she hadn't before. But in the two weeks since she'd been in Hartley-by-the-Sea she'd gotten to know people anyway. Lucy and Juliet and Abby, and even prickly Eleanor Carwell and the handful of schoolkids who came in. The boy who had tried to nick the sweets on her first day now smiled at her when he came into the shop. Claire hoped he wasn't pulling a con and still stealing sweets.

When she thought of the wide array of shallow friends she'd had in Portugal—all of them really Hugh's friends, with tinkling laughs and hard eyes—she felt as if she'd actually put down some roots here. Thin, little things, perhaps, but still. Roots.

"I could do the Easter Fair."

Dan stopped counting receipts. "You?"

"Why not?" She lifted her chin in challenge. "It might drum up a little more business."

He hesitated, then shook his head. "No."

"But why not?" Claire pressed, and Dan's expression hardened into its familiar, implacable scowl. She hadn't seen it for a while, but it still possessed the power to make her fall instantly silent.

"Because I said no."

She didn't try to reason with him after that.

The next day she and Lucy took the train into Whitehaven. It was early April and almost starting to feel like spring, at least when the wind let up for a moment. Claire had forgotten how green everything became in Cumbria, thanks to the rain. The grass looked almost fluorescent, and the leaves on the trees were bright against the blue sky.

"I remember doing this in school," Claire said as they watched the sheep-dotted fields stream by for the seven-minute journey into town. "Honestly, I don't know what we actually did in Whitehaven. Walk around in too-high heels and try on all the lipsticks at Boots, I suppose."

"That's right. Abby said you were one of the in girls," Lucy recalled with a rueful smile. "I have to say, I never knew how that felt."

"I'm not sure I did, either."

"What do you mean?"

Claire shrugged, wishing she hadn't mentioned school. "I just went with the crowd. They chose me, and so I followed."

Lucy looked at her curiously. "But didn't it feel good to be chosen?"

"It had nothing to do with me," Claire said bluntly. "If your parents are rich and put on parties for your class, you're pretty much guaranteed to be popular."

"I don't know about that," Lucy answered. "My mother was well-off and she put on a birthday party for my class when I was six. I still wasn't popular."

Claire shook her head. "It didn't mean anything. I never felt like they were really my friends."

"So why did you stay with them, then?"

She shrugged. "Because it was easier. Not the best reason, I know, but school was hard for me. I was ill a lot of the time as a child, and I didn't feel very . . ." She blew out a breath. "With it."

"Ill?" Lucy frowned in sympathy. "I'm sorry."

Claire shrugged again. "It was a long time ago."

Lucy must have sensed that she didn't want to talk about it, because she fell silent, but as the sheep pasture gave way to neat rows of White-haven's terraced houses, Claire found herself remembering more than she wanted to. The push and pull of friendships she didn't really understand. The feeling that she was underwater and everything was happening on dry land. The poor reports from school, the teachers with their pitying smiles, saying in hushed voices to her parents, "Claire's not really an academic girl, is she?" Her father's compressed mouth, his hand heavy on her shoulder, her mother's fluttering movements, and over all of it the sense of always disappointing people that rested on her like a leaden mantle.

Those years in primary school with Rachel had been the one bright light amidst all that oppressive darkness. But she'd turned away from it, for no good reason. Not that Rachel had really minded. They'd both dropped their friendship as if it hadn't meant anything, and maybe it hadn't. They'd been little kids, after all.

Whitehaven with Lucy was far more enjoyable than the pointless afternoons and evenings Claire had spent with a gaggle of Wyndham girls, standing by uncertainly while they nicked makeup and tried to get into the dance clubs with fake IDs. Lucy regaled her with a story of how she'd had to buy a bra for the head teacher's daughter, which made Claire both laugh and shake her head in amazement at Lucy's determined meddling and endless good cheer.

"But it all worked out in the end, because we're dating now," Lucy finished.

"You're dating the head teacher?"

"Alex, yes. It's still somewhat early days, though, so . . ."

"If you've bought his daughter a bra, you have a deeper relationship than I ever did with my fiancé."

Lucy looked at her with a cringing mixture of compassion and curiosity. "Why do you say that?" Lucy asked, her voice terribly gentle.

"Oh, it just wasn't that deep a relationship," Claire said, trying to sound dismissive. "Which makes me sound terribly shallow, I realize. I'm sure Hugh is an interesting and dynamic person, but I never really got to know that part of him."

She snuck a glance at Lucy, who was now looking both fascinated and appalled. "But why did you agree to marry him, then?"

"Because . . ." Claire bit her lip. There was nothing she could say that would make her come out looking good in this scenario. "Because I knew my parents wanted me to," she finished. "And I haven't had too many real romantic relationships. We got along on the surface, and that seemed enough."

Lucy nodded slowly. "I spent years trying to impress my mother. Trying to win her love, really. I've finally stopped, mostly, but it was hard. I think it's human instinct to want to gain our parents' approval and love, especially if they seem reluctant to give it."

"Maybe," Claire agreed. She'd never had her parents' approval, but she thought she'd had their love. Their overwhelming, suffocating, sacrificial love.

She and Lucy spent a happy hour in the art shop, buying supplies for the Easter crafts at the fair, and then over huge cups of coffee at the Costa on King Street Claire worked up the nerve to tell Lucy about her idea of the shop having a stall at the Easter Fair.

"I think that's fab," Lucy exclaimed.

"Dan doesn't—"

"Let me work on Dan. He's had a hard time, you know."

"Has he?" Claire was curious about her boss, but she kept herself from asking for details. "Don't pressure him into doing it," she said. "He seemed quite . . . final. I think it would annoy him, actually, to know I'd been talking to you about it."

"He could come around. . . ."

"I'll talk to him again," Claire said. Even if the thought of it made her toes curl in trepidation.

Sunday Claire spent pottering around the house, tidying up even though Rachel had left everything spotless and then making herself a curry from scratch. She'd bought the ingredients while she'd been in Whitehaven with Lucy, and she enjoyed cooking for herself. When she'd lived with Hugh, they'd always eaten takeaway or in restaurants.

Everything about their life had been glamorous and yet transient; Hugh's flat had come furnished in a lot of black leather and marble and chrome, and Claire hadn't put much of a stamp on it.

When he'd asked her to move in with him, after they'd gotten engaged, she'd put her clothes in the guest bedroom's cupboard because Hugh's perfectly pressed shirts and hand-tailored suits had filled the one in the master bedroom. She'd kept her toiletries in her wash bag and had only put her toothbrush in the glass with Hugh's with trepidation. Her carbon footprint on Hugh's apartment, even on his whole life, had been incredibly light. She suspected it was already gone. And even though it made her feel a little bit ashamed, she didn't mind. Losing Hugh had never hurt; in fact, it had been almost a relief.

He still hadn't rung her, and Claire recognized that she would have to call him at some point. She wondered what he would say, if he would prevaricate or bluster or just plain lie. She decided she didn't want to find out. Not yet, anyway.

After she'd cleaned up her curry, she decided to take a walk along the coastal path that ran along the sea for the whole length of the village. It was spectacular on a sunny spring evening; although the wind off the water was chilly, the sunlight was brilliant, gilding the sea in gold. In the distance Claire could see the violet smudges of the Isle of Man. The cliffs leading down to the beach were yellow with budding gorse; rabbits darted in and out of the tussocks, and the waves crashed onto the shore below. Claire couldn't see a single person anywhere, and she felt herself relax, her breathing evening out, her shoulders losing the tension she felt as if she'd been carrying it forever.

This was so much better than a hot-rock massage at Lansdowne Hills. She sat down on a weathered bench by a lookout point, the tufty gorse-covered cliff jutting out towards the sea. Gulls wheeled above, their cries still audible over the crash of the surf. At that moment Hartley-by-the-Sea seemed like one of the most beautiful places on earth, and she wondered why she'd ever left.

Then Claire saw there was a person sitting right on the edge of the cliff, legs dangling down towards the beach fifty feet below. Alarm jolted through her, because she might feel like an offcomer, but she knew the cliff eroded a few inches or more every year, and if you walked too close to the edge, the clay soil could crumble beneath you.

"Excuse me . . ." she began uncertainly, fearing some ignorant tourist was about to meet an untimely end. When the figure turned to look over her shoulder, the words died on Claire's lips. It was Rachel.

Rachel's shoulders sagged and she let out a sigh that even Claire could hear. "Oh," she said flatly. "It's you."

"Yes. Me." Claire managed a smile. "What are you doing out here?"

"It's a free country."

"Of course. I know. I'm sorry." She cut off the pointless apologies. "I meant, sitting out there, right on the edge? It's dangerous—"

"I'm fine." Rachel turned back to stare at the sea, and Claire sat there for a moment, wondering if she should try to make conversation. Rachel looked small and vulnerable, sitting on the edge of the cliff, the sea spread out before her in an endless, undulating slate gray blanket.

"It's a bit like the rhododendron bush, isn't it?" Claire blurted. She didn't know where the words came from; the memory felt like snatching at a snowflake, slippery and fleeting and yet possessing its own beauty.

Rachel had stiffened at her words. "I didn't think you'd remember that."

"I do." Scrambling under the bush, trying not to get her knees dirty. Whispering to each other, gossiping about the other kids, making up stories. Blissful solidarity. Claire swallowed hard, and then, after a moment's hesitation, she rose from the bench and started picking her way through the gorse, the thorns snagging on her jeans. "How did you get through all this?"

Rachel glanced back at her, lips pursed. "Not easily."

Claire finally made her way through the bushes and stood about a foot away from the edge of the cliff, not sure if she should join Rachel by sitting down, or even if she wanted to. It didn't seem like Rachel wanted her to.

Then Rachel scooted over, and Claire saw she was actually sitting on the thick, twisted roots of the gorse patch. They'd jutted out from the soil and provided a nature-made bench. With seeming reluctance Rachel patted the space next to her, and gingerly Claire sat down. She didn't like the sensation of her legs dangling down, touching nothing, but Rachel didn't seem to mind it.

"So what do you remember about the rhododendron bush?" Rachel asked.

"I remember us sitting under there," she began. "Talking."

"Right." Rachel stared out at the sea. "Do you even remember us being friends, Claire?"

"Yes, of course I do."

"But not much."

"Do you have a lot of memories of when you were seven?" Claire asked, slightly stung.

"Enough," Rachel answered flatly, and looked away.

13

Rachel

"I DO REMEMBER." CLAIRE'S voice sounded strong, for her anyway. Rachel glanced at her.

"We were friends for four years. I'd hope you'd remember *something*."

"I remember lots of things. It's just that it was a long time ago—"

"Trust me, I know that." Next to her Claire shifted a little, clearly uncomfortable. Rachel wished she hadn't started the conversation. What did she want Claire to say?

"I was just remembering the other day how you always waited for me at the bottom of the school lane," Claire said. "So we could walk up together."

Ridiculously, Rachel felt a lump form in her throat. She stared hard out at the sea, her eyes starting to water.

"Do you remember that?" Claire asked.

"Yes." Rachel took a deep breath. Enough with this little stroll down memory lane. She didn't want to go there, didn't want to revisit those bittersweet memories. They'd both moved on.

"Do you hate me?" Claire asked abruptly, and Rachel turned to her, discomfited by her rare bluntness.

"No . . ."

"Because you seem angry with me—"

"I'm not angry." It would be pathetic to be angry about a friendship that had ended nearly twenty years ago. And yet sitting there together, both of them staring out at the sea, Rachel couldn't keep herself from asking abruptly, "Why did you dump me in Year Six?"

Claire stared at her, blinking, her mouth open. "What do you mean . . . ?" Claire looked so blank that Rachel almost laughed. Almost.

"Are you bloody well joking, Claire? Don't you remember?" She sounded far too angry for this conversation. Rachel took a deep, calming breath. "How else do you explain that one day I came to school and you weren't even talking to me? You had your posse of Wyndham wannabes surrounding you like a flock of highlighted crows. You didn't even look at me."

"I . . ." Claire shook her head. "It wasn't like that."

"It felt like that to me."

"But you never . . . You never came over," Claire burst out, and Rachel knew Claire remembered that moment just as well as she did.

"Why would I come over? You were surrounded by a bunch of snobs who couldn't even bother to sneer at me." They'd simply ignored her instead, Rachel Campbell with her secondhand uniform and free school dinners.

"I never liked any of them," Claire said in a low voice.

"You spent enough time with them." The hurt was audible in Rachel's voice, bubbling over from a deep well of emotion she had never wanted to access again. "This is so stupid," she said, impatient and furious with herself. "It was years ago. I really don't give a damn about it anymore."

And yet even now she remembered sitting alone at lunch, watching Claire surrounded by her flock of in girls. She remembered the burning sensation in her chest and the way she refused to show how hurt she was. She remembered her mother breaking her back, her family falling apart, and having absolutely no one to talk to about it. She even remembered crawling under the rhododendron bush by herself one afternoon, clutching her knees to her chest and rocking back and forth, feeling lonelier than she ever had in her life. But of course Claire didn't have those memories.

"I didn't mean for things to happen that way," Claire said. Her face was pale and pinched, her eyes huge, making her look even younger. "I never wanted to stop being friends with you."

"Oh, really? It didn't look that way from where I was, sitting alone at lunch and feeling like Johnny No-Mates."

"But you never talked to me——"

"Because you never talked to me," Rachel burst out. "And you were the one with all the friends. It was as if they just appeared one day. . . ." As if the popular girls of Year Six had descended from Mount Olympus and taken Claire over.

Claire bit her lip. "After the school acceptances came through, my mother arranged for all the girls going to Wyndham to have a day together, at a spa in Ambleside." She grimaced. "Basically they were bribed to be my friends."

"But you went along with it," Rachel pointed out. Was she really surprised by that? Claire went along with everything. The girls would have all have gossiped and bonded over manicures. By Monday they had become an impenetrable clique, the in group with shiny nails, impossible to breach. School politics was brutal and ruthless.

The realization made Rachel feel tired. "It doesn't matter anyway," she dismissed. "We're adults now."

"But you're still angry——"

"No." She wouldn't admit to that. "Look, I realize I've been acting like a bitch," Rachel said. A gust of wind lifted her hair away from her face, and she squinted as she kept her gaze on the sea; the sun was starting to sink towards the horizon, and in about fifteen minutes it was going to be very cold and windy and dark up here.

"I didn't mean to say that . . ." Claire began.

"No, it's true. I am a bitch." Rachel leaned back, bracing her hands against the ground, only to mutter a curse when a thorn from a gorse

bush burrowed deep into her palm. "I'm a bitch to pretty much everyone these days," she continued as she plucked out the thorn. "My sisters, you, even your brother."

"My brother . . . ?"

"We had a drink in Whitehaven." Rachel decided not to tell Claire
about Andrew's request to watch over her. "Anyway, it's my problem. I
realize that. My life is stressful and overwhelming and I've got a chip on
my shoulder"—she repeated Andrew's indictment with a burning sensation in her chest—"about all the things that didn't happen for me. And
I suppose when you swanned back into the village with your expensive
clothes and perfect hair, able to relax for however long you liked, with
that huge house all to yourself and so much freedom, well, it got to me."
She glanced at Claire, who was staring at her, openmouthed. "So I'm
jealous. It's as simple as that."

"Jealous . . ." Claire sounded wondering.

"Does that really surprise you?" Rachel demanded, exasperated.
"You're pretty and rich and if you don't want to lift a finger you don't have
to. Meanwhile I'm working ten or twelve hours a day, cleaning toilets,
including yours, just so my sister can go to a school she's telling me she
doesn't even want to go to. Is it no wonder I'm jealous?"

The words had exploded out of Rachel and seemed to fall on Claire
like hammer blows. She blinked, looking as if she'd just been beaten up.

"I never thought of it like that."

"No? How do you think of it, then?"

"I think how lucky you are to have your own business and be so
smart. . . ." Rachel let out an incredulous laugh. "You knew all the
answers to the pub quiz."

"I'll go far in life, then, shall I?" she said, and struggled up from her
perch on the gorse roots. She needed to get back home. Nipping out for
an hour's walk would come with a price to pay: dirty dinner dishes left
out and Lily no doubt wasting time on her doodles without Rachel to
nag her. "I know the answers to the questions on the pub quiz," Rachel

proclaimed, spreading her arms out. "Therefore my life is sorted. Look, Claire, I'm sorry I've taken out my frustrations on you. It isn't about when we were little—at least, it's not just about that." She took a deep breath. "I'm sorry. Okay?"

"I'm sorry——" Claire began, but Rachel couldn't listen. She didn't want to spend another second thinking about those painful years; it hurt too much.

"It's fine," she said. "It's all fine." She began to walk away, suppressing the flicker of guilt she felt for leaving Claire there; if they'd been kids she would have helped her up, even brushed the dirt and gorse bits off her clothes. But they weren't kids anymore, and Claire needed to start taking care of herself for a change.

Back at the house Rachel found Meghan in the hall, doing her lipstick in the tiny mirror above the table littered with unopened bills and the detritus from everyone's pockets.

"You're going out?"

"Just for a little bit."

"Not another four a.m. return, Meghan, please——"

"What's it to you?" Meghan tossed over her shoulder.

"I had to sleep in your bed with Nathan——"

"Which I do every night."

"Because he's your *son*." Rachel lowered her voice, conscious that Nathan was probably upstairs. "Is he asleep?"

"Yes." Meghan gave her a sudden, fierce look. "All I'm asking is that you listen for him, okay, Rachel? You'd be home anyway."

"What if I had plans?"

"Then ask Lily! I haven't gone out except to work in years. You know that. Why can't you let me have a little fun?"

Her emotions, already raw from her conversation with Claire, felt even more scraped. "Do you see me having a little fun?" Rachel demanded.

"You go to the pub quiz every week."

Except this week, because she'd been too overwhelmed. It felt as if nothing in her life was going well. With a sigh, Rachel waved Meghan towards the door. "Fine. Go out. Enjoy yourself."

"You said that with so much heartfelt emotion," Meghan answered, and Rachel rolled her eyes.

"At least I said it."

The house felt very quiet and empty without Meghan, even though Rachel knew Lily and Nathan were both upstairs and her mother was asleep in the downstairs bedroom. She went into the kitchen, heartened to see that it was actually mostly clean, if she didn't count the grease splatters across the stove top. Both Lily's and Meghan's attempts at tidying were lackadaisical at best. They never could have taken over Mum's house-cleaning business.

She switched on the kettle and sat at the little metal table in the dark, her chin propped on her hands. The only sound was the hiss of the kettle and then the creak of the stairs. The moment was almost peaceful, despite the tumult of the day's encounters: Claire, Meghan, even Henry Price's bathroom. Rachel let out a gusty sigh.

"Rachel?"

Rachel glanced up to see Lily standing in the doorway, her slight form illuminated by the hall light. They hadn't really talked since the bust-up about Lily's cartoons, and now Rachel felt her chest expand with a maternal mix of love and guilt. Standing there, Lily still looked little, almost as little as she'd been in primary school, when Rachel had sat next to her and helped her sound out words in her reading book. When she'd stood by the school gate to make sure Lily had a friend to walk into school with, had given the stink eye to a Year Three she'd seen was a bully.

"Hey, Lil." Rachel managed a tired smile and went to the kettle, which had switched off. "Tea?"

"All right." Lily took a step into the darkened kitchen, her head ducked low. "Test me on my biology?"

It was, Rachel knew, a peace offering. She nodded, her back to Lily, and then, emotion getting the better of her, she sniffed. "Of course I will," she said, her voice a little thick. "Anytime."

By the middle of the week Rachel felt as if her equilibrium was mostly restored. She wasn't snarling at everyone at least. She'd kept herself from snipping at Meghan when she came in at an almost-respectable one o'clock in the morning, and had even gotten up early to give Nathan his breakfast.

She'd spent three days with her head down cleaning, and as she arrived at Four Gables, she breathed a sigh of relief that Andrew West was gone and Claire was at work. She wasn't ready to face either of them yet, or perhaps ever. She was able to clean the huge house without any interruption, although in actuality there wasn't much to do. Claire did her own dishes and, by the looks of it, the bathroom too. The house looked practically pristine.

By the time she arrived at Emily Hart's on Wednesday afternoon, she was as much in need of a cuppa as the harassed mother.

"Riley and Rogan are up to their usual tricks, I see," Rachel said cheerfully as she nodded at the streaks of marker on the walls.

"They've discovered felt tips," Emily said as she sank into a chair at the kitchen table. "No matter where I put the box of them, those two manage to find them."

"I just found them," Rachel remarked. She'd been putting away the loaf going stale that Emily had left out on the counter and retrieved the box of markers from the bread bin. "I'll put them up here, shall I?" She slid the box onto the top of the fridge and then switched on the kettle.

"You look tired," she said as she handed Emily her mug and leaned against the counter with her own. "Are the twins sleeping?" She could hear them chattering to themselves in the next room, over the musical din of the *Chuggington* theme song on the telly.

"They are," Emily admitted. "I don't really have an excuse—"

"The twins are an excuse in and of themselves. You'll probably be knackered for the next five years."

"Or longer," Emily said on a sigh. "Tom's been talking about having another."

"Easy for him, isn't it?" Rachel had met Emily's husband on a few occasions, a cheerful, blunt-faced man who left his dirty socks in the hall.

"We always wanted a big family," Emily said, but she didn't sound convinced.

"Things change, though. Do you still want a big family? The twins aren't even two yet."

"I know. I know." Emily put her mug down, her soft blond hair falling in front of her face. "Sometimes I don't know what I want anymore."

Rachel could sense a big heart-to-heart coming on and discreetly she checked her watch. Not that she didn't like Emily, but she had another house to clean this afternoon, and by the looks of it Emily hadn't done any cleaning all week. Besides, she didn't know how much emotional energy she had left. Lily, Meghan, and Claire had taken it all up.

Emily continued to gaze down at her mug, and so with a mixture of sympathy and exasperation, Rachel asked the inevitable question. "Why do you think you don't know what you want anymore?"

"Because I have it all, don't I?" Emily looked up, a wry smile trembling on her lips. She looked like she was caught between self-deprecation and total tears. "I mean, look at this." She waved an arm towards the kitchen with its granite counters and top-of-the-line appliances, the dirty dishes littering most surfaces, crusts cut off from the twins' sandwiches in a jammy pile by the sink. "Everyone wants what I have, don't they?"

"Not everyone," Rachel allowed. "I'm quite sure there is a significant part of the population that could do without taking care of nearly two-year-old twins, lovely though they are."

"True," Emily agreed, and with relief Rachel noticed that the threat of tears seemed to have passed. "But the big picture. The house, the husband, the kids. I have it all."

"And?" Rachel asked after a moment. The needlelike prick of envy she felt was surpassed by a deeper curiosity.

"I keep thinking, 'Is this all there is?' Seriously?"

Rachel took a sip of tea, considering her response. "What more do you want?" she asked.

"That's the stupid thing. I don't know. I honestly don't know what I want, what could make me happy. I know I just want . . . more." She shook her head and gave her a guilty smile. "You must want to slap me."

"Why would I want to slap you?" Rachel asked, and Emily flushed and looked away.

"I only meant that I must seem ungrateful, compared to, well . . ."

"Ah." So she must want to slap Emily Hart because she was moaning about her perfect life while it was glaringly obvious that Rachel's life sucked. "I don't want to slap you, Emily," she said. She wanted to slap herself, for being so obvious about her jealousy and dissatisfaction. And *then* maybe she'd want to slap Emily. Although Emily was so tired and overwhelmed that Rachel couldn't really feel anything but sympathy for her. She was definitely not jealous of her having toddler twins.

"Do you ever think like that?" Emily asked after a moment.

"Is this all there is?" Rachel leaned back in her seat. "I suppose everyone thinks that once in a while." Although actually she didn't think she had, mostly because she knew the answer. *Yes, it bloody well is.* "I've been too busy with everything to stop and ponder about the meaning of life," she said with what she hoped passed for a rueful laugh.

"But do you hope for more?" Emily pressed. "I mean, I don't know, a different job or a new relationship, something to give your life more excitement, *anything* . . ." Rachel couldn't tell what the expression on her face was, but it must have gone strange, because Emily let out an embarrassed laugh and shook her head. "Sorry. Sorry. I'm rabbiting on. Don't mind me, Rachel, honestly. I'm seriously sleep-deprived." She finished her tea, leaving the mug on the table. "Do you mind stripping the beds today? I didn't get around to it this week."

You never do, Rachel thought as she murmured her assent, and then took both mugs to the sink.

Rachel might have dismissed Emily's question to her face, but it rattled around in her mind as she went about her jobs for the next few days, hoovering, scrubbing tiles and toilets, stacking dishes and folding clothes. Picking unknown hairs out of a stranger's shower drain and dusting photographs of weddings and baptisms and parties of people she didn't know but thought looked deliriously happy had a way of making her think about her own life.

Was this all there was?

She knew the answer to that question, which was why she'd never struggled with it the way Emily Hart had. But now she let herself consider how Lily would be going to university in a few months. Would that be her chance to have some freedom? But no. There was still Meghan and Nathan and her mother. Janice Campbell might be an invalid, but Rachel suspected she would need more and more care over the next several decades.

And don't you want her to?

She was shocked by her selfishness, the fact that she was practically begrudging her mother her life. What was *wrong* with her? So many people had it far worse than she did. She had a job that paid most of the bills and that she liked at least some of the time. She had a family she loved, even if they drove her crazy on occasion. She had friends, a small social life, her health. She was fine. It was only because Claire West had breezed back into Hartley-by-the-Sea that she was feeling so unsettled.

Friday evening she trudged up the path to her house, bracing herself for the din of noise she knew would greet her upon her arrival. Lily's music. Her mother's groans. Nathan's wailing. And Meghan probably on her way out somewhere; out of the last five nights she'd been gone three, coming home smelling of beer and smoke and men's cologne.

Deep breath, and she opened the door and was greeted with . . . silence.

Carefully Rachel shut the door behind her. She poked her head in her mother's bedroom and saw she was dozing. The kitchen was empty and fairly clean, and then Rachel went into the sitting room and came up short. Lily was sitting on the sofa, talking to Andrew West.

"What . . . ?" She trailed off and simply stared at him, looking completely at ease on the overstuffed sofa with the shiny worn patches on the armrests. He wore a pair of chinos with knife-edge creases and a blue shirt that was open at the throat. The most boring clothes imaginable. As Andrew caught sight of her, he raised his eyebrows.

"What am I doing here?" he finished. "Saying hello."

"I thought you were in Manchester."

"I was. I've come back for the weekend." The words hovered there for a moment. He'd come back to check on Claire.

"Well, you don't need to check on me," Rachel said. "I'm fine."

"I know you are," he said with a small smile. "I've actually come to extend an invitation."

"An invitation . . . ?"

"Claire and I are going to go hiking this weekend, maybe try to conquer Scafell Pike. We thought you, and any of your family"—he glanced at Lily—"might like to join us."

Rachel gaped at him. Literally gaped, mouth hanging open, eyes bulging, speechless. "I . . ." she finally said, uselessly, and Lily jumped in.

"I'd love to go," she said. "And so would Rachel."

14

Claire

CLAIRE WASN'T AN OUTDOORSY person. Growing up she'd been deemed too fragile for sports because of her health, and in any case, her parents weren't exactly the fell-walking type. Andrew was, though; he'd run track at Wyndham, and when he'd gone to uni, he'd always come back and hiked through his holidays. He'd had a goal of conquering all two-hundred-odd peaks in the whole of Cumbria. Claire didn't know how many he'd actually managed.

Apparently he was going to attempt one today, along with her, Rachel, and Rachel's sister Lily. It felt like an odd assortment of people packed into Andrew's usually roomy Lexus. Claire watched Rachel covertly, noticing the way she'd stroked the leather of the seats before jerking her hand back and then folding both arms and staring straight ahead. She hadn't said much, and Claire couldn't tell if she was still angry or not.

Why did you dump me in Year Six?

The question had been so unexpected, and it still made Claire inwardly squirm with a mixture of guilt and confusion. She hadn't remembered it exactly like that. Back when she was eleven, it had felt like Rachel had been turning her back on her. Admittedly she'd gone with the Wyndham girls, but she'd been waiting for Rachel to elbow her way in and join them. She never had.

Lily was seemingly oblivious to the tension that Claire could feel from Rachel and even Andrew, although he looked relaxed enough, driving the alarmingly narrow road by Ennerdale with ease. Claire flinched every time they passed a car; the side mirrors nearly brushed each other.

"I've never actually climbed a fell," Rachel announced from the backseat. She had insisted on sitting in the back with Lily although Claire had offered her the front seat.

"And you a born-and-bred Cumbrian?" Andrew said, arching an eyebrow, a small smile playing about his lips. For a second Claire wondered if her brother was actually flirting. With *Rachel*.

"You are too," Rachel pointed out. "Even if you don't act like it."

"Yet I've climbed one hundred and ninety-two fells."

"Andrew wasn't actually born in Cumbria," Claire chipped in. "He was born in Leeds. I'm the only one in the family who was born in Cumbria."

"Have you ever climbed a fell?" Rachel asked.

"No, I never have."

"So what are we all doing out here, then?"

"Having fun," Lily said, and lightly punched her sister's arm. "It's an absolutely glorious day."

Claire gazed out the window at Ennerdale in the valley below them, the water a brilliant blue in the sunlight, the fells, some still snowcapped, providing a backdrop so stunning it looked like a set piece from a play. It was so different from London or Portugal, and she had to remind herself that she'd actually lived here for most of her life. "It reminds me of the backdrop in *The Sound of Music*, when they do that song about the goats," she said, and Andrew let out a laugh.

"You're comparing all of that out there to a painted bit of cardboard in a film?"

"Well, sort of . . ." she began, and Rachel caught her eye. "Yodel-lay-he-hoo," she sang off-key, and they shared a surprising, complicit smile before Rachel glanced back at Andrew.

"So we're not actually climbing Scafell Pike, are we?" Rachel asked.

"Why shouldn't we?"

"Because I'm wearing trainers and it's about five thousand feet high."

"Three thousand and sixty-eight, actually."

"I stand corrected."

Andrew shrugged, his gaze on the narrow, winding road. "If we ascend from Wasdale Head it shouldn't be too taxing, although it would help if you'd brought the right kit."

"It would help if I owned the right kit," Rachel returned tartly, and Claire smothered a smile. She rather liked Rachel's sharp sense of humor when it wasn't directed at her.

"How about we just have a picnic?" Claire suggested. She wasn't all that keen on hiking herself. Plus she was also wearing trainers, and they didn't look as serviceable as Rachel's.

"Why didn't you come prepared?" Andrew asked Rachel with a frown. "You could have borrowed some boots from someone, I'm sure."

"No one I know owns hiking boots. Or any of the other kit you've got on."

Besides his top-of-the-line hiking boots Andrew had brought a waterproof anorak, a varnished walking stick, and a rucksack with a first-aid kit and a titanium water bottle. He looked like an advert for *Cumbria Life*.

"I'll walk up the fell while you lot lounge at the bottom, then," he said. "I want to get a view."

"We've got a decent view from the car," Rachel returned. Andrew just shook his head.

Half an hour later they were parked by the Wasdale Head Inn, where a gate marked the way to the Hollow Stones trail, which was, according to Andrew, the "non-hiking route" up Scafell.

He glanced at Claire's shoes as they assembled by the gate. "Seriously?"

She looked down at her Mint Velvet plimsolls. "These are all I had."

He let out a sigh. "I should have checked before we got in the car."

Which made her feel like a child, and she could tell that Rachel had noticed. She was frowning as she observed the interaction between her and Andrew, a conversation like a thousand others they'd had over the years.

"You wouldn't have found a pair of hiking boots at home," Claire said. "We don't have any. Mum and Dad never did this kind of thing, you know."

"I know," he said, and pushed open the gate. "We'll go as far as we can. The conditions are dry, at least."

They walked in silence for a few minutes, navigating the rocky trail, the vista stunning and yet barren, with the steep sweep of tree-less fells and the blue flash of the still lake. The air was colder than it had been in Hartley-by-the-Sea, and after fifteen minutes both Claire's legs and lungs started to burn.

"So how come you're the outdoorsy type?" Rachel asked Andrew. She was walking next to him, keeping up with his brisk pace, her arms swinging by her sides. Lily was behind her, and Claire was behind Lily, walking more slowly than anyone else. She could already tell that her plimsolls were not up to the job.

"I like being outside," Andrew answered. "But I didn't get into hiking until I was in uni and had my own car." He glanced at Rachel. "How come you aren't the outdoorsy type?"

"Oh, I don't know," Rachel answered. "I didn't have the holiday time, or my own car, or even the boots. Kind of tricky, without all that."

Andrew didn't answer, and Claire couldn't tell if he was annoyed by Rachel's comeback or chagrined by his own assumptions. Did he, like Claire, feel like he had to apologize for being rich?

The conversation she'd had with Rachel last Sunday had been picking at her all week. Rachel—confident, brassy, in-your-face *Rachel*—felt Claire had dumped her. It seemed laughable even as Claire recognized the truth of it. At the time she'd felt as if Rachel had abandoned her to the mercy of the Wyndham girls; she'd wanted Rachel to rescue her. She still remembered the stony look on Rachel's face when she'd stopped short in the school yard and stared straight at Claire, surrounded by the in girls. Then she'd set her jaw, turned on her heel, and walked away. They'd never spoken again.

Claire could still remember glancing covertly at Rachel across the Year Six room during lessons, wondering why she was so stubbornly ignoring her. During a field trip Rachel had picked Oliver Cakewell as her partner even though he picked his nose and wiped it on his trousers. Claire had been partnered with a Wyndham girl—Michaela or Shelly, she couldn't remember. The gaggle of girls who had been her best friends in secondary school had blurred together into one faceless mask. She hadn't seen any of them since she'd left Cumbria for university.

She wished she could say something about all that to Rachel, but she suspected it would sound pathetic. The moment for sharing memories about their childhood days had passed, up on the cliffside overlooking the sea.

Andrew asked Lily about school, and they started chatting while Rachel fell back so she and Claire were almost, but not quite, walking together. Claire tried for a smile, something like the one they'd shared in the car, but Rachel looked away.

Claire tried to concentrate on the view. Having Andrew show up last night had given her a weird, mixed-up feeling of disappointment and relief; she'd had a good week, but she'd been starting to feel lonely. Three days of enduring Dan Trenton's silence had been hard, although admittedly he was talking more than he used to. He'd even trusted Claire alone in the shop for an hour while he'd walked his dog, whose name, she'd learned, was Bunny.

"You named your dog Bunny?" she couldn't keep from saying, trying not to laugh, and Dan had grimaced.

"She came with the name. She's a rescue dog."

Which made her even more curious about him. Why did the unfriendliest man in the village have a rescue dog? It hinted at a depth and sensitivity to him that she realized she'd sensed even as she'd doubted it was there. And Dan certainly didn't give many opportunities for her to see it. When he'd returned from the walk he'd shouted at her for jamming the Lotto card dispenser, and Claire had cowered almost as much as Bunny did.

He'd given her a terse apology and then comforted the dog before taking her back to his kitchen. For the rest of the day Claire had been on tin-stacking duty.

Even worse than Dan Trenton's was the silence of Four Gables when she'd returned at night. Room after pristine room, all of them empty, the only sign that anyone lived there the faint indentation of her footprints in the thick cream carpets.

She'd had a few pleasant interactions over the week: coffee with Abby down at the café, a walk with Lucy. But the majority of her time was spent alone, fighting off the loneliness that threatened to sweep over her like the waves that crashed onto the shore, icy-cold and overwhelming.

And now she was being melodramatic. She'd spent most of her life alone, even when she was with people. She'd always felt on the periphery, almost like a ghost. She'd chosen it, because it was easier to exist on the sidelines than to fight for the middle. Yet since coming to Cumbria, since meeting people and getting a job and actually living her own life, even if just a little, that sense of isolation had bothered her more. She didn't want to live that way forever.

"Why does your brother treat you like a child?" Rachel asked abruptly.

Claire turned, yanked out of her melancholy reverie. "Because he's my older brother?"

"No, seriously. He acts like you're . . . I don't know, mentally deficient or something."

Claire let out a dry laugh. "Wow. Thanks."

"Actually, everyone does. Or did. *I* did." She turned to give her a hard stare. "Why was that? Why have you always seemed so helpless?"

Claire could feel her cheeks starting to burn. Now both her face and her feet were throbbing. "You really know how to lay on the compliments, Rachel."

"Seriously, Claire." Rachel stopped walking, and she forced Claire to stop as well by laying a hand on her arm. Andrew and Lily continued on ahead, oblivious. Claire couldn't hear what they were saying, but they were both waving their hands, engrossed in some discussion. "Why?" Rachel demanded. "You're smart. . . ."

"Actually, I'm not. I never did very well in school."

"You went to university."

"I was tutored through all my A levels. I barely scraped by with three Cs."

"That's not that bad," Rachel objected. "You still got in somewhere." Claire shrugged. "Why does Andrew baby you?" she pressed.

"You said you did it too," Claire answered after a moment. "So why did you?"

"I don't know. I've thought about that. There was something so helpless about you when we were growing up that made me want to reach out. There still is." She pursed her lips. "I liked it back then. I liked taking caring of you and how much you seemed to appreciate it. But, frankly, now it's annoying."

Claire tried for a laugh. "I knew I annoyed you now."

Rachel shook her head impatiently. "Don't you want to stand up for yourself? Tell Andrew to shut it? Tell me to shut it, for that matter—"

"All right," Claire retorted, and for once her voice came out strong. "Shut it, Rachel."

Rachel grinned. "Okay, I will. But you need to stand up for yourself more, Claire. Make your own decisions. Live your own life."

"Noted." She kept walking, even though she was developing blisters on both heels, because she didn't think she could stand there and listen to Rachel tell her what to do, even if it was well meant, for another second. She was trying, for heaven's sake. Didn't anyone see that?

"Shall we stop here?" she called up to Andrew. Her feet were killing her.

He turned around, looking surprised at how far Claire and Rachel were lagging behind. "Are you all right, Claire?"

"I'm fine," she snapped. "Quit worrying about me, Andrew." She flopped onto the stubbly grass and yanked off her shoes. Her feet felt like they were on fire.

Andrew, Lily, and Rachel all came to join her, Andrew grimacing at the state of her feet. "Honestly, Claire. Let me get you some plasters." He took out his first-aid kit while Rachel unpacked what looked like revolting tuna sandwiches, all smooshed and damp, from her rucksack and handed one to Lily, who took it with a slight grimace.

"Couldn't we all eat at the inn on the way back?" Claire suggested. She didn't want to eat one of Rachel's sandwiches, but she hadn't brought any food herself.

"I thought you said you wanted a picnic," Andrew said as he handed her a couple of plasters.

"I did. In the beer garden." She ripped open the plasters and stuck them on her blisters, sucking her breath in sharply at the sting of pain. Why did anyone walk up a mountain? What was the *point*?

As if reading her thoughts, or perhaps just the expression on her face, Andrew said, "If you'd had the proper footwear, Claire . . ."

"None of us have the proper footwear except for you," Rachel interjected. "So stop picking on Claire."

"Picking on Claire?" Andrew looked incredulous. "I'm just looking out for her."

"Maybe she can look out for herself."

Andrew's eyes narrowed. "We've had this conversation before, Rachel."

"Wait . . . You have?" Claire jerked upright, the pain in her feet forgotten for a moment. "You've been *talking* about me?"

Andrew hesitated, and Rachel waited, saying nothing, but she looked guilty. They both did. "I just wanted to make sure you were looked after," he finally said.

So he'd asked Rachel to be her nursemaid? No wonder Rachel thought Andrew treated her like a baby. "Damn it, Andrew," she said, and then, because she didn't trust herself not to burst into tears, which would prove both their points, she got up and walked a little distance away, towards a creek that was tumbling down the hillside. She stood there, staring at the clear, cold water streaming over the stony ground, feeling like a child who had just stomped off because someone had taken her toys. Rachel was right. She was helpless. And she still didn't know how to change.

"Claire." Andrew came up behind her, managing to sound both conciliatory and reproving. Only he could manage that tone, along with their mother. "I'm sorry if it seemed as if I was interfering."

"Seemed?"

"All right, I have been interfering. But I've told you before, we're all worried about you."

"And I've told you before, you don't need to be."

"Really? Because when your sister ends up in rehab for a month due to a drinking problem, it's understandable to be a bit worried."

She closed her eyes, humiliation seeping from every pore. Andrew had spoken loudly enough for both Lily and Rachel to hear. "I don't think I actually have a drinking problem, Andrew," she said, her voice squeezed out from her constricted throat.

"Oh, Claire." He sounded so weary, so disappointed. "Don't."

"I'm not in denial." She opened her eyes and took a deep breath. "I know it seems like I am. I know everyone listens to Hugh rather than me because, well, he's Hugh and when has anyone listened to me? But it's true, Andrew. I drank too much. Once. *Once.*" Actually, twice. But she'd been feeling stressed and miserable, and maybe she *did* have a problem, or even several. But she didn't think she was an alcoholic. "I wasn't sneaking vodka into my orange juice or blacking out or anything like that—"

"Having a drinking problem doesn't necessarily mean you black out. Or sneak alcohol or any of the stereotypical signs. You know that, Claire. It can manifest itself in—"

"Oh, stop. Please, just stop. I heard it all at Lansdowne Hills for four whole weeks. I don't need it from you."

"Maybe you do, considering—"

"I said to *stop!*" she said, and then, because she couldn't think of anything else to do, she went back to where Rachel and Lily were sitting in rigid silence, yanked on her shoes, and started back down the trail, her feet throbbing with every step.

"Claire," Andrew called. "Where are you going?"

"Home," Claire yelled over her shoulder, and kept walking.

15

Rachel

RACHEL WATCHED CLAIRE STOMP down the trail with a mixture of bemusement and pride. Claire's feet had to be killing her. Then she glanced back at Andrew, who was standing there, mouth hanging open, arms akimbo. It was particularly satisfying to see him looking like he didn't know what had hit him. As satisfying as knowing it was *Claire* who had.

After a few seconds Andrew closed his mouth, shook his head, and then walked back towards Rachel and Lily. "We should go after her."

"Why?" Rachel asked. Andrew gave her an incredulous look.

"Because she's in no state—"

"She seemed fine to me. A little pissed-off, maybe." Rachel hadn't heard the whole conversation, but the words "drinking problem" had practically bounced off the mountains. Rachel glanced at Lily. "Lil, you want to keep going?"

"Well . . ." Lily glanced between Rachel and Andrew, clearly trying to decipher the undercurrents flowing between them. Her feet were probably hurting too, just as Rachel's were. "All right. Sure."

"Good." Rachel clambered up to standing, trying not to wince. She was doing this for Claire's sake, even if she'd never realize it. "Onwards. It's time to conquer my first fell."

"You'll never get to the top in trainers," Andrew stated, and Rachel gave him a long, level look.

"Try me," she said, and they started walking.

After half an hour her feet started to chafe and then to throb, and then into their second hour of walking they went blissfully numb. Maybe she'd rubbed the skin clean away.

Andrew attempted to chat with Lily about her schoolwork, but Rachel could tell he was distracted. He kept looking back down the trail, as if expecting to see Claire hurrying after them. Several times he took his phone out, until Rachel said in exasperation, "Surely a civil engineer such as yourself realizes there is no way to get phone reception up here."

He gave her a sheepish look and put his phone back in his pocket. "I'm worried."

"Why? I think she can manage to walk down the trail we just came up."

"But by the time we get back it will have been hours—"

"So? She'll go into the inn and have a drink. If she has any sense, she'll have several and be properly *kaleyed* by the time we arrive."

Andrew frowned at her. *"Kaleyed?"*

"Cumbrian for 'drunk.'"

"That's the last thing she needs." Andrew sounded outraged.

Rachel gave him a conciliatory smile. "Does Claire really have a drinking problem?"

"You shouldn't have heard that."

"Considering you were practically yodeling it, it was hard not to. Seriously, though—"

"It's none of your business," Andrew said, and started to walk faster. Rachel lengthened her stride to keep up with him.

"It's none of my business and yet you asked me to look out for her? You can't have it both ways."

Andrew sighed. Lily was behind them, snapping photos, but he still lowered his voice. "She was in rehab for a month before she came back to Hartley-by-the-Sea."

"For alcoholism?"

"Yes."

"Did she check herself in?"

Andrew glanced at her sharply. "Why do you ask?"

"Just curious."

"As it happened, her fiancé, Hugh, called my parents and shared his concerns. They checked her in."

Rachel nodded her understanding. "So everyone managed Claire, as usual."

"She needed help, Rachel."

Rachel knew she should drop it. She didn't know what Claire had been up to these last few years. Maybe she'd been knocking back a bottle of gin every night. Maybe she still was. "Even so, I think you should give Claire a little space to make her own decisions."

"I agree with you in principle, but as I told you before, now is not the time." Andrew sighed and gave her a semiapologetic smile. "Claire's not as strong as you, Rachel."

She felt an irrational pulse of pleasure at the implied compliment and quickly squelched it. "Maybe she's never been given the chance."

"Maybe," Andrew allowed. "But maybe there is a reason for that. I know you were friends with Claire a long time ago, but you don't know her now. Or our family."

"That puts me in my place," Rachel murmured.

He shook his head, sighing. "I'm sorry. I didn't mean it that way."

"Actually, I think you did." Rachel shrugged. "It's true anyway. No one in Hartley-by-the-Sea really knows any of you. But then you Wests never tried to fit in, did you? You lived here for decades, but you always acted like offcomers." Andrew frowned, and Rachel continued lightly.

"Up in your house high above us all, going to the private school in Keswick, swanning off to Cambridge, your parents to London. We didn't stand a chance."

"I suppose not," he agreed after a moment. "We kept to ourselves, for better or worse. Yet you were still friends with Claire."

And it always seemed to come back to that. "I have a kind heart," Rachel answered flippantly. She turned back to her sister. "Don't I, Lily?"

"Umm . . . sometimes?" Lily ventured, and Andrew gave a small smile.

"Even your family condemns you."

"Damned with faint praise."

"Why didn't you go to university, Rachel?"

The suddenness of the question threw her. "Because I had to work." She glanced at Lily, whose expression had turned wary. "I had better things to do," she said, because the last thing she wanted to do was make Lily feel guilty. But when she saw a certain glint enter her sister's eyes, she realized that might not have been the best answer. "Lily's going, though," she stated firmly. "Right, Lil? She has a conditional offer from Durham."

"That's great news." Andrew turned to Lily. "To study art?"

"Um, no." Lily bit her lip, and Rachel stared at her in surprise. "Biology," she muttered, not looking at Rachel. "Probably."

Probably? The offer from Durham was for biology only. Still Rachel said nothing, and Andrew murmured, "I see," and they kept walking.

Art? Was this about those cartoons? Had Lily talked about them with Andrew? For a reason Rachel didn't want to examine too closely, the thought made her break out in a hot, prickly flush. Why had Lily been talking to Andrew about her stupid cartoons?

They weren't stupid, Rachel knew; in fact, even from one cursory glance she'd seen they were quite clever. So, fine. When Lily was at Durham she could do a cartoon strip for the *Palatinate*, Durham's student newspaper. Rachel had no problem with that.

They were nearing the top of the fell, or at least Rachel hoped they were. The air was sharper and colder, and snow dusted the ground. She might not have worn hiking boots, but at least she had a warm coat. She dug her hands into its pockets as she carefully picked her way over the rocks, her gaze on the ground below. The last thing she wanted was for Andrew to have to call Mountain Rescue because she'd sprained her ankle or worse. Although he wouldn't be able to call Mountain Rescue, because he didn't have reception on his phone.

"Careful." Andrew cupped her elbow with his hand and Rachel instinctively tried to jerk away, making him hold her more firmly. "I don't want you to break a leg."

"I was just thinking the same thing." She let him help her across the stony ground, even though it went against her instincts. There was something rather pleasant about being helped, held, even in such a small way.

"You could look up, you know," Andrew said, and she realized, belatedly, that they'd actually reached the summit. She sucked in a hard breath, shaking off Andrew's hand as she slowly moved in a circle, taking in the stunning view in every direction. Barren fells, rocky, rust colored, and unrelieved by any trees or bushes, swept to an endless horizon. She could see the glint of Wastwater in the distance, a hard, bright blue. It was beautiful, but there was something lonely and bleak about it too, something that made Rachel's chest feel tight in a way that had nothing to do with the cold air or high altitude.

"Amazing, isn't it?" Andrew said quietly. From behind her Rachel heard Lily snapping pictures.

She didn't answer Andrew, because "amazing" wasn't the right word. It was awe-inspiring, incredible, and yet also painful. Looking at that endless view made Rachel realize how small she was, how utterly insignificant. There was a whole world out there to explore and conquer, and soon enough she'd be cleaning Henry Price's toilet.

She closed her eyes, shutting out both the vista and the thought of Henry Price and his unhygienic habits. She wanted to savor this moment and at the same time run away from it. Lily came to stand next to her, and Rachel opened her eyes. She saw Andrew gazing at her thoughtfully, a look in his eyes that Rachel feared was too close to pity.

"I suppose we should head back and find Claire," she said.

The walk back down Scafell Pike was as onerous as the journey up, each downward step jolting Rachel's knee joints and sending loose pebbles skittering down the path.

"People underestimate how difficult it is to walk down a mountain," Andrew remarked, and Rachel didn't bother to answer. She was trying not to whimper in pain. She didn't think she'd ever wear trainers again.

By the time the gate at the start of the trail came into view, she could have wept with relief. They'd passed a few hikers along the way, all of them decked out in the same sensible kit as Andrew. No one looked like they were in the kind of pain Rachel was. Lily, however, had managed all right. She'd borrowed a pair of hiking boots from a friend.

"Claire's probably inside," Andrew said, nodding towards the inn, and they all trooped inside the large whitewashed building. Rachel glanced around the wood-paneled bar with its deep booths and full array of wines and beers and thought she'd do just about anything to sink into a seat with a large glass of red.

Andrew, however, didn't look inclined to linger. He was walking around the room, looking for Claire, but after just a few seconds of searching it was clear she wasn't there.

"Maybe she got a room?" Rachel suggested. After her glass of wine she'd like a bubble bath and a twelve-hour nap upstairs. She imagined Claire would like the same.

"Look." Lily pointed to a notice board by the door, where various people had pinned adverts for secondhand hiking equipment or guided tours. There was a torn-off piece of paper with a few words scrawled on it: *I went home. —Claire.*

"How on earth did she get home?" Andrew demanded. "It's not as if a bus comes through here."

"Maybe she got a lift with someone," Lily ventured, and Andrew scowled.

"Let's go," he said, and strode out of the pub.

They were all quiet as they got into his Lexus, Rachel taking the front seat. She let out a quiet yet deeply felt sigh of relief when she sat down. She was desperate to take off her shoes, but she wasn't about to do it in Andrew's car. She'd assess the damage privately, at home.

"I'm sure she's fine," she said as Andrew pulled out onto the road, his face set in grim lines.

"Hitchhiking with some stranger? Right."

"Did you guys read that book about the fell walker who was a serial killer?" Lily asked as she leaned forward, one hand on each of their seats. "Seriously creepy." Andrew did not reply and Lily sat back. "Sorry," she murmured. "It was really unrealistic. Completely stretched my suspension of disbelief. How would he fit two women in the boot of his car?"

Rachel almost laughed, but a niggling worry kept her from it. What if something had happened to Claire? She was the one who had goaded Claire up on the fell, telling her not to let Andrew baby her. If Claire ended up chopped into pieces in the boot of some murderous hiker's car, it would be Rachel's fault.

They'd just turned onto the A-road towards Egremont when Andrew's phone trilled with an incoming text. He glanced down at it, his expression clearing even though the set of his shoulders remained rigid. "She's back home."

"Well, then." Rachel settled back into her seat. "I knew she'd be all right."

Clouds were starting to roll in from the sea as they reached Hartley-by-the-Sea, and Rachel's mood turned with the weather. Despite the various tensions, she'd enjoyed the day out, an escape from real life. With every mile they came closer to home, the pressures and worries she'd kept at bay for a few hours started to hound her.

She'd forgotten to do her weekly food shopping online, and tea still had to be made. Rachel doubted Meghan would have lifted a finger. Her taxes were due in a few weeks, and all her business expenses were kept in a shoe box that she hadn't so much as looked in for about nine months. Lily's final lab work was this week, and Rachel had forgotten to ask her about the soil samples. Her mother had a doctor's appointment in Whitehaven on Thursday, and Rachel would have to rework her day to take her, or ask Meghan to do it. Both options were unpalatable.

She wanted to run away from it all, back up to that view of freedom from the top of Scafell Pike, drink in the emptiness of it like a glass of cold, clean water, and forget about the pressures that were already crowding in on her, making it hard to breathe.

The car slowed, and with a hollow sensation Rachel saw they were back home. The terraced house she'd lived in her whole life looked smaller and shabbier after spending a day out in wide spaces with long views. Slowly she unbuckled her seat belt.

"Thanks for a lovely day out."

"Was it lovely?" Andrew said, one eyebrow cocked. "I'm glad you think so."

"I think so," Lily said as she got out of the car. "It was fab."

Lily was already walking inside, and yet Rachel hesitated, reluctant to end the day. She knew the second she stepped through the doorway she'd be sucked into the chaos and clamor of her life.

"I take your point about Claire," Andrew said quietly, and she turned to look at him in surprise.

"You do?"

"I'm not that blind or stupid. I know she's an adult and that she needs to make her own decisions. But . . ." He let out a sigh and rubbed one hand over his face. "I've been looking after Claire for my whole life. It's hard to stop."

"The perils of being a big brother, I suppose."

He dropped his hand with a weary smile. "You have no idea," he said with a grim quietness that unnerved her.

Rachel almost asked him more, but then she heard Lily go inside, and with a sigh she got out of the car.

"Thanks for taking us out today. We needed the break."

"I'm glad I was able to give you one." He smiled wryly. "And that it truly was a break."

She gave a little laugh. "I know I give you a hard time. I'm sorry."

"It's only because you like me, right?" He shook his head, still smiling, and Rachel schooled her face into an equally smiling-yet-neutral expression. She didn't like Andrew West. Not like that.

"Well, bye, then," she said, and for some reason it felt awkward. Date-like and yet so not. He nodded goodbye and she got out of the car. She'd just started up the path when Lily wrenched open the front door and stood on the stoop, her face pale and shocked.

"Rachel," she said, and her voice sounded like a child's, small and scared. "Something's wrong with Mum."

16

❧

Claire

CLAIRE STOOD AT THE sink and stared out at the twilit sky. She felt exhausted, every muscle aching, and yet also absurdly proud of herself. She'd gotten home.

She'd walked back down the fell, limping the last part of the way, and headed towards the inn. She'd been considering her options as she'd walked and realized they were extremely limited. She didn't have any cash on her or even her phone, which she kept in a drawer in a bedroom and checked once a day for messages from her mother, like taking medicine. Nasty but quickly over.

Wasdale Head was one of the Lake District's most remote outposts. It wasn't as if she could catch a bus or a train, even if she'd had the money to do so. So she'd stood in the doorway of the inn and gazed around at all the hikers with their walking sticks and pints of beer and then, clearing her throat, she'd issued her challenge, or really, her plea.

"Is anyone heading towards Hartley-by-the-Sea?"

A dozen heads had swiveled towards her, no doubt taking in her ruined plimsolls and desperate expression. She really did not want to have to wait for Andrew to come back down Scafell Pike, shaking his head in a sanctimonious I-told-you-so way.

"I'm going to Workington," a woman called out. She was in her mid-fifties, kitted out in high-tech hiking gear. "If you can wait for me to finish my lunch, I'll take you."

So Claire had waited, her stomach growling, as the woman finished her steak-and-ale pie. Claire almost wished she'd taken one of Rachel's tuna sandwiches.

Finally they set off, the woman introducing herself as Anna Linhart. She unclipped a dog's lead from the post outside, and Claire glanced at the enormous, slobbering wolfhound with some alarm. She was not much of a dog person, and definitely not a big dog person. Even Bunny made her a little nervous.

"He wouldn't hurt a fly," the woman assured her, but Claire still kept a good five feet between her and the half horse that the woman put in the backseat of her Mini. The car was so small that the wolfhound's head was practically on Claire's shoulder, his hot breath steaming into her ear.

"He likes you," Anna remarked. Claire did not reply. She could tell by Anna's few, careful questions that the older woman thought Claire was fleeing some breakup or abusive boyfriend, rather than an irritating older brother.

"You do have a safe place to stay?" she asked for the third time as they neared Hartley-by-the-Sea.

"Yes, definitely. I'm not in any danger, honestly." Claire smiled weakly, not wanting to admit she'd begged a lift simply to save face. "Really, I'll be okay."

"Call this number if you need anything," Anna said, and gave her a card for the Good Samaritans. Claire took it with murmured thanks.

She stepped into Four Gables with a sigh of relief, for once relishing the emptiness around her. Then she ran a deep, hot bath, eased off her ruined plimsolls, and sank into the foaming water.

An hour later Andrew still wasn't home and Claire felt mostly restored. She knew she could expect a lecture from Andrew about not accepting rides from strangers, and that would really make her feel like a child. What if she told him she'd accepted a chocolate bar from a stranger too? Anna had shared the bar of Cadbury's she kept in her glove box.

The thought made Claire smile, and the fact that she could see the humor in a situation for once made her feel strong. Maybe Rachel was right, and she didn't have to creep and inch her way through life, head ducked down, apologizing for everything. She'd been doing it for so long she'd forgotten how to do anything else, but she could learn. She could try.

Andrew finally came in at ten o'clock, when Claire had just been about to head up to bed. He looked tired and distinctly hassled, and in a knee-jerk reaction Claire babbled out an apology.

"Sorry to make you worry. I really was fine though, Andrew."

"It's not that." Andrew flung the car keys on the granite counter-top, where they skittered and bounced. He raked his hands through his hair and then dropped them wearily.

"What . . . what took you so long?"

"Rachel's mother had a stroke."

"What?" Claire stared at him, appalled. "When . . . ? How . . . ? I mean . . ."

"Lily found her when we got back from Wasdale Head. She was lying on the floor of the sitting room."

"Is she okay? I mean, now?"

"I don't know. I stayed with them until she was settled, but they'll have to do tests, and of course she'll have to have some rehabilitation." He shook his head slowly. "Not an easy situation."

"Is there anything we can do?"

"I doubt it. Rachel doesn't want help, anyway. At least she doesn't want to admit she needs it." Andrew smiled wryly. "She's too proud." Claire heard a note of affection in his voice and wondered again at Andrew's interest in Rachel. "I'm completely shattered," he continued, "not to mention starving. Is there anything to eat?"

Claire had made a cup of instant noodles for herself several hours ago. "Toast?"

Andrew grimaced and closed the door of the fridge. "Maybe I'll just go to bed."

"Okay."

He stood there a second, his palm flat on the fridge. "How did you get home, anyway?"

"I hitched a ride."

"And did you consider how dangerous that is?"

"Yes, actually, I did. But the woman who gave me a lift seemed perfectly safe and she was. So." She took a deep breath. "Don't baby me, Andrew, please."

"Is that you or Rachel Campbell talking?"

"Did you even *hear* what I said?"

"Yes, actually, I did," he parroted back at her before he sighed heavily. "Look, Claire, I'm not trying to annoy you. But you've always had someone looking out for you, usually me. It's hard to know how to stop, or if it's a good idea. Especially now."

"I know," she said softly. Even in primary school Andrew had been there, watching in the distance, a tough-looking Year Six to her scared Year Two. "You didn't . . . ? You didn't ask Rachel to look out for me back in primary school, did you?" she asked suddenly, and Andrew smiled, bemused.

"Are you kidding me? That would have seriously ruined my street cred."

But he'd walked home with her every day, held her hand as they walked down the steep school lane. He hadn't been too fussed about street cred. And then later, when she'd been at Wyndham, he'd been there, a steadying presence, older, wiser. He'd taught her to drive, until her mother had insisted Claire shouldn't drive because of her ear. As if being deaf in *one* ear made you a liability. But then, to her mother, it had. In so many ways.

"I'm sorry," she blurted.

"For what?"

"For needing to be looked after for so long. I get that I've seemed helpless to you. To everyone."

"I'm hearing Rachel again."

"But it's true, isn't it? Just because Rachel said it doesn't matter. She said it to help me, and I am trying to change, actually—"

"But this isn't your life, Claire." Andrew turned to face her. "Living in our parents' house, working in a village shop? I understand you need a break. But this isn't real life."

She blinked at him, absorbing his words. "And you think Portugal was real?"

"You had a decent job. You were engaged to be married. It stands to reason—"

"I was miserable in Portugal, Andrew. *Miserable.*" Her voice choked a bit, and she took a deep breath, willing the emotion back. "That's why I drank too much. Once, at a party. Or twice, if I'm honest. But it was because I felt like my life was spinning out of control. Everyone had made all my decisions for me, and I'd let them. I understand that. I accept my responsibility for it. But I was looking at the rest of my life, and I didn't want any of it."

Andrew stared at her for a moment. "What about Hugh?"

"What about him?"

"Didn't . . . ? Didn't you love him?" The question sounded diffident, uncomfortable. The Wests didn't use the L-word very often.

"No," Claire admitted. "I don't think I did." She paused. "I know I didn't."

"Did he love you?"

"I doubt it. Andrew, I haven't even spoken to him in more than a month." What had she shown him of herself to love? "I think he just liked having me on his arm. And I've always been eager to please." She smiled wryly. "Something else I'm trying to change."

Andrew stared at her. "Why did Hugh call Mum and Dad, if he wasn't genuinely concerned?"

"Because he wanted rid of me, I think." Claire shrugged. "I'd embarrassed him in public and become a nuisance." She winced at the recollection. "I admit it. I was loud and drunk and stupid at a party. I don't even remember half of what I said. And Hugh wanted to . . . to punish me, I suppose."

"*Punish* you? He sounds like a complete ass."

Claire smiled at Andrew's look of outrage. "Not a complete one. He could be quite charming, when he wanted to be."

"He didn't . . ." Andrew paused. "He didn't . . . mistreat you, did he?"

"No, not like that. Never like that." She tried for a laugh. "You sound like Anna Linhart."

"Who?"

"The woman who gave me a lift today. She handed me a card for the Good Samaritans before I got out of the car. I think she thought I was fleeing an abusive boyfriend."

Andrew rubbed a hand over his face. "And you didn't think to enlighten her?"

"And say what? That I'd gone off in a strop and left my brother on top of Scafell Pike?"

"We weren't even close to the top then."

She laughed, something lightening inside her. She couldn't remember the last time she'd talked like this with her brother. Maybe never.

"Rachel made it to the top," he said as he opened the fridge again and peered inside. Claire had a feeling it was just a tactic to avoid looking at her.

"There's nothing more in there since the last time you looked. Lily did too, I assume?"

Claire noticed Andrew's quick, almost guilty look before he closed the fridge again. "Yes, of course. Lily too."

"Hmm." She decided not to tease him about Rachel. She didn't even know how she felt about Andrew and Rachel as a concept. "I'm going to bed," she said. "But I'm glad everyone got back in one piece." She took a step towards him and laid a hand on his arm. "Thanks, Andrew."

"For what?"

"For easing off a bit."

He grimaced. "I must be really bad."

"I know you mean well—"

"Ouch."

"But I'm okay. Really. I'm okay." She stood on her tiptoes and kissed his cheek, and then she went upstairs to bed.

The next morning, while Andrew slept in, Claire decided to do something for Rachel. She wanted to be helpful, and after recalling how Andrew had mooched about, looking for something to eat last night, she decided to make a meal. Preferably something simple.

There were no trains running on a Sunday, so she walked to the village shop for ingredients, steeling herself against another abrupt encounter with her boss. At least she was a customer rather than an employee today, although Dan hadn't shown himself to be particularly friendly to customers, either.

"What are you doing here?" he asked as she came through the door. "You're not working today."

"I know. I'm a customer. I want to make a meal for Rachel Campbell. Macaroni and cheese, I think."

Unsmiling, he pointed to the shelf Claire had dusted and stacked several times. "There's a tin over there."

Claire followed the direction of his pointing finger, and when she saw the tin with its picture of rubbery orange macaroni and cheese, she burst out laughing. Dan stared at her nonplussed while she clapped a hand over her mouth.

"Sorry. Sorry. I'm not laughing at you, honestly. It's just . . ." She couldn't explain what she found so funny, and Dan obviously didn't see the humorous side to the situation.

"How about the beef stew with minty peas?" he asked, and then he actually cracked a smile.

Watching Dan Trenton smile was like seeing the snow melt in Narnia. Was it really happening, after all this time? Winter was over?

"Wait," she dared to tease. "You actually have a sense of humor?"

"No. I just want to shift my inventory." He jerked a thumb towards the back. "The milk and cheese are in the refrigerated section, you know."

"Okay." She walked over to the refrigerated section, conscious of Dan watching her. The shop felt smaller than usual, even when they shared the single room for eight hours at a stretch.

"So why are you making macaroni and cheese for this Rachel Campbell?" Dan asked.

"Her mother's had a stroke. I thought she could use a meal." Claire picked up a wedge of plastic-wrapped Cheddar. "Do you know her?"

"Her mother?"

"Rachel."

"No."

"Do you know anyone in this village?" she asked, and Dan's expression hardened a little.

"I know Robin, the milkman. And Sue, who delivers the meat pies. Lucy Bagshaw. And you." She saw a glint of challenge in his eyes, and he folded his arms repressively.

"I wasn't meaning to sound rude, but . . ." She shrugged, not sure how to explain how odd it was that Dan was so reclusive. Although she was hardly one to talk. "Where did you live, before here?"

"Leeds."

"Why did you move to Hartley-by-the-Sea?"

"What is this, an interrogation?" He fiddled with the Lotto card dispenser for a moment before answering. "The village shop was for sale, and I fancied trying my hand at running it."

"But you don't want to get to know people."

"No. Do you?"

The blunt question surprised her. "Well, yes, sort of . . ."

"Because you don't want to go to the pub quiz, and when Lucy Bag-shaw corners you, asking you for coffee or what have you, you look like a frightened rabbit. Although come to think of it, you always look like a frightened rabbit."

"I think that's the most I've heard you say in one stretch since I've known you," Claire said. She was trying to joke, but she felt flayed by Dan's flatly stated assessment. She had no idea he'd noticed so much. "I didn't say it wasn't hard," she said after a pause. "I've been away a long time, and I've never been good at making friends."

"Why not?"

"Now you're the one interrogating me."

"Shoe's on the other foot, is it?"

"I guess it must be, since I only had enough money to buy one shoe." She smiled, hoping he'd smile back, but he didn't. "I don't know why not. Why do you have trouble making friends?"

He looked affronted. "I never said I did."

She rolled her eyes. "You didn't have to."

"I don't want any friends," Dan said after a moment. "They're more trouble than they're worth." He nodded towards the milk and cheese she held in her hands. "Now, are you going to pay for that before the milk goes sour?"

Conversation clearly over, Claire paid up and then walked back to Four Gables. She was half amazed by what Dan had shared and more than a little unnerved by how much he'd noticed about her. Were they friends now? Maybe not quite. Maybe not at all.

A couple of hours later she headed up the street towards Rachel's house, holding a foil-covered casserole dish of slightly soupy macaroni and cheese. The only time she'd been to Rachel's house had been yesterday, when they'd picked her and Lily up for the hike. Now she stood on the concrete stoop, uncertain as to whether this was actually a good idea. Rachel might be annoyed that she'd come around, offering what she might consider pity. Maybe she'd turn up her nose at homemade mac and cheese.

Before she could contemplate beating a silent and cowardly retreat, the door jerked open and a woman stood there, hands planted on her hips. She looked a lot like Rachel, minus the height and the red hair.

"Well, well, well. Claire West." A catlike smile curved her lips.

"Hi. You must be Rachel's sister."

"You don't remember me from school?" Meghan raised her eyebrows, her smile widening.

"No, sorry."

"It's Meghan. I was four years younger than you. But I guess you were too cool to notice me."

Not the cool-girl thing again. "I'm sure you were too cool for me," Claire answered lightly. "Is Rachel in?"

"Rachel!" Meghan yelled over her shoulder. "Someone to see you." She stepped back inside, and Claire followed, feeling faintly ridiculous carrying her foil-covered dish.

"Meghan, Nathan has pooed his pants again. I thought he was potty trained?" Rachel came striding out of the kitchen, looking tired and harassed, only to come up short when she caught sight of Claire. "Oh. You."

Which was what she'd said the last time Claire had come across her unexpectedly.

"Hey . . ." Claire began, but Rachel was already turning to Meghan.

"He needs to be cleaned up. Now."

"He's regressing because of all the stress around here," Meghan muttered. "Oy! Nathan." She disappeared into the kitchen, and Claire tried not to wrinkle her nose. Now that she was in the house, she realized it reeked.

"Sorry," Rachel said, and picked up a woolen beanie that had been lying on the floor and hung it on a coat peg. "So, not to be rude, but . . . why are you here?"

"I thought you could use a meal." Claire nodded towards the dish in her hands. "With everything going on."

Rachel stared at her for a moment, unspeaking, and Claire smiled back uncertainly. Meghan barreled past them, holding a very smelly little boy aloft.

"Coming through with nuclear waste," she announced, and headed upstairs.

"Come into the kitchen," Rachel said, and Claire followed her through to a tiny room, every surface cluttered with dirty dishes and . . . stuff. Crumpled papers, makeup, sweet wrappers. She'd never seen so much rubbish.

"Sorry. I haven't had time to tidy up," Rachel muttered.

"You're starting to sound like me, saying sorry all the time."

"Well. It is a tip in here." Awkwardly Rachel held her hands out, and just as awkwardly Claire put the casserole dish into them. She hadn't expected this to be quite so weird.

"It's macaroni and cheese. I had a taste, to make sure it wasn't revolting. You're not vegan or anything, are you?"

"Vegan?" For a moment Rachel looked amused. "No. Definitely not."

"Okay, then. Good." They stood there for a moment, staring at each other, and Claire felt the weight of the years between them, decades of silence she found it hard to break now. "How's your mum?" she asked finally.

"Not very well at the moment." Rachel opened the fridge and slid the casserole dish inside. "She's going to be in the hospital for a few days while they do some tests."

"It was a stroke?"

"They think so, yes. She's a smoker, so I suppose it's not really surprising."

"It must be hard, though. Is your dad . . . ?" Claire trailed off as she saw Rachel stiffen.

"My dad hasn't been around for years, Claire, but I don't know why

I'd expect you to know that. You were in uni then, and we hadn't so much as spoken for seven years. But I thought you might have heard the *crack* through the village grapevine."

"The *crack* . . . ?"

"Cumbrian for 'gossip.' Surely you knew that?" Rachel gave a half smile. "You were born here, after all."

"I'm afraid I never got the hang of the dialect."

"No, I don't suppose you would have."

"If there's anything else I can do . . ." Claire offered. Rachel gazed at her for a moment and then shook her head.

"I really don't think there is."

"Okay. Well." Claire took a backwards step towards the hall. "You must have loads to do. I suppose I'll go . . ." Another step, and Rachel just watched her. This whole conversation was becoming more awkward by the second.

"I really mean it," Claire blurted. "If there's anything I can do . . . anything at all . . ."

Rachel's mouth twisted in a wry smile. She looked exhausted, with violet smudges under her eyes, her hair caught up in a messy ponytail. "Unfortunately," she answered with a sigh, "I don't think there is. But thank you, Claire."

17

Rachel

MEGHAN CAME IN AS Claire was leaving, tossing Nathan's dirty clothes towards the washer with an alarmingly wet splat.

With a sigh Rachel picked them up and shoved them in. "Couldn't you have put them in the washer?"

"Close enough," Meghan answered breezily. "What did Claire West want?"

"She made us a meal."

"A meal?" Meghan raised her eyebrows. "Are we her charity, then?"

"Actually, I think she was just being nice." Which had felt kind of strange—and nice. Rachel hadn't had much experience of Claire West taking care of or looking out for her. "Come on," she said to Meghan. "We need to get going. Mum's waiting."

They drove to the hospital in silence, the four of them crammed into the hatchback, Nathan in his car seat behind Rachel, kicking his legs against the back of her seat. Meghan angled the rearview mirror away from Rachel to do her lipstick.

"Seriously, Meghan? I'm driving."

"Use your wing mirrors. That's what they're for."

"When can I get driving lessons?" Lily asked from the back.

Driving lessons cost about two hundred quid. "I'll teach you," Rachel said, and Meghan guffawed.

"Just like you taught me? You lasted all of two lessons."

"You were impossible."

"So were you. You grabbed the wheel from me to do a right turn and we ended up on the curb."

"You practically stripped the gears changing from second to third."

"I was *learning*."

Rachel angled the rearview mirror back towards her. "I'll teach you, Lily," she said. "Promise." Lily didn't reply, and no one spoke until they'd reached the hospital.

"Why do hospitals always smell?" Meghan asked as they walked through the sliding-glass doors.

"Because they're hospitals," Rachel answered tartly. It had taken her twenty minutes to find a parking space, and she'd ended up on a grassy verge. She was worried about what the doctors were going to say about her mother and what the prognosis was. She didn't think she could cope with her mother being even more bedridden and ill. And she was starting to feel bad about not being nicer to Claire this morning.

"I know they do," Meghan said, "but what is that smell? Cleaning fluid? Medicine? Flesh rotting?"

"All three," Lily answered, and let out a nervous laugh. Rachel knew they were all tense about their mother, not knowing how to act, what to feel. Last night had been a blur of fear and helplessness; when Lily had come out of the house, her face so pale and shocked, Rachel had run inside, stopping short to see her mother collapsed on the floor of the sitting room, her limbs at weird, awkward angles, her face contorted in a grimace of pain.

Rachel had stood there, frozen for a few seconds, until Andrew came in behind her, calmly took out his phone, and dialed 999.

"I can do that," Rachel had protested, her voice rising in panic and anger, and Andrew hadn't bothered to reply.

She had crouched by her mother, wiping a few lank strands of gray hair away from her face. "Mum? Mum, can you hear me?"

Janice had blinked up at her and then tried to speak, but only an animal-sounding groan came out. Fear had clutched at Rachel hard, so she couldn't speak either. She couldn't believe this was happening, and just after she'd resigned herself to her mother having thirty or forty years of bedridden existence ahead. She'd been practically wishing her mother dead, and now this. . . .

"An ambulance is coming," Andrew had said.

Rachel had taken her mother's limp hand in hers. "I don't think we should move her."

"Probably not. They'll be here soon, and they can put her directly onto a stretcher." He'd sounded so calm and reasonable, as if he saw grossly overweight women sprawled on floors every day of the week. Rachel noticed that her mother's old nightgown had rucked up to her thighs, showing the pasty, dimpled flesh, and she'd gently pulled it down again.

"Is she going to be all right?" Lily had asked in a whisper. She was standing in the doorway of the sitting room, her face as pale as Janice's, her hands clenched into fists at her sides.

"Yes, of course she is," Rachel had said with far more conviction than she felt. "She'll be fine." She looked around the room, taking in the dirty dishes on the coffee table, the TV still on, a din of canned laughter and corny music she hadn't even registered. Andrew found the remote control and switched the TV off.

"Where's Meghan? And Nathan?" They should have been there; Rachel had asked Meghan to stay with Janice while they went hiking. They all knew Janice couldn't be left alone. "Lily?" She glanced back at her sister, who hadn't moved from the doorway. "Do you know where Meghan is?"

"No. She wasn't here when I came in." In the distance they heard the wail of the ambulance's siren.

The paramedics were briskly efficient, unmoved by the sight of Janice Campbell sprawled on the floor in a worn and stained nightgown; four of them were needed to load Janice onto a stretcher and then into the ambulance. Andrew had offered to drive Rachel and Lily to the hospital, since they weren't allowed in the ambulance, and numbly Rachel had refused.

"I can drive. . . ."

"I don't think you're in a condition to drive," Andrew had said firmly. "And I don't mind driving you."

And so she had accepted, because she did feel dazed and weird, and she didn't want to handle this alone. She didn't think she could. They'd gotten back into his Lexus and driven in silence to the hospital.

The next few hours had passed in a terrible blur of doctors and waiting; an hour in Meghan had phoned, panicked, and Rachel had yelled at her.

"Where the bloody hell were you, Meghan? Mum fell. They think she's had a stroke, and you just left her alone—"

Andrew had removed the phone from Rachel's hand, and she stared at him in shock. "We're at West Cumberland," he said into the phone. "Can you drive here? No, actually, let me come and get you." He'd disconnected the call and handed the phone back to Rachel; she'd stared at the dark screen in disbelief.

"What was that?"

"Getting angry at your sister serves no purpose," Andrew had said calmly. "I'll go fetch her. I'm sure she wants to be here."

Rachel had sat back in her seat, her arms folded, feeling both furious and chastised. Maybe she shouldn't have yelled at Meghan, but it wasn't up to Andrew West to tell her so. And yet with a rush of guilt, she knew he'd done the right thing. It didn't mean she had to be grateful, though.

"Do you think she'll be all right?" Lily asked. She'd asked the same question at least a dozen times since they'd first seen Janice on the sitting room floor, and Rachel still had no answers.

"We'll see, Lil," she had said tiredly, and put an arm around her sister's shoulders. Lily had pressed her face against Rachel's arm.

Twenty minutes later Andrew had returned with Meghan, who'd looked dazed and pale, Nathan clinging to her, his thumb stuck firmly in his mouth, his eyes huge and unblinking.

"Where were you?" Rachel had asked, her tone level.

"I went out with Nathan for a bit." Rachel saw her sister's eyes were red, and she realized Meghan had been crying. She'd never seen her sister cry, not when Mum had fallen or Dad had left. Not when Nathan had gotten croup when he was four months old and had had to be hospitalized. Meghan always presented a breezy front. Rachel had come to depend on it, even as it exasperated her. "Just for a little while, to the beach," she whispered. "He'd been climbing the walls all day, and even Mum was getting fed up." Meghan's voice was pleading, so unlike her usual stroppy sass.

"It's okay, Meghan." Rachel had taken a deep breath and gestured to the seat next to her, hard and plastic. Meghan had sniffed and sat down. "I'm sorry I yelled at you."

Finally a doctor told them their mother was stable; she'd almost certainly had a thrombotic stroke and would have a battery of tests the next day, to determine the extent of damage to her body, her brain. She was sleeping so they couldn't talk to her, and eventually they'd all trooped home, exhausted and overwhelmed.

Andrew had walked her to the door, almost like it was a bizarre, awful date. "I'm sorry," he said in a low voice. Meghan and Lily had already gone inside.

"You don't need to be sorry. You didn't do anything. Thank you for all your help." She spoke stiffly, the way she would to a stranger at the supermarket who had fetched something for her from a high shelf. "You've been very kind."

"Let me know if there's something I can do. I could drive you tomorrow. . . ."

"We have a car," Rachel said. "Thank you, Andrew, but we don't need any more help." She'd gone inside without looking at him, shutting the door with him still standing on the stoop, because she didn't trust herself not to throw herself into his arms and ask him to stay, to help, to take over. For a moment she wanted to be like Claire, letting other people do the heavy lifting. Letting other people do everything.

Now she, Meghan, Nathan, and Lily all sat in the consultant's office and waited to hear Janet's prognosis. They'd seen Janice, who had been dopey with painkillers but had managed a weird rictus of a smile; the consultant had said the left side of her face and body were paralyzed, perhaps temporarily. Perhaps not.

The consultant, Mr. Greaves, looked up from his notes with a conciliatory smile that made Rachel dig her fingernails into her palms. This wasn't going to be good news.

"Your mother's health is very compromised," he began. "I'm afraid her lack of mobility, along with her smoking, has contributed to her suffering from a thrombotic stroke." Which was what he'd told them last night.

"What's the outlook?" Rachel asked bluntly. She didn't care about the medical details. She needed to know how things were going to change. How they were all going to cope.

"It will take some time to assess the full damage," Mr. Greaves said carefully. "She'll be in the hospital for several weeks, undergoing tests and beginning rehabilitation. When we feel she can be released, she'll be able to go home, but she'll have to attend a rehabilitation clinic several times a week."

And how on earth was that going to happen? Rachel would have to drive her. She took a steadying breath. "Okay."

Mr. Greaves looked back down at his notes. "I understand your mother's mobility was already limited, due to her back injury."

"Yes . . ."

"We'll do our best to work within the limitations of her condition.

But . . ." He hesitated, and Rachel felt all four of them go tense as they waited for what felt like a verdict. "You should be prepared for the probability that she will not make a full or even partial recovery."

"Even partial?" Rachel repeated, her voice hoarse. "What do you mean?"

"I mean, considering your mother's prestroke condition, it seems unlikely she will recover much mobility."

"She didn't have much mobility in the first place," Rachel said. "What about her speech and . . . cognitive function?"

"That remains to be determined."

Half an hour later they were back outside in the car park, all of them dazed and unspeaking. Rachel yanked the parking ticket stuck beneath the windshield. "Seventy pounds for parking on the grass, when there were no bloody parking spaces." She ripped up the ticket and let the pieces flutter to the ground while Lily and Meghan watched, mouths open.

"Won't you get in trouble for that?" Lily asked.

"I don't care." She unlocked the car and got in, staring straight ahead as Meghan buckled Nathan into his car seat and Lily got in the back.

"Are you going to start the car?" Meghan asked after a moment. Rachel realized she'd just been sitting there, her hands clenched on the steering wheel, for several minutes.

Wordlessly, she jammed the key into the ignition and reversed off the verge, scraping the muffler with a screeching sound as she came off the curb. Meghan winced. Rachel cursed. And kept driving.

18

Claire

"ARE YOU DEAF?"

Claire jerked around from where she'd been stacking milk bottles, wiping her hands, cold and damp from the condensation, on her jeans. "Pardon?"

Dan stared at her from behind the counter, his arms folded. "I said, are you deaf?"

She thought he was being rude, but as he stood there expectantly she realized he meant the question, and he was waiting for her to answer it. "No, not . . . not exactly. Why do you ask?"

"Because I've noticed you have trouble hearing me when there are people around, and you always tilt your head to one side when someone is talking. So I wondered. Are you deaf? Partially, I mean?"

She blinked, discomfited by his perception. "Yes, actually, I am. But you're the first person who has noticed." She never talked about her hearing problems. Her mother had insisted it didn't matter, people didn't want to know, and Claire shouldn't limit herself by acting as if she had some sort of disability. Claire didn't think her mother was *ashamed* of her, not precisely, but Claire's ear troubles, the endless operations and illnesses, weren't something she bandied about. Even Hugh hadn't known about it; Claire hadn't meant to keep it a secret, but he

179

hadn't seemed like someone who would be interested in any kind of weaknesses or deficiencies, and disability or not, she knew instinctively that's how it would be viewed.

"I knew some blokes in the army," Dan said. "Blew out their eardrums when they were too close to an explosion. Went deaf in one ear."

"Oh. Right."

"What happened to you?"

"I had loads of ear infections as a child. Eventually one became bad enough that it developed into a cholesteatoma."

"A what?"

"A tumor sort of thing. Anyway, it dissolved the bones in my ear and made me deaf. In one ear." Just in case he thought she was *really* deaf.

Dan nodded slowly, his expression unchanging. "That's tough."

The last thing she expected was Dan's sympathy. "It's not too bad. I'm kind of used to it now. But I suppose when I was younger . . ." She shrugged, not used to going into the details. The endless doctor's appointments and medical procedures she'd had in an attempt to rebuild the bones in her ear and restore her hearing; none had been successful. The bouts of pneumonia and flu, the suffocating concern of her mother. The feeling that she had to be wrapped in cotton wool, and she was still fighting her way out.

"Why didn't you tell me?" Dan asked. "About being deaf?"

"Partially deaf—"

"Even so. It would have been good to know."

"I don't tell anyone. It doesn't really affect me." Dan gave her a disbelieving look. "We haven't been sharing confidences, have we?" Claire challenged. "The only things I know about you are that you're from Leeds and that you were in the army."

"And I have a dog named Bunny."

"Right." They stared at each other for a moment; Claire felt as if Dan was weighing her up.

"All right," he said. "What do you want to know?"

"About you?"

He shifted where he stood. "Yes."

And of course now she couldn't think of a thing. "Who's Daphne?" she finally blurted, recalling his tattoo, and Dan stilled.

"My ex-wife."

"Oh." His tone did not encourage further questions. Still, an ex-wife. Claire wouldn't have expected it. She could not imagine Dan Trenton with a wife, *in love*. Of course, there was a reason why the woman was an ex.

"Why do you have the word 'sapper' tattooed on your arm?" She'd stick to asking about the tattoos.

"Because I was one."

"A sapper? What is that?"

"A position in the army. I cleared minefields."

"Oh." She blinked. "That sounds . . . dangerous."

"It was."

She couldn't sound more inane if she tried. "Where did you serve?"

"Afghanistan." He paused. "That was dangerous too." And then he smiled, barely the quirking of the corner of his mouth, so tiny she almost missed it. She wasn't even sure it was a smile, and yet . . .

"Do I sound as silly as I think I do?" she asked.

"Sillier," Dan told her, and now he was definitely smiling. It looked strange, as if he were using muscles that were stiff and atrophied.

"Oh. Okay. Well, good to know." Dan didn't seem inclined to say anything else, and so Claire turned back to the milk. After about ten minutes he spoke again.

"You can do the stall at the Easter Fair if you want."

She turned around, suspicion warring with hope. "This isn't some . . . pity gesture, is it?"

"Why would I pity you?"

She hesitated. "Because . . . because of my ear." Among other things.

"Get over it, rich girl. I knew plenty of soldiers who had it loads worse than you. I just want to increase revenue."

He turned away, and she realized she was smiling, a big, sloppy grin. "Okay. Great. Well, thank you."

Dan didn't answer.

A week later Claire was setting up her stall in the playing field outside the school. The sun was shining for once, and Alex Kincaid, the head teacher, had decided the grass was dry enough for the fair to be held outside.

Claire had spent a lot of time, probably too much, deciding how she wanted the stall to look. In the end she'd bought some old-fashioned glass jars and metal scoops online and filled them with a selection of sweets from the post office: jelly beans, humbugs, licorice whips, gummy worms. She'd also bought some red-and-white-striped paper bags and brought her mother's expensive brass kitchen scales to weigh the filled bags, fifty pence for twenty-five grams of candy. She'd even gotten herself a matching red and white striped apron, and had embroidered SWEETS FROM THE VILLAGE SHOP on the front. Sewing was one thing she'd always been able to do.

Now that she was here with all of her crazy kit she felt a little ridiculous. No one else had gone to nearly as much effort as she had.

"This all looks absolutely fantastic," Lucy exclaimed as she came up to Claire's stall. "Like an old-fashioned sweetshop. Amazing."

"Well, that was the look I was going for." Claire smiled self-consciously as she glanced around at the various people manning the other stalls. No one had anything remotely like a costume on. "I feel a bit over-the-top though."

"Nonsense, you can't be OTT for this." Lucy leaned forward conspiratorially. "I asked Alex to wear an Easter bonnet, complete with ribbons and bows."

"You did not." Claire had seen the stern teacher from a distance, and she couldn't imagine him in any such getup, even if he was dating Lucy.

"Well, I asked," Lucy replied with a grin. "He refused, though."

Claire looked down at her candy-striped apron. "No one had to ask me."

"You look great," Lucy said firmly. "The kids will love it." Her eyes sparkled with kindly mischief as she added, "I'm pleased Dan came around to the idea."

"I was surprised he did, to be honest."

"Maybe he's taken a shine to you."

Ridiculously, Claire blushed. "Maybe," she agreed, and Lucy grinned. Claire could imagine what she was thinking; Lucy Bagshaw seemed exactly the kind of person who delighted in playing matchmaker. And the idea of her and Dan together like that was utterly ludicrous. "I'd just like to be his friend, Lucy," she said. "So don't get any ideas."

"Me? Get ideas?" Lucy batted her eyelashes in exaggerated innocence. "Why on earth would you think that?"

"Oh, I don't know, because I can see the hearts in your eyes?" Claire teased before dropping the banter. "Seriously." The thought of Dan overhearing any part of this conversation made her inwardly cringe. She did not even want to imagine the kind of scathing smackdown he was capable of in that scenario.

"Okay, okay, I promise," Lucy said. "But as I said before, he has had a hard time of it. He needs someone who—"

"Trust me, I am not that someone," Claire cut her off. She was curious about Dan Trenton's past, but she didn't want to hear about it from Lucy Bagshaw. She wanted Dan to tell her himself, and maybe, just maybe, one day he would.

"I'd better go check the face-painting stall," Lucy said with a glance over her shoulder. The children were coming towards the field from the school, a bobbing sea of checked pinafores and gray flannel. "Apparently they always go there first, although your sweet stall might give face painting a run for its money." She hurried off, and Claire tugged on her apron and then stood up straighter, trying not to feel intimidated by the several hundred waist-high people surging towards the field.

Within minutes she was besieged by pupils, all who seemed quite taken by the idea of filling the striped bags with a variety of sweets and then thrusting grubby fifty-pence pieces towards her. She saw the boy who had tried to nick sweets from the post office saunter towards her stall, hands held up innocently when she gave him a knowing look. It would be pretty difficult to sneak a sweet from one of the high jars Claire was keeping well out of the children's way.

"It looks like you need help," a red-haired teacher remarked. "Oy, you lot. Step back." She came around the table to Claire's side and reached for a metal scoop. "How about I scoop sweets while you take the money?"

"Bless you," Claire answered with deep gratitude, and within a few minutes they had developed a natural rhythm of working together, and the line of children snaking towards the middle of the field began to shorten.

"I'm Diana Rigby," the woman said in between scoops. "I teach Year Three."

"Claire West, and I work in the post office shop."

"You're new to the village?"

"Sort of." Claire handed fifty-pence change to a girl with plaits and a pinafore before turning back to Diana. "I grew up here. I went to the village school myself, actually, about twenty years ago."

"But you've been away," Diana surmised. "Oy! Jacob Peterson! Keep your hands to yourself!"

Claire glanced back to see a lanky boy in Year Six jam his hands into the pockets of his trousers. Next to him a girl with plaits was looking annoyed as she retied the ribbon on one end.

"Rob Telford used to yank my plaits," Claire recalled. "Or so he told me when I saw him at the pub. I don't actually remember it."

"Rob seems the type to get into trouble as a lad, although he's on the straight and narrow now."

"Is he?"

Diana nodded solemnly. "He bought the pub a few years ago and lives with his mum in the flat above. Works hard, he does. Jacob Peterson, I'm still watching you."

Jacob slunk off, and the girl with the plaits, clearly not as annoyed as Claire had thought, ran after him.

"You seem to know everyone around here," Claire remarked.

"Not everyone, but Hartley-by-the-Sea is a small place. Surely you know that, since you grew up here?" Diana gave her a look of smiling curiosity.

"Yes, I suppose I do," Claire answered. "Although to be honest, I don't think my family got very involved in things." Diana waited, clearly wanting to hear more, and hesitantly Claire continued. "My brother and I went to secondary school in Keswick, and my father worked in Manchester."

"Ah," Diana said, nodding, and Claire felt as if she'd understood more than she'd actually said. "But you're getting involved now, it seems?" She twisted a bag of gummy worms closed and handed it to a sticky-faced Year One.

"Yes," Claire said slowly. "Yes, I think I am."

Two hours later she'd sold all her sweets, made seventy pounds, and was aching all over. Diana had left to take her Year Threes back into the school, and the other people were starting to dismantle their stalls. The field was festooned with stray bits of paper, more than a few crumpled, empty sweet bags, and a good deal of pink ribbon from the Easter-bonnet decorating competition.

Although Claire had spent the entire fair behind her stall, she'd enjoyed watching all the activity, including a nail-biting egg-on-a-spoon race and a hair-raising three-legged one, with many of the children collapsing, laughing, onto the grass.

Plenty of people had stopped by her stall, not just for sweets, but to say hello. Abby had come with Noah, and Claire had given him a licorice bootlace that he'd chewed happily. Meghan and Nathan had also stopped by, somewhat to Claire's surprise. She'd braced herself for Meghan's acerbic remarks, but Rachel's sister had only looked tired.

"How's your mum?" Claire had asked, and Meghan's face tightened a bit.

"Still in hospital. It'll be a while yet, they say, until she can come home."

"But making progress?"

Meghan shrugged. "She's trying to talk, so that's something, but the left side of her face and body is paralyzed. They don't know how long that will last, or if it will be permanent." Her voice wobbled a bit at the end, and impulsively Claire leaned over and touched her arm.

"I'm so sorry, Meghan. If there's anything I can do . . . another meal . . ."

"The macaroni and cheese was great," Meghan said, shaking her arm off. "Thank you. But we're fine."

"Tell Rachel I'm thinking of her."

Meghan gave her a rather funny look before nodding. "I will," she said, and moved on.

Claire hadn't seen Rachel all week, although when she'd come in from work on Thursday she could tell the house had been cleaned. It smelled strongly of lemon polish and lavender, and the floors had seemed shinier than usual. But other than that Claire had no idea how Rachel was coping, or if she'd want to see her again. And she wasn't quite brave enough yet to find out.

Even though Claire was tired, she was reluctant to pack up and trudge back to Four Gables and another evening alone. Andrew had left several days ago, although he'd promised to come back on the weekend. Claire was looking forward to seeing him again; now that they'd started breaking through their usual roles with Andrew as caretaker and her as supplicant, she found she enjoyed his company.

She was just reaching for the canvas holdalls she'd stuffed underneath her stall when a familiar figure loomed above her.

"Looks like you did well."

Claire blinked up at Dan. "What are you doing here?"

"Helping you bring all this back."

"But who's in the shop?"

"I closed it for ten minutes. It won't kill me." He reached for the empty glass jars. "You put the sweets in these?"

"I wanted it to look like an old-fashioned sweet shop," she explained, bracing herself for the expected, scornful dismissal of such a silly notion.

Dan nodded slowly. "That's a good idea. Maybe we could use the jars in the shop."

"Oh . . . yes, of course you could."

"I'll reimburse you."

"You don't have to—"

"I will," he stated, his tone final, and he reached for one of her bags and started loading things into it.

A few minutes later, holding several bulging bags each, they left the field and headed down the high street to the post office shop. The sun was still high above, but a slight chill had entered the air and a few dark clouds scudded across the pale blue sky.

"At least it didn't rain," Claire remarked as Dan unlocked the front door of the shop and then held the door for her to squeeze past him inside.

For some reason, as she was sucking in her stomach to move past him in the narrow doorway, she remembered Lucy's kindly teasing and felt a prickly heat sweep over her.

It was utterly absurd to think of Dan that way. For one thing, she was still a bit intimidated by him. And two, he seemed like the least romantic person she had ever encountered. She glanced at him as he took the bags into the back of the shop. He wore his usual black T-shirt and dark jeans, which emphasized his massive biceps and body like an oak tree. His dark hair was buzzed short, his face clean-shaven and un-expressive. She supposed he was handsome, in a massive, intimidating way. He was certainly strong.

"I'll rinse these jars out in the kitchen first," he called over his shoulder, and she realized she was staring.

"Okay." She followed him back, intending to help, but the kitchen was barely big enough for both of them. Bunny scampered under the table.

"Hey, Bunny." She crouched down to stroke the trembling dog's silky head while Dan unloaded the jars onto the counter by the sink. "What do you think happened to her?" she asked.

"She belonged to an old lady, and when she died a relative took her and left her out on the M6."

"Oh, that's horrible," Claire exclaimed.

Dan nodded grimly. "She was half her normal weight too. I could see all her ribs."

"Do you think she'll ever stop being afraid?"

Bunny had submitted to Claire's gentle stroking, but she still trembled.

"In time. I've only had her a year." He glanced down at the dog, his face softening. "She was loved for a long while. It hasn't all been bad for her."

Claire straightened, her shoulder brushing Dan's. "It was kind of you to take her on."

He shrugged so his shoulder brushed hers back. "I wanted company." He turned back to the sink and started rinsing out the jars. Claire watched and then took one as he handed it to her, drying it with the dish towel that had been hanging on the stove's rail.

They worked in silence for a few minutes and when the jars were clean and dry Dan jerked his head back towards the shop.

"We should go back in." He'd left the door to the kitchen open so they could hear if anyone came into the shop, but even so Claire knew he didn't like leaving it empty for long.

She followed him out of the kitchen. "What do you want me to do now?" She still had an hour left of her shift.

"I think you've earned a break," Dan answered as he took his place behind the till. "You can go home."

"Oh." She couldn't keep the disappointment from her voice, and Dan glanced at her.

"Don't you want to?"

"Well, there's nothing much for me at home besides a lot of empty rooms with carpets I'm afraid to walk on."

"Seriously?"

"And pillows I don't want to crumple. My mother keeps her house very neat."

"But your mother isn't here, is she?"

"No, thank goodness." Claire pretended to shudder, although she wasn't actually sure how much she was pretending. The thought of Marie West descending on the little life she'd built here was terrifying.

"Well, you can stay if you want," Dan said with a shrug. He sounded indifferent to the idea. "And start filling those jars with sweets, if you want something to do."

"Okay," Claire said, and with a ridiculous smile on her face, she headed back to his kitchen to get the jars.

19

Rachel

AS FAR AS WEEKS went, it had to be up there with her worst. Not as bad as the week after her father had left, when Meghan had called her, telling her she needed to come home from Durham. Not as bad as the week after her mother had broken her back, when her father had stumbled home from the hospital every night and Rachel had slept with Lily's bassinet next to her bed, one foot dangling down to rock it whenever Lily stirred.

So this was probably the third worst week she'd ever had. Rachel pulled in front of the house and briefly rested her forehead on the steering wheel. She didn't want to go inside and deal with Meghan's attitude, made inexplicably worse by their mother's stroke, and Lily's sullen silences, and Nathan's near-hysteria. He'd completely regressed with his toilet training, and Meghan refused to let him wear nappies, insisting they could ride through it. Rachel would rather have Nathan encased in non-biodegradable plastic.

With a sigh she switched off the engine and opened the door. A chilly breeze buffeted her; spring had come and gone again, as it often did in April. Easter was this Sunday, and last year they'd gone to church and she'd actually made a roast dinner. The prospect seemed laughable now.

"Hello?" Rachel called as she opened the door. The house was eerily silent, until Lily thundered down the stairs.

"Meghan's gone off and Nathan has been a complete pain," she said as she grabbed her jacket.

"Wait—where are you going?" Rachel watched as Lily yanked on her jacket and shoved her phone and keys into one of the pockets.

"Out."

"Out where? Lily, it's a school night—"

"It's six o'clock," Lily protested. "I've got loads of time."

"Your exams start in three weeks—"

"Loads of time," Lily insisted, and disappeared out the door. Rachel registered Nathan's postsob sniffles from upstairs.

Slowly she climbed the stairs, wondering if it was worth texting Meghan and demanding to know where she'd gone. Meghan had disappeared often in the last week, first the late evenings out after Nathan was in bed, and then during the day, leaving Lily or Rachel in charge as often as she could. Rachel couldn't keep the creeping fear from taking hold of her that one day Meghan might leave and not come back.

She stood in the doorway of Meghan's bedroom; Nathan was sitting in the middle of the bed, his face tear-streaked, his eyes watchful.

"Guess what, Nath," Rachel said with as much cheer as she could muster, which admittedly wasn't much. "You're going to wear a nappy."

Three hours later Nathan was bathed and in bed—with a nappy on—and Rachel had started cleaning the kitchen. Usually Meghan kept things at a minimum level of tidiness, but without Janice here to care for, her sister seemed to have forgotten she had any responsibilities at all. The drain of the sink was choked with soggy cereal, and dirty plates were stacked in a teetering pile on the counter by the dishwasher. At least she'd stacked them.

Rachel heard the front door open and called, "Meghan?"

"It's Lily." Lily slouched into the room, and Rachel leaned against the counter, her arms folded.

"Nine p.m., Lily, and you haven't done any work tonight. What about your biology course work?"

"I turned it in last week, Rachel. And study leave starts soon. I'll have all the time in the world to study, honestly."

"No, you'll have two weeks." Briefly Rachel closed her eyes. "You know I'm nagging because I care about you, right?"

"Yeah," Lily answered. "In theory."

"What is that supposed to mean?"

She sighed. "Nothing."

"No, seriously—"

"It's just . . . you want me to go to Durham, right? But sometimes it feels like *you* want to go to Durham." Lily bit her lip, flinching slightly as if waiting for Rachel to scream at her. And maybe once she would have.

"I did want to go to Durham," Rachel said slowly. "Once. I went, actually."

"You did?" Lily frowned uncertainly.

Of course Lily didn't remember. She'd only been seven, and no one ever talked about Rachel's aborted academic career. No one wanted to feel guilty or responsible for her failed dreams.

"Yes, I did. For all of two weeks. And then Dad left, and so I came back."

Lily stared at her for a moment, still nibbling her lip. "For me."

"For everyone."

"Why didn't you go back?"

"When?" Rachel asked, exasperation creeping into her voice. "When could I have left you all to manage on your own?"

"I don't know, when I was fifteen or sixteen? Old enough to cope?"

"Meghan had had Nathan by then."

"So? Nathan's her son, not yours."

"It doesn't feel like that at the moment." Rachel turned back to the sink and fished out a few more disintegrating Cheerios. "I don't regret my decisions, Lily. I wanted to be here for you and Mum and Meghan. And Nathan too."

Lily was silent for a long moment. "Do you miss him?" she asked, and with a jolt Rachel realized she meant their father.

"No," she said out of instinct, because she hadn't ever let herself miss Joss Campbell. He'd chosen to dump them all in it when he'd walked out on an invalid wife and three children, the youngest of whom had been only seven years old. How could she miss someone who did that? And yet how could her beloved father, the man who had shown her how to use a lathe and told her to hold on to her dreams, have done that?

"I don't even remember him, really," Lily said. "I mean, a little. I remember seeing him sleeping on the sofa when I came downstairs in the morning. I remember him being really tired and grumpy."

"He wasn't always like that," Rachel said. "He used to be a lot of fun, before Mum's accident." But of course Lily couldn't remember life before their mother's accident, when things had been chaotic and hard and *normal*. So wonderfully normal.

"Tell me?" Lily asked, her voice soft.

Rachel hesitated. She hadn't accessed those memories in a long time. She never let herself, because they hurt too much. "He was funny," she said slowly. "He used to tell these ridiculous knock-knock jokes. They weren't funny, but he was." A tightness had formed in her chest, and she focused on the Cheerios in the sink for a few seconds while she waited for it to ease.

"Knock-knock jokes," Lily repeated. "I don't remember those."

"No, you wouldn't. He stopped when you were little."

"When Mom fell?"

Rachel nodded, her back to Lily. "Damn Cheerios clogging up the drain. I suppose Meghan just dumped Nathan's bowl straight in."

"Actually, that was me. I was in a hurry this morning. Sorry."

Rachel's breath came out in a rush, and she shook her head. "It doesn't matter."

"Do you remember any of his jokes?"

"Oh no, I don't think so. . . ." Rachel trailed off, because of course she remembered them. She remembered everything. "Knock, knock," she said.

"Who's there?" Lily sounded as expectant and eager as Nathan would have.

"Impatient cow."

"Impatient—"

"Moo," Rachel interjected, and realization dawned across Lily's face. She started laughing, and then Rachel started, and then they were laughing way too hard for a stupid knock-knock joke, both of them holding their sides and wiping tears from their eyes.

"That's really bad," Lily said on a gasp when she'd finally subsided.

"Yeah," Rachel agreed. "They were all like that. And Meghan used to make them up, and hers were ridiculous. They didn't make sense at all. But Dad—" She stopped abruptly, because she hadn't actually said the word "Dad" in a long time. Not like that. "He always used to pretend they were funny," she finished. "He always said, 'That was a good one, Meg-o.' That's what he called her. Meg-o, and I was Rach, and you were Lil-lil." The tightness was back, and she turned to the sink even though there were no more Cheerios to fish from the drain.

"You miss him," Lily said quietly.

"Not anymore."

"But you must have. It sounds like you were close."

"We were, a long time ago. But I don't miss someone who could do what he did. I won't let myself."

"Did he ever . . . ?" Lily hesitated, and Rachel tensed. "Did he ever get in touch? With you? Or Mum? I've never even asked. It always seemed like a complete no-go area."

"I suppose it always has been. Easier that way. And no, he never got in touch." Not one phone call or postcard or even a lousy text. Nothing.

Sometimes Rachel had wondered if he'd died, if he'd had some kind of accident. She'd even, way back when, called the police, who had told her to come in and fill out a missing-person report. Then his mobile phone bill had come in the post, and she'd seen that he was still using it. A withdrawal from the bank, collecting his dole, and she'd known he was alive and well. Known he could be found if she tried, but she didn't. She wouldn't let herself.

"Do you mind me asking about him now?" Lily asked. She looked worried, and Rachel shook her head.

"No, of course not." But she did, because talking about their father was like picking at a scab, only to discover the skin hadn't healed over nearly as well as you'd hoped it had, and all of a sudden you realized you were bleeding. A lot.

"You must be angry at him," Lily said. "For leaving. Do you think he knew you would come back from uni to take care of everyone?"

"I don't know." It wasn't an avenue she'd let herself wander down, because she didn't like where it led. Her dad had always been excited for her to go to university. When she'd had her offer from Durham, he'd taken her to the pub, just the two of them, and he'd ordered a whole bottle of champagne and toasted his wonderful, talented daughter. She'd had half a glass and he'd drunk the rest.

How could he have *not* realized she would come back? He'd known all along that Janice couldn't cope on her own, and Meghan wasn't much use. She'd only been fifteen then. He had to have known Rachel would come back, had probably been counting on it. And that realization was one she couldn't bear to accept, not even ten years later. "I don't know," she said again, and started loading plates into the dishwasher.

Lily went upstairs to study, and an hour later Rachel heard the front door open again, very quietly, like someone was trying to sneak in.

"Not so fast." She stood in the kitchen doorway, arms folded, while Meghan froze mid-tiptoe upstairs.

"What? I'm shattered."

"I bet you are. Partying all night is exhausting, I'm sure."

Meghan made a face. "It's not even eleven yet."

"Where were you, Meghan?"

"Does it matter?"

"Yes, actually, it does," Rachel snapped. "We all need to pull together now that Mum's in hospital, and instead you're doing a runner."

Meghan sighed impatiently. "I just went out with a friend, Rachel. Chill, okay?"

"Chill? *Chill?*" Rachel's voice rose, and she took a steadying breath. "I'm not going to chill, Meghan. I don't have time to chill. I'm working all hours and—"

"Oh, please spare me the I-work-so-hard spiel yet again. We all know you do, Rachel. Trust me." The vitriol in Meghan's voice surprised her. It went beyond the usual snippy sarcasm into something that felt almost like hatred.

Meghan went back downstairs and into the kitchen, and after a second Rachel followed her. "Fine," she said as Meghan reached for a glass and filled it with water from the tap. "I won't give you that spiel."

"Thank God for small mercies."

"But in return how about you tell me what's going on? Where have you been going at night? And who with?"

Meghan shrugged, her back to Rachel. "Just to the pub. With a friend."

"What friend?"

"A bloke I met."

"Someone from the village?"

A pause. "No."

"Meghan." Rachel rolled her eyes. "Why are you being so cagey about this?"

"Maybe because I don't want people interfering in my life?"

"When have I ever interfered in your life?" Rachel demanded. "I've never even asked you who Nathan's father is."

"You just did."

"That was not asking." Rachel blew out a breath. "Look, I'm not trying to pry, but your behavior affects us as a family. I need to be able to count on you."

Meghan let out a sharp laugh as she turned around to face Rachel. "Count on me? Are you serious? When have you ever done that?"

"What are you talking—" Before Rachel could finish Meghan was pushing past her and then clumping up the stairs in her high-heeled boots. So much for tiptoeing.

Rachel listened to the door close upstairs—just short of a slam— and then Nathan's predictable sleepy cry, quickly silenced by Meghan.

Rachel let out a long breath, sagging against the counter. There was so much she didn't understand or even know about her sister, and she felt her ignorance keenly now. Meghan was right; Rachel had never felt she could count on her. She'd never tried, and Meghan had most certainly never offered to step up and go the extra distance for the sake of the family. She worked her nights at the pub, did the minimum work at home Rachel asked of her, and spent the rest of her time watching telly or going out.

What on earth was going to happen when their mother returned from the hospital? Mr. Greaves had made it clear that Janice would need much more care than she had before. She could never be left alone in the house, and she'd have to go to rehab several times a week, driven by either her or Meghan, which meant a reshuffling of her cleaning jobs.

And what about Meghan? Her sister might be lazy and unreliable, but at least she was there. If Meghan took off, who could stay home with Janice?

The sound of her mobile ringing brought Rachel out of her grim reflections. She didn't recognize the number, but she answered it anyway. Someone who called at eleven o'clock at night either was drunk or had an emergency.

"Hello?"

"Rachel?" The cultured male voice didn't register with her for a moment, and then he clarified with a touch of impatience, "It's Andrew. Andrew West."

"Is Claire all right?"

"And you think I baby her?" he returned with a touch of amusement.

"I can't imagine why else you'd be calling me," Rachel answered. "Especially so late at night."

"Is it that late?" Andrew sounded surprised.

"It's after eleven."

"Oh, sorry. I was working from home and I didn't realize the time. Were you in bed?"

The question, ridiculously, made Rachel's cheeks warm. "No. I was just in the kitchen reading Meghan the riot act, as usual."

"As usual?" Andrew repeated, and Rachel surprised herself by explaining.

"We always fight. I don't think she does enough to help out, and she thinks I'm being sanctimonious." She gave a little laugh. "You probably agree with her."

"I think you have a great many demands on you," Andrew answered. "Besides, I'm hardly one to talk about being sanctimonious."

"Wait. Did you just make a joke?" Rachel dared to tease.

"No, actually, I was simply stating a fact. I'm aware of how I come across, especially with Claire."

She walked into the sitting room and sank onto the sofa, distantly noticing the empty crisp packets and soda cans on the coffee table. "So if you're aware, do you think you'll back off for a bit? With Claire?"

"I'll try. Claire asked me to, so I suppose I should respect her wishes."

"Good."

"Have you seen her lately? Is she all right?"

"This is you backing off, is it?" Rachel returned dryly. "And no, I haven't seen her since last Sunday. I've been a little busy."

"Of course. I'm sorry. How's your mother?"

"Still in hospital. We're not sure yet what the long-term prognosis is going to be."

"That must be difficult."

"It is, but to be honest, it's a bit of a relief not to have her at home." Rachel gave a guilty laugh. "I suppose that makes me sound awful."

"No, just human. It can be exhausting, always looking after someone."

Like he looked after Claire? Rachel didn't ask. She hadn't spared too much thought for Claire, although she had a niggling sense of guilt that she hadn't been friendly enough when Claire had brought over a meal. She was trying to help, maybe even to make amends, and Rachel knew she wasn't meeting her halfway. But she couldn't add yet another person to her life who needed her to care for them.

"So what do you think?"

"Sorry. What?" Andrew had been talking and Rachel hadn't heard a word he'd said.

"I was asking if you'd like to come to Manchester," Andrew told her, his tone turning overtly patient.

"Come to Manchester? What on earth for?"

"You really didn't hear anything I said, did you?" Andrew said, and Rachel couldn't tell if he sounded amused or exasperated. "I was inviting you to visit, Rachel."

"Visit . . ." She was still coming up blank.

"Me. There's a new photography exhibition at the Whitworth Gallery, which just reopened. I thought you might like to see it. With me."

"Why would you think that?" Rachel blurted.

Andrew gave a dry laugh. "This conversation is a little more ego bruising than I would have liked."

"Oh. You mean . . . Do you mean . . . ?" Rachel's mind spun as she stammered out her reply. "Do you mean visit you, as in a *date*?"

Silence. "It could be a date, if you wanted it to be."

Which was a complete nonanswer. "What do you want it to be?"

Rachel asked. She had no idea what she wanted. She'd never thought of Andrew West that way, had never even considered it, not really.

"I asked you to visit, didn't I?" Andrew returned. "You can come up and down in a day, or you can sleep on my sofa if you prefer."

Rachel wasn't prepared for the fluttery feeling in her stomach at that suggestion. A day out, away from Hartley-by-the-Sea, from house-cleaning, from all the demands and stresses of her life. An actual date.

"Rachel? Are you still there?"

"Yes. Sorry. I'm just . . . I wasn't expecting this."

"I kind of got that."

She laughed then, a lightness she hadn't experienced in a long time buoying her spirits. "I haven't been to Manchester in years."

"So now may be a good time."

And then reality set her down with a thud. "Actually, it isn't. With Mum in hospital . . ."

"That's partly why I thought of it. She's taken care of, isn't she? Surely you can spare a Saturday."

Rachel thought of Meghan and Nathan and Lily, all of them need-ing her in their different ways. But maybe they didn't need her as much as she thought they did. Maybe they could manage for just one day. Maybe their world wouldn't come unglued if she wasn't there to hold it all together. "All right," she said, feeling heady with the reck-lessness of it. "But just for the day."

"All right, then," Andrew answered, and he sounded pleased, which made a goofy smile spread over Rachel's face. "I'll meet you at the sta-tion on Saturday."

They made a few more arrangements before disconnecting the call, and then Rachel sat there in the silence of the sitting room, her phone held in her hand, the smile still on her face.

20

Claire

THINGS HAD CHANGED. SHIFTED just a little, but Claire noticed. The tension that had existed between her and Dan while they worked had eased. It wasn't gone completely, and they were hardly palling around, but things felt gentler somehow. Friendlier.

Dan had given her more responsibility at the shop, and now he took Bunny out for a walk every day for an hour or so while Claire manned the till. He'd even suggested he train her to be a postal assistant, so she could work the post office as well as the shop counter.

"I'm just getting the hang of the Lotto cards," Claire had joked. "Are you really going to trust me with stamps?"

"There's a lot more to running the post office than stamping a few letters," Dan had answered shortly. So they definitely weren't palling around, but it was enough. It was good.

Other parts of her life had started to bloom and grow too; she'd had coffee with Abby down at the beach café a couple of times, and they'd taken to power-walking along the coast several evenings a week, while Mary, Abby's grandmother, watched Noah. It had started as simply a way to get some exercise, but Claire thought they both enjoyed the conversation. Abby had returned to Hartley-by-the-Sea less than a year ago and felt almost as much of an offcomer as Claire did.

"If you leave here, no matter for how long, it's not the same as staying," she said as they descended from the coastal path to the beach on the far end of the village. The tide was out, and the beach was a lovely long stretch of wet sand that glimmered under the evening sunlight, the rocks smoothed to shining darkness. Claire breathed in the salty, sea-damp air, every part of her reveling in the purity of the moment.

"Why did you leave?" she asked Abby.

"University. I went to Leeds to study medieval literature. Not the most useful of subjects."

"I studied art history, so I'm not one to talk."

"No. Well. Coming back has been harder than I expected, especially with Noah."

"Noah's dad . . . ?" Claire ventured to ask, and Abby's expression closed up.

"He died when Noah was a baby. Motorcycle accident."

"Oh, I'm so sorry—"

"I'm not sure he would have stayed around, if he'd lived," Abby answered with a shrug. She sounded diffident, but Claire recognized the slump of her shoulders, how sorrow weighed on her like a mantle. "But coming back to a place like Hartley-by-the-Sea with a kid in tow has its challenges."

"There are a few single mums around though, aren't there? Rachel's sister Meghan . . ."

"Yes, I'm not alone there. But it's still not easy."

"And will you stay? Keep running the beach café?" Abby had already told her that she'd taken over the café when her grandmother had had a heart attack six months ago.

"Probably," Abby answered with a rueful laugh. "I'll probably still be here thirty years from now, slinging toasted sandwiches and trying to make the espresso machine work. Well, it could be worse."

"You've done a lot with the café, from what I've heard. Lucy's art on the walls . . ." Claire had admired a watercolor of a field of buttercups, with a single baleful sheep in the distance.

Abby smiled. "Yes, Lucy's art is brilliant. And I'd love to do more of that. Add local books, have mini exhibitions . . ." She trailed off with a sigh. "Right now it's all I can do to keep the place running, never mind make improvements."

"Maybe when Noah starts school . . ."

"Yes. Maybe." Abby turned her curious gaze on Claire. "What about you? Are you going to be stacking tins forever?"

"I hope not. Dan's mentioned training me to be a postal assistant." She had a rather ridiculous desire to get behind that Plexiglas counter to weigh and stamp letters.

"You know what I mean, though. You're not going to work in a shop for the rest of your life?"

"Why not?" Claire challenged. "Everyone has this idea that I'm too good or too smart to work in a shop, but plenty of people do, and I actually enjoy it. Why shouldn't I work there forever?"

Abby laughed and shook her head. "I don't have an answer for that one."

Of course eight hours of doing inventory in the tiny, airless storeroom the next day made Claire reconsider her declaration. Dan had been in a particularly surly mood, snapping at her and finding fault with everything she did. It was as if the last few weeks of friendliness hadn't happened.

"That's me finished," she announced as soon as it hit four o'clock. She'd been finding semiplausible excuses to stay at the shop a little later each day, simply because she enjoyed it. Today, however, she practically ripped off her apron and made for the door.

"See you tomorrow, then," Dan said. He was restacking packs of cigarettes, his back to her, and he didn't turn around as he spoke.

Claire hesitated, one hand on the door. "Dan . . . you're all right, aren't you?"

His big shoulders stiffened, but he didn't turn around. "Why do you ask?"

"Because you've been biting my head off all day?" Claire suggested.

"You were slow," Dan answered. "And I'm fine."

Claire stared at his back, as hard and broad as a brick wall, and with a sigh she opened the door. "All right, then. Bye."

She started down the street towards the beach road and Four Gables, facing the prospect of an evening alone, when she abruptly turned around and headed back up it instead. She might not be able to breach Dan's black mood, but there was someone else she needed to talk to.

Claire hadn't seen Rachel since she'd been in her kitchen, and she'd been semi-avoiding her to avoid any more awkwardness. But a week and a half on and she knew she needed to own a few of her mistakes.

She stood in front of Rachel's house just as she had ten days before, minus the macaroni. And once again she wondered if she was making a mistake, and if Rachel was going to go ballistic on her again.

"Oh. You." Rachel opened the door to her cautious knock and then stood there, unsmiling.

"Your greetings always make me feel so welcome," Claire returned dryly. "Yes, it's me. I wondered if you fancied going out for a drink."

"A drink?" Rachel's gaze narrowed. "It's a bit early, isn't it?"

"Nearly dinnertime," Claire replied. "Besides, it's Friday and I just got off work."

"Aren't you a teetotaler now?"

"In theory. But since I've decided I don't actually have a drinking problem, I think I can have a glass of wine with a friend." She held her breath, bracing herself for Rachel's setdown.

A steely glint had come into Rachel's eyes, and her jaw looked tight. She looked completely stressed, now that Claire looked at her properly. Shadows under her eyes, her shoulders practically up by her ears, her features seeming blurred with fatigue. "All right then," Rachel said, and yanked her coat from the peg. "If you're buying."

"I am." She stepped outside, closing the door behind her, and Claire couldn't keep from asking, "Do you need to check in with anyone? Lily? Or Meghan?"

"No, why should I?" Rachel returned. She sounded rebellious and sulky, like a child playing truant. Then she took her phone out of her pocket. "I'll text Lily."

They walked in silence down to the Hangman's Noose; it was a golden afternoon, the sky a pale blue, the air still holding the day's warmth. A few commuters were trickling from the train station, but otherwise the street was peaceful and quiet.

The Hangman's Noose was nearly empty at four o'clock in the afternoon; a few farmers were huddled with their pints of bitter by the fireplace, although the grate was swept clean of ashes. Rob Telford was behind the bar, polishing glasses, and he raised his eyebrows in eloquent surprise as they came into the dim, low-ceilinged room.

"What can I get you two ladies?"

"A bottle of red," Claire said firmly, and Rachel shot her a bemused look.

"A whole bottle? Really?"

"Why not? It's cheaper, anyway, than two or three glasses."

"A bottle it is," Rob said, and took a bottle down from the rack behind the bar. "Cabernet Sauvignon do you?"

"That's fine," Claire said, and took the bottle and paid.

They sat at a small table in the back of the near-empty pub, the open bottle and two wineglasses between them.

"So let the debauchery begin," Rachel drawled, and Claire managed a laugh as she poured.

"What shall we toast to?" Rachel asked as she took her glass.

"To . . ." Friendship didn't seem quite right, and Claire couldn't think of anything else. "To new beginnings," she finally said, and Rachel nodded and hefted her glass.

"To new beginnings."

They both sipped their wine, the mood far more awkward than Claire had hoped. She'd asked Rachel out for a drink because she wanted to make amends, maybe even become friends again, but both possibilities seemed beyond her now.

"Right." She put her wineglass down with a *clunk*, and Rachel stopped in midsip, eyebrows raised. "I want to say sorry for what happened with us in Year Six." Rachel stared at her, her glass suspended halfway to her mouth, and resolutely Claire continued. "I should have said it before. I know it was my fault, at least initially, that we fell out. I should have spoken to you. I shouldn't have hidden behind those awful Wyndham girls."

Rachel gazed at her for a moment and then shook her head. "I appreciate what you're doing, Claire, but this really is ancient history."

"I know it happened a long time ago, but it still matters. And when you spoke to me about it, you seemed upset. . . ."

"If I've seemed upset it's because my mother has had a stroke," Rachel cut in. "And my life feels like a trap that is closing in on me, because I'm never going to be doing anything other than cleaning toilets and taking care of my family for the rest of my life." She broke off abruptly, pressing the heel of her hand to her eyes before she resolutely dropped it. "I'm not upset because you hurt my feelings when we were eleven. I'm not quite that pathetic."

"I know that," Claire said. "I don't think you're pathetic. If anyone's pathetic, it's me, for not being brave enough to keep the best friend I ever had."

Rachel pressed her lips together, her eyes bright with what Claire thought might actually be tears. "I suppose I was the same. I was too proud to go and talk to you." She took a quick, sharp breath. "I didn't want to be rejected."

"I wouldn't have—"

"Are you sure about that? You stayed with those girls for the rest of Year Six. They came to your blasted birthday party."

Claire closed her eyes briefly as a memory washed over her. "That was an absolutely wretched party. My mother arranged it all—"

"Including the invitations?"

Claire's mouth parted soundlessly as realization crept in. "You weren't invited . . . ?"

"No, but I hardly care now. It's not about that." Rachel let out an impatient sigh. "It was a hard time in my life, that's all. My mother broke her back and my father was out of work, and I wanted—needed—someone I could count on."

"Oh, Rachel." Claire swallowed hard. "I should have been that person." Rachel didn't answer. "I hate that I was so *weak*," Claire said abruptly, her tone vehement. "I hate it. I've been so bloody weak my whole life, going where someone points, even to rehab!" She laughed, a choked sound, and shook her head. "You must despise me. *I* despise me."

"I don't despise you," Rachel said. "I can understand how you might have wanted to be popular."

"It wasn't that. I've never wanted to be popular in my life."

"No?" Rachel glanced at her, eyebrows raised. "What, then?"

"I wanted to please my mother. She wanted me to be friends with all the Wyndham girls. To be popular. But I never really felt like part of their group."

"You looked like you were, from the outside," Rachel said as she reached for the bottle and poured herself another glass of wine. "You looked like you were having a ball."

"Did I really?" Claire shook her head. "Actually, I was miserable." She paused and then continued starkly. "I think I've been unhappy most of my life."

Rachel stared at her, nonplussed. "Oh?"

"I know you think I had the whole silver-spoon thing going on," Claire continued stiltedly. It was hard to hold on to her conviction with Rachel looking so unimpressed. "And I know I've been lucky in a lot of ways. But . . ." She took a deep breath, wondering how she could explain everything without seeming like she was asking for pity. Maybe she was. "I also know there's no excuse for dropping you as a friend. I do realize that."

"I'm glad, and I get that you want to make up for all that," Rachel said, "but there's really no need. I lost my temper the other day, but trust me, I have not been crying into my pillow every night, wondering what went wrong."

"I know you haven't. And this is as much about me, and trying to be the person I want to be, as it is about addressing something that happened a lifetime ago. So let me do this, okay?"

Rachel sat back in her chair. "Fine."

"My whole life . . ." Claire began slowly, searching for the right words. "I've felt . . . fragile. And useless, like you said. And I haven't known how to stop."

"Okay," Rachel said cautiously, eyeing her with wary curiosity. "And now?"

"Now I'm trying to change," Claire answered. "I'm trying by working in the shop, and I'm trying with you right now. But it's hard to break old patterns. From the time I was four years old my mother wrapped me in cotton wool and treated me as if I could break. I didn't go to Reception or Year One because she thought I was too fragile. And so I started acting fragile, because that's how everyone seemed to see me. Even you, unbuttoning my coat the first day of Year Two. I remember that."

"You didn't stop me."

"I *know*. And I suppose part of me expected it, even. I remember being relieved that I'd have someone to take care of me. Because that's what I was used to."

Rachel shook her head slowly. "So why did your mother treat you that way? It seems a little OTT, even for Marie West."

Claire took a deep breath. "When I was little I was always getting ill. Ear infections, colds, just low-level stuff. But then when I was four I developed a tumor thing in my ear. It started out small, but it went undiagnosed, and I ended up having a whole bunch of surgeries and then I went deaf in that ear. It freaked my mother out, I suppose, and so she kept me off school and obsessed over everything." She released her breath in a long, low rush. "And I mean everything."

Rachel was frowning, looking like she didn't even know Claire anymore. "Why did you never tell me about all that? When we were little?"

"I didn't tell anyone. It didn't feel like a secret exactly, more something you shouldn't mention in polite conversation."

"Your mother said that, I'm guessing?"

"It was more just a feeling." A very strong feeling. "You must have noticed how much school I missed."

"I suppose." Rachel was still frowning, lost in thought. "You had pneumonia for a couple of weeks in Year Three. . . ."

"I was always getting sick or having surgery. It felt like that, anyway. And my mother was always flitting about me, obsessing about every little thing. She stopped work when I first got sick, and I think she made me her career. And I don't think I was a particularly satisfying one." Claire let out a humorless laugh and drained her glass of wine.

"And when you grew up? Went to college, to Portugal? Didn't you ever feel like breaking that pattern?"

"It took me a while to realize there was a pattern to break. I know this doesn't put me in a good light," she added, for Rachel's expression had gone a bit skeptical, a little sour. "I just . . . drifted. My father arranged for me to work in an art gallery in London, so I went. And then my mother's friend had a villa in Portugal, and they thought I should go there. I think my mother was hoping I'd get together with Hugh."

"Hugh." Rachel said his name like it was a foreign country, a place she'd never heard of. "You haven't mentioned him very much."

"No."

"Did you love him?"

Claire gazed down at her wineglass. "No."

"But your mother wanted you to marry him, so you said yes."

"It seemed like the next step."

"Did he love you? I have to admit he doesn't sound like a stellar guy, checking you into rehab without your consent."

"Well, I did have a problem," Claire said, and nodded towards the wineglass dangling from her fingertips. Rachel finally cracked a smile, and Claire slumped in her seat, leaning her head back against the chair. "I don't know. I don't know what he saw in me except that I was biddable and eager to please. When I moved in with him, I asked if I could put my clothes in his bedroom cupboard. He said no."

"Seriously?"

"I used the guest bedroom's cupboard instead. But everything was like that. And I didn't make a fuss. I'm not sure I even minded, really. When you're so miserable you don't mind anything, if that makes sense. I was just sleepwalking through life."

"So that's why you got drunk at that party. Because you were facing a lifetime of Hugh Hoity-Toity."

Claire grimaced. "Basically. But to be fair, he wasn't that bad. He was—is—very handsome and charming. And he could be funny too, when he turned it on."

"So what did you do when you were drunk?" Rachel asked. "I hope you embarrassed him terribly."

"I did." A smile slipped out, and Rachel leaned forward.

"Go on, then. Tell me everything."

"I don't remember it all, but I know I danced. On a table."

Rachel let out a bark of laughter. "I would so have liked to see that."

"And I sang along to the music. 'Roar' by Katy Perry, if I remember correctly. And I don't have a good singing voice."

Rachel looked fascinated. "And how did you feel when you were doing all that?" she asked.

"Wonderful," Claire admitted with a surprised laugh. "Absolutely wonderful."

"Spot on," Rachel answered, and then filled both their wineglasses to the brim.

A glass of wine was making her feel woozy, and Claire sipped the second one more slowly. She imagined the look of horror on her mother's face to see her drinking at the pub with Rachel Campbell, and then found herself smiling instead of wincing, a mental nose-thumbing at her mother from three hundred miles away.

"So are you going to see Hugh again?" Rachel asked, and Claire shook her head.

"No. We haven't spoken since I left Portugal."

"You should ring him. Make sure you're the one to end it properly."

Now that was a novel and surprisingly appealing idea. She liked the thought of shocking Hugh. Again.

"I might do that," she said, and then took a deep breath, offering Rachel a tentative smile. "So are we friends now?"

Rachel didn't answer for a moment, and Claire braced herself for the inevitable brush-off. One drink didn't change ten years of hard history.

"We were always friends," she finally said, and raised her glass in a toast.

21

Rachel

RACHEL HADN'T ACTUALLY LEFT the county of Cumbria in nearly a decade. She hadn't gone beyond Keswick in more than a year. Taking the train to Lancaster from Hartley-by-the-Sea and then switching to the express train to Manchester felt akin to scaling the Alps. The coffee shop at the train station in Lancaster was an adventure in itself, and she ordered a large mochaccino, feeling dangerously decadent.

Meghan and Lily had both been openmouthed with shock when Rachel had announced she was going to Manchester for the day.

"Manchester?" Meghan had said, as if Rachel had suggested she was going to Antarctica or Greenland. "Why? What will you do there?"

"I'm seeing a photography exhibition with Andrew West," Rachel answered. She'd been trying to sound airy, but the words came out defiant instead.

Meghan stared at her. "I don't know which part of that sentence surprises me more."

"Why shouldn't I go out?"

"With Andrew West?"

Rachel shrugged. She hadn't decided how she felt about going on a sort of date with Andrew West. On one hand, his occasionally pompous attitude irritated her. On the other, he was an attractive, intelligent man, and she could tell he really did care about Claire. And the thought of spending the day in Manchester had become like a drug, a fix she craved. A day of freedom, of escaping all the pressures and strains of life. No Nathan to cajole and change while Meghan disappeared. No mother to visit and endure a painful hour of garbled speech and frustration. No Lily to nag or worry about.

It took her a while to let go of all those concerns as the train chugged down the coast, and by the time she reached Lancaster and sipped her mochaccino she was starting to relax. Sort of. Now that she'd left Hartley-by-the-Sea behind, Manchester loomed in front of her, intimidating and unknown.

She'd done an Internet search on the exhibition she and Andrew were going to, and it hadn't looked too artsy, thank goodness. She wasn't sure she could talk intelligently about art or anything anymore. Her only intellectual outing these days was the pub quiz.

Then of course there was Andrew. How were they supposed to act around each other? This wasn't a clear-cut date, and Rachel didn't know if Andrew wanted it to be. There could be all sorts of awkwardness.

He'd said he'd meet her at the station, and so she disembarked from the train, blinking at the vastness of Piccadilly Station, the crowds of people surging around her as she clutched her handbag and felt like Country Mouse.

"Rachel."

Andrew stood before her, looking as boring as ever in pressed chinos and a blue button-down shirt. The man had absolutely no fashion sense, and this put Rachel at ease. This was Andrew West, not some gorgeous, urban stranger.

"I made it."

"So you did. I thought we could go right to the exhibition. It's about a twenty-minute walk. Unless you'd prefer to get a coffee first? I thought we could have lunch afterward." While speaking, Andrew had put his hands in his pockets and then taken them out again, jangling his keys; with relief Rachel realized he was as nervous as she was.

"We might as well go straight there," she said. She had a feeling chatting over coffee would be awkward. At least at the exhibition they would have a focus.

Andrew led her out of the station and Rachel tried not to gape at everything. It had been so long since she'd been in anything close to an urban environment; the sheer size of the station with the arched glass roof of the train shed was enough to impress her. Then they hit the city streets, and the noise of the cars and buses and trams made her want to cover her ears. And there were so many *people*, women in smart work outfits and high heels, men in skinny suits, everyone with smartphones and earbuds and looks of bland indifference on their faces as they strode purposefully down the street, clearly going somewhere important. Rachel dodged out of the way of a woman who was walking like a ship in full sail, a huge Prada handbag swinging from one shoulder, nearly hitting Rachel full in the face.

"Good grief." She pressed up against the side of the station and shook her head. "I feel like such a yokel."

"Come on," Andrew said, and took her arm. "We'll walk through the park. The gallery is on the university campus."

He slipped her arm through his, and it felt almost natural to walk arm in arm, navigating the crowded streets until after a few minutes they reached a quieter section of the city, the university campus with its vast swath of verdant parkland ahead of them.

Rachel had the urge to slip her arm from Andrew's, because now that the pavement was empty, it didn't feel quite so natural to be this cozy. But he was holding her arm quite firmly, and disengaging it would have required an awkward yank, and so she remained arm in arm with him, walking stiffly through Whitworth Park.

The sky was heavy and gray with the damp feel of rain in the air, and even in the park the air smelled of diesel and coal smoke. Even so Rachel felt exhilarated by how different everything was, how big and alive with possibility.

"I haven't been in a city in years," she confessed, and Andrew slid her a sideways, smiling glance.

"I can tell."

"You travel all over the world, right? So Manchester must seem like nothing to you."

"Cities can often feel the same to me, except for the infrastructure."

"The infrastructure?"

"Bridges, dams, motorways. That's the stuff that interests me."

She laughed, shaking her head. "Weird."

"Yeah, I know. I had a girlfriend back in America who broke up with me because I kept going on about the highway system. Have you seen Spaghetti Junction in Atlanta?"

"Um, no. I've barely been out of Cumbria."

"I mean in pictures. It's amazing. An aerial view makes it look like a flower. Five stacks rather than the usual four, and ramps for four side roads. It puts the original Spaghetti Junction in Birmingham to shame."

"You do realize you're sounding like a complete geek now?" Rachel asked, and he smiled wryly.

"Yes, I realize."

"But I admire your passion. Clearly you love what you do."

"I do," he agreed, and then gave her a wary glance. "And I realize what a privilege that is."

She laughed, shaking her head. "I'm not going to bite your head off about being rich. That would be rude, considering you invited me here."

"Oh. Phew. Disaster averted, then."

"Just." Were they flirting? It felt like it. It also felt weird. Fortunately they'd reached the gallery, a huge redbrick Victorian building, by then, and conversation was taken up with the logistics of stowing bags and getting tickets before Andrew led the way towards the new photography exhibition.

Rachel had spent an embarrassing amount of time on the Internet reading up on photography so she'd have something intelligent to say now. Yet as she stared at the black-and-white photographs, every erudite observation she'd read fled from her brain. All she could think was that she'd appreciate a little color.

Andrew was, as she'd suspected he would be, the kind of person who stood in front of a photograph for an inordinate amount of time, lips pursed, one finger tapping his chin, as he studied it carefully. Rachel stood next to him, shifting her weight, wondering how on earth you could look at a single picture for five minutes. What was there to *see*?

"What do you think?" he asked after a few minutes, and her mouth dried.

"Um . . ." She stared at the photograph of a ceiling fan taken from above, so its shadow could be seen on the white floor. "It's very . . ." She searched for a word. "Stark."

"Yes, I think so too."

"And very . . . monochrome." She glanced at him, wondering if he really was this pretentious, only to see with relief that his mouth was quirking in a small smile.

"Yes, I agree. Considering it's black-and-white photography, that is quite an astute assessment."

"I thought so." She laughed then, an uncertain hiccup, and Andrew grinned.

"I'm not actually a huge art fan."

"Then why did you invite me to an exhibition?"

"Because I figured you'd rather see this than the Worsley Braided Interchange."

"The what?"

"The motorway outside the city that connects the M61 with the M62. It really is a remarkable feat of engineering."

She laughed and shook her head. "You're right. I'd rather see this."

They breezed through the rest of the photographs, spending no more than a minute on each one, competing with each other for the most inane or over-the-top comment, before they were finished and back out in the lobby. It was half past eleven.

"We did that a bit more quickly than I anticipated," Andrew said as he glanced at his watch. "I thought we'd stay in the exhibition until one, and then have lunch in the café here until three. Then we were going to walk around the city until five. . . ."

"It's okay if we don't keep to your schedule, isn't it?" Rachel teased. She felt much more relaxed now that they'd gotten the photography out of the way. The realization that Andrew was less pompous and more geeky than she'd thought was a huge relief.

"I suppose," he said, and took her arm again. This time it didn't feel quite so awkward.

Rachel suggested a walk in the park until lunchtime, which was a mistake because they'd walked right to the center of it when the rain started bucketing down. Gallantly, Andrew put his coat over Rachel's head, leaving him soaked, and they sprinted for the nearest shelter, a public toilet that stank and had a homeless man sleeping off a binge in the doorway.

"The charms of urban life," Rachel said. "I almost miss Hartley-by-the-Sea."

Andrew glanced at her seriously. "Do you? There must be something quite nice about living in a place where everyone knows you."

"You lived there too," Rachel pointed out.

"But not in the same way. We were never really part of the village, as you remarked yourself."

"And you think I am?"

"Aren't you?"

Rachel gazed out at the drizzling rain, turning everything to gray, and shrugged. "I suppose. But there's a downside to everyone knowing you too. You can't start over."

"Have you wanted to?"

Andrew sounded so interested and intent; it made Rachel feel both gratified and embarrassed. "Sometimes. When . . . when I was growing up, I was the kid whose father was sometimes on the dole and whose mother cleaned half of the class's houses before she broke her back. No one turned their noses up at me, not exactly. Hartley-by-the-Sea has never really been like that. But they knew, and sometimes that's enough."

She'd said way too much. Rachel dug her hands into the pockets of her coat and nodded towards the rainy park. "How about lunch?"

Andrew thankfully had the sensitivity to follow her lead. "I'll call a taxi, and we can go into the city center to eat."

Twenty minutes later they were seated at a bistro on Booth Street, menus open in front of them.

"You're soaked," Rachel remarked. His button-down shirt didn't look quite so boring stuck to his chest. Andrew plucked at it ineffectually.

"I'll dry."

Rachel was more than a little damp herself, and she could feel her hair starting to frizz. In a few minutes she'd look like a six-foot-tall Orphan Annie.

"You know," she said after they'd both ordered, "I didn't think you actually liked me."

"Why would you think that?"

"I don't know. Maybe because of that huge chip on my shoulder you mentioned I have?" She tried to speak lightly, but an edge broke through anyway. "And because I was kind of bitchy to you. And to Claire."

Andrew glanced down, realigning his knife and fork with precise movements. "I wasn't at my best, either. I was worried about Claire. Too worried, most likely."

"She told me a little bit about why," Rachel offered. "The stuff with her ear, all the illnesses when she was a child . . ."

"Yes. Well. Old habits die hard and all that."

"So that's why you've been so protective of her? Because of her ear?"

"Not just her ear. Everything. My parents, my mother especially, have always been obsessive about Claire's health. I don't really remember when she had the tumor all that well, only that it was an emergency. Her face was partially paralyzed, and she had to be rushed to the hospital. They thought she might die."

"Goodness." Anything she said felt inadequate. "That must have been scary."

"I suppose it was. From a nine-year-old boy's perspective, though, I was more annoyed at my father missing my football tournament." He shrugged. "I don't think I realized how serious it all was until later."

"So Claire's health issues affected you," Rachel said slowly; it seemed obvious now. They would have affected everyone in a family. She'd seen the same kind of thing happening in her own. Yet she hadn't expected to feel such a point of sympathy with Andrew West. "You always had to watch out for her."

"That was my brief. That's every big brother's brief, like you said. But with my mother and Claire . . . it was a lot more intense. If Claire so much as grazed her knee at school, my mother thought it was my fault. I should have been watching her better, been more careful." He shrugged. "Not to moan about it, but it has an effect on you over time."

"Yes, I can understand that."

He nodded, his gaze training uncomfortably on her. "You've been looking out for your sisters for a long time."

"Since I was eleven."

"Is that when your mother got injured?"

Rachel nodded. "Broke her back falling down some stairs while cleaning a house in Egremont. Lily was six weeks old."

"That must have been tough."

"It wasn't much fun."

"And your dad," Andrew said quietly. "He left . . . ?"

"When I was eighteen." She paused and then confessed quietly, the words drawn from her reluctantly, "I'd just started at Durham. Two

weeks in and my sister Meghan called me, asking me to come home."
She shook her head, trying to stem the tide of emotion that threatened
to overwhelm her. The last thing she wanted to do was cry in front of
Andrew West, and especially on their first date. If this really was a date.

"Oh, Rachel, I'm sorry." Andrew reached over and covered her hand
with his own, the simple touch of another person adding to her emotional overload.

"It was a long time ago," she managed to choke out, and then had
to suffer the humiliation of dabbing her eyes with her napkin. "Seriously. I'm over it."

Andrew removed his hand and sat back, and Rachel let out a tiny
sigh of relief. This was getting way too intense. "And you've been cleaning houses ever since?"

"I took over my mother's business, Campbell Cleaners. She'd had
to stop it when she got hurt, and for a while we survived with whatever work my dad could get."

"Which was?"

"Carpentry, shift work. The dole." More than once she'd had to
collect one of the orange vouchers and go to the food bank in Whitehaven for the emergency supply of milk, bread, and tinned tuna and
rice pudding. Growing up she'd been entitled to free school meals, a
badge of shame that everyone had known about even though it was
never spoken of. Somehow you just *knew* which kids were so poor they
had to get free meals.

"None of that could have been easy," Andrew said.

"No, but we managed. When Meghan turned sixteen, a year after
my dad left, she quit school and started pulling pints at the pub." She
shrugged. "It worked out."

"But that was ten years ago, and Lily's almost finished school. What
are you going to do then?"

"My mother has just had a stroke and my sister has a three-year-old I suspect she is going to off-load on me," Rachel answered. "What do you think I'm going to do?"

Their meals came then, thankfully curtailing any more conversation, and they both kept to light topics after that. There was only so much emotional heavy lifting you could do in a single afternoon.

By the time they left the bistro it was the middle of the afternoon and the rain had cleared to a pale blue sky with wispy clouds. They walked through the city center, and Andrew pointed out every architectural and engineering feature, which, after about an hour, he finally realized was far more interesting to him than to her.

"Sorry. I'm boring you rigid, aren't I?"

"Not rigid, no," Rachel answered. "The rigor mortis won't set in for another hour."

"You have a high tolerance, then," he said with a laugh, and steered her towards the river. "But there's one more feat of engineering I want to show you."

"Uh-oh."

"You'll like this one, I promise." He'd taken her hand, loosely threading his fingers through hers, and Rachel felt a jumping sensation of awareness in her belly, something she hadn't felt in a long time. Flirting with Rob Telford at the Hangman's Noose had never made her feel like this.

They walked down Bridge Street, turning down the narrow St. Mary's Passage, before emerging in front of the River Irwell, with a narrow white footbridge with steel cables like gossamer strands stretching high above.

"The Trinity Footbridge," Andrew announced. "It joins Manchester to Salford. I worked on it back in 2010. Just some repair work, but I've always liked it."

"It's striking," Rachel said. She liked the way the bridge seemed suspended over the river, its arch deceptively simple.

"Come on," Andrew said, and tugged her up onto its narrow walkway. The sun was still high in the sky, but the wind was dying down so the surface of the river was placid and still, the sun's rays touching it with gold.

They walked to the middle of the bridge, stopping to gaze out at the city. Rachel let out a long rush of breath.

"It's beautiful. I've enjoyed today." She glanced at him, but he wasn't looking at her, his gaze on the cityscape spread around them. "I think I needed a day out of reality. To recharge."

"It doesn't need to be just a day," Andrew said, and Rachel tensed, her insides doing a weird flip-flop.

"What do you mean?"

He turned to face her, his expression intent. "You've given ten years of your life to your family, Rachel. Lily's going to university and Meghan can manage her own child—"

"And my mother?" she interjected sharply. She wasn't sure she liked where this was going.

"I don't know how her rehabilitation will go, but there might be solutions. Why shouldn't you go back to university, have at least some of the life you wanted? You've deferred your dreams for long enough."

She turned back to face the river, hating that he'd made it sound so easy. It *was* easy, for someone who had money and ambition and time, with no commitments, no strings. She had strings dangling all over the place, tripping her up at every step. "It's not that simple, Andrew."

"It could be."

"That's easy for you to say."

"Yes, it is easy for me. I'm not pretending it would be easy for you. But why won't you even think about it? You complain about being stuck in a rut, but you won't actually *do* anything about it."

"Wow, you're ending this day on such a terrific note," she drawled, sarcasm the cheapest defense. "Thanks so much for a lovely day out."

She turned and started walking, blindly, filled with a fury she couldn't articulate.

"You're heading towards Salford," Andrew called to her, and muttering a curse, Rachel turned around. "And you know why I think you won't even think about what I said?"

"Oh, you're a psychologist now too, are you?" Rachel snapped. Her comebacks sucked, but she couldn't think of anything better. She felt too raw to be clever.

Andrew had folded his arms and stood in the middle of the footbridge so she couldn't pass. A couple of pedestrians were coming behind him at a brisk clip, and in a few seconds he was going to be either pushed out of the way or cursed at, yet still he stood in the middle of the bridge, seeming to straddle the world.

"You're scared," he stated. Rachel jerked back.

"Scared?"

"Of trying and failing. Everyone is to some degree, but you've let it paralyze you."

"Hey," a man behind him called as he came striding forward, briefcase swinging at his side. "How about getting out of my way?"

"My thoughts exactly," Rachel snapped, and pushing past Andrew, she started walking back towards the city center.

22

∿

Claire

CLAIRE STOPPED IN FRONT of the post office, her hands on her hips as she surveyed its shuttered front. It was eight o'clock on Saturday morning, and the shop should have been open for an hour at least. She didn't work Saturdays, but she'd come in to get some milk and the Saturday paper—and to check on Dan.

He'd seemed his former surly self the last few days, since he'd growled at her about being slow with the inventory, and her few attempts to get him to open up had been met with stonewalled silence. Not exactly a surprise. Still, she'd thought she should drop by, make sure he was okay, even if he just snapped at her to mind her own business and insist that he was fine.

If the shuttered shop was anything to go by, he wasn't.

"Dan?" she called, and knocked on the door. The shop window was covered in a curtain of corrugated iron and the door's shade had been drawn so she couldn't see anything inside. She doubted Dan could even hear her, if he was in the shop, which she didn't think he was.

After a moment's hesitation Claire walked past the shop and down the alley that ran along its side, to the little courtyard in the back. She'd been there before to take out the bins, and she knew there was a door to the kitchen.

She peered in its tiny rectangle of window and saw that the

kitchen was dark, dirty dishes scattered over the usually pristine counters. Then she heard a scratching at the door and a heartrending whimper, and realized Bunny was in there.

"Oh, Bunny, you poor thing." She jiggled the door handle uselessly. Of course Dan locked his doors. He probably had some kind of jerry-rigged homemade trap for burglars that would have her dangling by her ankles with piano wire if she so much as stepped across the threshold.

Claire tapped on the glass, and then knocked loudly, and then finally kicked the door, hurting her foot in the process. Bunny continued to whine.

"Darn it." She rubbed her foot absently, wondering if she dared to break a window. Not that she'd even be able to wriggle into the one window above the kitchen sink. Without any better ideas, she started knocking again, and after about ten minutes, when her knuckles had started to bruise, Dan finally appeared in the kitchen.

He stood in front of the door, peering through the window, and all Claire could see was how bloodshot his eyes looked and the deep furrow between his eyebrows as he scowled.

Finally he unlocked the door and Bunny rushed out, tangling herself around Claire's legs before she hurried into the tiny garden to pee.

"You look terrible," Claire said. He wore sweatpants and his usual black T-shirt, his face pale and unshaven.

"Thanks." Dan turned around and went to the sink, pouring himself a glass of water and gulping it down. Finished, he tossed the glass in the sink, where it shattered, and he braced his hands against the edge of the counter, his head bowed.

"You smell awful too," Claire said as she came inside, Bunny scampering in behind her. "Are you ill?"

"I'm hungover," Dan said flatly. His head was still bowed, and he was taking deep, even breaths. Claire could see the sweat beading on his forehead.

"Are you going to be sick?" she asked in alarm, and wordlessly he shook his head. Now she recognized the sour, yeasty smell of metabolizing alcohol. She saw a whiskey bottle on the kitchen table, next to a single glass. The bottle was empty.

"Shall I feed Bunny?" she suggested, and Dan nodded. Gingerly Claire moved around him, finding Bunny's bag of kibble in the cupboard under the sink and pouring a scoop's worth into her bowl. She started to tidy up a bit, but Dan's bulk dominated the room and made it nearly impossible. "You should eat," she finally said. "Why don't I make you some tea and toast? You can go upstairs and make yourself presentable."

"That's not—"

"Necessary?" she filled in. "I think it is. Seriously, you smell rank."

Dan gave her a glare that lacked its usual malevolent force, and after a tense pause he turned and headed upstairs. Claire let out her held breath in a rush of relief and started to clean the kitchen.

She heard Dan's heavy tread above her and then the squeaky sound of the shower being turned on. She bustled around the kitchen, cleaning the broken glass from the sink and then washing the dishes. She put the bottle of whiskey in the recycling bin outside and then went in search of bread and tea.

By the time Dan came down the stairs the kitchen was clean and she had a mug of tea and two pieces of buttered toast on the table.

"I don't know how you like your tea. . . ."

"Milk, three sugars."

"*Three* sugars? Real builders' brew, then." She put the sugar bowl on the table along with a spoon and then stood back, conscious of how Dan's hair was damp and bristly. He'd changed into a fresh T-shirt and jeans and he smelled of soap.

"Thank you," he said as he sat down. He glanced up at her standing by the sink, her hands tucked behind her. "You want to join me, or are you just going to watch me eat?"

"Oh, all right, then." She fetched another mug and made herself a cup of tea while Dan started on his toast.

"You don't usually get hungover," she remarked as she sat down across from him and blew on her tea. "Do you? I haven't noticed . . ."

"No, I don't." He was steadily working through his two pieces of toast, his head down as he chewed methodically.

"Is everything okay?" Claire asked. Dan looked up.

"Sure, everything's fine," he answered, and she couldn't miss the sarcasm. "I normally empty a bottle of Glenlivet on a Friday night by myself. Who doesn't?"

"Maybe you do and I just didn't know it," Claire retorted. "You've never opened up to me about your life."

"Why would I?"

"Because we're friends?" Claire suggested. "Or becoming friends, at least?" Dan didn't reply, and she couldn't keep from feeling a needle prick of hurt. "But you don't really do friendship, do you?"

"I did," he answered gruffly. "Once."

"Once?"

He shook his head. "Leave it. And thank you for the tea and toast."

It sounded like a dismissal, but she didn't move. "What are you going to do about the shop? You can't miss a whole Saturday of business."

"I'll go out there in a minute."

"Why don't you let me?" He swung his head up, his gaze bloodshot, bleary, and narrowed. "I can manage the shop on my own," Claire said. "And you can dry out. Take Bunny for a walk. She looks like she needs it." Bunny was quivering under the table, her head nudging Claire's knee hopefully.

"I can't afford to pay you overtime——"

"You don't have to pay me at all——"

"I don't need your charity," he snapped. "I'm not that strapped."

"Is it charity if I want to do a friend a favor?" Claire demanded. Dan didn't answer, and she gritted her teeth. "Why do you have to be so difficult?"

"*I'm* difficult?" He looked both affronted and surprised. "I gave you a job when you were completely unqualified."

"So I can accept charity but you can't?"

He stared at her for a long moment, the only sound Bunny's nervous whine from under the table. Then he actually cracked a smile, the gesture so surprising Claire gaped back at him. "Fine. But don't open the post office."

"Of course I won't," she answered with stiff dignity. "I'm not a trained postal assistant yet."

It felt strange yet also surprisingly comfortable to be in the shop alone, turning on lights and unlocking the door. A note had been thrust through the letter box from Robin the milkman, stating he'd come back later to deliver the day's pints.

Claire had just gone behind the till when Eleanor Carwell stumped in, dressed in her usual twinset and tweed, looking decidedly disgruntled.

"So you finally decided to open, did you?"

"Better late than never," Claire answered cheerfully.

Eleanor stopped in front of the empty newspaper racks. "No newspapers," she stated in an aggrieved tone. She turned towards the refrigerated section. "And no milk, either."

"They'll both be here shortly," Claire assured her. "I could deliver them to your home, if you like, when they arrive."

Eleanor eyed her suspiciously. "I'm perfectly capable of walking to the post office twice in one day," she said. "It's merely inconvenient."

"Which is why I suggested delivery," Claire returned sweetly.

Eleanor glared at her for a moment and then nodded. "Fine. I live at number fifteen, just down the street. The house with the iron railings."

"All right." As Eleanor strode out of the shop Claire wondered what Dan would think about her offering delivery service. Maybe she wouldn't tell him.

The rest of the morning passed quickly; the milk and papers arrived, and she stacked them both in between serving the occasional customer. An elderly farmer threw a strop when he discovered the post office wasn't open as it usually was, but after quelling a bit under his beady glare, Claire managed to stand her ground. He rolled the *Westmorland Gazette* under his arm and left the shop in a huff.

At lunchtime Dan emerged from the back, looking sheepish. It was a new look for him, his hands jammed in the pockets of his jeans and a faint flush coloring his cheeks as he nodded towards the kitchen. "I've made lunch, if you're hungry."

"What about the shop?"

"We'll leave the door open. I can hear if someone comes in."

Which sounded rather cozy. It had started to rain, and drops splattered the kitchen window as Dan dished out tinned tomato soup and tuna sandwiches. Claire could tell he'd gone to some effort, with paper napkins placed beside the plates and a pitcher of water with a slice of lemon floating in it. Fancy stuff.

"Thank you," she said as she dipped her spoon into her soup. "This is very kind of you."

"Thank you for waking me up this morning," Dan answered gruffly as he sat down across from her. "I don't normally . . . do that."

"Get drunk on a whole bottle of Glenlivet?" He nodded, and Claire asked in a gentler tone, "Why did you, then?"

Dan didn't speak for a moment, just spooned soup into his mouth until Claire thought he'd ignore the question completely. "My ex-wife is getting married," he finally said. "She texted me to let me know."

"Oh." Claire gulped down a mouthful of soup. "I'm sorry."

He shrugged. "Happens to a lot of people."

"But it upset you."

He sighed and leaned back in his chair. "What upset me is that she's marrying my brother."

"Oh, no, that's awful. Are you going to go to the wedding?"

He gave her a look of scathing disbelief. "Do you really not know the answer to that?"

"I guess not," she murmured. "Very awkward."

"Awkward? Awkward is having a piece of lettuce stuck in your teeth or laughing at the wrong part in a joke. This wasn't *awkward*." She stared at him, wide-eyed, shocked to hear the emotion in his voice. "This was devastating," he continued quietly. "I came back from Afghanistan to find Ted, whom I'd asked to look after my wife, was screwing her instead." He rubbed a hand over his face. "Trust me, that wasn't just awkward."

"I'm sorry," Claire whispered. "I shouldn't have said anything."

"It's not your fault." He dropped his hand and glanced at her bleakly. "That's why I came out here. To get away from it all."

"And did you?"

"Physically, yes. The rest I'm not so sure about." He rose from the table, dumping the rest of his soup in the sink. "That kind of thing leaves its mark. I don't know if you ever recover."

"I hope you do," Claire said. "I have to believe you do. If you can't recover from the blows life deals you, what hope is there?"

"I'm not sure there is any."

"Oh, Dan, you can't believe that," Claire protested. "You can't believe that and go on living."

He turned around with a wry smile. "Hence the bottle of Glenlivet."

"Look, I understand about drowning your sorrows. I ended up here for the same reason."

He cocked an eyebrow, waiting, and Claire plunged ahead. "I got drunk at a party and my fiancé dumped me and I ended up in rehab for four awful weeks, but at least it got me back here. I feel like I'm finally figuring myself out, and considering I'm twenty-eight, it's about time."

Dan filled the kettle and switched it on. "Your fiancé dumped you?"

"More or less. He didn't actually say it in words, but considering I haven't heard from him in two months, I consider myself dumped. I'm not heartbroken," she added quickly. "Maybe I should be, but I'm not."

"That's just as well. There's nothing good about being heartbroken." He paused, his gaze distant. "We were married for seven years."

"I'm sorry."

He shrugged aside her apology and reached for two mugs. "So am I."

Claire watched him make them both mugs of tea even though she hadn't asked for one. There was something natural and comforting about sitting in his kitchen, sharing a meal, accepting a mug of strong, sweet tea. "You know," she said when they were both sitting down with their mugs, "you could still try here. Make friends, a life—"

Dan shook his head wearily. "I don't really see the point."

"But you came here for a reason. And life does go on—"

"Does it?" Dan interjected, his voice sharpening. "I lost four men in Afghanistan. We were doing a search-and-clearance operation in the Nad Ali District and a hidden bomb exploded in an area I'd already swept. It was my fault. Completely my fault that those men died, and two of them had children. Three were married." He glanced away, his face set hard.

"Oh, Dan . . ." Claire whispered. She had no idea what to say.

"Life doesn't go on for everyone," he finished, and drained his mug of tea. "Why should it for me? Now you'd better get out there. I'm sure someone will come in soon." He rose from the table, taking their dishes to the sink, and then started upstairs. Claire watched him go, wishing she could say something, yet having no idea what to say or how to comfort a man who had far more depth and sensitivity than she'd ever realized.

Alone in the kitchen, she tidied up and then went out to the shop. It was raining steadily now, a thick mist lying over the high street. Claire doubted they would get many customers in such weather, and she decided to brave the mist and rain to take Bunny for a walk. She could deliver Eleanor Carwell's paper and milk while she was at it.

She locked the front door and hung up the BACK IN AN HOUR sign and then whistled for Bunny, who came quivering towards her. She'd gotten used to the dog in the last month, but she'd never walked her before. Although she didn't want to incur Dan's wrath again, she decided to ask his permission and tiptoed up the stairs.

"Dan . . . ?" she called, and received no answer. She went all the way up, Bunny at her heels, and crept down the narrow passageway, conscious that she was invading Dan's privacy and setting herself up for a serious smackdown. "Dan . . . ?" The door to what had to be his bedroom was ajar, and after tapping nervously on it, she poked her head around.

Dan was stretched out on the bed, fast asleep. Claire stood there for a moment, watching him. In sleep the grim set of his features was softened, his breath coming out deep and even. He slept like he'd been laid in a coffin, flat on his back, his hands folded over his chest. Maybe it was a military thing.

Claire glanced around the room, shamelessly looking for clues about this man, but the Spartan bedroom gave nothing away. Nothing on top of the bureau or bedside table, no photographs or books or even loose change. The only thing she learned about him was that he was very neat. That was probably a military thing too.

After another moment of watching him, strangely transfixed by the sight of him asleep, Claire tiptoed back downstairs and whistled for Bunny, who came scampering joyfully to her side.

23

Rachel

IT TOOK RACHEL ONLY about ten steps towards the Manchester side of the bridge to realize she was overreacting. She stopped, taking a few deep breaths, needing to control the emotion that had been bottled inside her. A few pedestrians slipped by her, clearly annoyed that she was standing there unmoving while they were forced to break their purposeful stride.

Finally, when the bridge was empty, save for her and Andrew, she turned around. Andrew stood a few feet away, his hands in his pockets, his expression unruffled. The man *never* emoted.

"Fine," she said. "I'm scared. Of course I am. Who isn't?"

"There's nothing wrong with being scared. It's when you let the fear control you—"

"Oh please. What self-help book did you steal that line from?"

"There's nothing wrong with self-help books, either."

"You know, I have thought about it," she said. Her chest felt tight again, and she took a few more deep breaths. "Of course I have. But it isn't fear that's kept me from trying to do something more with my life."

"What, then?" Andrew asked. He took a step towards her, and Rachel turned to look out at the river. It was easier to stare at the gently flowing water than at him.

"Exhaustion, for one. I feel like I can barely get myself through each day most of the time. But beyond that . . ." She braced her hands on the bridge's railing, her fingers curling over the cold metal. "I don't want to *settle*. I don't want to be the person who has to be thrilled she got a place at University of Cumbria's night school, doing some adult ed course on data entry or hospitality management. Yes, I've looked at the courses online," she said, cutting him off before he could say anything. "I haven't been completely paralyzed. But . . ." Her hands tightened on the railing, her gaze firmly on the river. "I was accepted on academic scholarship to *Durham*. I know it's not Cambridge or Oxford, but it's still one of the best universities in the country. I had plans. Dreams . . ."

"What were you studying at Durham?" he asked quietly.

"Chemistry." Her throat thickened alarmingly and she swallowed hard. "I wanted to go into research. I was going to get a PhD, find the cure for cancer. . . ." She let out a laugh, the sound just a little wild. "Oh, well."

"You're only twenty-eight, Rachel."

"Give it up, Andrew. I don't have the money for all that. The part-time chemistry course at West Lakes College was too much for my pocket. Anyway," she finished with a shrug, "it doesn't matter. I can't skip off to uni even part-time with my mother in hospital and my sisters needing me."

"Maybe they don't need you as much as you think they do."

She turned to face him. "And what is that supposed to mean?"

"I admit, I'm only seeing this from the outside, but you've done everything for them, Rachel. Meghan only works three nights a week, but you've let her. You've never demanded she have a full-time job, or that Lily help more with the housework. You've been doing it all, all the time, and I don't think you need to."

She felt a blush sweep over her body, hot and prickly. How had he seen all that? He'd barely stepped inside her house once. He didn't know her or her family at all. "I want Lily to study, not do dishes," she said stiffly. "She has so much opportunity. She could go to Durham—"

"So could you. Or if not Durham, then somewhere else. The University of Lancaster has loads of decent courses. It doesn't have to be settling, and frankly, settling for something is better than having nothing at all."

"Why do you care so much?" she blurted. "Am I your pity project or something?"

He held his hands up. "No pity. If anything, I admire you, chipped shoulder and all. But I've stood by and watched Claire waste her life."

"Because she's working in a shop?" Rachel interjected sharply.

"No, because she's been unhappy, letting other people make her choices for her. Don't do the same thing."

Shock made her jaw drop before she snapped it shut. "I can't believe you're comparing me to Claire."

"You have some surprising similarities."

Another rush of pedestrian commuters was starting down the bridge, and Andrew took hold of her elbow to move her to the side. "Come on. We have time to get a drink before your train."

Rachel let him lead her off the bridge and to a quiet wine bar near Piccadilly Station. They sat in a deep booth with huge glasses of wine and, thankfully, Andrew didn't continue with his pep talk. She'd had enough. She felt both raw and invigorated, and she was painfully aware that in less than an hour she'd be back on the train; in three hours she'd be in Hartley-by-the-Sea, cleaning up the kitchen, nagging Lily, and probably putting Nathan to bed. She leaned her head back against the plush booth and sighed.

"Tired?"

"More than you could possibly know."

Andrew placed his hand over hers, a deliberate act, his palm warm and dry. "Think about what I said."

Rachel glanced down at their hands, his covering hers. She wanted to ask him what was going on between them, if anything. Had this been a date? Would they see each other again? But she couldn't face the nonanswers she suspected he'd give, and she didn't know what her own answers would be. She didn't know what she wanted anymore, or what she was capable of.

An hour later Andrew walked her to the train and kissed her cheek before she got on board, a gentlemanly peck that still managed to make her skin buzz.

She sank into a seat, leaned her head against the window, and thankfully, after only a few minutes, fell asleep.

The house was quiet when she let herself in three hours later. Rachel tiptoed upstairs, not wanting to wake Nathan, and peeked in Lily's room. She was curled up on her bed, drawing.

"Adventures of a Mad Scientist?" Rachel guessed as Lily covered the paper with her hand.

"Yes . . ."

Rachel nodded. Words rose to the tip of her tongue about studying and having only two weeks until her first exam, but she felt too tired to say any of it. "Where's Meghan?" she asked instead.

"Asleep."

"Really? It's only nine."

"She'd had a few late nights."

"True." Rachel leaned against the door. She'd dozed most of the way back to Hartley-by-the-Sea, but she still felt tired. Tomorrow she was meeting with Mr. Greaves to discuss her mother's "next phase of reha-bilitation," whatever that would be. She also had to clean three houses.

"You okay, Rach?" Lily asked, and she managed a smile.

"Yeah, just tired."

"Did you have a nice day out with Andrew?"

Rachel thought of the museum, the bridge. "Mostly."

"He seems nice, to me."

"He is nice," she said slowly. She remembered his hand on hers, the intensity in his voice when he'd encouraged her to do something. "He's very nice," she said, and turned from the room.

It was strange to have the house so quiet, even peaceful. The kitchen was actually clean, and someone had switched the dishwasher on. Rachel stood in the center of the room for a moment, savoring the stillness, Andrew's words running through her head, and then turned and went upstairs to bed.

On Monday morning she sat in Mr. Greaves's office and listened to him drone on about cognitive function and rehabilitation options and best-case scenarios. She felt tense and edgy; she hadn't slept well to begin with, and then Nathan had woken up crying at five in the morning. Rachel had stumbled out of bed when he hadn't stopped after several minutes to find Meghan lying with a pillow clutched over her head and Nathan sniffling next to her.

"Meghan. Seriously. Can't you get him to stop?"

"No, I bloody well can't. Don't you think I've tried?" Meghan yanked the pillow off her head and glared at Rachel with bloodshot eyes. For the first time Rachel noticed how awful her sister looked. Admittedly, no one looked their best at the crack of dawn with a toddler screaming next to them, but Meghan looked . . . on the edge. She'd lost weight, so her body was stringy rather than svelte, her hair in a greasy clump, her face pale and streaked with last night's makeup. But beyond all that there was something desperate and reckless about her that made Rachel lean forward and scoop Nathan up into her arms.

"Come on, sweetheart. You can sleep with me."

Meghan rolled over and Rachel went to her bedroom, tucking Nathan up next to her. She thought of Andrew telling her how maybe she didn't need to do everything. Right then it felt like she bloody well did.

Now she tried to focus on the consultant's spiel, but all she really wanted were bottom lines. "So we'll have help. Day nurses . . ."

"Yes, you'll certainly be entitled to at least a few hours of home nursing each week, but you'll need to think about who will have the burden of care."

The burden of care. It was an awful phrase. And a few hours each week didn't sound like much help at all. "But there are forty hours in a working week," Rachel said. Not to mention mornings and evenings and weekends.

Mr. Greaves's expression tightened. "The National Health Service is very stretched financially. We will do all what we can, of course."

Of course. Fifteen minutes later Rachel sat next to her mother's bed and tried to listen as the nurse went through Janice's daily physical exercises. In the two weeks since the stroke, Janice hadn't progressed much, if at all. Her face and body were still mostly paralyzed, although she could twitch her muscles occasionally. Speech was garbled and limited, and cognitive function was, as one nurse had put it, "not operating at full capacity." Which made her mother sound like a machine that had more than a few rusty bits.

"Hey, Mum, you're doing so well." Smiling, Rachel took Janice's limp hand in hers. She forced herself to meet her mother's gaze; the frustration and fear in her mother's faded blue eyes both chilled her and made her want to cry.

She, of all Janice's children, could remember when her mother had been busy and hassled, banging saucepans on the stove and clipping kids on the ear. She'd been too stressed and frantic to be one of those nurturing, hands-on mothers, but Rachel had never doubted that Janice had loved her children and she'd worked hard to provide for them financially. Now she lay in bed, a terrible desperation in her eyes, and Rachel only wanted to back away. And she thought *she* was trapped.

After half an hour of murmuring encouragements while the nurse rotated Janice's limbs, Rachel finally cried off. She had Emily Hart and her terrible twins waiting for her.

When she arrived at the Harts', Emily was standing at the sink, staring out the window while Riley and Rogan sat on the floor and banged pot lids together. Rachel covered her ears for a moment as the clanging reverberated through the kitchen, and when Emily didn't so much as move, she swooped down and took the makeshift cymbals out of the boys' chubby toddler hands.

"That's enough of that, I think." She glanced at Emily, who was still staring into space. "Tea?"

"Pardon?" Emily turned around, blinking as if she'd been asleep. "Oh, yes, that would be lovely."

Rachel hustled the boys into the sitting room and turned on the TV. They sat down in front of *Thomas the Tank Engine*, immediately docile, their faces slackening as their gazes became glued to the flat-screen in front of them. Thank God for the CBeebies channel.

Back in the kitchen Emily was drifting around like she didn't know what to do with herself, and Rachel filled the kettle, steeling herself for another moan about the purposelessness of life for the middle-class British housewife.

"So," she said as the kettle started to hiss. "Should I ask how you are?"

Emily let out a wobbly laugh and sank into a kitchen chair, dropping her chin into her hands. "Probably not."

"That bad, eh?" Rachel reached for the tea bags that Emily kept in a ceramic jar shaped like a rooster. "Oh, dear."

"Well." Emily released a shuddering breath. "I'm pregnant."

"Oh." Rachel handed Emily a mug and sat down across from her. "This isn't a congratulations type of situation, I'm guessing?"

"Not really." Emily took a sip of tea, her face pale, her eyes downcast. "I wasn't . . . We weren't trying. Obviously."

"And?" Rachel asked cautiously. "What are your . . . ? What are your thoughts?"

"My thoughts?" Emily looked up, her forehead wrinkling. "My thoughts are I really am not looking forward to being pregnant again. *Bowking* for twelve weeks and then turning into a bloody beached whale . . . not to mention the varicose veins, the hemorrhoids . . ."

Rachel held up a hand. "Really, I get the picture."

"Sorry." Emily made a face and then took a sip of tea. "It's just that Riley and Rogan aren't even two, and I feel like I can barely manage them. And to do it all over again, and then have toddlers *and* a newborn . . ."

"Have you talked to Tom about it?"

"I haven't told him yet. He's going to be thrilled, I know."

"But if you're not thrilled . . ." Rachel suggested cautiously. "There are options, Emily."

Emily stared at her for a moment before a look of horrified comprehension crossed her face and she shook her head quickly. "Oh, no. No, I don't think I could do that. I mean, I might not want to be pregnant, but when I think of Riley and Rogan . . . There's a little person in there. A mini me-and-Tom."

"Okay." Rachel shrugged, not wanting to push it. Emily had placed her hand on her middle and was smiling tentatively, as if she needed to give herself permission to be happy.

"It's just going to be hard, you know? And I'm so tired. But I don't regret it, either, not exactly. If that makes sense."

"It does." Rachel had never really thought she and Emily Hart had much in common. She'd looked down on Emily a little bit, for being so well off and yet still moaning about life.

But now, for the first time, Rachel could see the conundrum Emily was in. It was the same one she was in: feeling trapped yet not quite sure she actually wanted life to be different. She wouldn't wish Lily away, or the years she'd spent taking care of her. She couldn't wish Nathan away either, or how much time she spent with him. Sometimes her life felt small and suffocating and intolerable, but it was still her life and she loved everyone in it. Even Meghan.

Sighing, Rachel rose from the table and put her mug in the sink. "You look knackered, Emily. Maybe you should go kip upstairs for a bit. I can watch the boys while I tidy up."

Emily looked up from her tea, her expression guiltily hopeful. "Oh, I don't know. Are you sure . . . ?"

"Yes," Rachel answered, suppressing a sigh. "I'm sure."

Of course, the second Emily closed her bedroom door, the theme music of *Thomas the Tank Engine* came on, signaling the end of the show, and Riley and Rogan came trotting into the kitchen while Rachel was getting out the mop.

"Hello, you two," she said. "Are you going to be helpers?"

Three hours later Rachel acknowledged what wishful thinking that had been. Riley and Rogan did not have the word "helpful" in their admittedly very limited vocabulary. Emily had slept for the entire time Rachel cleaned the house, wiping up the dirty water the boys spilled when they tipped over her pail and keeping their hands from reaching inside the toilet as she attempted to scrub it. By five o'clock she was both filthy and exhausted.

Emily staggered out of her bedroom just as Rachel was packing up, making a little more noise than she usually would in the hope that she'd awaken Sleeping Beauty.

"Had a nice nap?" she called brightly as Emily stumbled down the stairs, rubbing her eyes and yawning.

"Yes, yes. Thank you so much. . . ."

She smiled at Rachel as Riley and Rogan came tumbling towards her and then tackled her around the knees.

"It was no bother," Rachel said, and despite the three hours of total hassle, she meant it.

She was just getting into her car when her mobile rang and she saw with a wary ripple of pleasure that it was Andrew.

"Hey," she greeted him as she closed the car door.

"I was just checking to see if you got home safely."

"Considering it's two days later, you'd better hope I had." She found herself smiling.

He chuckled softly, the sound weirdly intimate on the phone. "True enough. That was really just an excuse, anyway. I wanted to talk to you."

"You did?" She felt another silly smile spread over her face.

"Yes. To make sure you aren't annoyed with me for nagging you."

"I wouldn't call it nagging, exactly."

"Irritating you, then."

"You were right, though," she answered. "Sort of."

"So are you going to think about what I said?"

"Maybe. I haven't had time, to be honest." That wasn't quite true. She'd powered up the ancient desktop computer in the sitting room and thought about doing an Internet search for courses. Nathan had come running in before she'd opened the browser.

"How's your mum?"

The switch in topics threw her. "Oh, fine. Well, no, not fine." She sighed. "Terrible, if the expression in her eyes is anything to go by. I can barely look at her, which makes me an awful daughter."

"A normal person," Andrew corrected. "When is she coming home?"

"Probably at the weekend." Rachel closed her eyes, not even wanting to think about what that meant.

"Would you like me to help?"

Her eyes snapped open, and she stared straight ahead at the Harts' muddy garden with its patchy grass and runty trees. "Pardon?"

"I asked, would you like me to help? I could come to Hartley-by-the-Sea for the weekend. Drive your mum home from the hospital, maybe."

"I have a car."

"I know." Andrew's voice was gentle. "But I thought maybe you'd like help shouldering the burden."

Quite suddenly Rachel felt as if she could cry. She dropped the phone in her lap and pressed her thumbs to her closed lids as she took a few deep breaths.

"Rachel?" Andrew's voice, coming from the phone in her lap, sounded tinny and alarmed.

"I'm here." She took one last deep breath and picked up the phone. She hadn't expected Andrew to offer to help. She hadn't realized she'd want it so much. "Yes," she said. "That would be great. I'd love for you to come back and help me."

24

Claire

"ELEANOR CARWELL DIDN'T COME in today."

Dan didn't look up from the Lottery cards he was feeding into the dispenser. "So?"

"So she's come in every morning since I started working here," Claire said. She straightened, rubbing the ache in her lower back. She was almost finished stacking the newspapers.

"Which is all of four weeks," Dan pointed out.

"Still, she's made a big deal of it. Haven't you noticed? She gets all dressed up. . . ."

"She wears the same thing every day."

"But she looks smart," Claire insisted. "Why wouldn't she come today?"

"She's on holiday?"

"She would have canceled her paper, then."

"She's ill."

"Exactly," Claire said. "What if she's really ill? She lives all alone—"

"Let me guess," Dan interjected dryly. "You want to go over there like some kind of Suzy Sunshine and check if she's all right."

"And if I do?"

"I assume I'm paying you to do this?"

"You don't have to. Dock my wages fifteen minutes if you like."

Dan shook his head. "What if she doesn't want to be bothered?"

"Then I'm sure she'll have no qualms about shutting the door in my face." Which was what Eleanor had done the last time Claire had gone to her house, after she'd given Eleanor her newspaper and milk. Claire had found two pound coins in a small brown envelope on the stoop, propped up against the previous day's empty milk bottle, underneath a sign demanding dog owners clean up their pets' "dirt."

"Fine. Go. It isn't as if you've been working for the last ten minutes anyway."

"I finished stacking the papers," Claire protested.

"Ten minutes ago." Dan shooed her towards the door with the indifferent flap of one hand. "Go on."

Claire smiled and reached for her coat. It had been nearly a week since she'd found Dan hungover, and since then their friendship had progressed to a friendly-yet-bickering sort of banter. At least she hoped it was banter. She was never quite sure when Dan was joking.

"I'll be back in fifteen minutes," she promised. Dan did not reply.

Outside the sun had decided to peek out from behind a bank of woolly white clouds, and everything still glistened from last night's thundering rain. Claire hummed as she walked down the high street, waving to a few people she now knew by sight, from her time in the shop. She came to number fifteen and saw the curtains were drawn, the lights off. Maybe Dan was right and Eleanor Carwell had gone on holiday.

Claire knocked, and then knocked again and was just debating a third time when the door was wrenched open and Eleanor stood there, clutching the front of a ratty old dressing gown together.

"What on earth?" she exclaimed. "I thought someone was trying to break down my door."

"Sorry," Claire said, and Eleanor squinted at her.

"What do you want?"

Not the warmest of greetings, but Claire refused to be deterred.

"I noticed you didn't come in for your newspaper and milk this morning, so I thought I'd check to make sure you were all right."

"The post office shop is a doctor's surgery now too, I suppose?" Eleanor grumbled, and turned and went back inside, leaving the door open.

Claire stood on the stoop for a moment, uncertain as to whether she should follow her in. Eleanor had disappeared down a long, narrow corridor towards the kitchen in the back, and after another second's hesitation Claire stepped inside and followed her down the hallway.

The house smelled a bit like her grandmother's in Leeds used to, of lavender water and cough syrup and mothballs. It was a potent mixture, and Claire tried to discreetly breathe through her mouth as she stepped into Eleanor's kitchen, which looked like it had been transported directly from a time machine circa 1972.

Eleanor glanced over her shoulder, seeming both surprised and annoyed that Claire had followed her in. "So why are you here exactly? You didn't bring my newspaper. Or my milk."

"Oh. Right. I suppose I should have." This really wasn't going very well. "Like I said, I just wanted to make sure you were all right."

"And now you can see that I am." Eleanor's clawlike hand trembled as she clutched her dressing gown. Her hair, gray and straggly, was loose about her shoulders instead of up in its usual bun, and in the pale sunlight streaming through the window, Claire could see the age spots on her hands and face.

"Why didn't you come for your paper?" Claire asked. "Or your milk?"

Eleanor's mouth twitched and then she looked away. "If you want the truth, I didn't see the point today."

"Why not?"

"Every morning I get dressed and primped for my big outing," she stated flatly. "A walk down the high street for my milk and newspaper, and then I come back for my cup of tea and two digestives while I read the front page." Her mouth twisted in something meant to be a smile. "The highlight of my day."

"And you didn't feel like it today?"

"No, I didn't. Why should I?" Eleanor sniffed. "You have no idea what it is like to be old."

"No," Claire agreed, "but I do know what it's like to feel purposeless and lonely."

The older woman's face contorted for no more than a second before she looked away. "You have some cheek."

"I spent four years in Portugal showing villas to retirees and planning to marry a man I'm not even sure I liked."

"You had a job and a fiancé," Eleanor returned shortly. "Those are two things that I don't have."

"Is this a competition?" Claire dared to tease, and Eleanor gave her a quelling look.

"It most certainly is not. But don't think you can compare your situation to mine, young lady. I am old and alone and will spend the rest of my days in this miserable little house." She swept a hand to encompass not just the dated kitchen, but the dark hallway and the sitting room, which Claire could see from the kitchen was a study in brown and plaid. "I don't even like this house," she added. "It was my sister's, and she left it to me in her will."

"Why didn't you sell it and buy something else?" Claire asked, and Eleanor's sparse eyebrows rose in indignation.

"You are impertinent."

"Probably. And I'm not normally like this, but . . ." Claire shrugged. "I do know what it's like to feel unhappy and wonder what you're doing with your life. Yes, I had a job, but I hated it, and I'm much happier now stacking newspapers in the shop. And yes, I had a man, but I think the only reason he wanted to marry me was because I looked good on his arm and I never made a fuss. I'd rather be alone."

Eleanor sniffed and said nothing.

"Look, it's no good staying cooped up inside all the time," Claire said.

"Why haven't you joined one of the village societies? You used to do embroidery, didn't you?"

"I can't anymore," Eleanor said stiffly. "My eyesight isn't good enough."

"Oh." Sympathy twisted inside her. Was there anything good about growing old? "What about another club? I see the notices on the board in the shop. Bridge club, gardening club, cake and coffee in the church hall on a Tuesday . . ."

"I don't garden and I fell out with Maureen Lemmon years ago," Eleanor said. "She runs the bridge club. And she cheats."

"Oh." Claire nibbled her lip. "What about the pub quiz?"

"The pub quiz?" Eleanor repeated, disdain dripping from her voice. "I do not—"

"It's tonight, and it's good fun." Even if it hadn't been for her. "I bet you're good at trivia quizzes. You might even win."

"I have never done a pub quiz in my life," Eleanor declared.

"Then it's about time. We can make up a team—you, me, Dan, and . . ." She cast about for another name. "Lily Campbell. She seems like the trivia type too." Claire had no idea how she was going to convince Dan to participate in the pub quiz, but she was determined to try. "Come on, Eleanor," she urged. "What have you got to lose?"

"My dignity?"

"It's *fun*."

"That is a matter of opinion," Eleanor retorted, but Claire could tell she was relenting. She saw it in the way her hand had relaxed on her dressing gown and her gaze had taken on a thoughtful, almost crafty look. "Very well. I suppose I could go once."

"That's the spirit."

"Do not condescend to me, young lady," Eleanor snapped.

"Sorry." Claire bowed her head in brief contrition. "I'll meet you here at seven, and we can go on to the pub. And," she added as she turned towards the door, "my name is Claire."

"No," Dan said flatly when Claire broached the idea with him later that morning.

"For Eleanor's sake," Claire urged. "One pub quiz. How bad can it be? You might, God forbid, actually have fun."

"You don't even like pub quizzes."

"I know. You see the sacrifices I'm willing to make?" She was hoping for a smile, but Dan's expression didn't change as he locked up the post office for the lunch hour. "Please, Dan," Claire said, and laid a hand on his bare arm, her fingers closing over his "sapper" tattoo.

He stilled, and Claire registered how warm his skin was and how touching him just on the arm made her feel kind of tingly inside. Hugh had never made her feel like that.

She thought she should remove her hand, but she didn't want to and Dan wasn't shaking it off.

"How about it?" she pressed, and he sighed.

"Fine," he said. "One pub quiz." And then he shook her hand off.

After work Claire walked up the high street to the Campbells' house to ask Lily if she wanted to come to the pub quiz that night. She hadn't seen Rachel since they'd had a drink together last week, and she felt a niggling sense of guilt for not reaching out to her. She didn't even know how her mum was doing or when she'd be able to come back home. Some friend she was being.

Meghan answered her tentative knock, and Claire drew in a startled breath at how awful she looked.

"Meghan . . . are you . . . ? Are you all right?"

"All right? Why shouldn't I be all right?" Meghan's face was blotchy, her eyes bloodshot, and her clothes hung off her wiry frame. "Rachel's not here if you've come over to do each other's nails."

"Actually, I'm here to talk to Lily."

"Lily?" Meghan's gaze narrowed. "What do you want her for? Are you turning into Lady Bountiful or something?"

Claire flushed, discomfited by the vitriol in Meghan's voice. "No. I just need a fourth person to make up a team for the pub quiz," she said. "Is she around?"

"She's upstairs," Meghan answered, and walked into the kitchen, leaving Claire standing on a stoop for the second time that day.

She stepped inside the cluttered mess of the front hall, unsure if she should go upstairs in search of Lily or ask Meghan to help. It felt wrong to nose through Rachel's house, but Meghan hadn't left her much choice.

After standing there uncertainly for a few seconds, Claire started up the steep, narrow stairs. She hadn't realized how small and shabby Rachel's house was. When she'd last been there she'd been so uncomfortable she hadn't registered the state of the house beyond the overwhelming smell of Nathan's soiled underpants. Fortunately, the house smelled clean now, even if it didn't look it.

She picked her way up the stairs, stepping over crumpled clothing and discarded shoes before calling cautiously, "Lily?"

A thump sounded from one of the rooms and then Lily poked her head out of a doorway at the end of the hall, her mouth dropping open at the sight of Claire.

"Claire? What are you doing . . . ?"

"I'm glad you're home—"

"I'm on study leave." Lily stepped out of her room. "Is everything okay?"

"Yes, it's fine. Meghan told me to come up. I just wondered if you wanted to come to the pub quiz tonight. . . ." Quickly Claire explained her mission, and after her shock at seeing her there cleared, Lily brightened and agreed to come.

"As long as Rachel doesn't mind me horning in on her territory."

"Oh, do you think she will?" Claire winced inwardly at the thought of facing Rachel's wrath yet again. "I didn't even think of that. . . ."

"I'm sure it's fine. The worst she'll do is nag me to study instead." Lily made a face and then ducked back inside her room, and Claire made her way downstairs.

She saw Meghan in the kitchen, sitting at the table with Nathan on her lap. Claire hesitated, torn between making her escape and reaching out to Meghan, whose features looked drawn in stark lines, her expression cringingly bleak.

Then Meghan turned and caught her staring, and her face hardened into an expression of simple malevolence. "Finished, then?" she demanded, and with a nod Claire took an apologetic step backwards.

"Yes, yes—"

"Go on, then," Meghan said, and hugged Nathan closer to her.

"Meghan . . ." Claire began, because she couldn't just leave her there. "Are you . . . ? Are you okay? Because you seem . . ."

Meghan let out a harsh laugh. "Seem what? You're the one who did a stint in rehab, love."

Claire recoiled, shocked. "Did Rachel tell you?"

"No, but things have a way of getting out in a place like Hartley-by-the-Sea. Didn't you know?" Meghan's smile was malicious.

"Right." So everyone knew she'd gone to rehab. Fine, she could deal with that. "Well, I'm glad you're all right," Claire said, and when Meghan didn't respond, she turned and left the kitchen, her head held high.

25

Rachel

RACHEL HADN'T BEEN INTENDING to go to the pub quiz. She hadn't gone in several weeks; somehow, amidst all the demands of life, the weekly entertainment had lost its cheap allure.

"Claire West is going to the pub quiz?" she repeated when Lily told her about her plans. "She organized a *team*?"

"Me, her, Dan Trenton from the shop, and Eleanor Carwell."

"Eleanor Carwell? Isn't she the lady who lives at number fifteen and has all the notices about dog poo?"

Lily wrinkled her nose. "Um. I'm not sure."

"I don't know, Lil." Rachel sank into a chair at the kitchen table. "I'm shattered."

"You'll enjoy it. You always enjoy the pub quiz. And maybe you need to go out."

"What about Nathan?"

"Meghan isn't working tonight."

"Is she out?" Rachel hadn't seen her sister since she'd dragged herself into the house fifteen minutes earlier.

"No. She's upstairs."

Rachel hesitated. She hadn't seen much of Meghan lately, but what she'd seen worried her. Her sister had become increasingly erratic and fractious since their mother's stroke. "Maybe I should see how she is."

"But you'll go tonight?" Lily pressed.

Rachel sighed. "All right, fine. But be prepared to have your arse kicked."

Lily grinned, and with a tired smile, Rachel rose and went upstairs. She knocked once on Meghan's door before opening it; her sister was lying on the bed with one arm thrown over her face, Nathan stretched out next to her, playing with her phone. He looked up when Rachel came in.

"Ray-Ray!"

"Hey, Nath." Meghan didn't move, and Rachel took a step into the room. "Hey, Meghan. You okay?"

Meghan dropped her arm from her face. "Why do you ask?"

Rachel hesitated. "Honestly? Because you seem . . . off."

"First Claire, now you. Can't a girl have a bad day without everyone stressing her about it?"

"Claire? What did Claire say?"

"She came over to ask Lily to the pub and she asked if I was all right." Meghan rolled over to give Rachel a sardonic smile. "She almost sounded Cumbrian, except for the upper-class drawl. She should have said *areet*."

"Seriously, Meghan, though."

Meghan's eyes flashed with challenge. "What?"

"Are you all right?"

She let out a gusty sigh and rolled onto her back once more. "I'm fine, Rachel. Not that you care."

"I'm asking, aren't I?"

"Only because you're worried that I'm going to off-load Nathan onto you."

There was enough truth to that remark for Rachel to stay silent. Nathan looked up from Meghan's phone. "What does 'off-load' mean?"

"Never you mind, Nath," Meghan said, and rested her hand on top of his head.

"You know Mum is coming home on Friday?" Rachel said, and Meghan didn't answer. "I know this is hard, but it's going to be all hands on deck when she's back here. We'll have to work out some kind of schedule. She can't be left alone. Not even for five minutes to go to the post office."

Meghan let out a shuddering breath, and Rachel wondered if she'd come down too hard. But the reality remained that she needed Meghan to step up. She couldn't do this alone. "You and lover boy might have to cool it for a little while."

"Fine." Meghan rolled over so her back was to Rachel. "Finished?"

Rachel studied her for a moment, noticing how thin she'd become, how tense. Her bedroom was a mess of dirty clothes, the wastepaper basket filled with dirty nappies. Even though Rachel had a nagging sense that she should stay and try to talk to Meghan, comfort her in some way, the room made her feel as if the walls were closing in on her, and she just wanted to escape. Besides, she and Meghan had never had that kind of relationship.

"All right," she said, and took a step backwards. "I'm finished."

In the cramped solitude of her own room she gazed dispiritedly at her odd assortment of cheap skirts and tops hanging on the back of the door; there was no room for a wardrobe. She wasn't in the mood for a pub quiz, and hadn't been for weeks. The happy fizz of Andrew calling her two days ago had left a while ago, and now she felt flat. Even though she was looking forward to seeing him on the weekend, she wasn't relishing bringing her mother home and coping with all the new demands her care would bring, especially since Meghan seemed to be checking out emotionally.

Sighing, Rachel reached for a clean hoodie. No need to wear a stretchy top to impress Rob Telford anymore. Not, of course, that she was actually dating Andrew West. She really wasn't sure what was going on there, if anything.

"Rachel?" Lily knocked on the door. "You ready?"

Twenty minutes later she walked into the noisy warmth of the Hangman's Noose and felt it envelop her like a hug from a boozy friend. Lucy, as usual, was waving from their corner table, a bottle of wine open, glasses already poured. Her sister, Juliet, was smiling, Peter Lanford's arm looped casually around her shoulders.

"We can't have five people on the team," Rachel chided Peter, smiling, and with his free hand he raised his pint.

"I'm taking Abby's place. She's home with Noah tonight."

"That's all right, I suppose." She sat down on the barstool, shoving her bag underneath, and reached for her glass of wine. Peter was whispering something into Juliet's ear and Juliet was, most uncharacteristically, blushing. Rachel wondered how much of their nauseatingly sweet lovey-dovey act she could stomach.

She glanced at the table next to theirs, where Lily had sat down next to Claire and two people who composed the most unlikely quiz team Rachel had ever seen.

Dan Trenton sat on a barstool, feet flat on the floor, arms ominously crossed, his massive form dwarfing the tiny stool. His expression was wooden, and the pint glass of Guinness in front of him was untouched. Next to him sat an elderly lady whom Rachel assumed was Eleanor Carwell; she was dressed in a twinset the color of an old orange and a tweed skirt in complementing browns. She had a thimbleful of sherry on the table in front of her and was looking around the pub, her lips pursed. Lily, Rachel saw, had a half-pint of cider. She'd turned eighteen in February, so Rachel could hardly protest her drinking, but she felt a strange prickling feeling at realizing just how much her baby sister was growing up.

"Right, shall we get going?" Rob came from behind the bar, his gaze skimming over the crowd and resting briefly on Rachel before he started on the questions and everyone grabbed papers and stubs of pencil.

Rachel didn't feel the usual rush of determination to get the answers faster than anyone else. Lucy and Juliet had both reached for pencils, but she simply sat there, cradling her wine, as Rob called out, "Right, first question. What is the capital of Mongolia?"

"Mongolia?" Lucy, designated writer, looked up from the paper. "Who knows that?"

"You've been doing the pub quiz every week for six months and you don't know the capital of Mongolia?" Juliet scoffed.

"Do you know it?"

"No. Why would I?"

They both turned to Rachel. "You must know it, Rachel," Lucy said.

"Ulaanbaatar," Rachel said without enthusiasm. "Rob's trotted out the capital-of-Mongolia question at least three times before."

"How do you spell it?"

Rachel spelled it out between sips of wine and then Rob cleared his throat meaningfully and moved on to the next question, which was about the Lake District's deepest lake.

"Now, that's just a freebie," Juliet scoffed. "Everyone knows it's Wastwater."

"And for an extra point," Rob called out, "how deep is it?"

Juliet fell silent, and Rachel sighed. "Two hundred forty-three feet deep," she said.

"How do you know these things, Rachel?"

"I'm a font of useless knowledge." And she'd done geography A level, along with chemistry, further maths, and biology. It seemed a lifetime ago. It *was*.

"You're not so keen tonight," Juliet remarked when Rob had called for an intermission and Peter had gone up to the bar to refill everyone's drinks.

"Just tired." Rachel glanced over at the next table; Claire was looking flushed and happy, and Lily was laughing. Dan's expression was as implacable as ever, but Eleanor looked like she might have smiled at some point in the evening. Restlessness stirred, along with the feeling that everyone was enjoying themselves, and she didn't think she could have a good time if she tried.

"You worried about your mum?" Juliet asked.

Rachel shrugged. "Worried about her coming home."

"It must be hard."

Rachel nodded. In the last few weeks plenty of people in the village had offered their sympathy, whether it was a smile in the street or a card popped through their door. Everyone's compassion had been tempered by the fact that Rachel had been dealing with her invalid mother for a decade. This was merely another step down a depressingly expected road. Juliet, despite her sympathetic smile, was the same.

"So I think we got them all right except number five," Lucy said as Peter returned with their drinks. "The one about who won Wimbledon in 1996 . . ."

"Surely it had to be Pete Sampras," Juliet said. "Didn't he win Wimbledon about ten times in a row?"

"I think it's a trick question." Lucy nibbled on the end of her pencil. "What do you think, Rachel?"

"I think I should go home." Rachel put her half-drunk glass of wine on the table. "Sorry. I'm tired and not in the mood. I don't want to bring you all down." She gave everyone an apologetic smile, but they all were looking shocked and then, worse, worried. "I'm okay," she said. "Just need a good night's sleep." She turned to Lily, who was frowning at her. "Stick to a half-pint of cider," she instructed sternly, and Lily rolled her eyes. Claire, Rachel saw, was talking to Dan, who had softened slightly in the last half hour, although he still resembled a slab of concrete.

Grabbing her bag, Rachel shouldered her way through the pub, only to stop when Rob called her name.

"You've missed a few quizzes lately," he remarked as she paused by the bar. "You areet?"

"I'm fine, Rob, just have a lot going on."

He filled a pint with foaming beer and pushed it across the top of the bar to a woman who was nearly spilling out of her top. Rachel didn't recognize her, and Rob didn't take his eyes off Rachel.

"Anything I can do?"

"No, not really." She felt a flicker of guilt for flirting with Rob a few weeks ago. His concern now made her squirm.

He nodded towards the door as he filled another pint. "Then maybe you want to go see what's parked outside your house."

She tensed with alarm as she thought of Meghan's bloodshot eyes, her blotchy face. "What . . . ?"

Rob smiled and shook his head to dispel the nameless fears that had been circling. "A navy Lexus. Andrew West's car, if I'm not mistaken. I saw it when I took out the bins a few minutes ago."

"Oh . . ." Heat flooded her face, and Rob smiled wryly.

"I think he might be looking for you."

Rachel nodded jerkily and walked out of the pub. Outside it was still light, although the sun had sunk behind the rows of terraced cottages and so the street was cast in shadow, empty except for a couple of spotty teens loitering in front of the shuttered post office shop with their skateboards. She looked up the street and saw the navy blue Lexus parked, incongruously, behind her beat-up hatchback. And Andrew West standing in the middle of the sidewalk.

She walked towards him, slowly at first, her heart beating too hard for the occasion, her mind feeling as if it were filled with cotton wool even though she'd had only half a glass of wine.

Andrew saw her coming and offered a wonderfully lopsided, uncertain smile. "I thought I'd just stop by . . ." he began, trailing off as Rachel kept walking towards him and then into him, wrapping her arms around his middle as she pressed her face against the starched cotton of his shirt.

Andrew's arms closed around her instinctively, but his body was tense. Rachel could feel his heart beating underneath her cheek.

"Rachel . . . is everything okay?"

"Yes. I just needed a hug."

"*You* needed a hug?" His arms tightened around her. "Things must really be bad."

"No worse than usual," she said, her voice muffled against his chest.

"I can certainly oblige you," Andrew murmured, and he fit her body more closely to his, so for a few seconds she felt as if she could relax, as if she could let herself not be in charge.

Then, eventually, he loosened his embrace and pulled back from her. "What's going on?"

"Nothing." She pushed a few strands of hair away from her face, the embarrassment of having thrown herself at him, even if only for a hug, starting to scorch her. No wonder Andrew had seemed so surprised. He'd been expecting a snappy comeback and instead she'd nestled against his chest. "Sorry," she muttered as she moved past him.

"Hey." Andrew reached for her arm and pulled her towards him. "Wait a minute. Don't think I don't appreciate a hug. I just wasn't expecting it."

"Obviously." She felt as if she'd jump-started their relationship, and not in a good way. "Look, I'm tired and I should probably go home. Long day tomorrow . . ."

"Rachel, it's eight thirty. How about a drink?"

"I just left the pub."

"We'll go to Raymond's, then."

"I thought you said it was overrated."

"Did I?" He smiled ruefully. "You must have thought me a complete snob."

"I did, actually. And a pompous ass."

"Dare I hope that your opinion has changed?"

"A little. Maybe." She smiled, exhaustion and hope crashing around inside her so she didn't know what she felt. "All right. One drink. But then I should get back to Meghan."

"What's up with Meghan?" Andrew asked as they fell in step together and started walking down the high street towards the old train station. As they emerged from between the terraced houses on either side of the street, the sky opened up and they paused for a moment to watch the sun sinking towards the sea, the puddles in the sheep pastures glinting under the golden light. A brisk wind was coming off the water, and Rachel shivered slightly before walking on.

"I don't know what's going on with Meghan," she said. "But she's not herself. Snappier and stressed and she's lost weight. And there's a man involved somehow."

Andrew held the door open for her, and as she walked into Raymond's, the quiet elegance of the place soothed her frayed nerves. "This is nice. I've never been here before."

Andrew ordered their drinks while Rachel sat on the deep, squashy sofa in front of the fireplace and leaned her head back against the velvet cushions. She felt as if she could fall asleep. When he returned a few minutes later with their glasses of wine, her eyes were closed.

"Is this going to put you over the edge?" he asked as he handed her a glass of wine.

Rachel opened her eyes and took it with a murmured thanks. "Maybe. You might have to carry me home."

"I wouldn't mind." His gaze held hers for one tingling moment before Rachel looked away. She wanted so much to lean on Andrew, to have someone to share the burden of care that had been placed squarely on her shoulders, but she was afraid to ask. Afraid to trust, because she'd seen what had happened before when she'd relied on her father to pick up the slack. He'd scarpered. He'd broken her heart.

"So. Tomorrow," Andrew said. "What time are you meant to pick up your mum?"

"In the morning." Rachel's stomach churned at the thought. "We have a home nurse coming for the first time tomorrow afternoon. But I honestly don't know how we're going to cope, Andrew. When I've visited my mum in hospital she's barely been able to move or speak. And she can't . . ." She swallowed hard, a blush rising to her face. "Control herself. If you know what I mean. So that will be two people in the house in nappies."

"You can't do it all yourself, Rachel."

"But I think I might have to." She could feel a lump forming in her throat, and she took a sip of wine, hoping to dissolve it. It only got bigger. "There's no one else. Lily needs to study, and Meghan is barely holding it together."

"What about me? What about Claire?"

She looked at him in surprise, discomfited by the question. "Last time I checked you live in Macclesfield and Claire . . ."

"And Claire?"

"Claire works at the post office shop."

"Only four days a week."

Rachel took a sip of wine, her mind spinning. "She hasn't offered."

"I think she'd like to help." Andrew paused. "And I think it would be good for her."

"So this is for Claire's benefit?" Rachel asked, her voice sharper than she meant it to be.

Andrew regarded her evenly. "Why can't it be a win-win situation?"

"I don't know." The thought of asking for Claire's help, depending on her, made Rachel feel uncomfortable. Exposed. Claire had dropped her once. She didn't feel like being dropped again, especially at a time when she could so easily start to rely on her. On anyone who was willing to step up. "How could she help, anyway?"

"She could check in on your mother—"

"She has no training for that sort of thing."

"Do you?"

"Ten years of it," Rachel retorted, although that wasn't quite true. Since their dad had left, Meghan had taken care of their mother the most. Rachel had worked.

"Or she could take some of your cleaning jobs while you help out with your mother—"

"I couldn't afford to pay her."

"This isn't about money."

"Charity, then?"

Andrew sighed. "Why are you getting so prickly?"

"Because this is hard on me." Rachel could feel tears starting in her eyes, and she put her wineglass down with a *thunk*, pressing the heels of her hands to her eyes even though the gesture was more revealing than she liked. "This is bloody, bloody hard, Andrew. A week ago you were telling me I had choices. I should go back to university. And I even looked at some courses online, but how can I manage it or anything else now? I can't depend on you or Claire or anyone for very long. You'll get another job in some exotic country and Claire will figure out what she wants to do. She isn't going to stay stacking shelves for the rest of her life."

"Maybe not, but we're here now—"

"And I don't want to start counting on you only to have you walk away when it suits. Trust me, I've been there before."

Andrew's face was pale, his eyes dark. "I'm not your father, Rachel."

"I don't know what you are," Rachel snapped. "What's really going on here?" She gestured to the space between them. "Why are you getting so involved in my life? My family's life?"

Andrew was silent for a moment, his gaze steady on her. "Because I care about you," he finally said.

Rachel's breath came out in a rush. "I'm not even sure what that means, considering how far apart our lives are."

"Can't we just take it one day at a time, one step at a time? I'm in Macclesfield for another couple of months. I can come up here on the weekends. And you could come visit me—"

"How? Leaving home for one day was hard enough." She shook her head, everything in her weighted down, heavy. "I appreciate all your offers of help, Andrew, I really do. I know you're sincere. But I can't start depending on someone only to have it all blow up in my face."

"Maybe it wouldn't."

But that required a level of trust she simply didn't have. She shook her head again and reached for her bag. "I should go."

"Let me walk you home."

"There's no need."

"My car is back there, anyway." He put his unfinished glass of wine next to hers and helped her on with her coat, a gesture that made Rachel feel worse. They walked in silence out of the restaurant and headed back up the street.

The pub quiz was over and people were spilling out into the street, laughing and joking good-naturedly. Rachel slowed her step, reluctant to be caught up in the moment.

She saw Claire and Dan walking Eleanor Carwell back to her house, and Lily heading up to hers. Juliet and Peter were holding hands as they walked down to Tarn House. Everyone looked happy.

"Let me come with you to the hospital tomorrow at least," Andrew said. "That's why I came home, after all."

"Home? Is this really home for you?" Andrew didn't answer, and she sighed. "Okay. Fine." Then, because she knew she sounded ungracious, she added, "Thanks."

They'd reached the house at the same time as Lily, and the smile slipped off her face as she looked at them.

"Is everything okay?"

"Fine," Rachel said. "But as it's only nine o'clock, you can get another hour of revision in."

Lily nodded glumly, and Andrew reached for his keys. "What time should I be here?" he asked.

"Eight would work," Rachel said, and turned towards the house without saying goodbye.

26

Claire

THE PUB QUIZ, CLAIRE had recognized, could have been a disaster. It hadn't started out well, with Eleanor disapproving of the alcohol and Dan utterly silent, seemingly set to stoically endure the evening. Lily's and Lucy's enthusiasm made up for a lot, but Claire could see, even before she left, that Rachel wasn't having a good time.

Still, she was determined to make the evening a success, and Dan eventually answered a few questions, mainly in monosyllabic grunts, and when Eleanor took charge of writing down the answers, she got into the spirit of the thing. They didn't come close to winning; they only got nine out of twenty questions right. Dan had gotten the sports questions, Eleanor had rocked geography, and Lily had managed the pop culture ones, but everything else had been a complete blank. Claire hadn't answered anything—and yet she'd had a good time.

As they left the pub, Dan offered to walk Eleanor home, and Claire went along while Lily headed up the street to her house.

"I'm perfectly capable of walking home alone," Eleanor snapped.

Dan, implacable as ever, had replied quite seriously, "I'm being a gentleman."

Eleanor had harrumphed at that, but Claire could tell she was quite pleased. Not, of course, that she'd ever show it.

They said goodbye to Eleanor and started walking back up to the

263

shop, when Dan glanced at her and said, "Your house is in the other direction."

"Oh." In the darkness Claire couldn't read the expression on Dan's face, but she was glad it hid her blush. "Right." What had she been thinking, that she'd go home with Dan for a quick nightcap? "Sorry. I wasn't thinking straight. I'll see you tomorrow?"

"Assuming you're planning to come to work."

"Of course I am." She hesitated, reluctant to end the evening and face Four Gables alone. Andrew had texted her to say he'd be coming home for the weekend, but she didn't know when he'd arrive. And even with Andrew for company, she'd rather have Dan. Which didn't really make sense, but there it was. "Did you have a good time tonight?" she asked, and he shrugged one massive shoulder.

"It was all right."

"I'm going to take that as an unreserved 'hell, yes,'" Claire answered. "Considering how often you show enthusiasm."

He cracked a small smile then, much to her relief. "You can think that if you want."

"I will." The moment stretched and spun out and started to turn into something else. Claire took a step closer to Dan, her heart trembling in her chest. She wanted him to do something. . . .

He gazed down at her, and for a thrilling second Claire thought he was going to kiss her. She was practically on her tiptoes, face tilted up in silent, yearning invitation.

Then he took a step back, towards the shop. Claire rocked back on her heels, her trembling heart going terribly still before it went into free fall.

"Good night, Claire," Dan said, and disappeared down the alley to his flat.

Claire walked slowly back to Four Gables, battling the overwhelming sense of disappointment she felt. Nothing had been going to happen with Dan. The idea was ludicrous, just as she'd told Lucy. And yet for a moment, a glorious few seconds, she'd actually thought . . .

"Dream on," Claire muttered, and kept walking. The beach road was lost in darkness, and a few sheep bleated in agitated misery; Claire couldn't see them in the dark, but she knew lambing had begun, and the mothers were calling to their young. In a few months the white, woolly lambs gamboling through the muddy sheep fields would be taken away to be slaughtered; Peter had mentioned it at the quiz, and Claire had been as horrified as if he'd said he was killing Bambi.

The fizzy feeling of satisfaction she'd had at organizing the pub quiz outing had gone, leaving her feeling flat and a little bit depressed. Why was she trying to be friends, or even something more, with Dan? It wasn't as if he'd given her much reason. And if she was honest, not much about her life in Hartley-by-the-Sea was set to last. A part-time job in a shop? A handful of sort of, now and then friends? Living at home? Not exactly what you built your dreams on.

It hurt to admit, but just as Andrew had said, her life here was more of a holding pattern, a waiting time until something else came up. Until she made a decision about what she wanted to do in life. And she had no idea what that was.

A car slowed down on the beach road, and Claire turned to see her brother's blue Lexus.

"Want a lift?"

"I didn't know when you were coming back." She got in the car, and Andrew drove on. Both of them were silent for the duration of the drive.

The next morning Andrew was up and showered when Claire came down at half past seven for work. "Are you going somewhere?" she asked as she got out a bowl for cereal.

"I'm helping Rachel. Her mother's coming home today."

"Oh." Claire glanced at Andrew, surprised; he looked as composed as ever, wearing his usual uniform of chinos and a well-starched button-down shirt. "That's nice of you."

"I want to help." He glanced up with a wry smile. "Not that Rachel wants me to."

"She is prickly about stuff like that."

"She's afraid."

"Afraid?" Rachel seemed like the most fearless person Claire knew. She always had been, even when they were children. A memory slotted into place: Rachel taking on Rob Telford in the school playground, when he'd pulled Claire's plaits and run away with the ribbon. He'd mentioned it when she'd first seen him at the pub, but now Claire could see the scene in clarity: Rob's boyish, taunting face as he held up her ribbon and Rachel's righteous fury, hands planted on hips as she commanded him to give it back. Claire had simply stood there, shocked into silence by the whole episode and then filled with gratitude and relief when Rachel had returned her ribbon.

"She's afraid of trusting me," Andrew said, bringing her back into the present. "Or anyone. She doesn't want to depend on anyone, in case they let her down."

"I suppose I can understand that, considering her father up and left her family."

Andrew's expression hardened. "Not everyone is like that."

Claire glanced at him curiously. "Do you . . . ? Do you *care* about her, Andrew?"

"Maybe I do," he said, and folded up his newspaper. "I should get ready to go. I'll drop you off at the post office, if you like."

Claire wasn't looking forward to seeing Dan after their weird interaction last night. What if he'd been able to tell that she'd wanted him to kiss her? He probably had. He was probably secretly laughing at her, although Dan didn't really seem the type. More like secretly— or not so secretly—disgusted by her pathos.

She came into the shop warily; Dan was in the back, getting ready to open the post office. The papers had already been delivered, and so Claire started stacking them on the shelves without a word. Dan glanced over at her but didn't say anything, and they both worked in silence until Eleanor Carwell came in for her paper and milk at a quarter to nine.

By lunchtime Claire was ready to quit. Her few forays into conversation with Dan had ended in grunts, until she wondered why she even bothered. She'd offered to walk Bunny when the post office closed at noon, but Dan had said he'd do it and had left her alone in the shop for an hour, which was a relief after the tense silence she'd endured all morning.

By the time he returned with Bunny, she'd worked up enough courage—and irritation—to ask him what was going on.

"Nothing's going on." He put Bunny back in the kitchen and closed the door behind him, coming out a few minutes later while Claire stood there, bristling.

"You're being so *silent*," she said when he returned and started opening up the post office again.

He glanced at her, nonplussed. "You're surprised?"

"I thought . . ."

"I was changing?" He filled in. "You were rehabilitating me? Sorry, no."

"Rehabilitating—"

A farmer came in for a meat pie and a Lottery card and so Claire fell silent. Dan had disappeared behind the post office's Plexiglas partition and she was manning the till, so even after the farmer left, it wasn't easy to have a conversation. Not that she even knew what to say. She was the one who had supposedly needed rehabilitation, not Dan.

By four o'clock they'd had no more than a handful of words between them, and Claire chastised herself for feeling so disappointed, and worse, hurt. Maybe Dan was right and she had been trying to change him. She'd wanted him to talk more, anyway. She'd wanted him to like her.

"See you on Monday," she said as she reached for her coat. It was mid-May, but the wind off the sea was still cold.

"Wait."

Claire's heart lurched ridiculously, and she turned around to see Dan handing her a check.

"Your week's pay."

"Right." She took it without enthusiasm and stuffed it in her bag. "Have a good weekend, anyway," she said, and Dan didn't reply. What a surprise.

She was at the door when he spoke again. "Claire." She stilled, one hand on the doorknob.

"Yes?"

"Have a good weekend."

Her shoulders slumped, and she left the shop without replying.

She was on her way home when she decided to stop by and see Rachel.

When Claire knocked Rachel opened the door, looking distinctly hassled, a tearful Nathan balanced on her hip. "What—oh, Claire."

"That's a bit better than 'oh, you,'" Claire answered with a smile. "How are things?"

"Hectic." Rachel shifted Nathan to her other hip. "Do you need something? Because I'm kind of busy."

"No." Claire wondered if she looked like she needed something, or if Rachel had just assumed so because she'd always been the needy one. "Actually, I wondered if you needed something. If I could help."

"You?"

"Don't sound quite so surprised. I can be fairly capable, on occasion." Claire spoke lightly.

"No, sorry. I didn't mean . . ." Rachel sighed. "Look, you'd better come in."

The house was far messier than it had been when Claire had come before; Rachel led her into the kitchen, which was filled with dirty dishes, and the smell of grease and old fried food hung in the air.

"Sorry," Rachel said as she shrugged at the disaster zone. "I haven't had time . . ."

"I have time."

Rachel simply stared. "Sorry. What?"

"I have time," Claire said again, her voice firm. "You look shattered. Why don't you go in the sitting room and have a moment to relax and I'll clean up in here? I'll make you a cup of tea while I'm at it and keep an eye on Nathan."

"But . . ." Rachel blinked, looking completely flummoxed. Was it so hard to believe she could manage to tidy a room and boil a kettle?

"I happen to like tidying up." Gently Claire shooed her towards the sitting room. "Go on. Can your mum manage without you for a few minutes?" She hadn't heard anything from the closed dining room door, so maybe Janice was asleep.

"Lily's sitting with her."

"That's all right, then. I'll come in with your tea in just a few minutes."

"That okay, Nath?" Rachel asked, and Claire gave him a bright smile. Children made her nervous.

Predictably, his lip wobbled. "Ray-Ray . . ."

"It looks like you've been doing some coloring," Claire tried. She reached for the cheap coloring book that had been left open on the kitchen table, a half-scribbled picture of Thomas the Tank Engine obscured by a coffee ring. "Can you do some with me? And perhaps I can find you a biscuit." Claire pulled out a chair and patted the seat, and Rachel tiptoed to the sitting room while she helped Nathan sit down.

It was surprisingly cozy and cheerful, cleaning the Campbells' tiny kitchen while Nathan colored and the kettle boiled. It didn't take long to rinse and stack the dishes in the dishwasher and then spritz the cleaning surfaces and give the cooker a good wipe down.

She found a somewhat stale digestive for Nathan, who munched it as he colored, only looking up when the kettle whistled.

"What's your name?"

Claire laughed. "Claire," she said. "And I know you're Nathan." He looked surprised but pleased by this, and Claire brewed two cups of tea and carried them into the sitting room, Nathan scrambling off his seat to follow her.

Rachel was sitting on the sofa, her feet propped up on the coffee table, her eyes closed. She barely opened them as Claire came in and tidied a few magazines away to make room for their cups.

"Here we are. You look like you're about to doze off."

"I think I just did." Rachel straightened with a yawn and took her cup of tea. "Thank you, Claire."

"I made one for myself. I hope you don't mind."

"No, of course not."

Nathan settled on a corner of the sofa with his coloring book, and Rachel and Claire both sipped their tea in surprisingly peaceful silence.

"How did this morning go?" Claire finally asked. "With your mum?"

Rachel grimaced. "Hard. We really need a wheelchair, but there's none available at the moment. Bloody NHS." She glanced worriedly at Nathan, but he seemed oblivious. "I don't know what we would have done without Andrew. He helped me carry Mum inside." She closed her eyes briefly. "Not something I want to ever have to do again, in all honesty."

"I can imagine." Although she wasn't sure she could. Janice Campbell was a big woman.

"Mum looked so miserable," Rachel continued, her voice catching. "I'm sure her back is absolutely killing her, although of course she can't say. She's on a million different meds now. I'll never get them straight, and they all cost a mint." She sighed and shook her head. "Sorry. I don't mean to moan."

"You have every right to moan, Rachel. It all sounds pretty awful."

"It is."

"Will your mum—will she improve? In time?"

"There's no saying. With rehab, maybe a little. But . . ." Rachel paused, her face contorting a little before she took a measured breath. "She's only fifty-one. She could live like this for God knows how long."

Which meant Rachel could live like this for God knew how long. It was a life sentence, and a very tough one.

"I'm sorry," Claire said quietly. "Are Lily and Meghan helping?"

"Meghan disappeared this morning and hasn't been back." Rachel glanced again at Nathan before giving Claire a pointed look. "I don't know when she will be."

"You mean . . . ?"

This time she looked pointedly at Nathan. "I don't *know*."

"Look, let me help—"

Rachel raised her half-drunk cup of tea. "You already have."

"I mean really help. Properly. How on earth are you going to cope otherwise?"

Rachel's face took on a pinched look. "Trust me, Claire, I managed fine before you came along."

"I know you did. Of course you did. But I want to help, and I have some time."

"That's what Andrew said."

Claire jerked back a bit in surprise. "What?"

"He said I should ask you to help. But you went ahead and asked me."

"Oh. Okay. Well, let me help, then."

"Doing what? Changing my mother's nappy? Wiping the spittle from her chin?" Her voice rang out, and Claire drew back, shocked, and then even more shocked when Rachel's face crumpled and she started to cry.

"Rachel . . ."

"Don't." Rachel held her hands up to her face as she drew in several shuddering breaths. "Honestly. Please don't."

Don't what? Help her? Comfort her? Claire saw Nathan looking like he was about to cry too, and quickly she scooped him up into her arms. "Back into the kitchen, I think. How about another digestive?"

"Ray-Ray . . ." he began, but he didn't protest as Claire deposited him in a kitchen chair and thrust another digestive into his grubby hands.

Then, for lack of anything better to do, she made Rachel another cup of tea. By the time she brought it into the sitting room, Rachel had gotten control of herself. Claire handed her the tea and Rachel took it, bringing the cup up to let the steam hit her face.

"Sorry about that," she said, her gaze on the tea.

"You don't have anything to be sorry for, Rachel. Life is hard."

Rachel just shook her head and then took a sip of tea. Claire perched on the edge of a chair, half listening for Nathan.

"Thank you," Rachel finally said. "I could use your help. If you wouldn't mind cleaning."

"Cleaning? You mean, for your housekeeping business?" Rachel nodded, and relief made Claire almost buoyant. "Absolutely. Cleaning is actually something I can do."

Rachel smiled sadly. "You can do a lot of things, Claire."

"Well, I'm adding to my repertoire every day. Just tell me when and where. I have Tuesdays free, and on other days I'm finished at the shop at four. I like cleaning, actually."

"I have noticed that I haven't had to do much up at Four Gables," Rachel said, and then gave her a proper smile. "Okay, then. Thank you. I can shift some of my jobs to Tuesday and you can start then, and try to tackle Henry Price's horrible loo."

27

Rachel

IT HAD BEEN AN emotional roller coaster of a day, and Rachel was ready to get off. She remained in the sitting room after Claire had left, finishing her lukewarm tea and savoring the silence. On Tuesday Claire would take her cleaning jobs and Rachel would try to sort out the home front. And maybe, just maybe, she could figure out some way to move forward. As a family, as well as a person. She wasn't ready to let go of her dreams, buried as they were beneath an avalanche of worry. She just wasn't sure if she could find them again.

The door to the dining room opened and Lily came out, looking subdued. Rachel straightened.

"Mum okay?"

"She's sleeping. I think." Lily sat opposite Rachel, her hands tucked between her knees. "It's kind of hard to tell."

"I know."

Lily was silent for a moment, her hair sliding forward to obscure her face. Rachel didn't press; Lily hadn't visited their mother much in hospital in the last two weeks, because of school, and the reality of Janice's condition had to be a shock.

"She's not going to get much better, is she?" she finally asked, her head still bowed.

"Honestly? I don't know. I've never dealt with a stroke victim before.

But I'm not optimistic." Rachel abandoned her tea on the coffee table and leaned her head back against the sofa. "I have no idea what the future is going to look like, Lily. Or how any of us are going to cope. But the important thing is for you to focus on your exams. They're coming up soon, and you can't afford to—"

"Don't worry about me, Rachel. Exams seem kind of trivial, considering—"

"But they're *not* trivial." Rachel leaned forward, her exhaustion replaced by an urgency that was tinged with anger. "Lily, these exams are everything. I know you don't believe me, that you don't even want to go to uni, but trust me, please, that I know better in this case. That I know you want to do better than live here forever and work in the pub or cleaning houses for the rest of your life."

Lily was silent for a long moment; Rachel couldn't see her face. "I don't have to go to university to make different choices than you and Meghan did." She looked up, and her blue eyes, the same blue as Rachel's, as their father's, blazed. "There are more options than uni or working in a pub, Rachel."

Rachel swallowed down the angry words that bubbled to her lips. "Maybe there are, but do they involve making a living? Being independent?"

"Is *that* why you want me to go to uni?" Lily exclaimed. "So you don't have to support me?"

She made Rachel sound selfish, and her instinct was to deny it. She'd sacrificed so much for Lily. This wasn't about her. "It's part of it," she finally admitted. "Of course it is. We're struggling already—"

"And university costs nine thousand pounds!"

"I don't care about that. There are student loans—"

"If this is about money, I should just quit school and start working."

"Lily, that is the last thing I want." Rachel closed her eyes briefly and pushed a hand through her hair, which had fallen out of the messy knot she'd put it in this morning. It had been an unbelievably long day. "Look,

I don't want to argue. I don't think I can take it on top of everything else."

"I don't want to argue, either. Actually, I want to help."

"You could help by studying—"

"With Mum."

Rachel's mouth nearly dropped open at this admission. Lily never helped with their mother; she avoided her as much as she could. To Lily, Janice Campbell had never been much of a mum. She'd just been a woman stuck in bed, draining their resources and time. It was awful to think, but Rachel recognized it as the truth. In those first few years after Janice's accident, she'd been in and out of hospital, often doped up on painkillers. Rachel and her dad had taken care of Lily, and when he'd left it had just been Rachel.

"Really?" she said when she'd finally found her voice. "That's very kind of you, but . . ."

"She's my mum, Rachel. I know it doesn't feel like it—you feel like my mum more than anyone else." Lily gave her a lopsided smile. "But sitting with her just now, seeing her so helpless . . . it's awful. No one deserves that. And I've hidden from the hard facts for long enough. I want to help."

"But your exams . . ."

"I'm on study leave for the next two weeks. I can take care of Mum *and* study. You don't need to do it all."

"Okay," Rachel said at last. She had more help than she knew what to do with now, and it felt strange. Uncomfortable. "Okay. And Meghan will help too."

Lily didn't reply, but she didn't need to. Meghan wasn't there, and Rachel had no idea when, or even if, she'd be back.

Not that she actually thought Meghan would abandon her son. Did she? Rachel mulled the question over as well as its impossible answer as Lily headed upstairs to study and she made chicken nuggets for Nathan. Would Meghan walk away one day like their father had? Rachel was half bracing herself for it, and yet she knew that was unfair. Meghan loved Nathan. She'd chosen to have him, after all. But her sister had always been unpredictable, from her six-year-old sulks to the silent retreat she'd beaten when Janice had fallen, to her choice to have a baby when there was no father in the picture and life was hard enough.

Rachel heard the front door open and then slow, quiet footsteps, like someone was trying hard not to be noticed. Rachel almost let her sister go upstairs undetected; she didn't have the energy for a battle, and that's what every conversation with Meghan ended up being. Besides, Nathan was happily watching the CBeebies channel in the other room; she didn't need Meghan to step up right this second.

The stair creaked and Rachel couldn't help herself. "Meghan." Silence. "Meghan, I know you're there. Can you come into the kitchen and tell me what the hell is going on with you?"

So it was going to be a battle, and Rachel had fired the opening shot. Meghan slunk into the kitchen, arms folded, face set in a sulk.

"Where have you been today?"

"Out."

Rachel stared hard at Meghan, nearly twenty-five years old and acting like a stroppy teen. "Come on, Meghan. Give me a real answer. You dumped your son on me for the entire day while I was dealing with Mum. Don't you think I deserve to know the truth?"

Meghan looked away, her greasy hair hiding her face. "I couldn't face it," she finally said, her voice low.

"It? You mean, *Mum*?"

Wordlessly, Meghan nodded, and Rachel held on to her temper. Just. "You think it's easy for me, Meghan? Andrew and I had to carry Mum into the house like she was a sack of potatoes. And with the way her back is, it can't have been fun for her, either." Tears started in her eyes, and she brushed them back impatiently, too angry to waste time on crying. "It was hard enough when Mum was bedridden. But now she's . . . now she's practically a vegetable. And you just scarper."

"I'm sorry." Meghan's voice was so low Rachel almost couldn't hear it. "I'm sorry, okay? I know I should have been here. But it was too hard."

Exasperated, Rachel turned back to the tin of beans in tomato sauce she'd been opening, to go with the chicken nuggets she'd shoved in the oven. "Why can't we eat proper food?" she said, and shoved the tin away, sending it spinning and spraying tomato sauce over the counter like drops of orange blood.

"You're the one who does the Tesco order."

"I *know*." She took a deep breath, willing the excess emotion down. There was no point to it now; she didn't have the luxury to indulge in tears or sulks the way Meghan did. She never had. "Look, Meghan. Something is going on with you. You don't look well."

"Thanks a lot."

"I mean it. I know things haven't been easy between us these last few years—"

"Don't you mean ever?" Meghan interjected, and Rachel sighed.

"Fine, ever. I know we haven't gotten along. I know I nag you about work and Mum and Nathan—"

"So basically everything."

"Yes. Fine. But what I'm saying is we've managed. Mostly. But now I feel like it's all starting to crumble and I need to know why. What I really need is to have you on board, ready to help, but if I can't have that, at least let me know what is going on." She lowered her voice. "And whether you're going to leave me here with Nathan."

"Leave?" Meghan stared at her, shocked. "You think I'd actually *abandon* my son?"

"What am I supposed to think? You abandoned him for the whole day without even telling me where you were—"

"That was one *day*. I'd never leave Nathan for good. Never." Meghan's chest heaved, and her eyes looked wild. Rachel held up a placating hand.

"Fine. I believe you. But tell me what is going on."

Rachel didn't think her sister would answer. She stayed silent, chewing her lip, her arms wrapped around her body as if she were cold. "I think it's my fault," she finally whispered.

"Your fault?" Rachel stared at her, uncomprehending. "What is your fault?"

"Mum's stroke. It's my fault."

A big part of Rachel wanted to dismiss Meghan's concern, tell her she was being ridiculous, but she also felt the cold wave of trepidation sweep through her body. "Why?" she asked. "Why on earth would you think that?"

"Because." Meghan bit her lip hard enough for Rachel to see a drop of blood well on it before she licked it away. "I upped her meds."

"You—what? You mean you got a higher dosage from the doctor?" A few years ago Janice had switched from Percocet to OxyContin, and then a few months ago her OxyContin dosage had gone from ten milligrams to twenty. But looking at Meghan's face, Rachel knew that wasn't what her sister meant.

"I gave her more OxyContin than was prescribed." Meghan's voice was low. "That time she said they fell in the toilet? They hadn't. She'd just taken them all."

"What?" Rachel's mouth opened and closed as she struggled to find the words, to form them. "Meghan, don't you realize how dangerous that was? OxyContin is a very strong drug—"

"I *know*. But you don't know what it's like—you've never known what it's like—to be home with Mum all day!" Her voice came out in a desperate screech, tears starting in her eyes, trickling down her blotchy face. "How much pain she's in, how hard she has it. How she moans and *begs*. You're never there, Rachel. You think you are. You think you're working harder than anyone, but you're *never there*."

The accusation in Meghan's voice made Rachel reel back as if she'd been struck. She felt the words like hammer blows, shattering her illusions. She'd thought Meghan had had it easy, lounging around with

Nathan and Mum, watching *Real Housewives* and eating crisps. And there had been some of that. Rachel had seen the evidence herself.

"If you had it so hard," she asked, "why didn't you tell me? Why did you just give Mum more drugs without even asking?"

"Because you never wanted to know. I know you think I'm lazy. And maybe I am. Maybe I should have worked every night at the pub or somewhere else, but you've never even listened."

"You've never told me!" Rachel's voice rose to match Meghan's. "How on earth could I know how difficult you were finding things, if you never told me?"

"Because you never asked. You come in every evening moaning about how messy the kitchen is, how Nathan is such trouble, doubting that I've even looked in on Mum. What am I supposed to think? That you'd believe a word I said?"

Rachel sank onto a chair. Her head was spinning and starting to ache. "Tell me when this started."

"Which part?"

"The OxyContin," she snapped. "The overdose."

"It wasn't . . . I didn't think of it like that. She wasn't overdosing."

"She was having more than her prescription, Meghan. That's called an overdose."

"But it wasn't like that," Meghan insisted. "It was just a little extra, to take the edge off. The doctor had upped it once, and he even said he might have to do it again."

"So you thought you'd prescribe it yourself?"

Meghan's expression hardened. "You really don't know what it's been like. How much pain she's been in."

"Maybe she hasn't told me because she didn't want to admit she's taking so many damn pills!" Distantly Rachel knew she was being unfair, even cruel. Distantly she recognized the truth of what Meghan was saying, wrapped up as it was in a lot of self-justification. Rachel *hadn't* been there. Working eight or ten hours a day scrubbing floors and cleaning toilets might actually have been easier than being stuck at home with a fussy baby and an invalid mother. Distantly she recognized that perhaps she'd always known that, and she felt a hot rush of shame.

"So how much OxyContin did you give her?" she finally asked.

"Just a couple of extra pills a day. Sometimes not even that. Only when she really seemed to need them . . ."

"She might have been addicted, Meghan—"

"I looked that up on the Internet. That whole addiction-to-prescription-pills thing is mostly a myth. It's not addiction if you actually need them to manage your pain."

"If that's the case, you go to your doctor and ask for more. Why didn't you tell the GP about this?"

"It was easier just to do it," Meghan mumbled. "And make excuses for why she needed more. You'd be surprised at how easy it is."

"I *am*. I am surprised by all of this." She subsided into silence; it felt impossible to order her thoughts. "So why do you think you're to blame for Mum's stroke?"

"What if . . . ? What if it was caused by too much OxyContin?" Meghan's voice was barely a whisper. "The last few weeks she'd been asking for more and more. I tried to fob her off, but . . ."

"So you do think she overdosed."

"I don't know," Meghan cried. "But that's what I'm afraid of. And I'm afraid of taking care of her now, of how much work it will be. You'll just go on cleaning houses. I'm the one who will pick up the slack."

"You've never picked up the slack," Rachel retorted before she could stop herself.

"See what I mean? You've never believed I do anything around here."

Rachel took a deep, steadying breath. "First things first. I don't think the OxyContin caused her stroke."

Wary relief flashed across Meghan's face. "You don't?"

"Mr. Greaves never mentioned it, and they've done loads of blood tests. Besides, she was a ticking time bomb, with her smoking and weight. But we can check. Have you looked on the Internet?"

"I didn't want to."

Sighing, Rachel heaved herself up and went into the sitting room. Nathan was curled up on the sofa, asleep. A CBeebies presenter was showing luridly colored birthday cards to the TV screen. Rachel turned the TV off and then booted up the computer in the corner of the room.

Meghan stood beside her, biting her already ragged nails and shifting from foot to foot.

Rachel clicked on the Internet browser and typed *OxyContin overdose causing stroke.*

"Isn't that a little biased?" Meghan muttered.

"Do you want to know or not?"

"An Internet search doesn't mean anything, anyway."

Rachel didn't answer as she clicked and waited for the results to come up. Hartley-by-the-Sea's Internet was, according to the *Westmorland Gazette,* the slowest in the county.

Finally the results came up, and she clicked on the first one, a question on one of the many self-help medical sites, and read the answer. "OxyContin is not associated with stroke, although it has a variety of side effects, including anxiety, sedation, insomnia, mood changes, et cetera. OxyContin in overdose gives pinpoint pupils, respiratory depression, and hypotension."

They were both silent for a second, and then Meghan let out her breath in a rush. "So it wasn't the OxyContin."

"So now you believe the Internet?"

Meghan managed a wry smile. "It's never wrong," she said, and Rachel let out a tired laugh. She glanced up at Meghan, ashamed to see how relieved her sister looked, how little she'd known about what Meghan was going through.

"You can knock that off your worry list, I suppose."

"Yeah."

They were both silent, staring at the computer screen. "I'm sorry, Meghan," Rachel said quietly. "I should have realized what you were going through. How hard it was for you."

Meghan lifted one bony shoulder in a shrug. "I could have said. And I know you work hard."

"Life's been pretty crap for both of us." Rachel sighed. "Maybe it will get better."

Meghan glanced towards their mother's bedroom door. "Maybe," she agreed without much conviction.

"I mean it," Rachel said, and she realized she was speaking the truth. "We've cleared the air and we can work together now. Things can get better. For all of us." And for once she thought she believed it.

28

Claire

HENRY PRICE'S BATHROOM SHOULD have been cordoned off, like Chernobyl. Claire surveyed the bristly hairs in the sink, the clogged drain of the shower, and the unflushed toilet, and decided this room definitely deserved a Zone of Exclusion. And she was required to clean it.

It was her first day taking on Rachel's cleaning jobs, and she'd actually been looking forward to it. It felt good to be helping someone, to be needed. She felt strong. Capable for once in her life.

Who knew? Maybe she could go into business with Rachel. Campbell and West Cleaners. She actually liked tidying things up, although Henry Price's bathroom was definitely testing her limits.

Forty-five minutes later she stripped off her rubber gloves in the kitchen and washed her hands, because it really had been that bad. Her mobile rang and she fished it out of her jeans.

"Hey, Rachel."

"How's it going?"

"I've survived Henry Price's bathroom. I think. The effects might manifest themselves later."

Rachel laughed, and Claire smiled. "I did warn you."

"Nothing could have prepared me for that. How are things at home?"

"Okay." Rachel didn't offer any more information, and Claire chose not to press. "If you're still game for this, you have Emily Hart this afternoon. I switched her from Thursday to Tuesday. Beware the twins."

"Riley and Rogan, right?"

"Yes. Good memory." Rachel paused. "Thank you, Claire."

"It's no problem. You don't have to keep thanking me."

"I know. I'm not used to accepting help."

"And I'm not used to giving it. This is good for both of us."

"If you say so," Rachel answered, and Claire could hear the smile in her voice.

As she hung up the phone, it occurred to her that she and Rachel were becoming proper friends, in a way they hadn't ever been when they were younger, when Claire had depended on Rachel and Rachel had done everything. Now they were starting to have a friendship of give and take, of mutual trust. It felt good.

The rest of Henry Price's house was on par with the bathroom. Claire worked steadily until her three hours were up, and she let herself out with the spare key he kept under a moldy-looking flowerpot on the front stoop. On to the Harts'.

She drove up the high street in Rachel's car, glancing briefly at the post office shop and wondering how Dan was. Yesterday he'd been as terse and monosyllabic as ever, and Claire had no idea how to get things back the way they'd been so briefly. Maybe they hadn't really been friends. Maybe Dan hadn't been warming up to her. She told herself she shouldn't care, that Dan Trenton was a miserable old sod who was going to live and die alone and unloved, but it didn't stop the twisting ache in her center at the thought of what she believed they'd almost had. She must have been delusional.

The Harts' house was as different from Henry Price's bachelor home as Claire could have imagined. The noise and mess hit her the moment she stepped across the threshold; she'd knocked twice but no one had answered, and so she'd opened the door herself. The TV was blaring, toddlers were screaming, and the front hall was littered with toys as well as two pairs of crumpled footie pajamas and two clearly dirty nappies.

"Hello?" Claire called cautiously, and followed the sound of the toddlers to the kitchen. Riley and Rogan were strapped into booster chairs with plates of what must have been lunch in front of them. Ketchup was smeared all over their faces and clothes and in their hair. Claire drew back at the sight.

"You must be Claire." A wan, harassed-looking woman smiled tiredly from where she was kneeling on the floor, cleaning up bits of hot dog and grapes that had been sliced in half. "Sorry. The twins have gone on a food strike. They won't eat anything."

"Just put it in their hair?" Claire surmised with a smile, and then bent to help retrieve the bits of food. "I guess Rachel told you I was coming."

"Yes. I didn't realize her mother was poorly. She never said anything."

"It's been going on for a while."

"Poor thing. She's always been so good about listening to me moan about everything." Emily straightened and touched her middle self-consciously. "I'm pregnant. I just found out."

"Oh. Congratulations."

"Rachel listened to me go on about it last week. We weren't trying, you see."

"Ah. Right."

"Of course, children are always a blessing, but I'm afraid I gave Rachel an earful last week." Emily smiled apologetically, and Claire tried for an understanding nod back. She'd never even thought about having children. Hugh had always said he didn't want any, and Claire had gone along with it because she couldn't imagine actually being responsible for another person. Yet another way she'd bent to someone else's will, and yet now she wondered if she actually would like children one day. Glancing at Riley and Rogan, she thought she might, far into the future.

"Shall I crack on, then?" she asked when Emily didn't say anything else. The twins had started banging their spoons on the table and Emily was still standing with one hand on her stomach, staring off into space.

"Oh, already?" she said, sounding surprised. "Rachel always makes a cup of tea...."

"Oh, of course." Quickly Claire moved to the shiny chrome kettle perched by the sink. "I'm happy to make you a cup of tea." She filled the kettle and, feeling acutely self-conscious, searched for a mug and tea bag while Emily watched. It seemed to take an age for the kettle to boil and then for the tea to steep, and then it took Claire a moment to find the fridge because it had a wood-paneled front like the cupboards. She fished the tea bag out with a spoon and looked around for the bin, but it seemed as hidden as the fridge. She lobbed it in the sink and then finally, thankfully, handed Emily her tea. Mission accomplished.

"Oh..." There was no disguising the disappointment in Emily's voice. What had she done wrong? Maybe Emily didn't take milk, or the tea was too weak, or... something. Claire wasn't Rachel, at any rate. "Thank you," Emily finally said, and with a little apologetic sort of smile, she put the mug down to wipe Riley's and Rogan's faces and then unbuckle them from their seats. "We'll be in the playroom," she said, sounding forlorn, and Claire breathed a sigh of relief when they all left and she could get on with things.

By the end of the day she was tired, dirty, and yet quietly elated by her success. She'd cleaned three houses and she'd done a decent job, although Emily Hart had looked a little let down. Her house was clean at least, even if it lasted for only five minutes. Riley and Rogan had dumped what looked like a vat of Play-Doh onto the freshly mopped, still slightly damp kitchen floor as Claire had been putting on her coat.

Now she parked in front of Rachel's house, hauled out the cleaning supplies, and knocked on the front door.

Meghan answered, looking slightly better than she had the last time Claire had seen her. Nathan was balanced on her hip, and her hair looked washed, her face clear. "You survived."

"Just." Claire grinned, still high on her sense of accomplishment. "Actually, it was fine."

Rachel came to the door, gently nudging Meghan out of the way. "Thanks again," she said. "I really appreciate it."

"I enjoyed it, actually, Henry Price's bathroom aside."

"You managed the Harts all right?"

"Yes, but Emily seemed a bit . . . I don't know, disappointed."

"She just wanted a chat, probably," Rachel answered. "Sometimes I think it's the highlight of her week."

"A chat?"

"Most days I make us a cup of tea and we have a natter for twenty minutes or so before I start cleaning. I think she appreciates the adult conversation, such as it is."

"Oh." Claire thought of the cup of tea she'd made for Emily, pushing it into her hands, clearly itching to get on with her job. "I think I botched that. Sorry."

"You'll know for next time." Rachel hesitated. "Although there doesn't have to be a next time. Meghan and Lily are going to help with Mum, so I can really—"

"I like doing it," Claire cut across her. "Really."

Rachel hesitated, torn, Claire suspected, between pride and need. "Okay," she said at last. "For now it helps. I'll pay you, of course—"

"You don't have to pay me—"

"You deserve it. And it helps, to keep the clients. So thank you."

Claire smiled wryly. "You don't have to keep saying thank you, Rachel. You've certainly done enough for me over the years."

Rachel raised her eyebrows. "Over the years?"

"I mean before. Back when we were little. You stood before me and the world, or at least the rest of the Year Two."

"I'm not sure that was a good thing," Rachel answered, but she was smiling. "Look, do you want to come in for a cup of tea?"

The invitation sounded awkward but heartfelt. Claire grinned. "Sure," she said, and stepped inside.

An hour later she headed down the high street, having had a somewhat surprisingly enjoyable time with Rachel, drinking tea and navigating the chaos of the Campbell household. Nathan had run in and out, sometimes with no pants on, and Lily had thrown herself on her sofa and moaned about her biology exam in two weeks' time while Rachel had, with seeming effort, restrained from nagging her sister about studying. It had been nice, in a strange and surprising way.

Now the sky was gray and the air fresh and damp with the promise of rain. It was chilly enough to warrant a coat, even though the flowers were out in the window boxes and the cherry trees down by the church had blossoms like giant pink puffballs. No matter how cold or wet it was, spring came anyway, a determined, relentless reawakening.

Claire's steps slowed as she came to the post office; it was just before seven, and Dan would be starting to close up. She could see the light was on, and if she stood on her tiptoes she could see the top of his head, standing as he was behind the till. She wanted to go inside, but what would she say?

She started to walk past and then stopped. She was trying to change her life. Trying to take control of it, hard as that had been, and accepting Dan's slouch back to the status quo was not being in control or being brave.

Resolutely she turned around and opened the door of the shop. The warmth and comfort of the place hit her first: the neat shelves, the old-fashioned sweet jars that had proved to be a big hit with the schoolchildren, even the smell of the leftover meat pies drying out under the heat lamps—all of it filled her with an ache of familiarity. She loved it here.

"What are you doing here?" Dan asked. He didn't sound unfriendly, but his voice was far from welcoming.

"Can't I come say hello?" He looked nonplussed. And he didn't say hello back. "Dan . . ." This was far more awkward than she'd hoped it would be. She didn't even know what she was going to say, what she wanted. "I thought we were friends," she finally blurted, and Dan stared at her.

"Friends?"

"Yes. Friends. But lately you've been so . . ." She searched for a word. "Surly." Dan didn't answer, and she continued, each word an agony. "Is it something I've done? To make you change—"

"You didn't do anything, Claire." Dan sighed and came out from behind the till. Claire thought he was coming towards her—to push her out of the shop, maybe—but he went outside and pulled the iron shutters down over the windows, leaving her feeling entombed in the shadowy interior. He came back in and started flicking off lights, and Claire realized he wasn't going to say anything else.

"So what's going on?" she asked.

"Why does something have to be going on?"

"Because you acted one way and now you're acting another. And usually that means something has changed."

He stood by the door, one hand on the main light switch, about to plunge them into darkness. Claire dared to take a step towards him, even to put a hand on his arm.

"I like you, Dan. I thought you liked me." Inwardly she cringed at how needy she sounded, but another part of her was registering the solid warmth of Dan's arm under her hand, the heat of his body. He was so strong he could crush her in one massive fist, and yet she didn't feel threatened or even intimidated. She felt . . . safe. And tingly.

She glanced up at him, realizing with a jolt how close his face was. He was looking down at her, frowning slightly, his eyes narrowed.

"Dan . . ." she began, and she imagined standing on her tiptoes, brushing her lips across his. She imagined him taking her in those massive arms, cradling her. Kissing her back. She almost did it. She came so close, her feet tensing as she went on her tiptoes, took a breath—

Then Dan flicked off the lights and moved away. Claire rocked on her feet, throwing out a hand to brace herself against the wall. With the shutters down and the lights off, she couldn't see a thing.

"Go home, Claire," Dan said, and stinging with rejection, she went.

The next morning Dan didn't mention that moment, if it had even been a moment, and Claire went about her work without engaging him in conversation. So Dan didn't want to be her friend or anything else. She'd get over it. He was a mean-tempered ass, anyway.

At lunchtime he took Bunny for a walk, and the sight of the springer mix—that's what Dan thought she was, anyway—leaning lovingly against his side practically put a lump in Claire's throat. He wasn't that much of an ass. But never mind.

She tended the shop alone, managing the cigarettes and Lottery cards, the cash register no longer the frightening and intricate machine it had been just a little over a month ago. She'd changed. She'd grown, even if it was just in small ways. Even if she wanted to change a little more.

Dan returned with Bunny and resumed his place behind the till; Claire went back to checking inventory. She opened a just-delivered box of groceries, surprised to see upmarket pasta sauces inside rather than the tins of Spam and Fray Bentos "Boozy" pies.

She glanced up at Dan. "This is new."

He shrugged, not looking at her. "I'm diversifying."

They spent the rest of the afternoon in silence, but Claire felt a little better. A little hopeful. She even dared to ask Dan if he'd go to the pub quiz on Thursday. "Eleanor Carwell is counting on you, you know."

"I don't think so."

"You're a wimp—you know that?" The words rang out before Claire could think better of them. Suddenly she was angry. It had been a long time since she'd let herself feel angry, since she hadn't assumed it was all her fault and tripped over herself to apologize.

"A *wimp*?"

"A coward. An emotional coward. It's cowardly to keep yourself from having friends. I get that you were hurt by your wife—"

"Ex-wife," Dan interjected, biting off the two words. He'd folded his arms in that menacing way he had, making Claire swallow hard before she continued resolutely.

"Ex-wife, then, and your brother. I've been hurt too. It sucks." She took a deep breath; her whole body was shaking. "But you can move on, Dan. You can. Otherwise you'll just atrophy here in this shop. You'll die in your bed upstairs, choking on a rubbery piece of Spam, and no one will discover your body for months."

"They would," Dan answered tonelessly. "Because they'd notice when I didn't open the shop."

"*I* was the one who realized something was wrong when you didn't open the shop," Claire exclaimed. "*I* was the one who cared enough to make sure you hadn't drowned in the bathtub!" Furious now, she crossed the shop to poke him in the chest. *Ouch.* "I'm the one who is trying to be your friend, you stubborn old . . ." She trailed off, at a loss for words, and Dan wrapped his hand around her finger still poking into his iron-hard chest.

"Stubborn old what?" he asked quietly.

"Poop," Claire blurted.

Dan arched an eyebrow. *"Poop?"*

"I've been around a lot of toddlers lately," she muttered. She was acutely aware of his hand wrapped around her finger. Her heart was hammering with anticipation, which was stupid because nothing was going to happen.

"Why do you care?" he asked, his hand still wrapped around her finger.

"Because I like you."

"What do you like?"

"You—"

"I mean about me." His tone was flat, his expression hard. "What do you like about me?"

"I like that you look out for people, even if you pretend you don't. I like that you have a rescue dog and that you have a sense of humor so dry it's like living in the Sahara. I like that you're neat, because I am too."

"That's it?"

"What do you mean, that's it?" she demanded. "You're asking me to bare my soul while you're not telling me anything. Do you care about me?" The second the words were out of her mouth she regretted them. Dan had never indicated that he cared about her. She'd just set herself up for a massive rejection.

"You're completely exasperating," Dan said. "And practically useless. You don't even realize how entitled you are, although you think you do."

"Right." Her voice wobbled alarmingly. Yet another person was telling her what a waste of space she was. Why should she be surprised?

"And you work harder than anyone I've known," Dan continued. "And you're stronger than you realize. And you care about people, even grumpy old women like Eleanor Carwell."

Claire managed a crooked smile. "She's not that grumpy."

"Not as grumpy as me?"

"Not by a long shot."

He smiled then, the corner of his mouth lifting, and Claire had to keep herself from running into his arms. "So . . ."

"So I'll see you tomorrow night," he said, and with a grin she realized he meant the pub quiz.

At the quiz Eleanor Carwell flirted with him outrageously, practically cooing and making Claire laugh. Dan met her gaze once, his mouth curving in the tiniest of smiles, and for a second it felt like they were sharing an in-joke, but maybe not. She was terrible at figuring relationships out. She'd never had to before; she'd simply done what she was told.

She thought of her first date with Hugh, how he'd come to the villa she'd been showing to a retired couple and told her he was taking her out to the best restaurant in the Algarve. It had been a statement, a command, and Claire hadn't thought to protest. He'd taken her to a restaurant that had minuscule portions of artistically arranged seafood; Claire had always hated fish, but she'd eaten the scallops Hugh had ordered for her because that was what she did. She hadn't protested when he'd insisted on ordering for both of them, so why would she protest when he ordered something she didn't like?

She'd been utterly spineless, an indifferent spectator of her own life, removed from everything going on around her. Thank God Hugh had gotten tired of her and insisted she go to rehab. At least he'd woken her up, jolted her out of her catatonic lethargy.

But being awake and alive was as hard as it was invigorating; she needed to act, and sometimes she wasn't sure *how*.

A week slipped by, and May marched into June, the days chilly and gray and far from what Claire, after four years in Portugal, thought of as summer, although the residents of Hartley-by-the-Sea still went about in short sleeves and shorts. Life had eased into a pattern; she cleaned houses, worked in the shop, and wondered how to shift the status quo.

Andrew came back on the weekend and spent an inordinate amount of time at the Campbells' house; Claire learned to sit down with Emily Hart and let her moan over a cup of tea. She even changed Riley's and Rogan's nappies; unfortunately, she put them on backwards.

Dan, Eleanor, and Lily came out for another pub quiz, and as a team they earned eleven points, their personal best so far.

And all the while Claire felt that something needed to shift, to change or hopefully to grow; she just didn't know what or how. Then she came back from work on Friday and saw a car in the driveway of Four Gables, a sleek black Mercedes that sent a tremor of trepidation ricocheting through her. Her parents were home.

29

~

Rachel

"ARE YOU DATING ANDREW West?"

"What?" Rachel glanced back over her shoulder to see Meghan standing in the doorway of the kitchen, her hands planted on her bony hips.

"I think you heard me."

"Dating?" Rachel repeated, simply to stall for time. "Of course not."

"He's been around here an awful lot."

"Two weekends," Rachel dismissed. "He's being kind."

"It doesn't seem like pity to me."

"I didn't say pity." She didn't know what was going on with her and Andrew, but she certainly wasn't about to talk to Meghan about it. Things had eased up a bit between them, but they were hardly confidantes. And she hated how Meghan had found her weak spot so easily and slipped the blade right in, all with a smile on her face. *Pity.* God, she hoped not.

"What's going on with you and Mystery Man, anyway?" Rachel asked. "You haven't seen him much this week."

"You asked me to be around."

"Since when does what I've asked make a difference?"

Meghan sighed. "The truth is, he's married."

The statement, delivered so flatly, so hopelessly, made Rachel turn around from where she'd been scrubbing a pan in the sink. "Seriously?"

Meghan's face was sober, all traces of sisterly malice gone. "Seriously."

"Oh, Meghan." Rachel sorted through all the responses she instinctively wanted to say—*How could you?* being at the top of the list—and came up with "That sucks."

Meghan gave a hollow laugh. "Yeah. It does."

"Why . . . ?"

"I didn't do it on purpose," Meghan said. "No one wants to have an affair with a married bloke."

"So what happened?"

"He came into the pub one night. He wasn't a regular. I'd never seen him before. He started chatting me up, and then he asked if I wanted to get a proper drink somewhere else, after my shift."

"And you went? With a stranger?"

"Just down to Raymond's. I wasn't going to get in his car or anything like that." Meghan drew a shaky breath and pushed a hand through her hair. "He was nice, Rachel, okay? And interesting. And even better, he was interested in me. Do you know how long it's been since someone's seemed interested in me?"

"Do you know how long it's been for me?"

"Are we having a competition about how unlovable we are?"

Rachel cracked a small smile. "Maybe." She turned back to the pan in the sink, its bottom blackened from about a thousand grilled sausages. "Did you know he was married then?"

Meghan was silent for a long moment. "I suspected," she said at last. "But I pretended I didn't."

"Pretended to yourself?" Rachel glanced back at her sister, and Meghan lifted her chin.

"Yeah. I did."

Could she really criticize? Rachel sighed. "Are you still seeing him?"

"I don't know." Meghan folded her arms, lowered her head. "He hasn't called in a while."

"You mean he broke it off with you?" Rachel had hoped her sister had had enough self-respect to break it off first.

"It looks that way. I told him about Nathan." She paused. "He didn't like that I had a kid."

"Why not?"

"Because I'd start thinking of him as a father for Nathan, I suppose. He wanted a fling, and he was afraid I wanted more. So he scarpered." She let out a hard laugh. "It's happened only about a million times before, all over the world."

Rachel hesitated. "Is that what happened with Nathan's dad?"

Meghan stilled, her arms wrapped around her middle, her expression turning guarded. "Not exactly. He wasn't in the picture to begin with."

"You've never talked about him."

"You've never asked."

"That's because it was glaringly obvious you didn't want me to." Rachel turned off the taps, leaving the blackened pan to soak. She'd had enough of useless scrubbing. "Do you want me to now?"

Meghan didn't answer for a moment. Rachel waited, not sure how to navigate this fragile peace. "He wasn't from here," Meghan said finally. "He was hiking with some friends from uni. I met him down at the beach."

"And?"

"And? What do you think?" Meghan rolled her eyes. "We had a couple of beers down on the beach and got it on. Nathan was the result. By the time I knew I was up the duff, he was halfway to Robin Hood's Bay."

"It only takes ten days to hike to Robin Hood's Bay."

"Whatever. He was back home, then, in Southampton or wherever."

"And you didn't try to get in touch?"

Meghan was silent for a long moment, her face averted. "I tried. I looked him up on Facebook." A pause as she twirled a strand of hair around her finger and then tugged hard. "He refused my friend request. Dangers of dating in the cyber age, I suppose."

Rachel processed that for a few seconds. "You didn't try to get in touch another way?"

"I sent him a message on Facebook. It's probably in his 'other' folder. Or he just ignored it. What else was I supposed to do?" She sighed impatiently. "He was eighteen, Rachel, about to start university. I don't think he wanted a kid with the tart he hooked up with while hiking."

"But you wanted a kid." Rachel paused, not sure how to ask the next question. Meghan guessed it anyway.

"Why did I keep Nathan?" she asked, her voice low even though he was safely asleep upstairs. "Because I wanted someone to love me. Someone who *has* to love me, because that's what kids do." She took a quick, hitched breath. "You're not the only one who was affected by Dad leaving the way he did. I know you were his favorite, but I missed him too."

They never talked about their father. Never talked about how he walked out one day, never to return or even to look back. Never to send a single e-mail or text or postcard. What kind of dad did that? Rachel remembered sitting on his shoulders while they watched the rugby in Whitehaven, flying a kite on the beach, the fierce wind reducing it to tatters. She remembered sitting with him outside in the garden while he whittled a piece of wood to make her a whistle. Meghan had memories like that as well; Rachel had simply never considered them before.

"Of course you did." She felt her throat close up. "I never meant to act as if you didn't. . . ."

"No? You acted like you were the only one who was hurt by Dad's leaving. Like he left you and not all of us." Meghan spoke flatly, without reproach, but Rachel felt skewered.

"Meghan, I didn't . . ." She trailed off, unable to continue. "I'm sorry," she said. "I think I felt I'd lost the most by having to leave Durham." The admission was both obvious and painful.

"I know. You were escaping." Meghan sighed, pushing her hair away from her face. "I thought about not calling you."

"What? How on earth would you have coped?"

"I realized I couldn't, not with Lily and Mum and school. But I waited." She paused, her level gaze meeting Rachel's. "I waited three days before I called you. Because I knew it would be worst for you."

Rachel blinked, stunned by her sister's admission. "Meghan, I'm sorry."

"For Dad leaving? That wasn't your fault."

"No, for—for being such a bitch." Rachel let out a shaky laugh. "For thinking I was doing it all when I really wasn't."

"Well." Meghan smiled and shrugged. "To be fair, you were doing most of it."

"I don't know about that," Rachel said quietly.

"Well." Meghan sniffed and looked away. "That's why I kept Nathan. Because I wanted someone to love me. Kind of hard for you to understand, I know—"

"It's not hard for me to understand—"

"You don't seem to need anyone. I always feel like a completely pathetic loser next to you."

Meghan spoke without spite, surprising Rachel with her hard honesty. "If I don't seem to need anyone," she answered, "it's because I don't let myself. I needed Dad, and look where that got me."

"You could do something else now," Meghan said after a moment. "You don't have to take care of us anymore, Rachel."

Rachel stared at her sister, the proud tilt of her chin, the need visible in her eyes. "I don't want to abandon you."

"You won't. I've been thinking about quitting at the pub and starting a child-minding business. I know it will be difficult with Mum, but the hours would be better for me and I can work from home, with Nathan there. Abby Rhodes has said she'd love to have Noah here."

"What?" Rachel shook her head slowly. "I had no idea."

"I know. And it might be too difficult." She glanced wryly around the kitchen. "We'd have to keep the house clean, for starters. Safeguarding rules and all that." She smiled uncertainly, and Rachel smiled back. She felt as if Meghan had just off-loaded a whole lot of information, and she needed time to process it.

"Well," she finally said. "Plans."

"You should have plans too. You could do a part-time course or something. . . ."

"Actually, I have looked into it." She'd written the University of Lancaster for information on part-time degree courses. The brochure had come last week, and she hadn't yet dared to open it. Hope was dangerous. Losing it was hard. "Mum is going to need full-time care, Meghan. We can divide it between us, but—"

"And don't forget Lily."

"Lily will be going to university—"

"Maybe," Meghan said quietly, "you'd better ask her about that."

Rachel felt a clanging inside her, as if she'd missed the last step in the staircase. "What do you know that I don't?"

"Nothing," Meghan answered. "Because I think you already know it. But you're pretending you don't, just like I did."

Rachel shook her head. "No . . ."

"She doesn't like biology, Rachel. She doesn't want to go to Durham. You can't foist your dreams onto somebody else."

"Her exam is in a *week*."

Meghan shrugged. "That doesn't change anything."

A little while later Rachel stood in the doorway of her mother's bedroom and watched as Lily showed Janice the Mad Scientist cartoon strip. Rachel had glanced at a few of the drawings, quick pen strokes that managed to capture the lovable ditziness of the scientist whose experiments always went wrong but managed to produce good results. Janice's eyes were following the cartoon, although she couldn't speak. She managed to nod in what seemed like approval, and Lily smiled.

"And here's another one. . . ." She showed her mother another drawing, and Janice's mouth jerked in a half smile; the left side of her face was still paralyzed.

Rachel leaned against the doorway, taking in a scene she'd never expected to see. Lily enjoying time with her mother, when she'd always avoided her before. Things actually working, even if it was in a completely unexpected way.

Lily looked up and caught her eye, and Rachel stepped into the room. "Hey there," she said, smiling at her mother, whose face jerked again in response. "Those cartoons are pretty cool, aren't they?"

"I didn't think you'd looked at them," Lily said. Her voice sounded guarded, unsure.

"I glanced at a few when I was taking your dirty washing from your room. May I see them now, though? Properly?"

Wordlessly, Lily handed the sheets over, and Rachel spent a few minutes silently studying the drawings, smiling a bit as Mad Scientist Girl's potion exploded in a sea of bubbles, creating a soft landing for her sidekick cat, who had been thrown up in the air by the explosion. "Clever," she murmured.

"You think so?"

"Yes." Rachel looked up, taking a deep breath. "How's your studying going?" She'd meant the question as an opener, a way to talk about things, but Lily's expression closed up and she reached for her drawings. Rachel handed them to her without a word.

"Fine." She glanced at Janice, who was drifting into a doze. "I guess she wants to sleep," she said, and tiptoed out of the room. Rachel followed.

"Lily," she called. Her sister was already halfway up the stairs. With a gusty sigh she stopped and turned around.

"What?"

Rachel stared at her, not wanting to ask her about what she wanted. Not wanting to shed doubt or project possibility into a situation that had been so certain. "Just a few more weeks," she said, knowing she was chickening out. "Then it will all be over."

Lily stared at her for a moment, her face expressionless. "Yes," she agreed. "It will."

In her own room Rachel reached for the thick white envelope from the University of Lancaster and slit the top. She pulled out the glossy brochure and thumbed through the pages, glancing at the photographs of laughing students with backpacks slung over their shoulders, everyone looking as if they were having the time of their lives.

And for a second she imagined how it could work. She'd go down to Lancaster twice a week; maybe Claire could take over some of her houses, even go halves in the business. Meghan could take more on with Mum, and Lily would be at uni. It would be crazy and hectic, but in a good way. They'd all be living their dreams. Even if Lily didn't realize what hers was yet. Why shouldn't she try for it? It was easy enough to fill out an application online. It was the hoping that was hard.

Impulsively, she reached for her phone and scrolled down for Andrew's contact.

He answered on the first ring. "Rachel?"

"I'm looking at the University of Lancaster brochure."

"And?" His voice was careful, cautious.

"And I'm thinking maybe it could work. Maybe." Her fingers were clenched around her phone and her heart had started thumping. Amazing how difficult it was to admit that much.

"That's great news," Andrew said, and Rachel could hear the genuine warmth in his voice. "Let me take you out to celebrate."

"To celebrate looking at the brochure?" Rachel said with a laugh. "I haven't done all that much, Andrew."

"To celebrate you getting in," Andrew answered. "And starting your course."

She felt dizzy, imagining it. Andrew had been right. Settling for something was better than having nothing at all. Why had she kept herself from it for so long?

She knew the answer to that. Because of fear as well as pride.

"Rachel?" Andrew prompted gently, and she realized she'd been silent, just breathing into the phone. "We'll go somewhere really classy," he promised her. "Like Raymond's."

She laughed then, a shaky relief pouring through her. "Okay," she said. "I'd love that."

Still high with possibility, Rachel fired off a text to Claire. *What do you say you take on part of Campbell Cleaners permanently? If you're really thinking of staying in Hartley-by-the-Sea?* She sent it before she could think better of it, before she considered how much of herself she was putting out there.

For once she wasn't going to hold herself back. She was going to let herself dream, and see where it took her.

30

Claire

CLAIRE LAY IN BED and listened to the murmur of her parents' voices downstairs. No doubt they were talking about her, trying to manage her as always. It had been paralyzing, coming into the house to confront them. Not that she'd actually done any confronting.

No, she'd stood there with her head bowed, practically cowering, as her mother fluttered around her and her father remained silent, radiating disapproval.

"Darling, we've been so worried," Marie had exclaimed, air-kissing both of Claire's cheeks before she stepped back and examined her. "You look pale and a bit skinny. Not that you can be too thin, but are you eating well?"

"I'm eating fine," Claire had said. She'd forced herself to look up and face them. Her mother's sharp features were pursed with that familiar mixture of annoyance and concern that Claire always seemed to cause. "I'm fine," she'd added, and her voice came out a little firmer.

"Claire, how on earth can you be fine? You've run all the way to Cumbria, and Andrew says you're working in the post office...." Marie had let out an uncertain laugh. "Honestly, I thought he was joking."

"What's wrong with working in the post office?" Claire had asked.

"Not that I'm actually working in the post office. I have to be trained to do that."

Her mother had laughed again, only to trail off uncertainly. "Claire, really. This isn't . . . Look, I understand you needed a bit of a break, especially after Hugh . . ." Her mother's voice turned tearful and tragic, and Claire had suppressed a sigh.

"I'm not actually all that broken up about Hugh."

"It's admirable, of course, to put a good face on it—"

"I'm not putting a good face on it—"

"But that's all in the past anyway." Marie brought her hands together in a sort of clap. "The reason we've come all this way is because Daddy has arranged a job for you down in London. A proper job."

Claire had felt a leaden sense of inevitability fall over her, weighing her down. "What kind of proper job?"

"Working for a charitable foundation. Something with sport . . ." Marie had glanced at her husband. "What is it, Edward?"

"The Foundation for Promising Athletes," he'd said, his voice a rumble, his arms folded. Sitting there so silent and disapproving, he reminded Claire of Dan. Except Dan was a lot nicer.

"Sounds very . . . sporty," Claire had managed. "So what does it do?"

"Oh, it scouts for athletes from all around the country," Marie had enthused. "It's found the number twenty-two-ranked tennis player—"

"And it's a charitable foundation?" Claire had interjected. "It sounds like a talent agency."

"It's not like that." Marie had drawn back, affronted. "It runs camps and things. For the disadvantaged. They just have to show ability. Isn't that right, Edward?"

Her father nodded. Claire had sighed. Her parents had been home for ten minutes and she already felt overwhelmed, knocked back by the sheer force of her mother's will. She didn't want to go to London and work for some tony foundation, but at that moment she didn't have the energy to explain that to her mother.

Fortunately, her parents had left it, no doubt assuming Claire would fall in with their plans as she always did. And after an interminable dinner at Raymond's, Claire had excused herself and escaped to her bedroom, glad not to have to face her parents till the morning.

Lying in bed, she wondered what they were saying about her. She hadn't possessed the courage to order a glass of wine with her meal that night; her parents had exchanged relieved looks when she'd asked for sparkling water. Now she imagined them whispering about her, how wan she looked, how much better her life in London would be. Telling them no was going to take all the strength she had.

The next morning her mother was in the kitchen when Claire came downstairs, ready to clean two of Rachel's jobs that she'd switched to Saturday.

"You're up early," Marie said brightly as she sipped a black coffee, her smartphone in her other hand.

"I'm going to work."

"Work?" Marie looked blank. "You mean at the post office? But, Claire—"

"No, not at the post office. I'm cleaning houses for Rachel Campbell." Marie gaped at her, utterly flummoxed. "I enjoy it," Claire said with an edge of defiance. "And I have responsibilities."

"Of course you do," Marie agreed. She sounded as if she were soothing a skittish colt. "Of course you do. But . . . you can tell Rachel you can't do it after today. And you can give your notice at the post office."

Claire didn't bother to reply. She just took a banana from the bowl and reached for her coat. Outside the sun was shining, but the wind was cold. She lowered her head against it, calling herself a coward. An emotional coward, just like Dan, because she hadn't disagreed with her mother. Because part of her felt it would be safer, easier, to slink back to London than to keep trying to carve out a life for herself here, with people she wasn't even sure wanted her around.

On the way to Rachel's she saw that Dan was in the post office when she arrived, and impulsively Claire stepped inside.

"What are you doing here?" he asked, and she just shrugged. Dan peered at her from behind the Plexiglas. "Claire? Is everything all right?"

"No." Her voice wobbled, and she mentally shook her head at herself. *Now* Dan actually showed a modicum of interest in her. "It's bloody awful at the moment. My parents just arrived."

"You don't get on with them?"

"Not particularly, although I doubt they would say that."

Dan came out from behind the post office counter. "What do you mean?"

"They've been managing my life forever, and they still think they can do it." She paused and then blurted, "They want me to go to London. My father's arranged a job for me, working for some sports charity."

Dan was silent for a long moment. "And?" he finally asked.

"And they're going to nag and pressure me to go until I cave, because that's what always happens."

"It's your choice, whether you go or not."

"I know, but it never feels that way. My parents are very forceful. And it isn't as if I've got a real life here." She glanced at him, daring him to object, to insist that she did. Dan stayed silent. "I mean, I'm not even a postal assistant yet," she half joked. "And working in a shop a few days a week? Living at home? I can't even afford to get a flat."

"So you want to go to London?"

"I don't know." But she did know, even if she didn't want to admit it to Dan. She wanted to stay in Hartley-by-the-Sea; she wanted Dan and Rachel and everyone else to tell her to stay. To insist on it, because they wanted her there. Because they needed her.

"It sounds like a decent situation," Dan remarked tonelessly. "Working in London. And it's more your thing, isn't it? City life. All that." He waved his hand vaguely.

"I've liked it here," she said, and then waited. Dan still said nothing. "But maybe . . ." She imagined taking the job, finding a flat her parents would pay for, falling in with her old circle of friends, a never-ending cycle of clubs and wine bars and parties. Maybe that really was her life. Maybe she'd just been playing at something different in Hartley-by-the-Sea.

"I think you should go for it, Claire," Dan said, and went back behind the post office counter. Claire couldn't make out his expression behind the Plexiglas. "It sounds like a good opportunity."

He almost sounded as if he wanted to get rid of her. And she was late for Rachel. "Okay then," Claire said finally. "Thanks for your input." She walked out of the shop without either of them saying another word.

Four hours later she'd finished her two cleaning jobs and stood in front of Rachel's house, pail of cleaning supplies in hand. Claire couldn't bear the thought of going back to Four Gables and facing her parents, and so she knocked on Rachel's door instead.

Meghan answered the door, looking unimpressed. "You've got a face like a lemon."

"Thanks."

"What's wrong?"

"Just life." Claire tried for a smile. "Is Rachel around?"

"Yes, but she's busy. I don't think she can fix your life on top of everything else."

Affronted, Claire drew back. "I didn't ask her to. I just cleaned two of her houses, actually—"

"Come in if you want," Meghan cut her off, and stepped aside.

The house was tidy for once, with all the coats on their hooks and the little hall table cleared of its usual drift of junk mail. Meghan looked better too, her face a little rounder, her eyes less wild. She inspected Claire for an uncomfortable moment before she nodded towards the kitchen. "She's in there."

Claire stepped into the kitchen to see Rachel sitting at the table, papers spread out in front of her.

"Claire—"

"Sorry. Am I interrupting you?"

"No, not really." Rachel tidied the papers into a pile. "Just going through a few things. How did the cleaning go?"

"Fine—"

Rachel looked at her more closely. "Are you all right?"

"Do I really look that awful?"

"No, but . . ." Rachel looked at her closely. "You look tired and—I don't know—lost."

Which was how she felt. "My parents came home yesterday."

"And?"

Rachel looked confused, which was just how Dan had looked. Having her parents return to their own house shouldn't be such a big deal. Such a tragedy. Of course it shouldn't.

"And they want me to move back to London. My father has arranged a job for me, working for a sports charity."

"Really?" Rachel rose from the table, taking her pile of papers with her. "So are you going to go?"

Why did everyone assume she was? Why wasn't Rachel or Dan or anyone expressing dismay that she might be leaving, and then urging her to stay? "I don't know."

"Why not?" Rachel's voice had hardened just a little. "I mean, what's keeping you here, really?"

Ouch. "Not much, I suppose," Claire said slowly. Had she really thought she'd keep working in the post office, helping Rachel out a bit? Neither job paid nearly enough to make her self-sufficient, no matter what kind of shoes she bought. And as for friends . . . Maybe she didn't have as many as she'd thought.

"So it seems like a no-brainer to me," Rachel said briskly. She'd shoved the pile of papers in a drawer and then slammed it shut. "You were waiting for the next thing to come along, weren't you?"

"I suppose . . ." Rachel couldn't make it clearer that she didn't care if she left. Claire half expected her to start pushing her out the door. "How's your mum?" she asked.

"Fine. Everything's fine here. Meghan's going to start a child-minding business so she can be home with Mum, and Lily's biology exam is on Monday. It's all happening at the Campbell house." She pinned a bright smile on her face, hands planted on her hips. "And it sounds like it's happening for you too, Claire. So good news all around, hey?"

"Yes, I suppose so." Rachel was nodding almost manically, and Claire couldn't think of a reason to stay. She'd come here hoping to be comforted and bolstered, and instead she felt as if she'd gotten a shove in the back. "Right. I suppose I should go back home. Make some plans."

"So you'll go, then?" More nodding. "When will you leave?"

Was she counting the days? The *minutes?* "I don't know," Claire answered. "Soon."

She walked slowly down the high street, shivering a little in the wind, taking in the rows of slightly dingy terraced houses, the post office shop with its peeling paint and Lottery adverts, the street opening up to sheep pasture that looked unkempt and forgotten; a few sheep bleated mournfully. Their lambs had been taken away.

She thought about going to see Abby down at the beach café, but she knew Abby was busy and stressed and probably didn't want to hear about poor, privileged Claire's troubles. Just like Rachel hadn't.

Claire turned off the beach road onto the steep lane that led up to Four Gables, the wind chillier now, sweeping in from the sea with nothing to break it.

The house was quiet when she entered, her footsteps muted by the plush carpet. Her parents had left a note on the granite island in the kitchen; they'd gone to Windermere for the afternoon to meet friends for lunch, they'd be back late tonight, and Marie had left a ready-made salad and sandwich from the supermarket for Claire's dinner, as if she couldn't make a meal for herself, as if she hadn't been doing it all along.

Claire opened the fridge and looked at the plastic bowl of lettuce wrapped tightly with cellophane, a few tomatoes and withered cucumbers nestled among its wilting leaves. The chicken salad baguette looked equally unappetizing. With a sigh she closed the fridge door and stood there, feeling lost in her own house, in her own life. All the strides she'd made, all the progress, felt as if it had disappeared. She was sliding backwards, faster and faster, and it felt as if there was absolutely nothing to keep her in Hartley-by-the-Sea. What did she have besides a poorly paying part-time job and a couple of wished-for friends who seemed glad to see the back of her? She didn't want to live in her parents' house, trying to make a place for herself when no one seemed to really want her there.

Better to go to London and work at a decent job, even if she suspected it existed only because her father had given a large donation to the charity. Better to fit into the world she knew and maybe try to make a place for herself there.

So why did the thought fill her with dread? She *wanted* to stay here. But she wanted other people to want it too. She wanted Rachel and Dan to want her to stay.

Claire sank onto her bed, gazing around the bedroom she'd called her own even though it had never felt like it. Her mother had had the whole house ruthlessly done over by an interior decorator years ago and had refused to allow Claire or Andrew to put posters on the walls or do anything to personalize the spaces.

For a second Claire imagined finding a cheap place to rent in the village, even if just a room. She'd never had a place to call her own; even the flat her parents had arranged for her in London had been stamped with her mother's signature of thick carpets and expensive throw pillows. Claire hadn't dared to change anything.

She'd never dared, period. About anything, ever.

She opened the top drawer of her bureau and reached for the mobile phone she rarely used. She needed Andrew's advice right now.

She had one new text, sent from Rachel several days ago: *What do you say you take on part of Campbell Cleaners permanently? If you're really thinking of staying in Hartley-by-the-Sea?*

Claire read it several times, the words hardly making sense. Why would Rachel have suggested she take over part of her business, only to wish her well in London a few days later? Why hadn't she even mentioned the text, the whole idea, when Claire had seen her?

A memory flashed through her mind: Claire coming into school at the end of Year Six, surrounded by stupid Wyndham wannabes, and catching sight of Rachel standing against the stone wall, her arms folded. She'd looked away the minute their gazes had met, and Claire had felt a second's rejection before her attention had been claimed by the other girls.

Now she remembered that Rachel had been standing there alone. That her mother must have injured her back around that time, that her life had fallen apart. And that Claire had been the one to walk away.

Just like she would walk away now, and Rachel would let her; Dan would let her. She'd let them let her, because she'd always, *always* let other people direct her movements. Make her choices. She'd thought she'd changed, but in that moment Claire realized she hadn't. Not enough. Not nearly enough.

She started to text Rachel back and then decided a conversation would be better. But first she needed to talk to her parents.

They came in at ten o'clock, murmuring to each other, and Claire heard her mother's low laugh—a sound she never associated with herself—before it abruptly stopped as Marie caught sight of her.

"Claire? Is something wrong?"

"No. Nothing's wrong." Claire took a deep breath and held her hands more tightly together, because otherwise she was afraid they would shake. She'd never stood up to her parents. Never in her whole life, except for coming to Cumbria three months ago, and then she hadn't had to confront them. To stare them down.

"Then why are you sitting here like—oh, I don't know." Her mother gave a false little laugh, and Claire saw her gaze dart to the liquor bottles in the cabinet in the corner of the room.

"I haven't had any alcohol, if that's what you're worried about," Claire said. Her voice sounded strange, harder than normal. "I don't actually have a drinking problem, Mum."

"Oh, Claire . . ."

"Why would you believe Hugh rather than me?"

Marie blinked at her for a few seconds. "You never denied it."

Which was unfortunately true. She'd just gone along, meek and shocked, half convinced. "No, you're right. I should have said something. I should have stood up for myself a long time ago."

"Stood up for yourself? Claire, what is this nonsense—"

"I'm not going to fall in with your plans this time, Mum. Dad." Claire moved her gaze to her father, who was still standing in the doorway, his expression stony. "I know it will be a disappointment to you, although maybe it will be a relief. Perhaps you're as tired of managing me as I am of being managed." Her parents simply stared, and Claire forced a smile. "I don't want to go to London. I don't want to work at some charity simply because Dad's paid them to hire me—"

"That's not true," Marie protested, and Claire looked at her father once again.

"Did you give them a donation?"

"That's irrelevant."

Which meant he had. "I appreciate what you've done for me," Claire said, although it was only half true. "All along. I know you've been worried about me, and I know I've been a disappointment in a lot of ways. But I'm twenty-eight years old and I need to see if I can stand on my own two feet. And I want to do that here, in Hartley-by-the-Sea."

Marie looked genuinely baffled. "But why? I mean, darling, you're working in a poky little shop. And you don't know anyone here. . . ."

"I do," Claire said. "I have friends. And I like it here. I want to try to make a life for myself. Here." She took a deep breath. "I'm sorry, but I'm not going to London with you."

31

Rachel

"SO WHAT DID CLAIRE want?"

Meghan stood in the doorway of the kitchen while Rachel stared down at the papers she'd shoved in a drawer. Her application to the University of Lancaster. She closed the drawer and turned to face her sister.

"She's got a job in London. Figures."

"So she's leaving?"

"Looks like it." Rachel shrugged dismissively and opened the fridge to look for something to make for tea. She wasn't surprised Claire was leaving, not really. She just hadn't expected it to hurt quite this much.

"So who will take some of your cleaning jobs?"

She'd forgotten she'd actually told Meghan her plans, after sending that stupid text to Claire, when the world had seemed as if it were shimmering with possibility. Now she recognized that as an illusion. Except she wasn't going to let Claire West ruin her plans. "I don't know. I'll figure something out."

"You'll still go to uni?"

Rachel closed her eyes briefly. "Why do you care?"

"Because I actually care about you," Meghan answered. "You dolt."

"Thanks."

"I mean it, Rach—"

"I know you do." Rachel took a deep breath. "We'll figure something out, Meghan. I wasn't depending on Claire to make it all work, trust me." Except she sort of had been, at least a little. She'd envisioned Claire taking over part of the business, stepping in when Rachel went to classes. *Being* there.

Sighing, Rachel closed the fridge door. "How about fish and chips for tea?"

Meghan brightened. "Seriously? We never get takeaway."

"Maybe it's about time."

"What about Mum?"

"You can stay with her while I go—" Rachel stopped. "Actually, how about you go? And I'll stay." Maybe things needed to change.

"Okay." Meghan's smile looked genuine, and almost strange because of it. No mockery, no taking the mick. "I'll be back in fifteen minutes."

While Meghan went out, Rachel settled Nathan in front of the telly and then went to check on her mother. Janice was lying propped up in bed, her face slack, her expression glazed and vacant. Just looking at her made Rachel's insides twist with sympathy and more than a little horror. To be so helpless, so trapped . . . It made her realize what a brave face her mother had put on her back injury all these years, trying to downplay the pain, not to fall apart when her husband left her alone, an invalid with three kids to raise. Rachel had been so consumed with how much she'd lost, she'd never really considered how much her mother had. A husband, a partner, a *life.*

"Hey, Mum." She took a step into the room, and her mother blinked at her, her face jerking in what Rachel had come to recognize as a smile. "You all right?" She sat on the edge of the bed, something she rarely did, and touched her mother's hand. Her flesh was plump and puffy, cool and slightly damp.

Surprise flared in her mother's eyes at the touch, and Rachel felt another twist inside, this time of guilt, because how often had she ever shown her mother affection? She'd stayed in the doorway; she'd busied herself as an excuse to keep from dealing with the difficult stuff. The stuff Meghan had had to deal with every single day.

"You have a rehab appointment on Monday," she said, and her mother gave a jerky nod—at least Rachel thought that's what it was. She and Meghan had taken their mother to rehab twice, both times requiring a monumental amount of effort simply to get her out of the house. A wheelchair had finally arrived courtesy of the NHS, but even heaving their mother from bed to chair was a Herculean task.

Even harder was the actual rehab; Rachel had noticed how much better Meghan was at it than she was. She sat with their mother, listened to the nurses, offered encouragement. Smiled while Rachel shrank back. She must have been doing similar stuff for years, and Rachel had never known. Rachel had tasked Meghan with taking Janice to most of her doctor's appointments, and then she'd breezed in once in a while to make sure everything was on track. Supervising without suffering.

Janice tried to speak, but Rachel couldn't make out the garbled words. She shook her head. "Sorry, Mum. I can't understand."

Janice tried again, and then again, enunciating each word as best as she could. "Oo . . . ah ree . . . ?"

Finally Rachel realized what she was trying to say. *You all right?* Or *areet*, if they were going to be Cumbrian about it.

Gently Rachel squeezed her mother's hand. "Yes, Mum," she said. "I'm fine."

❧

Rachel didn't see Claire for the rest of the weekend, and on Monday morning, when she drove by the post office, she didn't glimpse her inside. Had she already left, without so much as a goodbye? Wouldn't be the first time.

Monday afternoon Rachel canceled her last cleaning job so she could be back home when Lily returned from sitting her exam. She'd made a cake, a gooey chocolate mess that hopefully tasted better than it looked. Her heart was beating hard, although with excitement or nervousness she couldn't tell.

Then the front door opened, and Rachel came into the hall to see Lily trying to slip upstairs.

"Well?" Rachel asked eagerly, even though Lily's closed expression didn't bode well. Anticipation burst in her chest anyway. "How was it? Not too hard, I hope?"

Lily turned around, taking a deep breath. "I didn't sit the exam, Rachel."

For a few seconds the words didn't penetrate. Rachel simply stared at her, her mouth opening and closing like a fish's. Finally, stupidly, she said, "What?"

"I didn't sit it," Lily repeated, her voice clear and firm, and she walked past Rachel into the kitchen.

Rachel followed, anger and incredulity blooming inside her where once a wonderful anticipation had been. "You didn't . . ." She could barely get the words out. "You didn't sit the exam? You didn't *take* it?"

Lily was at the sink, pouring herself a glass of water. She shook her head.

"*Lily.* Why on earth . . . ? Did something happen? Were you ill—"

"No. I just decided I wasn't going to take the exam."

"You just decided," Rachel repeated.

Lily looked at her warily. "Yes."

"You just decided, even though you've spent the last two years preparing for this exam."

"Yes—"

"You can retake it anyway," Rachel cut across her, her mind racing. "We can say you weren't feeling well. You'll have to delay entrance a year, but you can still sit it next year." She closed her eyes briefly. "Damn it, Lily."

"I'm not going to take it next year, Rachel." Lily's voice was almost gentle. "Or ever. I don't like biology. I don't want to study it in university. I certainly don't want to take out forty thousand pounds' worth of student loans to study a subject I've never enjoyed."

"But . . . but you're so good at it."

"And you're good at cleaning people's houses. Does that mean you want to do it for the rest of your life?"

"It's not the same—"

"Maybe it is," Lily returned evenly. Suddenly she seemed very grown-up. "More than you've ever been willing to believe."

Rachel raked her hands through her hair, unable to formulate any coherent or measured response. This was so unexpected, and yet maybe that was simply because she'd been so willfully blind. Meghan had warned her. Lily had been trying to tell her. But for her sister to simply throw everything away . . .

"Why?" she asked finally. "Why didn't you at least sit the exam? Since you studied for it? You could still turn down Durham, but at least you'd have had the qualification."

"Because I knew I'd cave to pressure and go anyway if I did," Lily said.

"Pressure? You mean . . . from me?" Lily nodded. Rachel's breath came out in a rush. "Is that how you see me?" she asked. "As someone who is pressuring you? Nagging you?"

Lily hesitated. "Sometimes," she said. "Yes."

Rachel walked into the sitting room and sank onto the sofa next to Nathan, who immediately curled into her, leaning his head against her shoulder. Absently Rachel stroked his hair, and Lily followed her into the room; she sat opposite and waited, her hands tucked between her knees.

"Are you angry with me?" Lily asked in a small voice.

"Angry?" Yes, she was angry. She was bloody furious, but even more than that, she was sad. So terribly sad. "I'm not angry, Lily," Rachel said wearily.

"Really?" Lily sounded skeptical—and no wonder.

Rachel had spent a lot of time being angry or irritated or just impatient, so sure that she was doing the right thing. The hardest thing. And it hurt to think that maybe, all along, she hadn't been.

"I don't know what I feel," Rachel admitted. "Sad, mostly."

"Because I'm not going to Durham?" Lily's voice had thickened, as if she was fighting back tears.

"Yes," Rachel admitted. "I had such plans for you. And I still think going to Durham is the best thing for you." She sighed and leaned her head back against the sofa. "But I recognize that decision is not one for me to make. You have to make your own choices, Lily, and that means making your own mistakes."

"So you think staying at home is a mistake."

"I'm afraid it's a mistake," Rachel corrected carefully. "You don't realize the opportunities you could have. . . ."

"Actually, I do. I went to Durham, Rachel, remember? I saw the beautiful old buildings and the student union and all the rest of it. I know what I'm giving up. Mostly."

"Then why . . . ?"

"Because I don't like biology. I don't want to be a biologist—"

"You know a degree from a good university can get you just about any job—"

"Not the kind of job I want."

Rachel fell silent. She knew there was no point to this argument; Lily had already made her choice. "So what is your plan exactly?"

"I'm going to apply for a part-time course at the Lakes College, in art and design."

Rachel closed her eyes, struggling not to wince. To give up a place at Durham for a part-time course at a community college. It felt wrong. "And live at home?"

"Yes. I thought that might be better." Lily's voice was hesitant. "I could help with Mum."

"Is *that* why—"

"No. I told you. This is what I want, Rachel. Honestly."

Rachel shook her head, unable to speak for a few seconds. Her throat felt thick with disappointment and sadness, and she struggled to find even the semblance of a smile. "Like I said, you need to make your own choices."

"I wish you could be happy for me."

"I will, eventually," Rachel managed. "Give me time."

"Hey." Meghan's voice rang out from the kitchen. "Who made the cake?" Lily winced. "Because the top layer is sliding off."

Rachel rose from the sofa. "I guess we don't need a cake anymore," she said, her voice brittle.

"We're not celebrating?" Lily sounded sad.

No, they weren't bloody celebrating. Rachel took a deep breath. "I suppose we might as well eat it before it slides onto the floor."

As soon as they came into the kitchen Meghan sussed what was going on, simply from their faces. "Uh-oh." She stuck a finger in the dripping icing and sucked it off .

Lily made a face. "Eww, Meghan. That's vile."

"So you told her?"

"You knew?" Rachel whirled around from the cupboard, and Meghan took another fingerful of icing

"I knew she was thinking about not taking the exam," she said, and swallowed.

Rachel banged the plates onto the table. "Did it have to come to this? Couldn't you have told me before, Lily—"

"I tried. You never wanted to listen."

Which was probably true.

"The only person in this family who wants to go to Durham, Rachel," Meghan said, her voice surprisingly gentle, "is you."

Rachel closed her eyes. "And I can't."

"Maybe not Durham, but why not Lancaster? You've filled out the application—"

"I know." Rachel opened her eyes and sniffed. "We'll see," she said.

A couple of hours later Rachel remained downstairs, wiping kitchen counters that had already been wiped as Meghan and Lily went upstairs to get ready for bed. The pipes clanked and the floorboards creaked, but otherwise the house was quiet, the last of the sun's rays slanting through the kitchen window even though it was ten o'clock at night. Rachel used to love the late-summer evenings; when she'd been little she and her father had walked to the beach at nine o'clock at night, the sun still glinting off the sea. It had felt magical, like a secret they shared, to be out so late.

When had she lost the pleasure in summer nights, in sunlight glinting off water, in anything? For years she'd simply been slogging through each day, head lowered against the rain, the wind, the world.

Lily was right. She had been a nag. And Meghan was right too; she'd been a grumpy git. She wanted to change, but at that moment she didn't know if she had either the energy or the will.

Her phone buzzed with a text, vibrating on the kitchen table like an angular insect, and wearily Rachel picked it up. When someone texted this late at night, it usually meant the cancellation of a cleaning job.

Can we talk?

It was from Andrew. Rachel stared at her phone for a few seconds before she thumbed a reply. *We can text.*

The phone buzzed back with another text. *No. Talk. I'm standing outside your door.*

Her heart felt as if it were clambering up her throat as she flung the phone onto the table and hurried to the front door. She opened it and saw Andrew standing there with a sheepish smile.

"What—"

"My parents asked me to come home this weekend, and I wanted to see you before I went."

"Why—"

"Because," he said simply, and stepped into the house.

Rachel stood there, the smile that had bloomed when she'd opened the door to Andrew threatening to slide off her face. She felt way too emotional for this moment.

Andrew frowned at her. "Rachel? Are you okay?"

"Yes. No. I don't know." She let out a strangled laugh, and then, to her horror, she felt tears start in her eyes. Too many tears to blink back, they spilled down her cheeks before she could keep herself from it, and she turned away, burning with embarrassment. "You must think I'm a nutter. I'll be all right in a sec. . . ." She wiped her palms across her cheeks, trying to will the tears back, but it was too late for that.

Then she felt Andrew's hands on her shoulders as he turned her gently around to face him and brought her into the comforting embrace of his arms. Which only made it harder to get herself together.

"What happened?"

"Everything." She could barely get the word out. "Lily's not going to Durham and Claire's leaving and I'm a bitch." She let out a hiccuppy half laugh, half sob. "Everything's wrong, Andrew."

"Let's take one thing at a time." He steered her into the sitting room and then sat on the sofa and pulled her onto his lap.

"I'm not really a lap sitter," Rachel mumbled, and Andrew chuckled softly and shifted so she was sitting next to him, his arm around her, her head tucked against his shoulder.

"That better?"

"Yes."

"So what happened with Lily?"

Briefly Rachel told him, and he listened without speaking. Finally he said, "I know it's disappointing."

"But," Rachel cut across him. "I know. It's her life. I was pushing the whole thing on her. I do realize that. I knew it all along, I guess, but it was such an opportunity."

"Knowing something doesn't make it any less disappointing."

"No." Rachel sniffed. The tears had thankfully stopped, although her face was no doubt blotchy and puffy from crying. Just the way she wanted Andrew to see her.

"And Claire?" Andrew asked.

"She's going to London to take up some pretentious job with a charity."

"Arranged by my parents, no doubt."

"Yes."

"Did she seem happy about that?"

"Happy?" Rachel paused, considering. "No, not exactly. But she seemed like she was going to do it. And I'd actually texted her, asking her to go into the housekeeping business with me, so I could have time to do a part-time course at Lancaster." She felt her eyes fill again, but this time she could blink the tears back. "I'm not dependent on Claire. I realize that, but . . ." Her voice wobbled, and then she started to squeak. "It's just that everybody *leaves*."

"Everybody?" Andrew asked gently. "Or just your dad?"

The simple question felled her. The tears came again, worse this time, and she buried her face in fistfuls of Andrew's shirt as her shoulders shook. "I miss him," she gasped out, a confession she'd never made to anyone, not even to herself. "I don't want to. I hate that I do, but I do."

"Of course you do," Andrew said. He was stroking her back and her hair, and for a few seconds, in his arms, she felt incredibly safe.

Finally she eased back, embarrassed again by how much she'd lost it. "Sorry . . ."

"Oh, Rachel." Andrew touched her chin with his forefinger. "You've had a pretty raw deal in life, haven't you?"

"So I'm not the only one who thinks my life sucks?" Rachel managed to quip, and Andrew grimaced.

"I know I sounded like a bit of an ass back then—"

"A *bit*?"

"All right, a complete ass. I'm sorry."

She shook her head. "I'm sorry. I've been ratty for too long as it is."

"You've had good reason. But things can change now, Rachel. You can still go to Lancaster."

"If they accept me."

"Are you joking? Of course they will. And you'll sort the house-cleaning. Maybe Meghan can help—"

"Meghan's going into child minding."

"Or Lily—"

"No. That's the last thing I want Lily to do. She can do her course and help with Mum."

"Something will work out. You could just do fewer houses."

"Maybe." But she'd liked the idea of going into business with Claire, of sharing something like they once had. Of being friends again, and better this time. Stronger. *Partners.* "I'll figure something out." She leaned her head back against the sofa, away from Andrew's arm. "Sorry to blub."

"You deserved a good cry."

She gave him a watery smile, and he touched her chin again. "And where do I fit into all of this?" he asked quietly.

"In Macclesfield?"

"Wherever I am."

"Let me guess. You have a job coming up in Papua New Guinea."

"Nope."

"Burma?"

"No, I'll be working in Macclesfield for a few more months. And after that . . ." He shrugged. "I could limit myself to the UK if I had a reason to."

Rachel felt her stomach dip, the way it did when she was on a roller coaster. It was not an entirely pleasant sensation. "Do you have a reason?"

"You tell me." Andrew rested his gaze on her, everything about him so steady and sure. So trustworthy, if she could summon the strength to trust him.

"Maybe," she allowed, and he laughed wryly.

"You're good for my ego, Rachel. You keep me from being arrogant."

"That's something, then, because I always thought you were a bit pompous."

"I know you did." He put his hands on her shoulders, and Rachel's breath hitched. "Maybe, eh?" he said, and then he leaned forward and kissed her. Rachel closed her eyes, savoring the sweetness of his mouth against hers, his breath warm and minty, his lips soft and yet hard at the same time. It had been a long, long time since she'd been kissed, and so tenderly.

He pulled back a little, smiling. "Still maybe?"

"You'll have to do better than that if you want a yes," Rachel said, and grinning, Andrew did.

32

Claire

"CAN I COME IN?"

Claire turned to see her mother poking her head around her door. She nodded warily. The last two days had been interminable, with all of the Wests inching round one another, speaking in staccato bursts. Now it was Monday and Andrew was returning to Manchester and her parents were planning to go back to London. Marie was still hoping Claire would come with them.

Marie came into the room slowly, glancing around. Quickly Claire checked that the curtains were straight, the pillows perfectly plump. Then she grimaced inwardly at the realization and deliberately sat on the bed, ruffling the smooth starchiness of the duvet.

"I need to go to work . . ." Although she didn't even know if Dan was expecting her. Maybe he considered their abbreviated conversation on Saturday her notice.

"I'm sorry," Marie said abruptly, and Claire gaped. Now, *that* was unexpected. "I think I made a mistake with you. A lot of mistakes."

This was new. Claire wasn't sure how to respond, and after a few seconds she asked carefully, "What kind of mistakes?"

With a delicate sigh Marie perched on the edge of a chair, her posture perfectly straight. "I coddled you. Protected you too much." She paused, her gaze distant. "You know before all the trouble with your ear I was a GP?"

"Yes . . ." She'd known that in an academic sort of way, but she'd never really thought about it. Her mother had never worked outside of the home in Claire's memory. She could not picture her in a white lab coat and stethoscope, being brisk and efficient.

"I stopped when you first became ill because you had so many hospital appointments, and it didn't make sense to continue. But I never went back because I suppose I felt guilty."

"Guilty?" That was one emotion Claire had never thought her mother felt.

"Yes, because I missed it, Claire." Marie's voice wobbled a little. "You had ear infections constantly and you kept complaining and I *missed* it. The reason you're deaf in one ear is because I didn't have you checked out soon enough. If I had taken you to a specialist sooner, they would have been able to remove the cholesteatoma and there would have been no damage to your ear." Her mother's mouth twisted. "No deafness."

"Anyone could have missed it, Mum."

"They're not usually as bad as yours was." Marie continued as if Claire hadn't spoken. "Cholesteatomas. Most children recover and regain full hearing. But not you, and that was my fault." She sighed, her manicured fingers brushing what Claire realized was a tear from her perfectly made-up eye. "So I went a bit overboard in protecting you. Keeping you off school and such. Trying to shield you from everything. From life."

And obsessing over every part of her life. Making her the career she'd given up, yet clearly missing what she'd had. For the first time it occurred to Claire that maybe she wasn't the sole cause of her mother's disappointment.

"I wish I'd known that before," she said.

"Perhaps I should have told you." Marie uncrossed her legs and rose from the chair. Their heart-to-heart, such as it had been, was clearly over. "So. You're not really thinking of staying here, are you, Claire?"

Claire nearly laughed. Had her mother actually been trying to guilt her into going by telling her that little sob story? Or did she simply have no other way to operate? It felt freeing, in a weird way, to be back on familiar ground.

"I'm not just thinking of it, Mum," she said. "I'm doing it." And for once she felt completely sure not just of what she was doing, but of *herself*.

Her parents left that afternoon, in a cloud of Chanel and martyred disappointment. Claire had some more sympathy for her mother now that she understood more about what had happened, but not *that* much. She wasn't going to live her life for her parents any longer.

And now she had to have a few hard conversations. The first one, she thought, might actually be satisfying.

Hugh picked up on the second ring. "Claire?" He sounded surprised and impatient and annoyed all at once. Claire smiled.

"Hello, Hugh."

Silence, save for the sound of him breathing through his nose. "I didn't expect to hear from you."

"I know. Although I thought you might want your ring back."

"Claire—"

"Shall I post it? You should use it again, Hugh. I'm sure you can find another appropriate socialite for a wife." She spoke without bitterness, almost lightly, and Hugh let out an impatient sigh.

"Look, clearly we need to talk. I wanted to give you some time. . . ."

"You're not asking me to come back, are you?" Hugh was silent, and Claire laughed. "I thought not. I embarrassed you too badly. And we never had much in common, anyway. You didn't love me, and I didn't love you."

Hugh was silent for a long moment. "You sound different," he finally said.

"I am different," Claire answered. "I'm trying to be, and I'm succeeding." Her voice came out strong, strident. "We both know it's over, Hugh. Thank God the disaster has been averted. I'll send you your ring."

"Make sure it's insured—"

She laughed, feeling lighter than she had in years. "Oh, Hugh. I can't believe I ever said yes to you." And then, smiling, she disconnected the call.

Next she tackled Dan. The door to the post office shop banged behind her on a gust of wind, just as it had on that first day. He looked up from the till, surprise or maybe even suspicion narrowing his eyes.

"I thought you were going to London."

"I didn't say I was going, did I?" He shrugged, and Claire planted her hands on her hips. "Do you *want* me to go?"

"It doesn't much matter to me."

"Ouch." For a few seconds Claire absorbed the sting of his indifference. "After nearly three months here, that hurts a bit, you know." Dan just shrugged again. "You know you're really difficult, don't you?" Dan simply stared at her. "You're a real . . ." She struggled to find a word. "Jerk." He blinked. "I liked you," Claire burst out. "A lot. I thought you liked me."

"Why did you like me if you thought I was a jerk?"

"I told you before."

"Because I have a rescue dog?" He sounded scoffing.

"Because I thought underneath that tough, silent thing you've got going you were soft. And sensitive." Dan let out a rasp of sound that Claire realized was a laugh. Suddenly she felt ridiculous. "Have I got it completely wrong?" she asked quietly. "Tell me the truth, Dan." She took a deep breath. "I liked you. I *like* you, present tense. I want to stay in Hartley-by-the-Sea. I want to keep working in this shop. I want to become a postal assistant. Seriously. I'm happy here. Or I was, until you practically shoved me out the door."

Dan was silent. As usual, Claire couldn't tell anything from his expression. "You seemed like you had one foot out of it already," he said.

"I was waiting for you to tell me to stay."

Dan shook his head. "You need to make your own decisions, Claire."

"I know, which is why I'm here now. I was waiting for everyone to tell me what to do, to rescue me, but I'm not waiting anymore. I told my parents I'm staying. I'm telling you I'm staying, if I still have my job."

"You do."

The shop was quiet all around them, the only sound the nervous click of Bunny's nails on the tile floor of the kitchen. Claire took a couple of steps towards him so she stood in front of the till. She laid her hands flat on the counter. "So how much do you like me?" she asked, and then held her breath.

Dan didn't answer for a long moment. Finally, his voice low and raspy, he confessed, "This isn't easy for me, Claire."

Her heart bumped in her chest. "Because of . . . because of your ex-wife?" He nodded, and suddenly Claire wasn't nervous anymore. Suddenly she knew exactly what to do. "It's easy for me," she said, and standing on her tiptoes, she leaned across the counter and brushed her lips across Dan's.

He stilled beneath her touch, and her nervousness came rushing back. What if she'd made a horrible, humiliating mistake? But his lips were so soft, and she wanted to feel them again, and more this time.

Still she waited, uncertain, and then his hands came up to grip her shoulders with a gentleness that hinted at his incredible strength and restraint, and he deepened the kiss. A few seconds—or perhaps it was minutes—later, the door creaked open and someone cleared her throat with loud deliberation.

"I don't suppose the newspapers have arrived?" Eleanor Carwell asked. "Because this might make the front page of the *Westmorland Gazette*."

She had one more conversation to have, and Claire hoped this one wouldn't be so hard. But maybe it would be harder, because she should have had it twenty years ago.

Claire stood in front of Rachel's house, summoning the strength to knock on the door. It was early evening, the sky a pale blue, the breeze surprisingly warm. Summer finally seemed poised to arrive, and in the distance Claire could see the twinkle of the sea, hear the laughter of children making use of the long, light evenings. Gazing around her, Claire realized Hartley-by-the-Sea had finally become home, the home she'd never felt she'd had growing up. She *liked* it here.

Rachel was home. Claire could see her car with its Campbell Cleaners logo parked on the street.

The net curtains in the house next to Rachel's twitched, and Claire knew she needed to stop standing there like a stalker.

Resolutely she walked up to the front door and knocked. A few minutes later the door opened and Rachel stood there; she looked unimpressed to see Claire.

"What—"

"Will you come with me for a minute?" Claire blurted. An idea had taken hold, a ridiculous, over-the-top idea that she knew she wanted to see through.

Rachel's gaze narrowed. "Come with you? Where?"

"Just . . . with me. Please." Claire tugged on her arm. "For five minutes. Are you free?"

Rachel glanced back inside, and Claire heard Meghan call, "Yes, you're free, Rachel. For heaven's sake, the house isn't going to go up in smoke if you leave for ten minutes."

"Five," Rachel said, and stepped outside. Claire started walking down the street, and Rachel followed. "So where are we going, then?"

"You'll see." She felt excited and more than a little nervous. Would Rachel think she was being absurd? Maybe she was. Suddenly she didn't care. She was going to do this, because she wanted to do it.

"What is this, Claire?" Rachel asked a touch impatiently, and Claire shook her head.

"Just wait a minute." She turned from the high street up the narrow lane that led to the school. Rachel's steps slowed.

"What are you doing?"

"You'll *see*."

"School's out—"

"I know." Claire had forgotten how steep the school lane was. Walking up it brought her right back to her primary days, when her legs had wobbled and ached from the walk and dread had pooled in her stomach at the thought of enduring an entire day of school. The only thing that had helped had been seeing Rachel standing at the top of the lane, smiling and calling her a slow coach.

"Almost there," Claire called, and with resolute determination, she headed across the school yard to the stretch of grass where the big rhododendron bush dominated the far side.

Rachel stopped at the edge of the yard. "I can't believe you're doing this."

"Believe it," Claire called back, and stood before the giant bush. Had she really scrambled under that thing? It looked so dirty.

"Claire . . ."

"Please, Rachel. Just humor me, okay? For my sake as much as yours."

"I have no idea why this would be for my sake," Rachel grumbled, but she crossed the field.

They both stood before the bush, staring at its dark green, glossy leaves, the bright pink flowers just coming into bud.

"Ready?" Claire asked brightly, and Rachel didn't answer. She crouched down and tried to lift the lowest branches up, getting smacked in the face in the process.

"I always held them back for you," Rachel said, and she sounded fond.

Claire grabbed a knobbly, inflexible branch a bit harder and pulled. "This time I'm doing it," she said, and forced her way under the bush. Rachel followed.

"It's dire under here," Rachel remarked as they crawled on their hands and knees towards the center of the bush, where there looked to be enough space at least to sit up. The ground was dirty and dusty and smelled strangely stale, littered with empty crisp packets and squashed beer cans. "Was it always this bad?"

"I can't remember." Claire crawled farther into the bush's heart. There was no going back now.

There was space at the center, enough when they'd been small to crouch or kneel, and now simply to sit, heads ducked low, knees tucked in. In other words, not very comfortably.

"So," Rachel said after a few seconds of scrambling into position. "What's going on? I get the symbolism," she added. "We're back under this damn bush. Back to being friends. Yay us."

All right, so it had been an obvious, over-the-top gesture. But still. Claire wanted it to mean something to both of them.

"Yes, we're under the bush," she said. "And I just wanted to . . . to say—"

"You don't need to say anything," Rachel cut across her. "Look, Claire, it's okay you're leaving. You need to live your own life. I get that. I'm not angry or hurt or anything."

Claire peered at her for a moment, blinking in the gloom. "What do you think I dragged you out here to say?"

"That you're sorry you're leaving, but . . . ?"

"I'm not leaving, Rachel. I don't want to leave. The truth is, I came over the other day because I wanted you to tell me to stay. Old habits die hard and all that."

"You're staying?" Rachel looked flummoxed.

"I'm staying and working in the post office shop and, if the offer is still open, joining Campbell Cleaners."

"But . . ."

"I didn't see the text you sent," Claire explained, "before I spoke to you. Not that it actually makes a difference. I should have just said what I felt, what I wanted. I thought I'd learned that much at least, but apparently I hadn't. Just like I should have said it twenty years ago." She took a deep breath, unable to see the expression on Rachel's face in the shadowy interior of the rhododendron. "I know we were just kids and it's old history and all the rest of it, but I should have fought for our friendship. I know that now. I always knew that."

"I should have too," Rachel said, trying for a smile. "I should have said something. It wasn't all your fault, Claire."

"I don't want to make the same mistakes now. I want it to be different. For us to be different."

Rachel wrapped her arms around her knees. "Well, I actually want to be different too. Not so bossy and bitchy."

"You bossy?" Claire smiled.

Rachel laughed, shaking her head. "It stinks under here," she remarked after a moment. "I think a dog must have pooed somewhere." Rachel gave Claire a direct look. "So are you serious about the cleaning thing?"

"Absolutely, if you're serious about letting me in on it."

"Yes—"

"Then it's settled." Claire held out her hand. "We can shake on it, or we can get out of here and go have a proper drink down at the Hangman's Noose."

"Drink, definitely," Rachel said, but after they'd scooted out from under the rhododendron, dusty and dirty and definitely worse for wear, Rachel pulled her into a sudden and surprising hug. "I've missed you," she said, her voice choking a little, and Claire returned the hug, felt the answering emotion tighten in her chest.

"I've missed you too," she said, and after a brief, hard hug, they pulled away, sniffing self-consciously.

"Right, we're sorted, then," Rachel said.

"Yes," Claire answered. "Sorted."

"Well, that took long enough," Rachel said, rolling her eyes and smiling. "Only about twenty years."

"Better late than never," Claire said, and laughing, she slipped her arm through Rachel's. "Now let's go have that drink."

The wind was picking up a little, the sun glinting off the sea that sparkled in the distance as arm in arm they headed back down the school lane.

Now and Then
Friends

A HARTLEY-BY-THE-SEA NOVEL

KATE HEWITT

A CONVERSATION
WITH KATE HEWITT

Q. In what ways did the Cumbrian setting inform these characters as you were writing
Now and Then Friends?

A. Having lived in an isolated village like Hartley-by-the-Sea, I know the impact of such a place on your psyche, both for good and bad. When I first moved to Cumbria, I struggled with some of the aspects of the region that the characters in the book also struggle with—the rainy weather, the lack of anonymity, the sense of remoteness. I learned to see the benefits of all these things, and I think my characters do as well—with time and effort!

Q. As an American living in England, did you experience any "outsider" moments that helped you relate to how Claire might have felt returning to Hartley-by-the-Sea after so many years away?

A. Yes, I have had many outsider moments, whether it is simply using the wrong word or not observing a traditional British custom (such as not eating birthday cake at a party—you wrap it in a napkin and put it all squashed in the party bag!). I've learned to laugh about it, and when I'm not sure what the protocol is, I say so up front. Just recently

I had a funny conversation with friends about the differences between British and American English, and we all laughed a lot at the differences that seem minor but still matter.

Q. The theme of sisterhood is so rich in this novel. Do you expect that Claire's personality would have been different if she had had a sister to share things with growing up, as Rachel did with Meghan?

A. Having a sister myself, I well know the joys and difficulties of that sibling relationship! I think Claire felt very isolated by her partial deafness and many illnesses during her childhood; in some ways Rachel acted like a big sister to her, helping and protecting her. Perhaps if she'd had someone at home to do that, she wouldn't have become such good friends with Rachel.

Q. Do you feel that early-childhood friendships can last well into adulthood? How do the changes we experience as we develop our adult selves impact these friendships?

A. I think childhood friendships can last when the people involved keep in touch and grow together. This didn't happen for Rachel and Claire until they reunited; even though they feel they were always friends, I think they had to develop a separate friendship as adults.

Q. How was the experience of returning to some familiar faces from your previous Hartley-by-the-Sea book in this novel? Did you enjoy giving readers another glimpse into Lucy's and Juliet's lives in Now and Then Friends?

A. Yes, I feel quite at home in Hartley-by-the-Sea, and the characters seem more real, their lives richer, with each story. It's always nice to follow up with characters from previous books, and I hope to include Lucy and Juliet (and Claire and Rachel) in the next book.

Q. Do you have any rituals in your writing day?

A. Grabbing as much time as I can! As the mother of five young(ish) children, it can be hard to find time to write. I find it most efficient to write in short bursts and then take a five-minute break before starting again. A cup of tea does not go amiss, either.

Q. As an author, what things most inspire you?

A. I'm inspired by what I see around me, whether it's a simple human interaction or a crisp sunny morning. I tend to get ideas while I'm walking my children to school or the dog in the local woods, and then let my subconscious untangle the knots. I think inspiration is everywhere if you are of a mind to look for it.

QUESTIONS FOR DISCUSSION

1. What did you most enjoy about *Now and Then Friends*? Who was your favorite character? To whom could you most relate?

2. Why do you think Claire and Rachel were drawn to each other as children? Does Rachel's response to Claire upon meeting her again seem understandable to you?

3. Claire struggles with feeling adrift in life and allows other people to manage her life. Can you relate to her predicament at all?

4. Rachel's relationship with her sister, Meghan, is fraught, due to the family struggles they had growing up. Have the issues your family had while you were growing up affected your adult relationships?

5. Why do you think Claire and Rachel stopped being friends in primary school? How did they both contribute to the end of their friendship?

6. *Now and Then Friends* has a colorful cast of secondary characters, including Andrew West, Dan Trenton, Abby Rhodes, Emily Hart, Rob

Telford, and Eleanor Carwell. Which of these characters did you enjoy reading about the most? Who would you like to read about in his or her own story?

7. Is Rachel justified in her actions toward Lily regarding her choices of subjects?

8. What do you most like about Hartley-by-the-Sea? What would you find the most challenging about living there?

9. Do you think Rachel made the right choice in leaving university to come home? Do you understand her reasoning about not wanting to "settle"?

10. How does Claire help other people in the village, such as Dan Trenton and Eleanor Carwell?

11. How do you think Rachel and Claire both grow and change through the story? How do they help each other to do this?

12. Which part of *Now and Then Friends* resonated the most with you? What will you remember about the book long after you've read it?

Continue reading for a preview
of Kate Hewitt's

RAINY DAY SISTERS,

Lucy and Juliet's story.
Available now!

LUCY BAGSHAW'S HALF SISTER, Juliet, had warned her about the weather. "When the sun is shining, it's lovely, but otherwise it's wet, windy, and cold," she'd stated in her stern, matter-of-fact way. "Be warned."

Lucy had shrugged off the warning because she'd rather live anywhere, even the Antarctic, than stay in Boston for another second. In any case, she'd thought she was used to all three. She'd lived in England for the first six years of her life, and it wasn't as if Boston were the south of France. Except in comparison with the Lake District, it seemed it was.

Rain was atmospheric, she told herself as she hunched over the steering wheel, her eyes narrowed against the driving downpour. How many people listed walks in the rain as one of the most romantic things to do?

Although perhaps not when it was as torrential as this.

Letting out a gusty sigh, Lucy rolled her shoulders in an attempt to ease the tension that had lodged there since she'd turned off the M6. Or really since three weeks ago, when her life had fallen apart in the space of a single day—give or take a few years, perhaps.

This was her new start or, rather, her temporary reprieve. She was staying in England's Lake District, in the county of Cumbria, for only four months, long enough to get her act together and figure out what she wanted to do next. She hoped. And, of course, Nancy Crawford was going to want her job as school receptionist back in January, when her maternity leave ended.

But four months was a long time. Long enough, surely, to heal, to become strong, even to forget.

Well, maybe not long enough for that. She didn't think she'd ever forget the blazing headline in the *Boston Globe*'s editorial section: *Why I Will Not Give My Daughter a Free Ride.*

She closed her eyes—briefly, because the road was twisty—and forced the memory away. She wasn't going to think about the editorial piece that had gone viral, or her boss's apologetic dismissal, or Thomas's shrugging acceptance of the end of a nearly three-year relationship. She certainly wasn't going to think about her mother. She was going to think about good things, about her new, if temporary, life here in the beautiful, if wet, Lake District. Four months to both hide and heal, to recover and be restored before returning to her real life— whatever was left, anyway—stronger than ever before.

Lucy drove in silence for half an hour, all her concentration taken up with navigating the A-road that led from Penrith to her destination, Hartley-by-the-Sea, population fifteen hundred. Hedgerows lined either side of the road, and the dramatic fells in the distance were barely visible through the fog.

She peered through the window, trying to get a better look at the supposedly spectacular scenery, only to brake hard as she came up behind a tractor trundling down the road at the breakneck speed of five miles per hour. Pulling behind her from a side lane was a truck with a trailer holding about a dozen morose and very wet-looking sheep.

She stared in the rearview mirror at the wet sheep, who gazed miserably back, and had a sudden memory of her mother's piercing voice.

Are you a sheep, Lucinda, or a person who can think and act for herself?

Looking at those miserable creatures now, she decided she was definitely not one of them. She would not be one of them, not here, in this new place, where no one knew her, maybe not even her half sister.

It took another hour of driving through steady rain, behind the trundling tractor the entire way, before she finally arrived at Hartley-by-the-Sea. The turning off the A-road was alarmingly narrow and steep, and the ache between Lucy's shoulders had become a pulsing pain. But at last she was here. There always was a bright side, or at least a glimmer of one. She had to believe that, had clung to it for her whole life and especially for the last few weeks, when the things she'd thought were solid had fallen away beneath her like so much sinking sand.

The narrow road twisted sharply several times, and then as she came around the final turn, the sun peeked out from behind shreds of cloud and illuminated the village in the valley below.

A huddle of quaint stone houses and terraced cottages clustered along the shore, the sea a streak of gray-blue that met up with the horizon. A stream snaked through the village before meandering into the fields on the far side; dotted with cows and looking, in the moment's sunshine, perfectly pastoral, the landscape was like a painting by Constable come to life.

For a few seconds Lucy considered how she'd paint such a scene; she'd use diluted watercolors, so the colors blurred into one another as they seemed to do in the valley below, all washed with the golden gray light that filtered from behind the clouds.

She envisioned herself walking in those fields, with a dog, a black Lab perhaps, frisking at her heels. Never mind that she didn't have a dog and didn't actually like them all that much. It was all part of the picture, along with buying a newspaper at the local shop—there had to be a lovely little shop down there, with a cozy, grandmotherly type at the counter who would slip her chocolate buttons along with her paper.

A splatter of rain against her windshield woke her from the moment's reverie. Yet another tractor was coming up behind her, at quite a clip. With a wave of apology for the stony-faced farmer who was driving the thing, she resumed the steep, sharply twisting descent into the village.

She slowed the car to a crawl as she came to the high street, houses lining the narrow road on either side, charming terraced cottages with brightly painted doors and pots of flowers, and, all right, yes, a few more weathered-looking buildings with peeling paint and the odd broken window. Lucy was determined to fall in love with it, to find everything perfect.

Juliet ran a guesthouse in one of the village's old farmhouses: Tarn House, she'd said, no other address. Lucy hadn't been to Juliet's house before, hadn't actually seen her sister in more than five years. And didn't really know her all that well.

Juliet was thirty-seven to her twenty-six, and when Lucy was six years old, their mother, Fiona, had gotten a job as an art lecturer at a university in Boston. She'd taken Lucy with her, but Juliet had chosen to stay in England and finish her A levels while boarding with a school friend. She'd gone on to university in England, she'd visited Boston only once, and over the years Lucy had always felt a little intimidated by her half sister, so cool and capable and remote.

Yet it had been Juliet she'd called when everything had exploded around her, and Juliet who had said briskly, when Lucy had burst into tears on the phone, that she should come and stay with her for a while.

"You could get a job, make yourself useful," she'd continued in that same no-nonsense tone that made Lucy feel like a scolded six-year-old. "The local primary needs maternity cover for a receptionist position, and I know the head teacher. I'll arrange it."

And Lucy, overwhelmed and grateful that someone could see a way out of the mess, had let her. She'd had a telephone interview with the head teacher, who was, she realized, the principal, the next day, a man who had sounded as stern as Juliet and had finished the conversation with a sigh, saying, "It's only four months, after all," so Lucy felt as if he was hiring her only as a favor to her sister.

And now she couldn't find Tarn House.

She drove the mile and a half down the main street and back again, doing what felt like a seventeen-point turn in the narrow street, sweat prickling between her shoulder blades while three cars, a truck, and two tractors, all driven by grim-faced men with their arms folded, waited for her to manage to turn the car around. She'd never actually driven in England before, and she hit the curb twice before she managed to get going the right way.

She passed a post office shop looking almost as quaint as she'd imagined (peeling paint and Lottery advertisements aside), a pub, a church, a sign for the primary school where she'd be working (but no actual school as far as she could see), and no Tarn House.

Finally she parked the car by the train station, admiring the old-fashioned sign above the Victorian station building, which was, on second look, now a restaurant. The driving rain had downgraded into one of those misting drizzles that didn't seem all that bad when you were looking out at it from the cozy warmth of your kitchen but soaked you utterly after about five seconds.

Hunching her shoulders against the bitter wind—this was *August*—she searched for someone to ask directions.

The only person in sight was a farmer with a flat cap jammed down on his head and wearing extremely mud-splattered plus fours. Lucy approached him with her most engaging smile.

"Pardon me—are you from around here?"

He squinted at her suspiciously. "Eh?"

She had just asked, she realized, an absolutely idiotic question. "I only wanted to ask," she tried again, "do you know where Tarn House is?"

"Tarn House?" he repeated, his tone implying that he'd never heard of the place.

"Yes, it's a bed-and-breakfast here in the village—"

"Eh?" He scratched his head, his bushy eyebrows drawn together rather fiercely. Then he dropped his hand and jerked a thumb towards the road that led steeply up towards the shop and one pub. "Tarn House's up there, isn't it, now, across from the Hangman's Noose?"

"The Hangman's—" Ah. The pub. Lucy nodded. "Thank you."

"The white house with black shutters."

"Thanks so much, I really appreciate it." And why, Lucy wondered as she turned up the street, had he acted so incredulous when she'd asked him where it was? Was that a Cumbrian thing, or was her American accent stronger than she'd thought?

Tarn House was a neat two-story cottage of whitewashed stone with the promised black shutters, and pots of chrysanthemums on either side of the shiny black door. A discreet hand-painted sign that Lucy hadn't glimpsed from the road informed her that this was indeed her destination.

She hesitated on the slate step, her hand hovering above the brass knocker, as the rain continued steadily down. She felt keenly then how little she actually *knew* her sister. Half sister, if she wanted to be accurate; neither of them had known their different fathers. Not that Lucy could really call a sperm donor a dad. And their mother had never spoken about Juliet's father, whoever he was, at least not to Lucy.

Her hand was still hovering over the brass knocker when the door suddenly opened and Juliet stood there, her sandy hair pulled back into a neat ponytail, her gray eyes narrowed, her hands planted on her hips, as she looked Lucy up and down, her mouth tightening the same way her mother's did when she looked at her.

Two sleek greyhounds flanked Juliet, cowering slightly as Lucy stepped forward and ducked her head in both greeting and silent, uncertain apology. She could have used a hug, but Juliet didn't move and Lucy was too hesitant to hug the half sister she barely knew.

"Well," Juliet said with a brisk nod. "You made it."

"Yes. Yes, I did." Lucy smiled tentatively, and Juliet moved aside.

"You look like a drowned rat. You'd better come in."

Lucy stepped into the little entryway of Juliet's house, a surprisingly friendly jumble of umbrellas and Wellington boots cluttering the slate floor along with the dogs. She would have expected her sister to have every boot and brolly in regimental order, but maybe she didn't know Juliet well enough to know how she kept her house. Or maybe her sister was just having an off day.

"They're rescue dogs—they'll jump at a mouse," Juliet explained, for the two greyhounds were trembling. "They'll come round eventually. They just have to get used to you." She snapped her fingers, and the dogs obediently retreated to their baskets.

"Cup of tea," she said, not a question, and led Lucy into the kitchen. The kitchen was even cozier than the hall, with a large dark green Aga cooking range taking up most of one wall and emitting a lovely warmth, a circular pine table in the center, and a green glass jar of wildflowers on the windowsill. It was all so homely, so comforting, and so not what Lucy had expected from someone as stern and officious as Juliet, although again she was acting on ignorance. How many conversations had she even had with Juliet, before that wretched phone call? Five? Six?

Still the sight of it all, the Aga and the flowers and even the view of muddy sheep fields outside, made her spirits lift. This was a place she could feel at home in. She hoped.

She sank into a chair at the table as Juliet plonked a brass kettle on one of the Aga's round hot plates.

"So you start next week."

"Yes—"

"You ought to go up to the school tomorrow and check in with Alex."

"Alex?"

Juliet turned around, her straight eyebrows drawn together, her expression not precisely a frown, but definitely not a smile. "Alex Kincaid, the head teacher. You spoke with him on the phone, remember?"

There was a faint note of impatience or even irritation in Juliet's voice, which made Lucy stammer in apology.

"Oh, yes, yes, of course. Mr. Kincaid. Yes. Sorry." She was not actually all that keen to make Alex Kincaid's acquaintance. Given how unimpressed by her he'd seemed for the ten excruciating minutes of their phone interview, she thought he was unlikely to revise his opinion upon meeting her.

And she was unlikely to revise hers; she already had a picture of him in her head: He would be tall and angular with short-cut steel gray hair and square spectacles. He'd have one of those mouths that looked thin and unfriendly, and he would narrow his eyes at you as you spoke, as if incredulous of every word that came out of your mouth.

Oh, wait. Maybe she was picturing her last boss, Simon Hansen, when he'd told her he was canceling her art exhibition. *Sorry, Lucy, but after the bad press we can hardly go ahead with the exhibit. And in any case, your mother's not coming anyway.*

As for Alex Kincaid, now that she remembered that irritated voice on the phone, she decided he'd be balding and have bushy eyebrows. He'd blink too much as he spoke and have a nasal drip.

All right, perhaps that was a little unfair. But he'd definitely sounded as if he'd had his sense of humor surgically removed.

"I'm sure you're completely knackered now," Juliet continued, "but tomorrow I'll give you a proper tour of the village, introduce you." She nodded, that clearly decided, and Lucy, not knowing what else to do, nodded back.

It was so *strange* being here with her sister, sitting across from her in this cozy little kitchen, knowing she was actually going to live here and maybe get to know this sibling of hers, who had semiterrified her for most of her life. Intimidated, anyway, but perhaps that was her fault and not Juliet's.

In any case, when Lucy had needed someone to talk to, someone who understood the maelstrom that was their mother but wasn't caught up in her currents, she'd turned to Juliet. And Juliet hadn't let her down. She had to remember that, keep hold of it in moments like these, when Juliet seemed like another disapproving person in her life, mentally rolling her eyes at how Lucy could never seem to get it together.

And she *was* going to get it together. Here, in rainy, picturesque Hartley-by-the-Sea. She was going to reconnect with her sister, and make loads of friends, and go on picnics and pub crawls and find happiness.

KATE HEWITT is the bestselling author of more than forty novels of romance and women's fiction, including the Emigrants Trilogy, set in Scotland and North America; the Hartley-by-the-Sea series, set in the Lake District; and Tales from Goswell, written as Katharine Swartz. Raised in the United States, she lives in the English Cotswolds with her American-born husband and their five children.

CONNECT ONLINE

kate-hewitt.com
facebook.com/katehewittauthor
twitter.com/katehewitt1
acumbrianlife.blogspot.co.uk